Caffeine Nights Publishing

G000147627

MY KIND OF JUSTICE

Col Bury

Fiction aimed at the heart

and the head..

Published by Caffeine Nights Publishing 2015

CONDITIONS OF SALE

Published in Great Britain by
Caffeine Nights Publishing
4 Eton Close
Walderslade
Chatham
Kent
ME5 9AT
www. caffeine-nights com

British Library Cataloguing in Publication Data.
A CIP catalogue record for this book is available from the British Library

ISBN: 978-1-910720-02-8

Cover design by
Mark (Wills) Williams

Everything else by
Default, Luck and Accident

Acknowledgements

With me every step of the way has been talented writer David Barber – in our teens we formed "Eccles Writers' Line", as there weren't enough of us to form a "circle"! For being a great friend and mentor, Matt Hilton deserves a huge mention, as does Graham Smith, whose drunken late night phone calls kept me going. Special thanks to Darren Laws and the team at Caffeine Nights for having faith in my writing.

The fantastic crime (and horror) writing community has been brilliant, especially… Paul Brazill, Richard Godwin, Lily Childs, Lee Hughes, Nick Quantrill, Howard Linskey, Pete Sortwell, Michael Malone, Sheila Quigley, Tony Schumacher, Luca Veste, Mandasue Heller, Kimberley Chambers, Bob and Carol Bridgestock, Maxim Jakubowski, and all those from online writing groups, ezines and social media sites, with whom I've 'chewed the fat' over the years.

Thanks must also go to legendary New York agent, Nat Sobel, for teaching me so much about the writing process and the business. Plus, those colleagues, whose eyes didn't glaze over and who didn't stifle yawns whenever I rambled on about writing!

A special mention goes to my mum, Vera Bury, brother Dek and sister Deb for their continued support and interest in my endeavours, and to the rest of my family for putting up with me! And finally, my wonderful wife, Mandy and our beautiful kids, Olivia and Joe – heartfelt thanks for your support, patience and understanding.

Praise for Col Bury's writing

"Fast dialogue and edgy plots, keeps you turning the pages. Cracking!"

Sheila Quigley, author of the Seahills series, and the Holy Island trilogy

"Bury is going places. He shows boldness by tackling different styles of writing which encompass humour, paranoia, action thrillers and urban discontent."

Crimesquad.com

"In 'The Cops of Manchester', Col Bury pulls no punches, landing a flurry of hard jabs to the solar plexus that leaves us breathless. This is tight, gritty, bare-knuckle writing."

Howard Linskey, author of The Drop

"Bury has the ability to draw you into a story fast, gripping the reader by lapels and not letting you go. With razor sharp dialogue and a vast array of grim characters, Col Bury epitomises the term 'Brit Grit'."

Luca Veste, author of Dead Gone

"Darkly funny, muscular prose with stark imagery. A must read."
Richard Godwin, author of Apostle Rising

"I've been impressed by Col's writing and been happy to have the opportunity to publish him, three times."

Maxim Jakubowski, author, editor and publisher

"Snappy and powerful with realistic characters."
Nick Quantrill, author of Broken Dreams

"I read 'Manchester 6' in one sitting, such was the intensity of the writing."

Graham Smith, author of Snatched From Home

For my mum, Vera Bury - my number one fan. Pity Dad wasn't here to see this. x

Prologue

"It's time, boys. Are you ready?" No answers, just steely expressions. "Right, let's do it." DJ flipped his hood up, covering his shaven head. "Jack, drive to the top level of the multi-storey."

Jack Striker felt the growing tension in his shoulders and neck stiffening, as the infamous Manchester rain spattered incessantly on the stolen Ford Escort's windscreen. The intermittent squeaks of the wipers did little to abate the downpour. A small part of Jack was relieved to leave behind the angry revs of impatient drivers clogged around Moss Range precinct's one-way system. He was pleased to see the back of the orange-and-white double-decker bus he'd been stuck behind, bound for Manchester city centre five miles up the A56. The bus proffered a parting shot in the guise of lead-laced fumes, prompting Jack to suppress a heave and wind his window up a notch, leaving a gap to allow their cigarette smoke to escape.

Beneath gloomy clouds, the crime-ridden high-rises looming over the precinct eased out of view as Jack took a left into the multi-storey. He flicked the wipers off and exchanged stern looks with each of his friends, DJ in the front passenger seat, then Wozza, Lenny and Ged in the back. All, DJ apart, seemed apprehensive.

Heading up the first incline Jack asked, "You sure about this?"

DJ clapped his hands confidently. "Course I'm sure. Chill, mate."

Jack felt uneasy at being in the stolen car, let alone driving it as part of DJ's 'master-plan'. The contents of the boot scared the shit out of him. Okay, so he was the best driver – the only one with a licence in fact, not that that mattered. He'd only reluctantly agreed to help because his dad had been made redundant from the now-defunct Bullsmead power station. Times were hard at home and the loan sharks had been knocking. Plus, these *were* his mates, right?

Up he drove, soon reaching the top of the incline. The first level was virtually full of cars, the odd shopper dotted about carrying their respective purchases back to their vehicles. Some pigeons cooed from makeshift perches on rusting girders supporting the floor above, bird shit spattering the graffiti on the wall below. The lighting on the low ceiling struggled to brighten the dowdy greyness of the vast car park.

Turning sharply right to avoid the yellow-and-black-striped crash barriers along the gradient, he heard a faint screech of rubber on concrete.

"What if they just take the gear without paying? We're not armed, so we'd be fucked," said Jack.

"We've discussed this already. Your arse twitching, Jack? Don't yer want yer cut then?" asked DJ with a sneer.

Jack's grip tightened on the steering wheel.

Level two.

This floor was three-quarters full, and Jack knew they were slowly reaching the point of no return. However, he still had nagging reservations.

"We all know what the Crew are like. Do we really trust 'em?" The silence answered his question. "Anyhow, it's too late now. Everyone watch each other's backs."

"That's the spirit, partner." DJ patted Jack on the shoulder.

"Yeah, come on, lads. Let's just get this done smoothly and we'll be on the ale counting the money in no time. I'm with you all the way, mate," said freckle-faced Wozza from the rear, reaching forward to receive a high-five from DJ.

"You up for it too, Lenny?" DJ turned, offering the same high-five to Lenny in the middle. Lenny obliged, as lightly as someone may tap a puppy on the head for being a good boy.

"What about you, Giant?" asked DJ, calling Ged by his nickname.

"Yeah, let's roll. Bring it on and stick together."

Jack mentally noted Ged hadn't given a high-five. He guessed that the cousins, Lenny and Ged, were as unconvinced as himself. He briefly regarded Lenny in his rear-view mirror; his boyish, pallid looks and cheeky smile momentarily relaxed Jack a fraction. Nonetheless, Jack could see trepidation behind his expression, echoing his own feelings. He seriously considered whether to just turn back.

Guilt pricked him, having twirled his parents, saying he

couldn't accompany them and his sister Lucy for the visit to their posh relatives in Hale, Cheshire. He'd lied about having a job interview, which had pleased his dad somewhat, secretly fuelling Jack's guilt. The way he felt now though, listening to Aunt Alice ramble on about herself would have been the safer option.

He knew the notorious Moss Range Crew were responsible for many of the recent shootings reported in Manchester, dubbed 'the gun capital of the North' by the papers. Tit-for-tat shootings had become commonplace with rival gang the Bad Bastard Bullsmead Boys. This year alone three young men had lost their lives in the area, and virtually every day the Manchester Evening News had run a new story of gang-related violence. He also knew that their little gang from the Bullsmead area – though in no way affiliated with the BBBB – were boxing well above their weight with this escapade. He just prayed they could duck and dive enough to avoid a knockout.

Level three.

Jack had tried to dissuade Wozza in DJ's absence, but he wouldn't listen. This had surprised Jack, since Wozza didn't need the money. His dad owned a sports shop in nearby Bullsmead, the biggest council estate in Manchester; business was booming as a consequence of its trendy, but reasonably priced, sportswear range. The five of them were testament to that in their branded hoodies, and all at wholesale prices. Jack had seen recent signs of Wozza becoming increasingly akin to DJ, especially when dabbling in the magic – or tragic – white powder.

Lenny was from a family of five brothers who, along with their dad, ran PSP – Powers Security Protection – a business successful enough to allow the family to escape Bullsmead. However, Lenny hadn't settled in 'Poshville' and kept returning to his roots. You can take the lad out of Bullsmead, as they say, but you can't take Bullsmead out of the lad. But now this wasn't Bullsmead, this was Moss Range: enemy territory.

Level four.

As for DJ, this was his baby. He was always up to something, forever dreaming up new ways to avoid the rat-race, this being the latest in a long list of money-making schemes. DJ wouldn't say where he'd acquired the gear in the boot, but Jack knew he'd made a few trips thirty-five miles along the lengthy East

Lancashire Road to Liverpool lately, to meet some 'business associates'.

"Come on, boys, there's five of us… the Sunnyside Boys. We'll be sorted. It's just business to the Crew, innit?" said Wozza enthusiastically.

Jack glanced at Wozza in the mirror; the expression reflecting back was not as chirpy as his words. *It's just business to the Crew…* He wondered whether his friends were really aware of what they were getting themselves into. What *he* was getting himself into.

Level five.

There was now a scarcity of cars, and Jack resisted the overpowering urge to yank on the handbrake and say, 'Sod this for a lark'. He'd never been one to shirk a challenge, especially where making a few quid and where his mates were involved. The many pool money matches in dodgy Manchester clubs and pubs proved that. They'd had a few bar room brawls after sharking the wrong type of guys. But something in his gut told him that in this game they were playing out of their league.

He turned to DJ, urgency in his voice. "There's CCTV cameras in here, mate."

DJ shook his head. "Relax, man. They're crap. I know lads who've nicked cars in here and never been caught." DJ glanced round at the others with a knowing smile. "Anyway, we're meeting at the opposite end to the cameras. It's a blind spot, so chill out, will yer?"

Jack eased the Escort onto the top level with another faint squeak of rubber on tarmac. As anticipated, only the odd car was dotted about and it was completely free of shoppers, creating an eerie feel. Gusts howled from the open sides like scared children. He slowed to five mph as he saw a black Mercedes parked beside a dark green Subaru Impreza on the far side. Both vehicles faced them and had tinted windows.

Shit. He could feel his pulse in his hands on the steering wheel. He drew the Escort to a halt ten feet from the two cars. The distant monotonous booming of rap music resounded from the Subaru.

"Here we go, boys. I'll do the talking," said cocksure DJ.

DJ got out with Wozza, 'Giant' Ged and Lenny close behind. Jack, as requested by DJ earlier, remained in the driver's seat with the engine running, 'just in case'. Despite there being enough smoke in the car to satisfy a chain-smoker, Jack lit another Benson and drew hard. He observed events through the windscreen, akin to watching a widescreen telly.

DJ was flanked by Wozza and Lenny, with Ged a couple of paces behind. They stood and waited about fifteen feet from the Crew's snazzy cars. Ged kept glancing at Jack. Nothing happened for a minute, as if Jack's telly had been paused.

The rap music stopped. Eight car doors opened, almost simultaneously. Five black and mixed-race males got out of each vehicle, as strictly no whites were allowed in the Crew. They lined up, ominously facing Jack's four mates, hard stares all round. He wound down the driver's side window some more to listen, getting a sickly whiff of car fumes drifting in. He could feel his pulse in his hands again as he gripped the steering wheel. His mouth was becoming parched. He swallowed.

One of the gang stepped forward a pace. Jack recognised his face and gangly frame. Jamo Kingston, the head honcho of the Moss Range Crew, his baggy jeans complimented by a black branded hoodie and snazzy trainers.

"Yo to the Sunnyside Boys," said Kingston, speaking in a hybrid Jamaican-Manc accent. "Nice to see you on the dark side of the street at long last. Top car, DJ." He nodded at the decrepit vehicle. "You white boys really look the part." A couple in the line grinned, one even laughed out loud, but instantly seemed to realise that wasn't so cool.

Lenny shuffled uneasily on his feet. Wozza looked briefly heavenwards. Ged appeared rigid, almost frozen to the spot, his face paler than the moon as he glanced back at Jack again.

"Just trying to stay low key, Jamo." DJ sounded almost jovial.

"Good, 'cos if you've been followed, man, me tinks me boys won't be too pleased." Jamo Kingston tossed a look at his boys.

Jack scanned the line: big fuckers for boys. He had seen one or two of them around, but most concealed their identity with bandanas, slightly skewed caps and hoods, some of the latter over their baseball caps. Like their leader, baggy jeans and dark sports jackets were prominent, but in essence they all appeared menacingly similar. Jack noticed two in the middle had their hands tucked inside their jackets.

"Yer got the money, Jamo?"

"Slow down, man. I'll call the shots. You got me charlie?"

"Yeah. Course I have." DJ gestured toward the Escort.

"Who's the shy boy?" Kingston pointed at Jack.

"He's cool, and he stays there."

"You hurt me feelings, DJ. Me tinks you don't trust me… respect me. You dissin' me, DJ?"

"Course not, man. Come on, let's just do the deal."

"Ok, white boy. *You're* the man." His sarcastic smile revealed a gold incisor.

DJ led Kingston to the back of the car. He was accompanied by two of his boys, who both tossed Jack the eye. Jack pivoted as the boot opened. He heard the holdall's zipper.

"Let me see. Cut the bag."

A few seconds passed.

"Let me taste it."

A few more seconds.

"Wicked. Top stuff, bro."

"What did you expect?" asked DJ.

Kingston shouted: "Yo, Jerome, Sniffer. Game on!"

Jack noticed the two in the middle striding toward the Escort. He recognised the stockier of the two, although his face was covered by a black bandana. It was Jerome Grant, the wanker who'd robbed him and DJ when they were kids on Bullsmead Park.

Jack saw Kingston carrying the black holdall containing the cocaine. He passed the front passenger side door purposefully, with DJ pursuing.

"Jamo, what about the money?"

Kingston ignored DJ and walked toward the Merc, passing Sniffer and Jerome, who both pulled out black handguns and pointed them at DJ, Ged, Lenny and Wozza.

"They've got shooters," yelled Jack out of the window, a tad too late.

"Back the fuck up or we'll bang you down," shouted Jerome.

Jack flinched, crouched in his seat. Ged, Lenny and Wozza scampered behind their stolen vehicle.

DJ stood his ground. "Jamo, you scamming bastard!"

Jerome pistol-whipped DJ twice across the face and he fell to the floor with a yelp, clutching his face. Some of the others joined in, kicking him on the ground amid a tirade of expletives. DJ squealed in pain, curled into a ball.

Jack revved the car noisily. He heard the rear doors open then slam shut seconds later. Ged, Lenny and Wozza were in a heap inside, panting and cursing. The remainder of the gang paced forward; at least two more, maybe three, had handguns at their sides. One, his face contorted, headed for the car, pointing a pistol at Jack.

"For fuck's sake, Jack. Do one. Go, go, GO!" cried Wozza.

Jack ducked. "Wait... DJ!" He leaned across, swung open the front passenger door, knocking one of the gunmen off balance. "Get in... quick..."

DJ had blood dripping from his nose but seemed to regain his senses. He scrambled into the front, legs dangling outside the swinging door. Cursing, Sniffer grabbed at DJ's feet. Dark faces sneered, contorting angrily, closing in.

Two of the Crew turned, pointing their pistols at the Escort. Jack reversed rapidly, twirling the steering wheel. Spinning tyres echoed throughout the car park as he negotiated a handbrake turn. Sniffer was thrown off balance, while DJ slid further out, but Jack grabbed his right arm. He struggled to control the car and slammed the brake with a resounding screech. He mustered the strength to drag DJ inside, Ged stretching across to assist, receiving a sturdy trainer in the face from the stocky Sniffer in the process.

Most of the gang surrounded the Escort, banging their guns and fists on the windows and bodywork, their twisted faces and manic eyes peering in like starved zombies after their prey. A couple more ran over swinging baseball bats. The two rear side windows smashed inward, showering those inside with small chards, causing screams that mingled with a cacophony of insults and threats. The vehicle rocked from side to side.

"LET'S GO, JACK, FOR GOD'S SAKE!" Lenny's voice crackled in panic.

A silver handgun dangled through the broken window, pointing at Wozza, who grabbed it hastily.

"Fuckin' gimme that." DJ snatched the pistol from Wozza.

Jack wheel-spun the vehicle forward, flicking Jerome into the air. He bounced onto the bonnet with a thud, his handgun clanging off the side of the car. A couple of hangers-on released their grips. DJ pointed his newly acquired handgun out of the window.

"No, DJ, don't!"

"Just fuckin' drive, Jack."

As the car sped toward the ramp leading to level five, there was a flurry of deafening bangs, whistling and pinging sounds.

DJ, arm out of the window, fired back manically, making Jack wince repeatedly as he drove. "WANKERS!" underlined each shot until the handgun was spent, the tiny wisps of acrid smoke instantly dispersing.

Jack's ears were still ringing from the gunshots when the rear windscreen smashed through and he felt something spatter on the back of his head and neck. He nearly lost control of the vehicle, feeling it lift onto its two rear wheels down the ramp. The car rebounded on return impact and they all bounced up, then down, in their seats. Jack managed to regain enough control for a swift right. The back end skidded to the left into the lengthy crash barriers, yanking off the bumper, which clanged noisily behind them.

Jack noticed red speckles on the windscreen and dash area. DJ wiped dripping blood from his swollen nose then stared into space. Confused, Jack continued driving.

Wozza began bawling inconsolably.

"No, no, NOOOO..." Ged's head was in his hands.

It was only when they reached the bottom of the multi-storey that Jack looked round. Lenny was slumped forward with a dark crimson hole in the back of his head.

***

After weaving frantically through the side streets, while checking the rear-view mirror as often as a fleeing bank robber, Jack finally eased off the revs. He drew the car to a halt on a dark cobbled road a mile from the precinct. Beneath the relative sanctuary of Bullsmead railway arches, Jack heard the rumblings of a tram above. The full moon offered scant light behind wind-dispersing clouds.

Jack took a deep breath, flicked on the interior light. Wozza's sobbing had reduced to sniffles. Ged stared ahead like a child in a war zone. Jack slowly turned round and saw the motionless Lenny. The back seat and footwell were soaked in blood, Lenny's hair matted carmine.

"Is he... still breathing?" asked Jack, struggling to comprehend the situation.

Ged was holding his cousin's hand. "Think I can feel a pulse. Aw... fuck... Len... What have we done? What are we gonna do now?"

Wozza looked forlorn, clearly in a state of shock, red dots sprayed across his face interspersing his freckles. Jack turned to the brooding DJ, who hadn't said a word for five minutes, congealed blood from his misshapen nose covering half his face. "We really need to drop Lenny at the hospital. What do you reckon, DJ?"

"I'm a dead man."

"What?"

"I said I'm a dead man."

Jack couldn't believe it. "Forget *you*, DJ. Let's sort Lenny first."

DJ pivoted, mad-eyed. "Fancy yer chances, Striker?"

"What are you on about? Lenny's dying here, you selfish prick. You and your bleedin' 'master-plan'."

DJ lunged for Jack, who instinctively swerved his upper body sideways. He gave DJ a swift uppercut, rocking the car. DJ cried out, his weakened nose exploding again. As he swung a retaliatory punch at Jack, Ged leaned forward, blocking it with his sturdy arms.

"Enough! Let's sort Lenny... Now!" Due to his size, when Ged raised his voice people tended to listen.

Jack's gaze was fixed on DJ, whose posture appeared to slump as he began his gazing into space routine again. "Right, DJ, you with us on this?"

An imperceptible nod, then he seemed to snap out of his self-absorbed trance. "Yeah, sorry, lads."

After all putting their hoods up, they headed for Bullsmead General Hospital two miles south. Jack prayed they didn't pass a police car; Ged prayed his cousin would live. Such was the state of the battered Escort, they'd stand out more than a bride at a funeral.

Jack avoided the main roads as best he could, opting for the side streets, the odd stare from pedestrians making him crouch in the seat. Lenny lolled with each turn, Ged and Wozza whimpering throughout.

They soon reached the brightly lit accident and emergency department, Jack pulling up beside an ambulance. A paramedic was having a sly cigarette beside it, acutely aware of the nicotine's damage capabilities, but clearly enjoying it as he puffed away.

"Ease him onto the floor, Ged, from your side."

"Aw… Jack…"

"Do it!"

Ged kissed Lenny on the forehead. He opened the back door and slid him out as gently as he could. "Soz, our Len."

The door still half open, Jack accelerated, purposely wheel-spinning, then sped off with his hand on the horn for a few seconds. He caught a snapshot of the startled paramedic looking over. In one movement the medic stubbed out his cig and headed for the prostrate Lenny.

Jack cringed as they left the hospital grounds, passing a police panda car entering. Luckily the lone driver seemed preoccupied enough to miss them flash by.

Soon they were under the gloomy arches of the disused Bullsmead railway station. After exiting the Escort, DJ retrieved a petrol canister that he had filled earlier, from behind a bush. Once all the lads were clear he expertly tossed a burning rag onto the petrol-doused vehicle. Within seconds, a whoosh of flames illuminated the area, as if the devil had turned the lights on to grass them up to God. They all ran like hell into the depths of darkness.

Ten minutes later, they collapsed against the inside of the decrepit wall surrounding Bullsmead Park, the ground damp and cold underneath them. They breathed heavily in unison, unable to speak for a minute or two. The dark expanse of the park before them revealed no footpaths leading out, only the void of the vast field surrounded by misshapen trees swaying and creaking eerily.

"Do you think… he'll survive?" asked Ged, sporting a developing shiner under his right eye from Sniffer's kick earlier.

"Well, he's in safe hands now. There's always a chance." Jack doubted his own words as he whispered them, mindful of people passing on the other side of the wall.

It was DJ's turn to sob.

Jack put a consoling arm around his shoulders, feeling him shudder fitfully. "Come on. We're all in it together, mate. Sorry for punching you." Wisps of the chilled night air followed Jack's reassuring words like cigarette smoke.

"S'alright. It was my idea, so it's my fault. Simple as."

Wozza, still appearing stunned, looked at Jack but didn't speak, his face pale in the moonlight.

Jack lit a cigarette, gave it to DJ, then asked, "When you fired those shots, do you reckon you hit any of them?"

DJ took a long drag, exhaled, blowing a thoughtful smoke ring before turning to Jack. "Yeah. I saw one fall down holding his face. I think it was Kingston."

More silence, more repercussions.

Ged shattered the silence, his deep tones incapable of whispering. "If Lenny dies, those fuckers will pay. Mark my words."

"I'm with yer on that, mate," said DJ, through snarling teeth. "Even if he doesn't die."

"And when my cousins find out, the shit will hit the fan big time."

Jack knew Ged was right about Lenny's brothers, but rationale was required. Despite Jack's grave concerns for Lenny, and criticising DJ earlier for his selfish reaction, he was now thinking of self-preservation.

"Lads, we really need to get our stories straight, you know. The cops'll be sniffing around soon. And I don't know about you, but I'm not going down."

They sat on the damp ground for hours, smoking and debating their options, until somewhat satisfied. All four of them clasped outstretched hands, pledging to stick together and to never speak to anyone else about tonight.

Jack trudged home, unable to shake the vivid flashbacks of the dark red hole in his poor friend's skull, wondering how he could possibly hide all this from his family. He hated lying and he knew, deep down, this would always be the biggest lie of his life.

It would haunt him forever...

Sixteen years later

Chapter One

Detective Inspector Jack Striker stroked a hand through his lightly gelled, raven-black hair, closed his eyes momentarily and took in a calming breath. He wasn't particularly shocked to find a young man whose face had been beaten to resemble a piece of rare steak. After all, this *was* Bullsmead, one of the largest and notorious council estates in Manchester, if not Europe, and he'd seen worse – much worse.

His apprehension stemmed more from the pending work ahead. It was his first case since returning to his old stamping ground on promotion as a substantive DI in the force's Major Incident Team. And he knew the eyes of the B Division's top brass would be scrutinising his every move.

Having cautiously entered the white SOCO tent, while wearing a matching protective suit, he stooped his six-foot-one-inch frame and studied the battered body at his feet, the crimson reflecting vividly under the bright portable lighting. The lad's denims were spattered in blood, his head swollen, misshapen. Visual ID was impossible at this stage, unless someone here knew him.

Striker shook off the initial apprehension, the excitement of the chase spurring him on. Time to get things moving. "Who is he? Any witnesses?"

Also in a white protective suit, portly, non-PC-DC Eric Bardsley held up a fat finger. He responded on his radio to the female comms operator asking if more troops were required at the scene. "Come 'ead, love. What do *you* think?" He rolled his eyes deridingly, his distinctive tones, gruff from years of chain-smoking, clearly revealing his Liverpool roots.

Bardsley's origin had been swiftly pounced upon by the many football-crazy Manchester City and United fans he worked with at Bullsmead nick. They had instantly labelled him a 'Scouser', his broad accent being the spark to ignite the fire of the Mancs, guaranteeing banter in abundance. Bardsley was well up for it though, being a supporter of bitter North West rivals Liverpool FC.

Striker studied the body and wondered briefly what the future held for his own children, Beth and Harry, when they became teenagers. He also wondered how his estranged wife Suzi would react to the news that he wouldn't be able to pick the kids up from school tomorrow, as it would have been the first time in two weeks. Knowing her, she would receive the news like a hungry lioness being denied her food.

Bardsley shook his head, a thoughtful hand smoothing his greying and somewhat dishevelled beard. "According to CID, there's no ID yet, Jack. No witnesses either."

Some DI's, the ones up their own arses, would insist on their detectives calling them 'Boss', but Striker wasn't one of them. He was from the streets himself, *these* very same streets. Respect was important, of course, but once out of uniform and into the confines of a plain clothes unit, he felt team morale was more important than the vanity of a power junkie. And providing the nasty bastard – or bastards – who'd killed this lad were caught pronto, his team could call him what the hell they wanted.

The double bleep of a text message prompted the DI to pull out his HTC mobile. He frowned at the message, sure that Suzie was a mind reader: *Don't forget kids 2moz – I'm at work so we're counting on U. And don't let us down… AGAIN.*

Striker forced family thoughts aside and exited the tent. Intermittent flashes of blue lights from panda cars parked around the crime scene illuminated the chilly autumn night. He scanned the noisy figures dotted about the area ogling the crime scene, recognising a dodgy face here and there.

All of these people and still no witnesses? Typical.

He spotted Jamo Kingston, a local gangster-turned-good-guy, whose face always seemed to pop up, ever since he'd been appointed as an Independent Advisory Group member. Striker thought it ridiculous that Kingston had been chosen as a link between the cops and the community. He certainly wouldn't be telling *him* anything about this case. Kingston, wearing an eyepatch from when he was shot years ago, was already sticking his nose in, talking to a uniformed officer on the far cordon. The loss of his left eye had apparently made him 'realise the error of his ways', but Striker wasn't so sure.

Moss Range Road ran from a slip road off the Mancunian Way, through urban sprawls and onto Bullsmead Road, where Striker stood, on the Bullsmead Estate in South Manchester. The Mancunian Way, a mini-motorway running high across the south edge of the city centre, offered its elevated motorists a flashing glimpse of Manchester in all its glory, providing them with a flavoured mix of old and new.

On view was a panorama of surviving cotton mills, factories and warehouses, many having been converted into hotels and apartments. The former were a constant reminder of Manchester's historic status as the 'international centre of cotton and textiles'. Formerly known as 'Cottonopolis', the city became *the* global supplier of textiles, via its large network of canals and railways.

Lying prominent in the city centre were two large universities and the mightily impressive Beetham Tower – the tallest residential structure in Europe – that was even visible to Striker now, four miles away in the distance. Two of the tower's vivid red warning lights peered back at him through charcoal clouds, like the eyes of the devil.

This stretch of Bullsmead Road had a row of shops opposite a long line of red-brick council semis, the street cast in an orange haze by staggered lampposts. Front gardens contained a mixture of colourful children's Wendy houses, slides and swings, a discarded bike and even a decrepit-looking sofa. Most houses were lit up as if electricity was free around here, and in many cases it probably was. Front doors ajar, family members congregated outside, some drinking cans of cheap lager. A mum cradled a baby in her arms while sucking on a cigarette. A couple of her other offspring were running boisterously around the front garden, despite it being gone ten thirty, a barking mongrel chasing them. Two of the houses overlooking the crime scene were boarded up.

Typical.

Striker glanced up and saw a pair of old trainers tied by their laces dangling bizarrely on a telephone wire. Beyond them the clouds were gathering, promising rain – another reason to get things moving.

Fortunately, the SOCO tent had been erected promptly, ensuring the scene was protected. However, if they were to find a discarded murder weapon he didn't want it to be rain-soaked and free of vital forensics. His initial assessment was that the uniforms, despite their limited numbers and the usual plethora of Friday night calls, had done a decent enough job. The cordon was a good forty metres wide, the road was closed and Traffic, in their high-visibility jackets topped with predominantly white hats, were diverting vehicles down side streets toward alternative routes. He could hear the inconvenienced drivers' curses before they'd begun: "Fuckin' pigs!"

A white-suited female SOCO – now supposedly referred to as a 'CSI', but they were still SOCO to UK cops, old habits and all that – was examining the general vicinity outside the tent, currently bagging a discarded bottle of lager. She peered round from her kneeling position, as though feeling Striker's eyes on her. They exchanged nods.

DC Bardsley gestured at a uniformed officer talking to two boys sitting on a garden wall. Their dark hoods concealed their features.

"They're our only hope so far," croaked Bardsley. "There's no suggestion they're directly involved, but they were here when we arrived so they may have seen something."

"Have you spoken to them, Eric?"

"No, I thought I'd leave that to the 'wooden top' while I…"

Striker cut him short, not liking the insinuation that all rookies lacked intelligence. "You were a probationer once, Eric. Never forget that."

Aware of the growing groups of noisy locals gawking around the cordon, Striker disrobed the protective suit and overshoes and walked over. He turned to Bardsley, who'd done the same and was following so closely that Striker smelled remnants of the DC's last cigarette on his breath. He fought the urge to ask him for one.

"Have they all been spoken to?" asked Striker.

"Most of the ones here when we arrived were very tight-lipped. I spoke to a shopkeeper who said there had been a gang of about a dozen lads loitering outside his shop. He said they ran off after all the commotion."

"Commotion?"

"Yeah, he said there was a lot of shouting and swearing, and people running around. But he didn't actually see what had happened."

"Didn't see, or was too scared to say?"

Bardsley shrugged.

Feeling a tinge of hope, Striker stopped to scan the row of shops, trying to shrug off an old memory of the newsagents in the middle, when as a probationer he'd disarmed a masked robber. He could still hear the crack of the handgun shooting perilously past his ear, even now, a little too close for comfort. In the end it didn't do any harm to his career prospects, he supposed. The divisional commander's commendation took pride of place on the living-room wall of his city centre apartment.

All the shops except for a Chinese takeaway were in darkness, clearly having shut for the night. "Anyhow, I thought you said there were no witnesses."

"I meant to the actual attack."

"Who's this guy that may be a witness then?"

"Khalid Khan from the newsagents. He was pulling his shutters down as I spoke to him. Like I said, he heard the attack, but was too scared to come out. He did peep through the shop window though, and saw a 'tall bulky figure' running from the group of youths in the direction of the petrol station."

Striker still felt a little uneasy as his unwanted memory of the newsagents nagged, but he managed to suppress it. "Just one lad?"

"Yes, just one, but it wasn't a lad, it was a man. Course he might've just been a scared passer-by. Mr Khan did say the boys were running in different directions, yelling, totally freaked out, but the tall bloke stood out somehow."

"Stood out?"

"He was the only one who wasn't shouting."

Striker absorbed this as they approached the constable talking to two lads sitting on a wall. It was rookie cop Ben Davison. Striker prided himself on knowing everyone at the nick and also took satisfaction in passing on his wisdom to the probationers.

He peered over the PC's shoulder, seeing a pen poised over a blank page in his pocket notebook.

"No joy, Ben?"

The fresh-faced Davison turned to Striker. "Huh? Oh sorry. No, not yet, sir."

The two pallid-looking youths were no more than sixteen – about five years younger than Davison, Striker guessed. The one on the left glanced up at Striker with shifty eyes, looking vaguely familiar. The other lad appeared to be sobbing under his dark baggy hood.

"You knew him, fellas?" Striker nodded toward the SOCO tent.

"Sort of," replied Shifty.

"Sort of?"

"Yeah, he's from the Moss. I don't know his name or anyfin' though."

Striker considered this momentarily. Moss Range was another town on the B Division and distinctly rival territory. *So what was the dead youth doing here?* "What happened?" he asked.

"What do yer fuckin' think, man?"

Striker resisted the urge to grab him by the scruff of the neck. Instead, he kept his tone measured. "We weren't here, so I don't know."

"Yeah, exactly. You 'weren't here', were yer?"

Sod this. "Were you involved?" Striker fixed his stare on the cocky one.

"No way, man," he insisted, somewhat panicky.

Striker recalled this character. He'd lifted him a couple of years ago for affray – a kick-off between local gangs, if he wasn't mistaken. A quick flick through the ever-growing files in his mind and a name popped up.

"Look, Grinley" – the lad looked surprised and instantly vulnerable – "we need to know what's happened so we *can* do something about it."

"I dunno anyfin'." Luke Grinley exchanged glances with the other youth. "Anyway, am no grass, copper."

"Right. So you do know something. Was it gang-on-gang?"

Striker swapped looks with Davison while Grinley dipped his head.

Eric Bardsley interjected, "Hey, lah... we have decent witness protection programmes these days, you know."

"Yeah, right." His reply was full of venom. "And am definitely not talking to a Scouser."

"You cheeky..."

Striker blocked Bardsley as the DC lunged toward Grinley. "Eric, go check on the Chinese chippy before it shuts." Bardsley eyed Grinley then walked away grumbling. Striker turned his attention to the other lad. "What about you, fella?"

"Say nowt, Mozo." It was almost a threat from Grinley.

"Zip it." Striker glared at Grinley.

The other boy looked up, his face streaked where grubby hands had seemingly been wiping tears. "I..."

Grinley appeared to nudge him with his elbow.

Striker lifted a warning finger and Grinley turned away huffily.

"Yes, go on."

"I saw nowt neither."

"Ever heard that withholding evidence is an offence?"

Mozo screwed his face up. "Yeah. So what? I've been locked up for 'obstruct police' before an' got off with it."

Crocodile tears? True colours shining through? "Oh, you have, have you? How about I lock you both up for murder, you cocky little shits?" Striker saw what scant colour there was draining from the boys' faces, but was disappointed he'd only lasted a matter of minutes in keeping his cool. Still, these pricks needed to show more respect. Despite his fourteen years' service in the Job – a perpetually expanding client base, a booming business even the credit crunch couldn't wane – some things never changed: the cocksure arrogance of the budding criminal.

"Where have your mates gone?"

"Dunno. They just ran off," mumbled Mozo.

"Where and why?"

"Dunno and dunno."

After an exaggerated sigh, mindful of other crucial avenues to explore, Striker said, "You've not heard the last from me." Turning to Davison and lowering his voice, he said, "PNC them both and verify their current details. Don't let them go anywhere until you've got signed first accounts. And if they don't assist you, threaten to lock them up for obstruct."

"Will do, Boss," said the young constable, a flicker of insecurity in his expression.

Striker thought for a moment, realising the officer's inexperience. "Give me a minute and I'll get you some help, Ben." Striker gave the boys a parting shot. "Tell this officer what you know or you'll be arrested."

He retraced his steps back through the outer scene, scanning the floor for anything eye-catching as five more uniformed officers tumbled out of a divisional van outside the main cordon. He was pleased to see DC Lauren Collinge with them, her friendly, pretty face and sweeping auburn locks lifting his spirits somewhat.

He smiled at Collinge, who reciprocated; the slight gap between her central incisors her only blemish, present perhaps because God thought she was *too* beautiful.

"Hi, Boss. Been a while."

"Lauren. Good to have you back."

"It's nice to be back."

"How was the course?"

"Nothing I couldn't handle."

"Apparently so. Believe you passed with flying colours. Congratulations."

"Yep. I'm a fully-fledged detective now, Boss." She flicked her hair confidently, her captivating smile enhanced by a subtle tan.

Realising the lull created by her arrival, Striker promptly refocused. "We'll catch up later, Lauren, but for now go and assist that constable over there" – he gestured at Davison and the hoodies – "and see what you can get from those two…" He refrained from calling them 'scrotes'.

"Sure. Whatever I can do to help," she said, giving him the smile again.

Striker watched her go. "And Lauren…"

Collinge stopped, looked round.

"Call me Jack. You're part of the team now."

She nodded and winked at him.

Striker smiled inwardly, pleased to have her on board. She'd been helping out on attachment from CID, having expressed her interest in MIT to Striker a few months earlier. Admittedly, he'd pulled a few strings, but he knew she was a willing worker and quick learner. Striker was aware of the occasional raised eyebrow from other female detectives who'd wrongly assumed something to be going on between Collinge and himself, but the rumours were unfounded. There was no way Collinge would go for a man ten years her senior, especially one with Striker's baggage. It was simply his prerogative to build a team he could trust implicitly.

He swiftly instructed the newly arrived officers to their assigned duties. He tasked two of them to conduct house-to-house, one to make CCTV enquiries at the petrol station, another to liaise with the response sergeant to help with the scene log, if necessary, and also to assist in preserving the scene from the ever-growing crowd. All the while Striker kept glancing over at Lauren Collinge.

The officers eagerly starburst to their various tasks as Striker weighed up the evidence so far, or lack of it. The sound of an approaching vehicle caught his attention. He fought off a feeling of deflation while watching the DCI's shiny, silver Mondeo park up.

Now, here was a woman he *wasn't* so happy to see.

Typical.

Chapter Two

Chisel weaved through the dark, dank Manchester alleyways like a sewer rat. He looked repeatedly over his shoulder as he fled the scene of his latest scrape with the law, the distant sirens diminishing into the night. On this occasion it wasn't planned, but these things just sort of happened to him, not that he gave a toss.

The guy shouldn't have objected to him jumping the queue anyway, especially when Chisel was hungry and wanted a Big Mac. Well that twat won't be doing *that* again in hurry.

No one else had objected, just dipped their heads, and a good job too. But there's always one – probably trying to impress his bird. Slowly scanning the back of the long line of terraced houses, Chisel replayed events in McDonald's.

"Erm, excuse me, pal. Do yer mind not pushing in?" said the scraggly-haired freak.

"You fuckin' what, Mr Big Shot?" Chisel saw the student-type physically shrink, pathetically clutching onto his bag of books.

The bird piped up, "He didn't mean it, go ahead, it's fine," stepping half in front of her shithouse boyfriend.

Chisel pushed the girl to one side like a rag doll and eyeballed the student. "Fancy yer chances? Want some?"

"I was simply pointing out that…"

The headbutt rudely interrupted the student's sentence and burst his nose, spraying the cowering crowd.

Staggering forward for more? "Okay, if you want some, you can have some." Chisel threw a flurry of punches and the student dropped like a sack of shit. The big right particularly pleased him, sending a shock-absorbing shudder up his arm. The girlfriend's screams and the pleas from the McDonald's staff were just a distant boring drone. Chisel was in the zone. The student was in a ball on the floor and his head was beautifully placed for a good stamping. And that's what it got, over and over. Something crunched on the sixth stamp.

It was only when some bloke in the queue, clutching the hand of his little, sobbing daughter, pulled at Chisel's shoulder and gestured at the CCTV camera pointing directly at them that he came to his senses a bit. He could now hear the unison of screaming as if someone had turned the volume up.

"The cameras in 'ere are crap," Chisel said to the bloke, before pulling his loose hoodie further over his face, just in case.

"The police are on their way," shouted a burger-flipper from behind the counter.

"Good. Well now there's plenty of fuckin' ketchup for those fat bastards, in't there?"

He left feeling a bit pissed off with himself. He was still hungry and had been really looking forward to that Big Mac. Like any cop-dodger worth his salt, seeing blue lights flashing in the distance, he quickly sought the sanctuary of the alleyways.

Ever the opportunist, Chisel finished scanning the line of rear windows, smirked in the darkness and slipped on a pair of leather gloves. His shadowy, hooded form slid between two wheelie bins and, despite his blood-spattered Nike trainers, he easily climbed over the wall into the back yard. Yet another unsuspecting householder had kindly left their kitchen window open for him.

People just never learn. No security light. No dog barking. A ladder, too... Fuckin' bingo! The house was in darkness and he carefully positioned the step ladder beneath the kitchen window. He wriggled his stocky frame through the generous transom window in quick time. The stale whiff of unwashed pots rose as plates clattered in the sink below, making him freeze for a second. He crouched like Spiderman's shadow on the kitchen unit, his senses heightened, his hand ready to withdraw his flick knife in an instant.

No return movement. No alarm. Definitely nobody home. It wouldn't have mattered anyway because he'd just stab whoever was unfortunate enough to disturb him. He'd done it several times before. That's how he got his nickname and how he became cock of the school before he was expelled. He didn't kill gobby Bobby Lomas in woodwork class, but he did shut the twat up with a chisel.

There had been no long stretch inside for Chisel, not with his boys doing their stuff when he was on remand at HMP Forest Bank. Nothing like a bit of witness intimidation to shut up a few blabbermouths. The 'not guilty' verdict was based on the fact that Lomas had lunged at him, and Chisel had had a legitimate reason for holding the chisel and had just 'reacted'. With the only witness testifying being Chisel's buddy, Jamie 'Johnno' Johnson, the judge and jury had no option and Chisel was freed.

He slid off the kitchen unit, withdrew a tiny torch and went for a mooch. Nothing heavy, just valuable – the golden rule of the lone burglar. The VW keys on the lounge coffee table were tempting, but he wasn't too arsed about car keys tonight. The cops would be knocking about, so best not. He'd stand out like a priest at a drug deal if he hit the streets in a stolen car. Anyway, he'd promised to meet Johnno, Bezzer and the rest of lads, and was running late. It was Bezzer's eighteenth so they'd all be stocked up with beer, coke and weed, and it was only right that Chisel brought something to the party.

Five minutes and as many rooms later, Chisel's pockets were filled with two gold rings, a mobile phone, three credit cards, a Nintendo DSi and forty-odd quid. The bonus of the latest Grand Theft Auto made him grin. Bezzer loved this shit so, all heart, Chisel would give his mate the game for his birthday.

Fifteen minutes of ducking, diving and skulking later, and Chisel felt secure in the sanctuary of his patch – Bullsmead.

He could hear Bezzer and the rest of Bad Bastard Bullsmead Boys before he actually saw them, their voices carrying in the cool night air. He felt charged up as he turned into the side street off Bullsmead Road and approached his boys. They'd already started on the booze, the twats.

Bezzer was sitting on a waist-high cable TV electrical box beside the wall of a 1950's gable-end terraced house. He wore his trendy baseball cap side on and was supping a bottle – Lambrini no doubt. The rest were hooded up, in a mishmash of black tracksuits and jackets. They gathered noisily around Bezzer under the streetlamp, jostling positions and generally larking about. An empty bottle flew through the air and bounced onto the road, the hollow clinking echoing between the two gable-ends of the side street that the gang occupied, then rolled to a stop at the kerb.

Chisel smiled. True to form, wannabe graffiti artist Johnno was spraying 'BBBB' in yellow on the wall of the end terrace while the unsuspecting occupant of the house was probably sat watching Newsnight reporting on yet another example of 'Broken Britain'. Chisel was proud of his boys.

He emerged from the darkness like a beast from a cave, striding toward the throng with a cocky swagger, his arms opening at his sides.

"Yo, Chisel, what's up?" One of the lads spotted him and their knuckles soon met in a macho greeting. He grabbed a bottle of Bud', downed it in one and wiped his mouth with his sleeve before lobbing the bottle into the night, ignoring the smash seconds later.

The other five repeated the knuckle greeting ritual, springs in their steps now their leader was here. They all gathered around Chisel, like flies round shit, as he told them about how he'd battered some student in McDonald's earlier because he'd misguidedly objected at Chisel jumping the queue. His re-enactment of the punches he'd thrown and the stamping he'd done on the lad's head produced roaring laughter and high fives from the boys.

He then told them, with a plethora of 'ra-ras' and 'innits', how the McDonald's staff were all pussies and had shit themselves. Plus, he'd left the lad motionless in a pool of blood on the floor with books strewn about and his girlfriend crying over him. Chisel's impression of the girl crying was hilarious.

"Hey, Bezzer. Happy birthday, mucker." Chisel produced Grand Theft Auto from his pocket. "Been doing a spot of shopping," he said, revealing tobacco-stained teeth.

Bezzer's face lit up. "Fuckin' awesome, mate. Nice one." He fizzed open a can of super-strength lager and gave it to Chisel, who again gulped it in one, and then squashed the can as he let out a long burp. He chucked the can over a wall into the back yard of the nearest terrace, causing a clatter, and held out his hand for another.

A light came on in the rear downstairs room of the house and the concerned face of a woman peered through the window, a hand raised above her eyes as if to aid her vision.

Johnno shouted, "Fuck off, you nosy cow," alerting the others, who all joined in the abuse, accompanied by V-signs and middle fingers.

A startled look zoomed across the woman's face. She

disappeared behind the curtain and was soon replaced by a man of about forty.

"Come on then, dickhead," yelled Chisel, his palms face up, repeatedly curling his fingers inwardly. The others also edged forward, bouncing on their feet, a couple doing the universal wanker gesture, goading the occupant.

The man's face wore a mixture of confusion, anger and fear. A few seconds later, the house's rear door opened and the man peeped out, the yard wall obscuring him except for his head.

"I've got kids asleep, lads. Could you please keep the noise down?"

"Get fucked, knobhead."

"There's no need for that. I've already called the police."

"Well that gives us another fuckin' hour then dunnit, you grassing twat," shouted Chisel, who thundered toward his prey. He clambered onto the top of the wall, spitting threats close up to the man, who stepped back wincing. On cue, *artiste extraordinaire* Johnno sprayed 'GRASS' in fancy yellow letters on the wall. Another threw a beer bottle, which smashed on the brickwork above the rear door, the shards falling close to the retreating occupant. Two cans clattered off the closing door as the man hastily slammed it shut.

When a brick shattered the window of what was probably the kitchen, the gang ran off, nearly pissing themselves with laughter.

Parked across the street, the engine of the black, tinted-windowed VW Golf GTI fired up, growled and followed them…

Chapter Three

DCI Maria Cunningham was a climber, and in Striker's estimation was welcome to the job. He felt anything above DI became too political, and he hated politics. Nor was he willing to shag his way to the top like she had. Admittedly, the way she'd overtaken him in the promotion stakes, despite having less service than him, did grate somewhat. They'd both served as constables together and, boy, were there fireworks back then, particularly when he became her sergeant. Soon enough, Cunningham's Manchester University qualifications – assisted ably by her sexual exploits – had given her an unfair advantage, providing an upward route via the force's 'High-Potential Scheme'.

However, that route didn't necessarily make you a good cop. Striker had a degree in being streetwise, which beat a sociology certificate every time in his book. His main disgruntlement stemmed from the super's unprofessionalism in allowing a good blow-job to influence his judgement. The paradox being that an officer could unintentionally make a Freudian slip or casual remark and the weight of GMP would squash them like an ant underfoot. But things like the super's and Cunningham's dalliance went unchallenged. He used to think they were all on the same team, though not now. The ground above him was way too political and, like some politicians, just as sleazy.

Cunningham had done nothing notable investigation-wise, yet she strutted her stuff like an old pro. She tried her best to look in her twenties, but Striker knew that with her being quite a late joiner, she was pushing forty. He recalled their 'little encounter' when Striker was in uniform on Response, though he tried not to dwell on *that* too much, which was easier said than done when it was the catalyst that changed his life.

It was fair to say, Cunningham wasn't on his Christmas card list.

He shook his head as the admittedly good-looking and fake tanned DC Brad Sterling got out of the driver's side, then rushed round the Mondeo to open the DCI's door. *Give me a bucket*, thought Striker. Rumours were rife about these two, and Striker had seen jealousy in the super's eyes more than once, knowing the old boy couldn't possibly compete with Sterling. Bardsley had cruelly dubbed Sterling 'Brad Shit', and the nickname had spread around the station.

Cunningham was dressed in a figure-hugging, slate-grey, pin-striped pencil skirt and jacket, her peroxide blonde hair in a bun, more than a hint of make-up – all business. Mutton and lamb sprang to mind.

"What have we got then, Striker?" Her voice was as hollow and emotionless as ever.

Striker pointed at the SOCO tent. "Mixed-race male, mid-to-late teens, clubbed to death. Maybe with a baseball bat, judging by the marks on his head and body."

"Witnesses?"

Striker nodded in the direction of Grinley and Mozo on the wall, being quizzed by Collinge and Davison. "Those two possibly, but don't hold your breath."

"Meaning?" She exchanged looks with Sterling.

"They're 'not grasses', apparently."

"Take them back to the station and get statements."

"They're juveniles and they're unwilling."

The DCI's eyes hardened, voice notching up a decibel. "Then arrest them and make them willing. What else?"

"The pathologist is just finishing an autopsy and he'll be down in half an hour."

"Get him down now. The body he's working on isn't going anywhere, is it?"

She had a point. "I'll have him called again." Striker glanced at Sterling.

"You do it, Inspector Striker," said the DCI. "It's your scene. What else?"

Cold inside, he appraised Cunningham of the ongoing enquiries, expressing his optimism about CCTV checks at the petrol station and the newsagent Khalid Khan seeing the man fleeing the scene. The robust Tactical Aid Unit – commonly known as TAG before 'group' was changed to 'unit' – were to undergo a line search; however, he was still awaiting adequate lighting to arrive from police stores at Openshaw on the other side of the city.

"Think about what you need and get it. I want this sorted. Mr Brennan is watching us."

Watching you more like, you insatiable cow.

Cunningham and her 'bitch' Sterling strolled off to inspect the body as the inevitable Manchester rain began to fall. Striker looked heavenward and cursed. He radioed a request for air support to take aerial shots of the scene at dawn. He also chased up Sidney Mortham, the forensic pathologist, who it turned out was already en route.

Striker had a bad feeling about this one, and not all of it to do with the DCI.

Not one of your everyday beatings, this. Someone had gone over the top. If the victim was from Moss Range then what was he doing around here in rival territory? Was it just another gangland feud or something else? Part of him hoped it was the former, as he'd had several successes as a DS in the gang unit. The alternative was what frightened him most.

"Boss."

Lauren Collinge's soft voice made him turn. She and Bardsley approached, with DCI Cunningham and DC Sterling just behind, dipping under the police tape from the crime scene.

"Bad news," said Collinge. "Both lads say they were in Khan's newsagents when the attack happened."

Striker clocked the DCI's stony expression.

Bardsley passed Striker an orange GMP memo. "Here's Mr Khan's number. At least we can check with him."

Cunningham's lips pinched. Striker dialled Khan's number. It went straight to answerphone. Cunningham exhaled loudly before walking away. She passed the officer who Striker had tasked earlier with checking the CCTV at the petrol station, now on his return.

"Sir, the man in the garage only speaks broken English and he can't work the CCTV system."

Typical. Striker checked to see if Cunningham was listening and saw her standing by the Mondeo within earshot. "So, who can work it?"

"The manager's not back in until ten-thirty tomorrow morning."

Cunningham shook her head. "I need a result with this one, Striker."

It was then that her phone rang – nothing fancy, just a boring Nokia tone. Striker watched intently as she answered it, seeing her stern face become granite in the moonlight.

Chapter Four

Chisel, Bezzer and Johnno scaled the locked gates of Bullsmead Park. The council locked them every evening to stop youths causing problems late at night. Yeah right, as if a locked five-foot gate would stop them.

The rest of the boys had scattered on seeing a lone panda car bumbling toward them along Bullsmead Road. It was probably a probationer, unsure of this patch. Chisel hadn't panicked like some of the others, since he knew how few patrol cops there actually were from his many encounters with them. He'd overheard and mentally noted snippets of conversations each time he'd been nicked. He'd gathered quite a bit of what they call 'intelligence' on them, because of their loose banter and blatant complacency.

Most of the filth would be tied up with the crime scene he'd adeptly created in McDonald's: a student with a face like an embarrassed Mr Potato Head. Now that *was* art, sod Johnno's shitty graffiti. Yeah, Chisel knew only too well just who actually ruled the roost around here and it certainly wasn't the cops.

Out of breath, they cut through the dense blackness of the park, lit meagrely by the moon's intermittent appearances behind pewter clouds. Just as the Manchester rain began to spit, they plonked themselves down on the woodchip beneath a large wooden, graffiti-stained climbing frame that offered shelter from the rain.

"Good buzz that," said Chisel. "We'll meet back up with those shit-bags later, and I'll have a word about sticking together. Fuckin' lightweights."

"If the cop had got out, we could've done him anyway," said Bezzer confidently. "It would've made me birthday that... kicking a pig's head in." He grinned. "Got any weed left, Johnno?"

"Hang on." Aided by Chisel's torch beam, Johnno reached into the inside pocket of his black hoodie and pulled out a ready-made reefer. "Ta-daah!"

"Nice one, mate."

The spliff passed between them and the conversation soon turned to the opposite sex.

"Hey, Chis, you still shagging that milf?" asked Bezzer, somewhat croakily as he exhaled smoke.

"Her name's Dorothy. And, yeah, now an' then I get the odd blow-job."

"Jammy bastard. Leanne wouldn't suck me cock if I paid her. Says it stinks of cheese." Bezzer's mobile phone did a burst of Eminem's Slim Shady and he checked the message. "Talk of the devil."

Chisel exchanged looks with Johnno, who smirked, obviously thinking the same thing.

"The devil? More like the angel. Anyway, she'd have to find your smelly cock first, wouldn't she?"

"Fuck you, Johnno. At least I've got a bird." Bezzer's fingers bleeped the keypad repeatedly in reply to Leanne's text.

"Look at yer, all loved up, kissy, kissy... aw..." Johnno retaliated.

"She swallows, too," boasted Chisel.

"Who, Leanne? How do you know, Chis?" Johnno laughed at his own joke and Chisel joined in, the marijuana taking effect.

"Hey. I mean it, you..."

Still giggling, Chisel thrust an arm across the lunging Bezzer. "Bez, chill man. We're just having a laugh. I was on about Dorothy. There's no hesitation what-so-fuckin-ever with the older birds." He snatched Bezzer's phone and opened the text inbox.

"Hey, what're doing, Chis? C'mon mate." Bezzer sounded worried and reached for his phone. Chisel shoved his protests away, and read what Bezzer had typed – soppy crap. The faint light from the phone illuminated mischief in Chisel's features when he replaced the text message with his own version, while Bezzer's head dipped into his hands.

Chisel held the phone up. "SEND."

"Aw, what have you sent, man?"

Chisel tossed him the phone and Bezzer frantically tapped away, until he reached the last outgoing message. He stared agape, his pale face lit up by the screen's light.

Johnno leaned forward, chuckling. "Read it out then, lover boy."

"Chis, you twat."

"What's he put… What's he put?" Johnno was getting giddy.

"Tell him, Bez."

"Well it's too fuckin' late now innit? He sent… 'How's about a birthday blow-job?'"

Chisel and Johnno fed off each other in a five-minute burst of uncontrollable laughter. After his initial curses, Bezzer joined in, such was the potency of the Moroccan Black.

The laughter was halted by Eminem.

"Oh shit. She's replied."

They eyed Bezzer, who grinned like a kid on Christmas morning.

Chisel exchanged bemused looks with Johnno.

"What did she say, man?" asked Johnno excitedly.

Bezzer's voice went up a note. "She said, 'Okay… but only if you shower.'"

"*Now* who's the jammy bastard?" Chisel grinned.

Bezzer got up. "Cheers, Chis." Their fists tapped each other's.

"Fuck me, Bez… You got a semi on already?" asked Johnno.

"Not quite, but soz, lads, am offski." He stood up, clutching the stolen game. "And thanks, Chis."

"You can always rely on Chisel to come up trumps. Don't blame yer, mate. Go get yer birthday blow-job."

Bezzer winked, then jogged off across the kids' play area and into the darkness.

Johnno shouted, "Don't forget to clean yer cock!" When Bezzer was out of sight, Johnno said, "Sucker," as he withdrew another joint from his pocket and lit it.

Chisel smiled. "You sly twat."

The glow of the spliff passed between them until it was spent and Chisel flicked it like a mini-meteor into the night, the drizzle soon extinguishing it.

"I'm gonna take a leak." Chisel stood up, his legs leaden momentarily, before walking a few paces into the gloom. Mid-piss, he heard a crunch of foliage behind him. He glanced toward the bushes that ran alongside the play area, separating the park from the high fence of Bullsmead Primary School.

"D'yer hear that, Johnno?"

"What, man? I'm cabbaged."

Chisel shook the dribbles off and slapped his cock away. "Sharpen up. That fuckin' noise. Someone's here."

Johnno sat up from his slouched position and Chisel could see that he was out of the game. "S'not the pigs, is it?"

Chisel took out his torch, shined it at the bushes. "Who the fuck's there?"

"I'm here, man... am..." droned Johnno.

Useless prick. Chisel flicked his knife out, stepped slowly toward the bushes. They rustled in the wind, the torchlight misshaping them into a hundred dark figures, the fine rain hindering visibility. *Fuck, I've had too much weed.*

"You're getting para... noid, Chis. It's just... this Moroccan, man. It always does..." A whooshing sound and dull thud ended Johnno's sentence.

Chisel shot his torch beam under the climbing frame and saw his mate sprawled face down in the woodchip.

"Shit." Feeling a rage and fear cocktail erupt from deep within, he zigzagged the blade in front of him, cutting though the darkness. "Do yer know who you're fuckin' with? Do yer? Fuckin' want some?"

"Yes of course I do, Chisel. That's why I'm here."

The calm, deep voice made him physically jump and pivot. Oddly, the casual tone and use of his name scared him more than seeing his mate out cold. He felt a sudden jolt of pain to his knife hand and dropped the blade. Then the same swift blow to his torch hand.

"Aaargh, you fuck..." Another whoosh of air was followed in an instant by something hard impacting Chisel's temple area, a sharp flare of light in his mind's eye as he fell onto the damp woodchip.

Hearing crunching footsteps, he shook his head fast, trying to regain his senses. He felt another whack across his back, the shooting pain sparking him into life. He rolled under the climbing frame, managed to clamber to his feet.

He could see the silhouette of his attacker about three metres away, legs slightly apart, with a backdrop of the full moon. The man wore a balaclava. "Who the fuck are yer? What do yer want?"

"You, Chisel… I want you," the voice replied evenly. The figure motionless, clutching a long thin weapon.

"Drop that metal pole and let's do it then."

No answer, still no movement, just a solid stance, weapon in hand. He was a big fucker, but so was Chisel.

Chisel glanced behind him at the gloomy expanse that was the football fields. For no more than a micro-second, he considered running. This angered him even more. The 'zone' feeling began to take over, building his rage.

"Fancy yer chances then, Mr Big Shot, eh? Want some… eh? Fuckin' eh?" Chisel ran forward and launched himself into the guy's midriff. It was like hitting a brick wall. He felt winded, but his fifteen stone managed to shift the man backward. They landed on the woodchip, Chisel on top, and he began pummelling the masked face. The first punch connected, a couple more missed as the target shifted from side to side. The next punch was caught. Chisel felt his right fist being squeezed, then twisted, and he let out a yelp. His enemy's ice-cool eyes glared menacingly from behind the balaclava.

Chisel felt a heavy punch to his left cheek. Recovering from the stinging blow, he realised that both his hands were now gripped. He used all his strength to force a head-butt, but the target moved, Chisel ending up with a mouth full of wet woodchip. They grappled and swiftly Chisel felt the man's strength roll him onto his back.

Shit. Roles reversed, the manoeuvre instant, the man was now on top. Chisel felt drained. Sturdy gloved thumbs pushed into Chisel's eyes sockets, his hands automatically shooting up to his face.

"Aaargh." The pain was excruciating. He could hardly see, aches all over, his fight ebbing away. The weight and strength of the mystery man pinned him down and Chisel felt both his wrists had been gripped tightly again. "What's your… problem… man?" he asked breathlessly.

"You… You are my problem." The tone was still surprisingly measured.

Chisel got a whiff of garlic from the guy's breath. "Why? What the... fuck... have I... done... to you?"

"It's what you've done to all your victims I'm interested in."

"What are yer... on about, man?"

"Citizens you've burgled, innocent people you've beaten up for no reason than for your own pleasure, that school kid you stabbed with a fucking chisel... *Chisel*. You and your fuckwit friends causing fear in the neighbourhood... Need I say more? Because there's much more, isn't there?"

"How do yer know... all this shit? And what... the fuck's... it gotta do with you anyway?"

"Where do you see yourself in five years, Chisel?"

"Eh? Dunno. What the... What are yer goin' on about, man?"

"Exactly."

"Fuck this." Chisel jolted a hand free and grabbed at the balaclava, yanking it up. On seeing the face, Chisel was gobsmacked and his mind drowned in mishmash of memories. "YOU?"

The smile on the familiar face was soon a grimace. A ferocious punch later and the lights in Chisel's world were switched off.

Chapter Five

Rookie PC Ben Davison had drawn a blank with his area search for the youths who'd smashed Mr and Mrs Wilkinson's kitchen window. He'd caught a glimpse of them running off, but once they'd hit the alleyways and backstreets he'd stood no chance whatsoever. He was the only free response patrol, since everyone else was tied up with the crime scene over on Bullsmead Road.

Sergeant Roache had freed Davison up from talking to the two hoodies on the wall with that sexy DC Lauren Collinge. "Go keep the wheel on," Roache had said. But Davison's radio was hot due to the flood of Friday-night calls. There simply weren't enough cops available, full stop.

Instead of catching the criminals who were blighting the local community with mindless acts of aggression, he was slowly realising that he just was a crime-recording machine. He'd dutifully taken a statement, their baby crying throughout, giving him a stinker of a headache. He'd tried to reassure the Wilkinsons that the police were "doing all we can". Just as he'd said that, another job boomed over his radio detailing "shouting and screaming on Bullsmead Park", which made him look like a bit of a tit, to say the least. Tumbleweed had passed over the airwaves and Davison thought, *I'm it*, as the last free cop standing would always say.

Having gleaned enough details to input a crime report of criminal damage later, he'd gulped half his lukewarm coffee, excused himself and headed out of the front door to his panda.

Thirty seconds later. "One treble-eight six en route," said Davison into his radio as he turned onto Moss Range Road, one-handed, blue lights flashing. No sirens though, stealth mode, because he wanted to actually catch criminals, not scare them off.

He was rather disgruntled that he'd yet again failed in the 'search' aspect of his job, with another negative area search now to his name. He'd recently been signed as competent by his tutor constable, after hitting the mandatory target of eighty per cent of competencies in his 'personal development profile'. The PDP, as it was known, was the bane of all student officers. Despite reaching the necessary percentage, he knew his searching of persons and property left a lot to be desired. And his supervisors had made him aware of this, in their inimitable way.

It hadn't helped when he'd done a short stint at Bullsmead custody suite as part of his training. Davison had searched an arrestee, fingerprinted him, then escorted him to his cell. Ten minutes later, one of the detention officers had been doing the hourly checks and had seen the detainee that Davison had supposedly searched. He was in his cell on his mobile phone, smoking a spliff! Oops. Davison hadn't used the hand-held metal detector which would've alerted him to the stash up this regular's arse. A schoolboy error on Davison's part, and word travelled fast of his poor performance, bringing the many piss takers on the division out of the woodwork.

Both the custody sergeant and Roache had told him in no uncertain terms that he needed to sharpen up, search-wise. He still had an ongoing 'action plan' that he was desperate to complete. Some of his peers had bragged about finding shell casings at shootings, screwdrivers and knives on offenders after a stop and search, as well as the more common snap-bags of cannabis. His discovery of the wet, porous brick on the Wilkinsons' kitchen table was useless in comparison. Maybe this job on the park would be his opportunity to shine.

He pushed the transmit button on the side of his police radio clipped to the top right of his body armour. "Where's the call come from, Mo?" he asked Maureen Banks, his shift's regular over at comms in Clayton Brook.

"Diane at number twenty-seven Park Road, but she doesn't want a visit."

"Any description?"

"Unfortunately not, Ben… just 'shouting and screaming'… I'll call her back."

"Cheers, Mo."

The thrill of speeding in a marked police car was still relatively new to him, having not long since passed his standard police driving test, and he milked it at every opportunity. He'd only been out of company from his tutor constable for three months, so even dressing up as a cop was still a novelty. The power of carrying a warrant card could easily go to your head, if you let it.

He'd like to think he hadn't, although some of his non-cop mates had said he'd changed. Inevitable really, since they now saw him differently and, like many people, they probably had stuff to hide. Be it no car tax or a house full of knocked-off gear that "fell off the back of a lorry" or was "bought from a bloke in the pub". He couldn't blame them though; Davison himself was still partial to the odd bargain, even now, credit crunch and all.

A couple of pedestrians looked up startled as he took a sharp right onto Park Road. He soon eased on the footbrake, anticipating the first of ten sleeping policemen he knew existed up to the park gates – a bid by the council to temper speeding motorists, with Bullsmead Primary School being adjacent to the park.

On his approach the park gates emerged between a long line of terraced houses. He clocked number twenty-seven to his left, the source of the call, but didn't stop. He switched off the emergency lights. His anxiety grew on envisaging the vast eeriness of the park at this time of night and he sought reassurance by fumbling for his flashlight on his utility belt. He clicked it out of its holder, while easing the panda to a halt outside the park gates.

Pressing the transmission button on his radio, he said, "One treble-eight six, state six, single-manned – sorry – *crewed*." He cringed knowing how politically correct some of his supervisors were. You never really knew just who was on air in the police from day to day. He'd simply wanted to let anyone listening know that he was alone, but deep down he knew no one was available to back him up anyway.

Checking his flashlight was working, he got out of the panda and clambered over the shoulder-high park gates. "Entering the park now," he informed comms, trying not to sound nervous.

The park's eeriness swamped him. With his torch beam sweeping from side to side, the bushes seemed to move on their own. He thought he saw the shape of a dark figure and flicked the beam back.

Nothing. He inhaled deeply, edging forward. Silence, except for his own footsteps and breathing.

He wondered whether this job had anything to do with those youths at the Wilkinsons'. He felt rather edgy and unclipped his retractable baton, before clicking it open. He briefly pictured his beautiful fiancée Louise, who he was taking to the Lake District tomorrow on his rest day. He planned on proposing to her on a boat trip on Lake Windermere. He'd got it all sussed: a cake with sparklers and everyone on the boat joining in with that old 'Congratulations' song, hopefully. The celebratory meal was booked at a swanky restaurant overlooking the lake.

His torch beam followed the narrow path to its end, where the park opened up to a vast darkness. He shined it to his right across the expansive field, then to his left toward the children's play area. The outline of a climbing frame and swings in the distance shifted bizarrely. In front of him was the start of another long path, leading to the exit near Bullsmead Primary School.

Now then… Which way?

The low growl behind him made up his mind.

Chapter Six

In his office, feeling somewhat fatigued, Striker ran his left hand through his hair and stretched his arms upward in front of the computer screen. Not long now until a good night's sleep to fully recharge him for tomorrow.

The office was modest with predominantly beige décor. There was the faint tick of a round white clock on the wall beside a map of the B Division. Through the window the bright city centre lights glowed five miles away.

Cunningham had shot off from the crime scene with her chauffeur-cum-lover boy Brad Sterling. Her last words: "There's been another attack... on the border with the A Division. I just hope it's not linked." Sterling had then done the obligatory wheel-spin and they were gone.

Like Cunningham, initially worried there may be a link with his case, Striker had kept one ear on the radio. He'd returned to the office and checked the computer log regarding the incident Cunningham had rushed off to. Reading it, his heart sank at the callous details. From a selfish viewpoint, he was both relieved and satisfied it was a random attack on a student and it fell into the jurisdiction of the A Division. Stories had been doing the rounds for years of hard-nosed detectives finding a floating corpse on their side of the canal. Such was the mindset of the over-worked Manchester cops, the body was supposedly shoved from their side to the other, making it the responsibility of the other division. He'd never believed such tales, until over a pint on yet another cop's leaving do an old Traffic sergeant insisted, vociferously, that it really did happen.

According to the computer log, the A Division's respective CID was currently going through some apparently decent footage of the incident, so the perpetrator would hopefully soon be caught. And, although the victim was in a bad way and had been rushed to Manchester Royal Infirmary, he had thankfully regained consciousness.

Reverting back to his own case, the cogs weren't exactly turning freely, more like creaking round. The oil he needed was more evidence, and sometimes that wasn't necessarily new evidence, but it could actually be gleaned by analysing what you already had.

It was too early to rule out the possibility that it could have been a racially motivated attack, though something told Striker this wasn't the case. Something didn't feel right, but he couldn't put his finger on it. So who the hell was this dead kid? And who had he annoyed so badly? Some parent, somewhere out there, would be fraught with worry.

He momentarily gazed at the photo of his own kids, Harry and Beth, before him on his mahogany desk. He should've texted Suzi to tell her there was no chance of him picking them up from school tomorrow, as agreed. He'd been too preoccupied and it was now probably too late because she'd be in bed. He'd not seen them for nearly two weeks, due to the conclusion of a recent rape case he'd led before his recent switch from CID. He'd have to sort the matter with Suzi in the morning.

His children's cheeky little faces gazed back at him from the photo, longing for their daddy. With a picturesque backdrop of the North Yorkshire moors, sheep and horses dotted about in the distance, Harry was proudly sporting his Manchester City kit with a raised thumb, resting his right foot on a Spiderman ball. Lucy was sitting on a picnic blanket listening to her MP3 player – probably Beyoncé or One Direction – while smiling as the sun reflected off her wavy, strawberry-blonde hair. Their piercing blue eyes, not too dissimilar to Striker's, were staring deep into his soul.

A pang of guilt began to bubble inside him and he had strong urge for a cigarette, the urge beaten only by his desire to hug his beautiful children there and then. Gazing into space momentarily, he was truly sorry he'd let his family down. He tapped his temples to refocus his brain.

A glance at the clock told him it was gone midnight and he plonked his cup of coffee onto the table, causing the dregs to plop upward and splash onto the desk. He reached across the desk for a tissue, while pondering what he had so far.

The dead lad must have been targeted because checks with the Manchester Royal Infirmary and surrounding hospitals had been negative regarding other youths being admitted with similar injuries. Not for the first time, or the last for that matter, he'd been frustrated by CCTV enquiries. On the surface, they seemed straightforward enough; however, there was always the matter of untrained staff and poor picture quality. If both those aspects were actually positive, then there was the manpower issue of trawling through the footage for anything relevant. A thankless yet vital job.

He dabbed the spilt coffee with the tissue, still reflecting, analysing.

It was typical of the bloody B Division that, despite all those people milling around, there still wasn't a decent witness in sight. What was he to expect though? After all, most people in Bullsmead had criminal records themselves.

He briefly wondered what the DIs in the plusher areas of GMP were currently dealing with, in the likes of Altrincham, Hazel Grove and Ramsbottom. He guessed it wouldn't be this shit. Nonetheless, this was the kind of work for which he'd joined up in the first place and he was more determined than ever to keep proving himself as a decent detective, and now a leader.

With Cunningham and the rest of the brass breathing down his neck, he knew he'd have to put the hours in on this one. It had already been a long day and he decided he would have a chat with newsagent Khalid Khan first thing in the morning. That was one of numerous outstanding actions they'd set up on HOLMES, the Home Office Large Major Enquiries System. The database offered greater inter-force co-operation, since the likes of the notorious Yorkshire Ripper, Peter Sutcliffe, and Soham child murderer Ian Huntley had slipped through the net.

The results of the fingerprint CSI had lifted from items scattered around the crime scene would be back late tomorrow at the earliest. The DNA from cigarette stubs and the discarded lager bottle, maybe the day after. But Striker was impatient and needed to know now so he could look for links, motives, and begin piecing the jigsaw together.

Home Office pathologist Sidney Mortham's initial examination had established the boy, as strongly suspected, had only just died, at approximately 22:15 hours. The deceased had been struck by a "long thin-ish weapon" at least a dozen times, about the head, face and upper body. This had caused extensive swelling to the brain and more fractures and breaks than Mortham as yet could count. In addition, there had also been repeated strikes to the kneecaps, shattering both.

Someone was seriously miffed, thought Striker, as he dropped the coffee-drenched tissue into the bin beside his desk. Cunningham, or Mr Brennan, would arrange a vague press release in conjunction with the Press Office, a necessity to prevent the media from speculating and possibly hindering the investigation.

Tapping away on his keyboard, he pensively concluded a laborious initial write-up on the crime of murder, when he heard a tentative knock on his office door.

"Come in."

Striker was pleased to see DC Lauren Collinge enter, clutching her turquoise A4 daybook.

Collinge had already proven herself as a thorough and competent investigator in her relatively short stint in the CID office with Striker. It was just over a year ago that she'd left the uniform behind after five years on the streets. Being the newest detective in the MIT office – Striker apart – he knew Collinge was probably as apprehensive as he was regarding this current case. After all, he'd only just filled his desk himself three days ago and didn't quite feel at home yet. A few eyebrows were raised when Collinge had been the one to follow him into the office to replace a retiree, considering her inexperience.

Throughout his career he'd always had faith in his team to produce and hoped this would be the same with the team he'd inherited. He knew a few of them well and was confident in their abilities.

Collinge's confidence had grown, under Striker's guidance, during their time in CID. Once she'd played integral roles in sending down several violent offenders, she'd blossomed as a detective and been quickly accepted by her colleagues. This was an achievement in itself, considering some of the hard-nosed characters in the office. She'd never once whinged at getting the shitty end of the stick when initially performing the more menial tasks. This had freed others up to do 'proper police work' and had enhanced her standing considerably.

Collinge was a single twenty-five-year-old and had her own apartment in prosperous Wilmslow, Cheshire. From what Striker had gathered, she ticked all the boxes any red-blooded male would require. She'd certainly turned a few heads when she first entered the CID office. On the occasional post-work do, Striker had seen her presence reduce his predominantly male workforce to a bunch of buffoons, stumbling over themselves to make drink-induced advances toward her. Of course, he'd remained the consummate professional, suppressing his own alcohol-fuelled urges, albeit only just.

They'd still not had a chance to catch-up since he'd sent Collinge to glean first accounts from Grinley and Mozo at their respective parents' homes because of their ages. He'd opted not to arrest them, despite DCI Cunningham's insistence. They'd agreed with him that they didn't mind him sending someone to their home addresses later as long as it was in an unmarked car. Still unconvinced about their accounts, but not enough to arrest them, he thought that Collinge may well get something notable from them.

Striker turned from the computer and the bright office lighting highlighted the DC's gentle tan. "Welcome back. How was your leave?"

"Oh, fine thanks, Boss. Glad to be back, really. Gives me a break from those Spanish waiters."

Striker raised his eyebrows.

"No. I mean they can ogle for England... well, Spain..."

"Ah, I know the type. Back to reality then. Talking of which, anything significant, Lauren?" He suspected from her look that the answer was a resounding "No".

"That Grinley's a right arsehole," she said in exasperation, placing her daybook onto the adjacent desk, her auburn tousles highlighted somewhat by the Spanish sun, swaying as she shook her head.

"Tell me something I don't know," said Striker.

"We can't prove that he saw something, can we? Even if we suspect he did."

"Try telling that to Cunningham."

Collinge rolled her eyes. "No thanks, I'll leave that to you." She smiled.

Cunningham had tried to block Collinge's advancement into MIT, but was overruled by Detective Superintendent Brennan after Striker had made a strong case for the DC.

"We'll work on him, soften him up a bit." Striker took a sip of his coffee. "What about that Mozo character? Thought you may have gotten around him."

"Meaning?"

"You know, your charm and winning smile." Lauren's grin, revealing the cute gap in her front teeth again, pleased Striker and he instantly pictured Mozo melting. "See."

"Well, he was the more talkative of the two, granted." She leaned slightly over the adjacent desk, placing a palm to the side of her daybook as she opened it and flicked a couple of pages, seeming to skim-read her notes.

Striker chided himself when he unintentionally caught a glimpse of her lacy black bra as she leaned forward, and he instantly averted his eyes. She was undoubtedly a bright girl, though he couldn't help wondering if she realised how much of herself she was presently revealing. It was a good job Bardsley wasn't in the room; he'd be dribbling by now. She soon appeared to locate what she was searching for.

"Ah yes. Mozo – or Nathan Mozerelli to us – said he'd popped into the newsagents for some fags, leaving his five or six mates outside."

Striker scratched his head. "Five or six? The newsagent Khan told Eric there were a dozen."

"Well, that's what Mozo said. Then he exited the shop because he heard a lot of shouting and saw everyone running in different directions. Some headed down the side street at the back of the petrol station. Then he spotted the boy lying in the road."

"So he doesn't know the lad?"

"Said he was from another gang who they were meeting up with to do 'some business', but he wouldn't elaborate."

"Ah, another gang. That explains Khan saying there were more. Did Mozo give you a name?"

"He only knew of him by his nickname... Wait for it... 'Gasbo'."

Striker hastily pulled his keyboard closer and typed in a person search for 'Gasbo'. He drummed his fingers on the desk while he waited for OPUS, the frustratingly slow local system, to produce a result of the search. It had been harshly referred to as "Hopeless" more than once, and plans were afoot to replace it.

Gazing at a blank screen, he turned to Collinge. "So, he didn't see the attack?"

"He said not."

"Well it's a start, of sorts. We'll speak with him again, see if we can squeeze a bit more out of him. I'll get the night Response lot to do preliminary house-to-house down the side street. I take it that's Spinney Lane?"

"Correct."

Striker stared impatiently at the screen.

"Boss, if you don't mind me saying, you look tired. Do you want me do the searches?"

Striker was touched, but just smiled and shook his head. "Lauren, you can call me Jack, you know," he said, eyes fixed on the screen, which had finally sprung to life.

"Okay. You found him… Jack?"

For a moment Striker remained quiet, checking the descriptions and records of the possible hits. "Well, there's six come up, but only four are teenagers and three of them are known on this division. Gareth Bolands is the only mixed-race one, so looks favourite… Jeez, five pages of crimes. He must have pissed a few people off." Striker hastily scrolled through forty plus pages of intelligence. "And guess what…" Collinge moved closer, leaning in, and Striker got a pleasant waft of her perfume. *Burberry Touch?*

"Gasbo's got an ASBO?" guessed Collinge, meaning an anti-social behaviour order. ASBOs were issued by the civil courts to people who'd repeatedly acted anti-socially, and a breach of their stringent behavioural conditions carried a power of arrest. However, they'd backfired on the government somewhat for two reasons. Firstly, breaches were so common that the UK's overcrowded prisons couldn't possibly house the offenders. And, secondly, many of their recipients wore the ASBO tag as a bad boy badge of honour, consequently enhancing their notoriety.

"Yes, he's a wrong-un... or was one. Keep this to yourself until we have forensic proof or a positive ID. Print results have been fast-tracked and should be back tomorrow."

"Do you want me to check to see if he's been reported missing from home?"

"No, Eric's still out and about, I'll get him to do it. Good work, Lauren. You've done your bit for today. I'll sort your overtime sheet. Now get yourself off home and get in for the briefing at eight-thirty tomorrow." He glanced at his watch. "This morning."

"No debrief tonight then?"

"No. I'll assess what we've got and we'll all get stuck in tomorrow."

He forced a smile, which Collinge returned, only better, before leaving. The waft from the closing door blew the remaining scent of her agreeable perfume toward Striker. Definitely Burberry Touch; he'd bought the same for Suzi the Christmas before their split.

An hour after Lauren left, Striker was still collating all the initial info gleaned, when his mobile sounded 'Blue Moon'. The anthem to his beloved Manchester City never failed to produce a sarcastic response from the many United fans in the vicinity.

"Change that bloody ringtone," emanated from the CID office across the corridor. A lone detective – aka the 'night DO' – took care of any serious jobs overnight.

Striker was fleetingly pleased to have wound up another Red. 'Eric' appeared on the HTC's screen, hopefully responding to the call Striker had made after Collinge left, about missing persons.

Eric Bardsley was old school and hated political correctness, even more than Striker, if that was possible. Bardsley was as down-to-earth a man as you would care to meet. Despite his fifty years – half of which was in the Job – a long-suffering wife and three grown-up kids, he was first in the queue when it came to ogling the likes of Lauren Collinge. However, unlike Striker, Bardsley didn't hide his wantonness. Regardless, he was a damn decent detective and had been in MIT for years, proving himself time after time. They went back a long way, being on the same shift when Striker had all 'the trouble' with Cunningham. Bardsley hadn't proved to be a bad lad at all… for a Scouser.

"Eric, did you manage to get anything from the Chinese chippy?"

"Yeah, a number twenty-one."

"Very droll. I suppose I asked for that. I meant did they see anything?"

Bardsley answered in a very poor Chinese accent. "We see nuffink. We wery, wery busy. No look outside."

Part of Striker was smiling within, since he knew Bardsley only too well. He was glad his dreary mood had been briefly lightened, but as a DI he felt obliged to say, "Eric, get a grip, fella. There's a dead boy, remember?"

"Sorry, Jack. That's why I phoned. A lad fitting the description's been reported missing. I'm just gonna check it out and go to his home address at seven Claythorne Street in Moss Range."

"What's his name?"

"Gareth Bolands."

"I'm on my way." No rest for the wicked, thought Striker, knowing his bed was now a good few hours away.

Chapter Seven

Pivoting toward the source of the growl, with his baton at the ready, PC Ben Davison's heart rate doubled. He shone his torch into the blackness of the park and a fearsome set of sharp, salivating teeth greeted him. He jumped back and stumbled over onto the wet footpath, his bottom now damp, his baton clattering out of reach.

A bright light blinded him momentarily. He tried to scramble to his feet, but was prevented by a wriggling weight on his midriff, frantic leathery wetness all over his face and manic, smelly panting. Helpless, he fumbled for the emergency backup button on top of his radio to alert all officers on this channel. Nonetheless, he struggled to reach the elusive button. With a mouthful of fur, he managed to glance up and saw someone shining a light upward from below their chin to illuminate their face.

Davison was both annoyed and relieved at the sight of the wide-eyed divisional dogman Bob the Dog donning his daft Billy Connolly grin and accompanying goatee.

"Woo-hooo!"

Hysterical laughter ensued.

Davison clambered up, wiped his face with his jacket's sleeve and began stroking the police dog, Rhys. "You baaa-stard, Bob," he cried, in between chuckles. Then reluctantly, "I'll give you that one."

The last time he'd seen the veteran cop, Davison had been on the loo in 'trap three' at Bullsmead nick, when the pitter-patter of excitable footsteps had been followed by a bucket of water, drenching him as he squatted at his most vulnerable.

"Bloody priceless that, Ben. Wait till I tell the lads." Bob the Dog also sounded much like the famous Scottish comic, having been brought up in Glasgow before his transfer from Strathclyde police many years ago to be closer to his Mancunian wife.

Davison was still bent over, stroking and attempting to calm Rhys. "But I thought I'd already had my initiation, Bob."

"You have, but when I heard this job come in I just couldn't resist it, mate."

"Anyway, I'm glad you're here. The park's too big for me to search on my own. Rhys and that dragon lamp will come in handy." He rubbed his eyes in an attempt to eliminate the dazzling effects of the powerful lamp.

Bob the Dog spoke into his radio and Davison smiled, knowing what was coming. "Four ..." Bob tweaked his voice to impersonate Sean Connery, "...double-O sheven... show me shtate shix at the park with Ben."

Mo tittered. "Received, Bob. Thanks for backing up. I was a little worried about him."

"Think she's fancies you, lad."

"Give over." Davison picked himself up, dusted himself down. "Come on then."

"You still got that action plan for searching hanging over you?"

"Yeah."

"Right, pal... Let's see what we can do."

With Rhys back on the leash, Davison held the somewhat heavy dragon lamp, its beam lighting up the park brilliantly compared to his meagre torch.

"Go on, Rhysy-boy," said Bob the Dog in his crisp Glaswegian tones, encouraging Rhys toward the open field to the right. Then a whisper, "Who's there, Rhysy-boy? Who's there?" Rhys pulled on the leash, making it taut, and the officers followed. A few small lit rectangles in people's homes grew larger as they did a sweep of the vast field. So far, there were no signs of anyone.

The damp grass and soil squished as they made their way across the field, the cold wetness seeping into Davison's right Magnum boot, reminding him he needed a new pair.

"Are you still seeing Louise then, Ben?"

"Yeah..." He paused for a moment. He'd not told anyone about his proposal plans. However, despite his practical jokes, Bob was a damn good mate, one who'd helped him immeasurably throughout the extremely steep learning curve of his probation. He was so excited, he just had to share the news. "Gonna pop the question tomorrow, mate."

Bob the Dog tugged Rhys to a stop. "Really? Good on ya, pal... Aye, good on ya. She's a bonnie wee lass."

"Cheers, mate. Just hope she says yes."

The lamp saved a lot of time and shortened the search significantly, with its beam reaching the far corners from the middle of the field beyond the just discernible white football posts.

"Ach, course she will, pal. You're a good lad." Bob the Dog guided Rhys around the field, then back toward the children's play area. "Best be thorough here. 'Shouting and screaming' could be something an' nothing. But in this job, ya never know, pal."

Davison knew his colleague was right, but with so many call-outs ending as 'no trace' jobs, it was easy to become blasé. "How are you and 'Mrs the Dog' doing?"

"We're fine and dandy, thanks. Think she's giving me my oats nowadays 'cause she knows my pension pay-off's coming soon. When the cash dries up, so will she. Woo-hoo!"

Davison laughed, shining the mighty beam at the play area. It was then that he saw an illuminated figure, with blood seeping from his head, staggering toward them like a stoned zombie.

"Jesus..." said Davison, agog, as Rhys began barking uncontrollably.

***

Striker eased the unmarked silver Vauxhall Astra to a halt behind Bardsley's older, dark green version of the same model. Claythorne Street was yet another terraced street, north of Bullsmead, in Moss Range. It was about three miles from the city centre, which was marked, as ever, by the huge Beetham Tower. Striker could see the hundreds of oblong windows high in the distance, probably half of them lit up, including Manchester's only 'sky bar' half way up, where Friday-night revellers would be having a good old shindig.

Meanwhile, Striker had to tell a mother and father that their son was dead.

He exited the Astra, as did Bardsley, faces solemn. They were outside number thirty-five, a good thirty metres from the Bolands' home at number seven. After a quick look over both shoulders, Striker asked in a hushed voice, "You got the missing report, Eric?"

"Yeah, it's in here." Equally tactful in tone, Bardsley opened his turquoise daybook and took out the report taken earlier by a uniformed Bobby.

"Where, when and by whom was he last seen?"

Bardsley studied the report, straining to see under the orange haze of the nearby streetlamp. "Er... Reported missing at just after midnight and... last seen at ten this morning by his mum, who also reported it."

"Okay." Striker thought for a moment. "What I don't get is why they'd report him missing? It's not like he's a little kid and I bet a bad boy like him normally rolls in at all hours."

"According to the notes, apparently he was supposed to meet his girlfriend at twenty-one thirty hours... It's her birthday and, well, he promised."

Striker raised his eyebrows, wondering how much weight Gareth Bolands' word actually carried, having earlier scrutinised his escapades on their database.

"How sure are you that he's our victim, Jack?"

"Ninety per cent, but we'll need an ID off the next of kin. You ready?"

"Always."

The night chill starting to bite, they paced down the street, dimly cast in an orange haze by the streetlamps, passing the line of flat-fronted, gardenless houses, and they were soon outside the Bolands' residence.

All the lights on show inside were switched on. Shouting emanated from within. Striker knocked on the dark wooden door and glanced at Bardsley, who was frowning.

More raised voices, then the door opened. A scruffy-looking, mixed-race man with a pot-holed face and ample beer belly greeted them, along with a waft of stale booze.

"You cops?" His voice was gruff, weary.

Striker flashed his warrant card, as did Bardsley. "DI Striker and this is DC Bardsley. May we come in?"

"Where's my son?"

"Are you Mr Bolands?"

"Yeah."

"Can we talk inside?"

"Who-da-fuck-is-it-Dougie?" yelled a woman from inside, clearly Irish.

"It's the police, so shut yer big gob will yer, woman?" Bolands senior nodded resignedly, turned and walked inside.

The detectives followed.

Chapter Eight

Davison recognised the staggering youth as Jamie Johnson, aka 'Johnno', one of the local Bad Bastard Bullsmead Boys, the four letter Bs on his knuckles confirming this. Johnson had blood oozing from a head wound and, for the first time since Davison had known this character, he actually looked relieved to see the police, rather than him making off in the opposite direction, as per usual.

Rhys added intermittent growling to his frantic barking.

Johnson held both hands up to his eyes. "Stop shining... that thing... in me face...will yer, man?"

Davison dipped the powerful dragon lamp.

Bob the Dog pulled Rhys in close and gave the German Shepherd a reassuring pat on the back to appease him. "What happened to you then, lad?"

"The swings..." Johnson collapsed on a graffiti-stained park bench, just pointing, his eyes empty.

"He's in shock, Ben."

"And on something too, by the looks of it."

Davison took a closer look at the head wound, using his Maglite this time. The laceration was surprisingly small, considering the blood loss and matted hair, but there was also clearly some swelling.

"Have your attackers gone, fella?"

Johnson just shrugged and stared at the floor. The two cops exchanged looks and headed for the play area, led by Rhys again.

Bob the Dog turned to Johnson briefly. "Stay on that bench, lad. We'll sort you an ambulance."

Davison was already onto it, depressing the transmission button on his radio and dipping his head slightly to the left toward the police radio clipped to his body armour. "Mo, one male, eighteen years, conscious and breathing, with a head wound. Ambulance to the park gates, please."

"Okay. You alright there?"

"Yeah, but something's clearly gone on and we're still searching. Standby."

Over the airwaves, brusquely: "DC Smith, comms. Talk-through with the officer in the park please."

"Go ahead."

Bob the Dog rolled his eyes at Davison.

"Update on those injuries. Are they serious?" It was the night DO.

Davison deeply inhaled the cold night air. "Negative. Small cut and slight swelling to head, and he's upright and talking to us."

"Okay. Keep me updated. Thanks, comms."

"They never trust us, do they Ben? Had it all my career. As soon as they ditch the uniform they become arrogant, interfering buggers, teaching us to suck eggs."

"S'alright. He's just doing his job, mate. I'm not arsed, really. Come on." Davison's cynicism hadn't yet reached the levels of 'old sweats' like Bob, though he knew that time would come eventually. His tutor constable warned him that years as a cop changed you irrevocably.

Reverting to the dragon lamp, they headed toward the play area. Rhys was sniffing the floor as though following a track. Davison shined the lamp, the shapes of the roundabout, climbing frame and see-saw, shadowing and shifting as they closed in. He could just about see the swings at the far end beyond the climbing frame. Five of them dangled from the horizontal bar above, swaying slightly in the wind. Woodchip crunched and squelched underfoot, some pieces dry, some wet, as they moved through the open metal gate into the play area.

Davison soon realised only four swings dangled and the lamp's beam lit up the fifth shape, twenty metres away. Rhys's barking intensified. Davison's heart nearly stopped at the sight before them.

A body hung there in the night, swaying and twisting ever so slightly, between the swings. Bulging eyes stared blankly at them, a bloated half-beaten face, pallid in the moonlight. The dead youth's tongue was protruding, as if to mock them.

The two officers gazed, momentarily mesmerised, Rhys straining on the leash, going berserk.

Davison hadn't seen anybody hanged before and obviously felt deeply saddened by the sight of the swinging youth. *But, hey*, he thought, both bizarrely and selfishly, and with more than a tinge of guilt, *at least my action plan for searching could be signed up and supervision would be off my back.*

He heard a noise behind him, glanced round and shone the torch to check on Johnson.

Shit – Johnson! He was now a potential murder suspect!

The park bench was empty.

***

Striker glanced at Bardsley as they entered the living room and wasn't surprised to see the DC rubbing his nose. They were greeted by an unpleasant concoction of sweat, stale alcohol and cannabis, topped with a hint of piss. Three bedraggled-looking blokes with flushed faces and baggy eyes, and donning sheepish looks, were squashed onto an equally scruffy sofa that Bullsmead tip wouldn't even accept.

Dougie Bolands stood to Striker's left and the loud drunken woman, who took size zero to another level, was belatedly clearing up the empty cans from the coffee table, popping them into a black bin liner. Striker noticed spliff-ends in an overflowing ashtray, but he ignored them, concentrating on the matter at hand.

"So-what-er-yer-here-for-officers?" The woman's voice was like runaway train, strong Irish lilt, in all likelihood a gypsy or, as the Job insisted you call them, 'a traveller'.

"Are you Gareth Bolands' mother?"

"Yeah-dat's-me-alright. Daisy O'Reilly. You-found-ma-Gareth -yet?"

Striker glanced at the three stooges on the settee, all avoiding eye contact.

"Can we speak in private?"

"Nah. We-speak-ere. A-don't-hide-anytin-from-ma-bruvvers."

"What's goin' on, Inspector?" Dougie Bolands sounded rightly concerned.

There was only one way to do this: straight to the point. "There's been a serious incident on Bullsmead Road, near the shops. A young man, fitting the description of Gareth…"

"What-da-fuck's-happened-to-ma-Gareth? Don't-ya-come-in-ma-home-an…"

Bardsley interjected. "Miss O'Reilly, please. Let the inspector finish." She picked up the ashtray and emptied it into the bin liner, a puff of ash drifting onto her wrinkly, flowery dress, the waft of stale cigarettes invading the detectives' noses further.

Striker continued, "Bad news. There's a young man at the MRI morgue, who I need one of you to identify. I'm really sorry, but we think it might be Gareth."

"Oh-no-be-Jesus!" Daisy O'Reilly collapsed and the ashtray clattered onto the laminate flooring. Her brothers assisted and comforted her in a cacophony of Irish slang, Daisy's wailing deafening.

Striker turned to the most sober of a drunken bunch. "Mr Bolands, would you kindly accompany us to the hospital?"

Bolands brushed a chubby hand through his short, greying afro, nodded and grabbed his coat from a hook in the hall as they left. Once outside, Striker checked his muted mobile and saw that he'd missed three calls from DCI Maria Cunningham.

"Eric, could you take Mr Bolands? I've just gotta make a call. I'll follow you up." He took his work mobile from his jacket pocket.

Striker left the haunting screams of Daisy O'Reilly, so loud that the lights of neighbouring houses came on, and he dialled as he walked back to his car.

"Maria, you want me for something?"

"Yes I do. Where've you been?"

"Just been telling Bolands' parents their son might be dead... that's all."

"The attack at McDonald's isn't connected."

"I know."

"But it still looks like a gangland feud. There's another body. This time in Bullsmead Park."

Shit. "I'm just off to the morgue, but I'll be straight there when..."

"No you won't. I've made the decision to call out Syndicate Two for this one. That's why I've been trying to phone you, so you didn't go when you heard. *We'll* speak tomorrow."

It just had to be DI Vinnie Stockley's lot. "But why? I can handle it."

"Cross contamination, of course, Inspector. You've been to the other scene and so have your team. Anyway, we'll speak tomorrow."

"Don't give me that, Maria. We both know there are ways round that. I don't have to enter the scene. I can even shower and change at the nick before Stockley rounds his troops together. Come on. If it's linked, I wanna know now. Like you said earlier, 'it's my case'. So why call out Stockley and his team?"

"I've just told you, and plus, it will give us a fresh perspective. Anyway, you've been on all day and you've enough on your plate with the first murder. The decision's been made, Striker. Like I said, we'll speak tomorrow." Cunningham ended the call.

He'd heard Stockley was in MIT and knew it was inevitable their paths would cross again... since...

He pictured Stockley years ago, before Striker had joined the force. The tall, bespectacled constable who'd called at his house when Striker's teenage antics had gone a little too far. But he tried not to think about *that* too much. He'd seen Stockley again, several years later, when they'd both been sitting their sergeant's exam at Sedgley Park, and there had been a moment's recognition. Striker had caught Stockley staring a few times throughout that day and they both knew where they'd last seen each other, all those years ago. There had been minimal encounters since, but Striker always felt Stockley harboured a grudge against him, stemming from that very first time when Striker had somehow wriggled from his grasp.

He'd known this time would come and felt rather vulnerable, that his past could finally catch up with him. He didn't like the feeling one bit. He also knew that Stockley was close to Maria Cunningham, enhancing his wariness of them both.

As Bardsley was just about to get into his Astra with Bolands senior, Striker shouted, "Eric, give me a cig, will you?"

Chapter Nine

PC Ben Davison's shock at seeing the hanging body was diluted somewhat because the park bench was empty. He ran past it in search of Johnson, knowing he'd definitely be late off now and the Lakes trip with Louise tomorrow would most probably have to be cancelled. There was a perverse relief in that he'd finally buried the nagging searching issue which had blighted his probationary period. However, if anything had happened to the injured witness he'd have some serious explaining to do. Found one, lost one, back to square one.

Having left Bob the Dog and Rhys preserving the crime scene, he'd called for back-up. He headed for the park gates, his Maglite frantically scanning the gloom of the park. Aided by the dropping temperature, a shiver crawled up his spine to prickle his neck and scalp, as the image of the hanging lad's bloated features pervaded.

He soon spotted the bright lights of the ambulance at the park's entrance, ricocheting off the house windows beyond, and relief flooded him when he saw a paramedic tending to Johnson at the rear of the vehicle. The medic was about to start wiping away the blood from Johnson's head.

Acting on instinct, Davison began sprinting and shouted, "Hang on... a minute... please."

The medic, in his green uniform, froze, looked up.

Davison stopped at the park gates to catch his breath. "We'll be needing... swabs... before you treat him. Give me... a minute."

He'd already alerted Mo at comms and asked for CID, SOCO and supervision to be made aware, but he'd not informed them he'd nearly lost the witness. Or was Johnson the murderer? He knew all eyes would be reading the computerised log over the coming days and once an entry was put on the log, it was basically cast in stone, hence his reticence over the air.

He made a radio transmission. "One treble-eight six, comms..."

"Go ahead, Ben."

"Mo, any ETA for SOCO?"

"Five minutes."

"Received, thanks." He turned to the medic and Johnson. "Obviously if you feel it's imperative to treat him now, I can't stop you, but I'd prefer it if you just sat him down and waited, so we can take swabs and maybe even photos first. And we'll probably need those surgical gloves you're wearing too."

The medic nodded and led the still groggy-looking Johnson inside the rear of the ambulance.

Davison was pleased to see a police van turn up as requested, and two sombre-faced officers he didn't recognize exited. One was a plain-looking white woman about thirty, with her blonde hair up in a bun and no hat on. The other was a much younger, slightly overweight Chinese bloke with an acne problem. They were reinforcements from the neighbouring A Division and their presence was clearly of a begrudging nature.

"Okay, so where do you want us?" asked the female cop, now holding a scene log and a roll of police scene tape, face like a smacked arse.

"If you could follow me and your colleague stays with this... er, witness." Davison paced toward them, away from the ambulance, his voice hushed. "He still could be a potential murder suspect, but I doubt it as he's made no attempt to escape."

The Chinese cop suddenly looked a little more interested and he unconsciously dropped a hand to caress his cuffs on the right of his utility belt.

The sulkier cop said in a hollow Geordie accent, "Okay, let's go then." She glanced down at her wristwatch. "Am supposed to be off duty in half an hour, like."

And I was supposed to be proposing to my girlfriend tomorrow, but we've a job to do so show some interest, will you?

Five minutes later and the play area of the park was cordoned off with long strands of police tape, juddering spasmodically in the wind. Davison was protecting the scene at the entrance to the play area, while the female A Division officer was virtually out of sight on the far side, nearer to the hanging body. It was her choice, since she wanted a "sly ciggie", the red end lighting up intermittently in the distance. Bob the Dog and Rhys were still patrolling the scene, protecting the perimeter, even though no one else was around at this late hour.

Davison's radio burst into life as a female CSI arrived, and he knew she'd be doing her bit regarding Johnson before the medic tended to the wound. Surprisingly, the young Chinese officer emerged behind a torch beam. He still donned a half-hearted look, his voice abrupt.

"Right then, where do you want me now?"

Davison was speechless and saw Bob the Dog passing, on yet another circuit of the scene.

"We want you with the bloody murder suspect, lad! The SOCO girl can't be expected to restrain him ya idiot," said Bob incredulously.

The light bulb above the officer's head was virtually visible, and he promptly swivelled and jogged back to the ambulance.

Bob shook his head, disappearing into the night, on another wander around the scene. Davison had sporadic chats with the dogman each time he passed, informing him of the A Division officers' reluctance to be there, as well as resignedly whinging about cancelling his Lake District trip.

Davison noticed a couple of approaching suits. He strained his eyes, trying to recognise them. As they got closer, he saw they were wearing the customary white over-shoes and the smaller of the two carried a torch, its beam haphazardly cutting through the gloom like a lightsabre.

"Right, what have we got?" asked an important-looking bespectacled chap with a pointy nose. Davison vaguely recognised him, but wasn't sure who he was.

"Er… Could you clarify who you are, please?" For the first time tonight, Davison noticed his breath was visible as he spoke and wished he'd put his GMP-issue fleece on underneath his jacket.

The man bounced looks with an almost cardboard cut-out of himself beside him, albeit a younger version with rounded glasses. Throwing Davison an icy glare, the older one fumbled in his pocket, then flashed a warrant card for a split second. "DI Stockley, MIT, and this is DC Barron. Now, you gonna tell me what we've got here, or what?"

"Oh, er, sorry, sir. It's a dead lad... a hanging." He shined his torch at the dangling body twenty metres away.

"Yes, I know that, constable. That's why I'm here. I do have a radio, you know. Evidence-wise, I meant." He rolled his eyes at DC Barron, who smirked.

Davison always felt a little uneasy when speaking with suits, especially bosses, but this guy was a knob. "Oh, right, there's a potential witness being treated in the ambulance, you probably just passed him, sir."

"We'll need a statement off him then. Anything else found? Scene preserved? Incident log started?"

"No weapons or anything's been found. And yes, we've cordoned the area off and a scene log has..."

Stockley brushed past Davison, cutting his sentence short, and lifted the taped cordon before heading into the scene saying, "Don't go off duty till I say so, and make sure you've done a statement. Now, put your hat on, Constable, there's a good lad."

Davison cursed to himself and did as he was told, despite no members of the public being present and it not really mattering. He raised his jacket collars around his neck to ward off the night chill, then heard footsteps and the hum of voices as someone else approached. He recognized these two suits from the other crime scene earlier. He'd briefly interacted with them on various works dos and these two seemed decent enough blokes. It was DI Jack Striker and that old Scouser whose name escaped him.

"Hi Ben. You okay, fella?"

Davison fleetingly considered telling the DI that he had been until that power junkie Stockley had arrived, though decided against it.

"Fine thanks, sir. DI Stockley's over there, with the deceased." Davison again shined his Maglite toward the scene and Striker's face stiffened.

"Looks like you've done a good job, finding and preserving this scene in quick time. Believe you've got a witness too. I'm impressed, Ben. I'll be speaking to Paul Roache about this."

Davison felt uplifted. "Thank you, sir."

Striker regarded the PC, then the crime scene. "What time you supposed to be off duty?"

Davison withdrew his smartphone and checked the time, the screen lighting up his face momentarily. "Er, about two hours ago."

"I'll see if I can get you relieved by the night shift, when I get a minute." Striker gave a subtle nod and headed along the left side of the flapping police tape.

"Cheers, sir."

"Well done, fella," said Bardsley, as he passed the probationer and followed Striker parallel to the low perimeter fence of the play area, both mindful that they'd entered the previous scene on Bullsmead Road earlier.

Ten seconds later, about five metres from the swings, Bardsley withdrew a small torch, alerting Stockley to their presence by shining it his way, the beam briefly reflecting off his and Barron's glasses as the detectives turned.

"What are *you* doing here, Striker?" Stockley pinched his lips and glared from the other side of the low fence separating the field and the children's play area.

Striker took a deep inhalation on seeing the silhouette of the hanging body shifting slightly in the wind. He swiftly composed himself. "Just back from the morgue and wanted to see if this was linked to my case."

"Don't enter this scene or you'll mess up *my* enquiry before it's begun."

"For God's sake, Vinnie, I know that." He considered asking why his colleagues were only wearing overshoes and not full protective suits, but decided against it.

"Anyway, it's too early to tell if there's a link, though I doubt it. Yours was beaten and, as you can see by the rope around his neck, Striker, this lad has been hanged."

"Cut the sarcasm. We're supposed to be on the same team, aren't we?" Striker spotted a female constable on the far side of the cordon, and within earshot, so lowered his voice. "You need a hand with anything, Vinnie, like cutting the body down? You'll need a ladder by the looks of it."

"I know! There's one on the way with CSI. And no – you're not supposed to be here. Maria's already told you that."

"Oh, been having a nice little chat with her have we? Surprise, surprise."

"And what do you mean by that?"

"Doesn't matter. You know there's a school behind you, don't you? Wouldn't want the local infants seeing this, would we?"

"Of course, I know that. He'll be down before dawn, once we get a stepladder and Mortham arrives. And if he's not, we'll just close the school, okay?"

Bardsley coughed for attention, shining his torch at the hanging body and then the nearby climbing frame. "With respect, Boss, we just wanted to see if it was linked to ours and backed up the gangland theory. I see the Moss Range Crew have been here." Bardsley's torch lit up 'MRC' in yellow on the side of the climbing frame. "Is that still wet?"

Stockley looked heavenward. "Look, stop interfering will you? This could be suicide for all we know. Let us begin our investigation and we'll liaise tomorrow."

"Suicide? I doubt that very much," said Striker, rolling his eyes. With both Bardsley's and Barron's torches lighting up the dead lad's bloated face, it was clear from his blooded nose and bruised eye that he'd been in some kind of fight recently.

"Boss, you might want to come here," said Barron. "He's got four Bs tattooed on his knuckles."

"Okay Striker," said Stockley, "since you're here, make yourself useful and go to the hospital to interview the witness, so we can get a quick ID on this lad."

"No need, Boss, I know him."

Stockley turned to Bardsley. "Who is he?"

"I dealt with his case a few years ago, when he stabbed a schoolboy with a chisel. It's Steven Bowker, aka Chisel. And he has plenty of enemies."

"Right. Could you put that ID in writing before you go home?" He looked thoughtful for a moment. "So, did you get *your* body ID'd then?"

Striker answered, "Yeah, it was Gareth Bolands and obviously his dad took it real bad. Do you know him? Nicknamed Gasbo."

Stockley shook his head.

Barron said, "Yeah, I know him. He's got an ASBO, hasn't he?"

Striker nodded. "That's right, Steve."

"And so has Chisel…" said Bardsley.

There was an audible silence, Striker wondering about the connection, albeit tenuous, as no doubt the other detectives were.

Stockley broke the lull. "I suggest you disappear now. Cunningham and Brennan won't be at all happy you've attended here."

"Even though our local knowledge has just given you a swift ID? I think the word you're looking for is 'thanks'."

The four detectives pivoted on hearing a kerfuffle at the play area's entrance. Striker and Bardsley headed toward the raised voices.

Davison, awkwardly clutching the scene log, was struggling to prevent a group of irate-looking men from entering the scene.

"Where's my fuckin' son? I want to see him, now!" shouted a stocky, middle-aged man, pushing Davison, who was now frantically speaking into his radio.

"It's Chisel's dad, Dessie Bowker. He's a right handful, Jack." Bardsley ran over, and grabbed Bowker's arms, managing to swing him to the floor. Two beefy lads about twenty headed for Bardsley, but Striker blocked them off, a palm in each chest. One swung for Striker, so he dipped his head and stung the lad with a left uppercut to the chin. He instantly hit the deck.

"Now calm down, all of you." Scowling, Striker faced the others, in case they wanted some of the same.

Bardsley helped up Dessie Bowker from the floor and held aloft a placating hand; the semi-retired gangster wore a face of thunder. "Dessie, we'll talk, but please control yourself first."

"What, like you two just fuckin' did?"

More uniforms streamed into the park, their footfalls audible on the stone path, like a burst of amateur tap dancing. They soon surrounded the six irate men, who looked around warily when a couple of batons clicked open.

The lad Striker had punched got up, rubbing his chin, still somewhat stunned and having second thoughts now. He mumbled expletives under his breath.

"Entering a crime scene is a criminal offence. Now walk with us, away from the scene, and we can talk… calmly," said Striker curtly.

En masse, the mixture of cops and civilians strolled out of the park, leaving Davison wondering whether he'd ever get off duty, while Chisel's body swayed in the distance.

***

Outside the park gates, in between a long row of semis – some with occupants outside or peering through their windows – Bardsley tried to place an arm around Dessie Bowker's shoulders, but was pushed aside.

The line of uniforms across the park gates would suffice for now. Striker had asked two of them to cover the entrance on the other side of the park, even though it was Stockley's crime scene. The ambulance had taken the lad, Johnson, who Ben Davison had told Striker about, to the hospital. Once these characters before him had gone, maybe Striker could catch a couple of hours of shut-eye.

The five young men accompanying Bowker were leaning on a short metal fence on the kerb of the pavement, facing the line of cops, who they eyed cockily.

Striker made eye contact with Dessie Bowker, then beckoned him over with a nod of the head. Bowker returned the gesture with a dirty look, though still followed the DI a few paces up the road, out of earshot of the others. The nearby streetlamp lit them up enough for Striker to see Bowker's craggy face and forlorn expression.

"Mr Bowker, how did you know about this?"

"Steven's mate Johnno phoned me. Sounded stressed."

"Right. What did he say?"

"That some maniac must've attacked them and that he'd been knocked out. And when he woke up, he saw my…" The big man started to sob, then punched a nearby garden fence, but didn't even flinch, despite it being metal.

"Okay, okay. I'm sorry, Mr Bowker. Please, just go home now and let us try to catch the bastard who's done this to your son. Someone will be in touch soon about a formal ID."

He hesitated, glaring at nothing, pain contorting his face. "Well, you'd better catch him before I fuckin' do," he growled, before storming off. His troops filed in behind him, jeering at the line of uniforms, then they all clambered into a white transit van and sped off.

Striker didn't think for one minute that he'd seen the last of them. Someone out there clearly had gigantic balls to have killed Bowker's lad. Either that or whoever it may be was just plain bloody crazy.

After updating Stockley by mobile on what Bowker had told him, Striker's last job was a gesture for the officers on the scene. He'd been there, done that and it was no fun standing in the cold dying for a piss, feeling forgotten and unappreciated. He radioed the late shift sergeant, Paul Roache to let him know Ben Davison and the others would need relieving by the night shift at some point soon. As it happened, Roache, being a decent bloke, was already onto it.

He shouted for Bardsley, who was chatting to the uniforms, and they headed for Striker's Astra. Bardsley had dropped his older Astra off at the nick after the morgue trip, when they'd both managed to pick up a quick coffee to keep them going.

"I don't think that's the last we've heard from Dessie Bowker and his cronies," said the detective.

"My feelings exactly."

"What do you reckon then, Jack? Gang related or something else?"

"They've both got ASBOs, Eric, which could be just a coincidence, but..." Striker tailed off in thought, knowing anti-social behaviour orders were common around these parts, weakening his premature theory regarding gangs somewhat. Striker opened the Astra's central locking and they both climbed in.

"So you don't think it is gang related?" asked Bardsley, lighting two Bensons, passing one to Striker.

Striker took the cigarette and opened the electric windows on both front doors to allow the smoke to escape. "Unfortunately not. The MOs just don't fit with gangs do they?"

Bardsley shook his head. "That's what I was thinking."

"I mean, a knife and a gun, yeah, but using a metal bar or something similar on Bolands. Then going to the trouble of messing about with a rope and hanging the kid Chisel... That's gotta be some kind of statement, don't you reckon?"

"Symbolism?"

Striker shrugged, glanced at his colleague. "Could well be. If it were the gangs, then a few bullets would've been discharged and they'd be outta there pronto. They wouldn't start hanging someone up like that. Somebody's given this a lot of thought, Eric."

"You think we're looking for a serial killer?"

"It's too early to suggest this to the others, as that's the last thing the brass would want to hear before we have conclusive proof. But it's highly likely the murders are linked and we've got some sort of vigilante ASBO killer on the rampage."

Bardsley drew hard on the Benson, blew a couple of smoke rings, then looked intently at Striker. "There are hundreds of these knobheads with ASBOs, Jack."

"I know, mate, and I do hope I'm wrong." Striker fired up the Astra. "But something is telling me our man is just getting warmed up."

Chapter Ten

After four hours of broken sleep, Striker was back in his office on his umpteenth phone call of the morning.

"What do you mean, you can't bloody make it? It's Beth's school play remember? You promised, Jack."

Striker cursed himself for forgetting about the play. "Something really important has come up, Suzi. You know if I could—"

He could hear the emotion in her voice as she interrupted. "That's the problem with you, isn't it, Jack? Something's always coming up – something more important than your children's upbringing?"

"Look, Suzi, there's this case and it's—"

Suzi jumped in again. "Oh, there's always *this* case or *that* case! You're gonna lose them, Jack."

Her words cut Striker real deep and for once words failed him.

She continued, "Well, if it's more important than your own flesh and blood, then so be it. If you wanna see your kids again, you can go through the damn courts."

And with that, the phone went dead.

"Suzi… Suzi? Shit."

He was just about to conduct the morning briefing with Cunningham and this was the last thing he needed. It would have to go into the box at the back of his brain. The only problem was that the box was getting rather full and he was struggling to shut the lid, what with this escalating case, the smoking relapse and his non-existent sex and social lives. At least the curse of being a Man City fan over the years had been diluted immeasurably since the Arab oil men's takeover of his beloved football club. The tag, 'the same old City' had waned. Nonetheless, finding the time to go to the odd game would be nice. Typical that he'd supported the sky blues through thin and thinner and now they were half-decent he was missing out.

However, more importantly, he knew his kids were slipping from his grasp when they should have been his highest priority.

Elbows on the desk, he dipped his head in hands, tapped his temples. He promised himself he'd make it up to them and consciously shut the box lid in his mind, for now. Compartmentalising was the only way he could manage the extremes of his life.

What was crucial to the over-worked office's flagging morale was for him to present a positive image, in order to motivate his team sufficiently enough to achieve a successful start, and hopefully a swift conclusion, to the inquiry.

He'd tried the newsagent Khan's mobile three times this morning, in the hope of having something positive to rouse the troops during the briefing, but frustratingly it kept going straight to answerphone. Khan didn't live in the rented flat above the shop, his home address was unknown, as yet, and typically the mobile phone database had it registered as an unnamed pay-as-you-go.

Striker needed to know more about this "burly man" Khan had seen running off. The sooner that guy was interviewed and eliminated, the easier it would be to focus fully on the gangs and who they'd pissed off so much. Why hadn't the man come forward voluntarily? Was he scared of repercussions? Or was there a more sinister reason?

His mind awhirl, Striker headed into the adjacent major incident room.

The MIT office was a good forty feet by twenty, and desks were positioned in clusters for the various teams. Filing cabinets ran virtually the length of one wall, along with a fax machine, a photocopier and a printer. A couple of wide one-way windows offered the not-so-stunning view of Bullsmead in all its 'glory': basically a mass of terraced rooftops, broken only by the odd tree or commercial premises.

Mugshots of numerous bad guys filled the bland, pale blue wall opposite. Some of the photos had vertical bars crudely drawn on in black felt tip, to signify the offender's incarceration, the odd sarcastic comment underneath: "See you in twenty years", "Don't wait up, luv", "Let me out", "Missing from home", "I want me mummy" and "Crime pays... the penalty!" amongst Striker's favourites. On each desk were a phone and a double-screened computer terminal, some accompanied by pictures of partners and children. All the desks had three-tiered trays containing fat, fawn-coloured pending files and multiple black-trimmed box files.

The air was filled with conversations from the dozen or so detectives dotted about the room – some sitting on desks and chairs, others standing, most drinking coffee.

Striker had formerly introduced himself to his new team just four days earlier, most of whom he already knew from his various stints and roles on the B Division. He briefly chatted with Eric Bardsley and Lauren Collinge before the buzz of conversations diminished and the DCI strolled in.

"Okay, okay, people," hollered Maria Cunningham, with two sharp attention-grabbing claps. She wore her usual charcoal grey, pin-striped pencil skirt and matching jacket, her shirt's two top buttons undone revealing the start of a considerable cleavage.

The room was instantly silent, but Bardsley continued whispering an incomplete story about the new barmaid at the Rock Inn and how he'd kept ordering stuff from the bottom shelf of the fridges in order to get a better view of her arse. Striker raised his eyebrows and nodded purposely toward Cunningham.

As if waiting for Bardsley to turn her way, the DCI, now standing at the head of the room, threw a glare that silenced Bardsley. Then she began.

"I'm sure you are all aware of the first murder last night – a particularly brutal one, I know you'll agree. On the face of it, it appears to be gang related."

Striker wore a puzzled look. On the phone earlier, he'd told the DCI about the man Khan had seen running off and they'd briefly discussed the subsequent murder.

"As for the second murder scene, the hanging in Bullsmead Park, DI Stockley and his team have already taken charge of that one, so a separate meeting will take place later. For now, we're not linking it to the one on Bullsmead Road, which we'll be focussing on in this briefing."

A few whispers could be heard, though soon diminished.

"And, as the other syndicates are stretched with the recent spate of shootings, this one will be run by DI Striker, who most of you in Syndicate One have already met. Team Two are also assisting today, to help get the ball rolling."

A few detectives glanced his way, so Striker nodded with a half-smile, before Cunningham continued.

"Getting back to the Bullsmead killing, DI Striker has informed me that the deceased's body was ID'd last night by the father, and by all accounts, Gareth Bolands is – was – as most of you will already know, a particularly nasty piece of work himself, being a member of the Moss Range Crew. But before we start viewing things the wrong way, this boy was still a human being and has a family, and he didn't deserve such a fate."

Bardsley whispered, "Well that's open to question," and Striker gave him a nudge with his elbow.

Cunningham went on, "The press are already onto this, so I want your heads fully focussed on the inquiry. Any questions from pushy journalists should not be answered by you, but should be referred to the Press Office. It's going to be a busy day, people. Now, over to DI Striker for an update on the Bolands investigation and your actions."

Striker stepped forward, turned a page on an SRA2 flip chart to reveal a crudely drawn bird's-eye view of the crime scene. It was another sign of the budget cuts the force had no choice but to make. He'd tried the overhead projector earlier and it was playing up; plus, the colour printer in his office was broken, preventing him running off the Google Maps image. The more professional photos were yet to be taken by air support, so this would have to suffice for now. He saw Cunningham frown and clocked a few suppressed smirks around the room.

"Morning everyone and thanks to Syndicate Two for turning out early and dropping whatever you're working on. Initially, we thought this was another gang-on-gang fight, and it may well still be the case." His glance bounced back hard from Cunningham. "However, experience tells us to always keep an open mind and we potentially have a witness who saw a tall, burly man dressed in black fleeing the scene, then running down" – Striker pointed at the map – "Spinney Lane, which leads to Bradburn Street. We don't know if he turned left or right, nor whether he'd parked a getaway vehicle nearby—"

Cunningham interrupted. "Getaway vehicle? Are you saying he's our murderer, Jack? Witnesses don't drive getaway vehicles, do they?"

Striker couldn't hide his sigh. "I'm just imparting the info we've collated so far. This man may or may not be local, so perhaps he had a car" – he tossed a glance at Cunningham – "parked around the corner. He was wearing a long black trench coat and is aged twenty-five to forty. Sorry, that's the best we've got. The problem is, we don't know his ethnicity or if he's involved at all, and up to now no one else has seen this guy. However, I'm hoping to speak with the key witness after this briefing. I'll let you all know of any developments."

A few mumbles were exchanged among the detectives.

"Look, I know this isn't ideal and that this man may well have just been fleeing the scene because he was scared, but we really need to know who he is. It also appears that not only were members of the Bullsmead Boys present, but also possibly half a dozen or so of the Moss Range Crew. Why? We're not sure yet. There's been a mention they were meeting up to do 'business', which seems unlikely, since they're bitter rivals. If that's the case, then it may have been the old classic 'drug deal gone wrong' scenario. The more probable line is they were meeting up for a fight, although at this early stage it's hard to say. But we also need to find this out.

"There were potentially about twelve people who saw the attack, and that's excluding door-to-door results that, apart from the aforementioned witness, have so far proved negative. So today we need to vigorously go about our business and discover exactly who was present at the scene and what transpired.

"The murder weapon appears to be a long thin object. TAG did conduct a negative search for it last night, but will be conducting a more comprehensive search in daylight this morning. Air support will be taking aerial shots of the scene so" – he turned to gesture at the drawing on the flip chart – "hopefully next time we'll have a decent photo. And no, my six-year-old lad didn't do this one. He'd have done a better job."

There was awkward laughter and grins all round, except for Cunningham, who looked like a headmistress with a grudge.

"Back to business. All but two of the eight shops overlooking the incident were shut, so we still need to check to see if any had cameras left running overnight. There's a pod set up at the scene that will obviously remain open, and leaflets appealing for witnesses are being printed as I speak. SOCO seized a few cigarette stubs and a beer bottle from the scene, but we've nothing back on them as yet. Any questions before I issue the initial actions?"

The athletic-looking, short-haired DS Rebecca Grant raised a forefinger. Striker had worked in the gang unit a few years ago with the Jamaican, before she'd left for MIT. Many regarded Grant as an extremely competent officer, including Striker himself.

"Becky?"

"You mentioned a 'tall burly man' was seen fleeing the scene, so have we considered trawling Bolands' crime queue for victims, in case it was a revenge attack?"

"Good question, Becky. I have browsed through Bolands' list of crimes and there are twenty-eight victims, another nine witnesses, as well as family members of the victims. Nothing obvious jumped out at me, but as we know there are no details of the victim's appearance." Striker thought for a moment. "Maybe contacting the officers in each case would have some mileage."

Grant nodded slowly.

Striker saw Cunningham looking ready to pounce again. "Although I certainly won't dismiss the revenge possibility, for the moment, I'd like to focus our attention on finding more witnesses and evidence from the incident itself and establishing Gasbo's movements, any recent arguments, et cetera. I will add, however, that in all the gangland stuff I've dealt with before, knives, guns and even knuckle-dusters are the weapons of choice. Not ropes, thin metal poles or batons."

Cunningham pounced. "Ropes, Jack? I've already said that there are no obvious links between the two murders."

"Okay, slip of the tongue, Maria, but we do need to keep an open mind on that."

"And you mentioned 'batons'. Why not baseball bats? They're common in gang fights."

"Yes, Maria they are sometimes used, however, I've spoken to the pathologist, Sidney Mortham on the phone this morning and he reckons the marks represent something thinner, like a baton."

Yet another interruption from the DCI: "Oh? And did it not cross your mind to let me know of this?"

"Well, you know now, Maria." Striker saw one or two smirks in front of him, which counteracted Cunningham's stony glare; Bardsley's was the pick of the bunch and bordered on a grin.

"Anyway, it's not absolutely clear yet and it could still have been a metal bar." He paused, glanced at Cunningham. "Or a *thin* baseball bat, perhaps. So let's all keep an open mind and get our heads on."

Aware that another nearby hand was up, Grant quickly asked, "Would you like me to send an email to all the officers who've had dealings with Bolands?"

"If you would, Becky, thanks. In fact send out a mass email to all officers, in case we miss someone." Striker turned to another detective with his hand up. "Go on – Wayne, isn't it?"

"Yes, Boss. Have CCTV checks been done at the garage? The pictures are pretty decent in there I believe."

"The night worker couldn't operate the system, one of those multi-formats, and the manager's not in till ten-thirty today, but I'll sort that later." He saw Cunningham motioning to speak again. *What now?* "Maria?"

"Jack, I noticed there was absolutely no mention of your murder on the morning electronic briefing site. Why not?"

Shit, he knew she'd put him on the spot. The fact he'd not finished till nearly four a.m. wouldn't wash, as this should've been done.

Think, Striker, think.

"Since we've had very little to go on and all we have are dark figures fleeing the scene, I thought it best to clarify this with other potential witnesses, hopefully this morning, with a view to a more comprehensive entry for the afternoon EBS."

Cunningham gave an imperceptible nod, her unyielding face expressionless.

Playing hard to get are we? thought Striker impishly, satisfied with his speed of thought under pressure.

He soon began issuing the actions, allocating two DCs to do CCTV checks at all the shops. Another four were designated to check the movements of Gasbo's main associates and another pair to conduct house-to-house enquiries along Bullsmead Road, Spinney Lane and Bradburn Street. All painstaking jobs that needed doing and he didn't see anyone pulling their faces, which was good.

As the buzz in the office grew louder, he overheard Becky Grant reallocating the email job to another DC. Delegation: one of the perks of being a supervisor. Lauren Collinge and Eric Bardsley were left gazing at Striker with 'What about us?' looks on their faces.

Striker turned to his left and Cunningham was suddenly there, up close. It was quite a shock. "Maria?"

"I want you to focus on the gangs, Jack. You're obsessed with this 'burly man'. There's nothing to suggest he wasn't just another gang member. How can your key witness say he was up to forty years old from him running off in the distance when it was dark?"

"Well, I've not spoken to him yet, so I'd have to—"

"WHAT?"

"Eric had a quick word with him and I've been trying the witness's mobile ever since."

"Let's get this right. Half your briefing was based on flimsy evidence from a witness you've not even spoken to yet?"

The DCI had a knack of making him, and he was sure others too, feel like a schoolchild. He assumed she must get off on it.

Bardsley coughed. Cunningham chucked a dirty look at him, before returning her icy gaze to Striker.

"You hardly touched on the gang issue. And, come to think of it, why didn't you arrest those two Bullsmead Boys sitting on the wall, like I asked?"

"They've been spoken to twice and they insist they were in the newsagents at the time of the attack. I can check this when I speak to the shop owner, then arrest them if necessary."

The DCI scoffed. "After they've got their heads together and their stories straight? When were you going to inform me of all this?"

"Look, if they'd been offenders, then why didn't they run off, instead of awaiting our arrival? Just like Johnson at the park murder?"

Cunningham ignored the questions. "Mr Brennan won't be at all impressed with this. I want to know every single name of these gang members and I want those two boys arrested. The

press are already sniffing and I want something solid for Mr
Brennan. Do you hear me?"

*From what I've heard, Mr Brennan usually has 'something solid' for you,
Maria.* "Loud and clear, Maria... and so do I. Though getting all
twelve of the names is a little unrealistic. You know all about the
wall of silence within the community."

"I want the names, Jack." The DCI turned abruptly, headed
for the door.

Striker noticed half the room had stopped what they were
doing. *Great. That's just bloody great for morale, that is.* Striker
approached Bardsley and Collinge.

Bardsley whispered, "Don't let that tart bother you, Boss.
She's bleedin' clueless."

"Get your coats," said Striker tersely. "You two are coming
with me."

Chapter Eleven

"I still can't see why I have to trawl the CCTV, Boss," moaned Bardsley, as Collinge pulled the unmarked Vauxhall Astra onto Bullsmead Road. The traffic was heavier than normal, due to the crime scene further up the road.

Striker turned from the front passenger seat. "Look, Eric. I want to ensure nothing is missed and I know I can rely on you to check it thoroughly." He gave the DC a little wink with the compliment.

"Okay, okay. You know I'm a sucker for flattery. Believe me, I don't get much. Just ask the missus. Anyway, I still reckon if I had an arse as good as Lauren's, I'd not only be in the front, but I'd be coming with you too."

Striker saw Collinge half-smiling, shaking her head, before he pivoted and said, "Now that's unacceptable. No more. Do you understand?"

"Oh, come on. It's just banter."

"Be careful. I'm getting…"

Collinge interjected, "It's alright, Boss. I can take it."

Bardsley raised his eyebrows. "Really? That sounds promising."

Striker frowned. "You're not in the damn pub with the lads now, Eric. Show a bit more respect or we'll make this official."

"Okay, okay. Point taken."

"Drop him here, Lauren."

Collinge pulled the Astra onto the petrol station forecourt, the crime scene in view fifty metres away, and Bardsley was soon heading for the entrance.

As the Astra pulled away, Striker said softly, "I'm sorry about that, Lauren. He's been like that since he joined. He's harmless, but God only knows how he's still a cop."

"Really, it's not a problem. I've heard it all before and I'm genuinely not offended. Like he said, 'it's just banter'."

Striker wasn't convinced, though admired the fact she wasn't kicking up a fuss. "Alright, before we go to Moss Range, let's just try the newsagents." He was mindful Mr Khan still hadn't answered his mobile.

En route a few minutes later, Blue Moon chimed on Striker's mobile and before answering, he saw that it was Bardsley. He was probably calling to apologise, having thought about his comments. This was typical of the DC – speak first, think later.

"Bad news, Jack. The manager's phoned in sick."

***

"What do you mean he's gone to Pakistan?" Aware of Collinge shaking her head beside him, Striker looked at Mrs Khan incredulously. His edginess, brought on by stirred-up memories from his wrestling match with an armed robber in this very shop years ago, were instantly quelled by this revelation.

In broken English, with a strong Pakistani accent, Mrs Khan explained calmly. "We've had very many problems with boys around here. Breaking windows, writing in paint on walls, racist shouts…" She dipped her head. "Khalid been very, very down in his mind and he just wanted break."

Striker's annoyance was tempered by concern for the woman. "Have you reported this?" he asked, wondering why a grown man had deserted his family in their hour of need. Another question arose too: *Had Striker himself done the same with his own family?* He quickly refocused on Mrs Khan.

"We did report early in year, but boys saw police car outside and painted 'grass' on side of shop. Khalid think about shutting shop forever. We live very, very scared, Inspector."

Striker reassured her that they were in an unmarked car, so nobody would know they'd been, and also that he'd speak with the uniform inspector for this neighbourhood. He switched back to his agenda. "When will Khalid be home?"

"Two weeks."

Great.

Collinge asked, "Can you give us a telephone number to contact him?"

"No, I'm sorry, but he said he will call to check on me and my sons in few days, so I will tell him then to call you."

Striker left her his card and stressed the importance of speaking to her husband as soon as possible. Before leaving, he bought a pack of Silk Cut and a cheap disposable lighter, and Collinge looked at him disapprovingly.

As they returned to the car she said, "They'll kill you, Boss."

"So will Cunningham when she hears about Khan."

Collinge fired up the Astra. "I take it we're picking Eric up now?"

"Yeah, then over to the Moss to see if any gang members are hanging out."

***

Striker and his two detectives had cruised around Moss Range scanning for gang members to quiz, but they'd been sparse to say the least. With it still being morning, most would be 'chilling' indoors, smoking a spliff or two; some were probably still in bed, as they 'worked' at night, preferring the shadows.

Mugging the local students was an ongoing battle that officers in the Robbery Unit, another of Striker's old haunts, were finding increasingly difficult to win. Regular inputs were given by well-meaning officers to each new batch of freshers who came to the trendy city of Manchester at the start of term with Daddy's credit card in their back pockets. Despite the stark warnings, once they were into the swing of the buzzing nightlife, and a few drinks had been mixed into the equation, their inhibitions and memories, it seemed, deserted them. Many would become yet another depressing stat for the chief super' to choke on, while scoffing his scones and supping his tea in those high-powered meetings.

Manchester's two universities would take ten thousand plus students at any one time and nearly fifty per cent would experience a robbery. Whether they themselves were the victim or witness was more down to chance than good judgement on their part.

The robbers hunted in packs, many in groups on BMX or mountain bikes, dressed in black, hoods up, approaching from behind, the threat of weapons usually deterring the odd brave victim. Others would skulk in the shadows, as word spread of how easy it was to make a decent living preying on the vulnerable. They would wait to pounce on the unsuspecting and engage them in conversation with the opening gambit of, "Have you gotta light, mate?" or "Give us a cig, man," to test the water. Before the victim knew what was going on, they'd be surrounded, having their pockets frisked. Ironically, increased stop-and-search powers had allowed cops to return the act by rooting through these dodgy characters' pockets, sometimes retrieving stolen items. Alas, not nearly often enough.

The rise of the smartphone had been a drain on resources, since it offered such easy pickings, whereby the robbers simply would cruise the streets on their bikes until they saw an unsuspecting student on their phone and then snatch it from their grasp. Five of these a day and you had a business, especially if you knew a dodgy techie guy who could unblock the phone. The cops secretly wished that the mobile phone owners were half as 'smart' as their phones.

The odd robber would be caught; nonetheless, for every detection for the crime of robbery, both the cops and the perpetrators knew that umpteen robberies would go undetected. The prisons were full and the magistrates and judges had their metaphorical hands tied tightly behind their backs, resulting in inadequate sentencing. Often the defendant would walk free under some kind of supervision order or probation, which simply didn't protect the public like prison did. So the bad boys knew that making a good few hundred quid before being caught, and slightly inconvenienced, was worth the risk. After all, though the stats sometimes lied, the facts didn't. Along with these robberies, the burglaries of student houses – where laptops and iPhones aplenty were stolen – were draining the force immeasurably.

Jobbing drug addicts apart, these perpetrators were usually small fry, the runners who'd give large cuts of their profits to the main gang members. The latter would be behind many a business robbery, which was obviously where the bigger money was. The targeting of a carefully selected residential property was also an option, yet rarely would the main men take the risk of actually committing the act themselves. They were too busy counting the proceeds from these crimes, plus their lucrative protection rackets, drugs and arms dealing.

Striker's days in the robbery and gang units had provided a few notable successes, but it had been a tough old battle. For every criminal they'd put away, such was the state of today's society, two more would inevitably take their places.

The Astra drifted along the heavily residential Upper Moss Road and Striker pointed a finger, prompting Collinge to take a sharp right onto Barkwood Road.

"Seen someone, Boss?" asked Bardsley from the rear.

"Yeah... Pull up now." Collinge hit the brakes and the tyres squeaked on the dry tarmac created by a rare sunny day. Striker threw the front passenger door open, causing a gangly black youth in baggy clothes to wince, then raise his arms protectively.

"Jerome, get in."

"Fuck that, man." Jerome Jackson casually strolled off.

"Get in or you're locked up."

"What for, man?" He clicked his tongue on his teeth with a hiss, in what Striker knew was a gesture of disdain.

"How about sus' murder?"

Jerome stopped on the spot. "Bollocks."

"Get in. Now." Bardsley opened the rear door.

Jerome looked around with shifty eyes, then climbed in through the back door. They drove for a few seconds in silence, until they reached a disused bowling green at the bottom of the road. Gravel crunched under the tyres and Collinge parked up behind the decrepit clubhouse.

"Where were you last night?" asked Striker, spotting swelling to the youth's right cheekbone. He wondered whether it was a result of trying to intervene in last night's attack.

"Rah, you're not pinning that shit on me, man."

"What shit? I only asked where you were."

"You know, that boy being battered good style, innit."

"Nothing's been on the news yet," Striker lied, trying to catch him out, "so how the hell do you know? And where did you get that injury from on your cheek?"

Silence.

"Jerome. Time to talk, and we'll consider not arresting you."

"Just the word on the street, innit."

"Specifics, Jerome."

"Fuck that, man. I'd rather do time than give *you* 'specifics'. At least I won't get smoked."

"So you do know something?"

"All I know, right, is that everyone's talking about it, like gossiping, 'cos word gets about, dunnit? No one knows what happened though, honest man."

"Who's said what?"

"Loadsa people. Torture me if yer wanna, but am not naming names."

Bardsley edged closer and, looking sheepish, Jerome sidled nearer the door.

Striker snickered. "You've been watching too much TV, Jerome. I wouldn't do that to you, fella. But I can't speak for my friend beside you."

Jerome glanced at Bardsley, who eyed him and inched closer still.

Striker continued, "We'll let you go if you tell me why members of your crew were meeting up with the Bullsmead Boys."

Jerome looked down, then out of the window, warily. "If I tell you, I'm free to go, right?"

"Of course. I'm a man of my word."

"Remember Meat Balls getting smoked?"

Striker nodded, recalling the shooting of the city centre bouncer earlier in the year. A power struggle over who ran the lucrative nightclub doors, he recalled.

"A few lads went up there to chat about joining forces, to take on the Salford lot."

Striker was surprised. The two gangs on his patch had been shooting each other up for years, so this was unprecedented. "Okay. Do one."

Bardsley looked disappointed and Jerome couldn't believe his luck. The gang member promptly 'did one', with a slam of the rear door.

"Boss, he knew something. Why leave it at that?"

"It's not enough, Eric. I just wanted to test the water. Let them know we're sniffing. Try and ease the risk of tit-for-tat killings and buy some time. But I've got what I wanted from him. Anyhow, I need to speak with someone else before getting too heavy. Drive, Lauren."

"Where to, Boss?"

"Stoker Avenue. I'm gonna pay my big sis an overdue visit."

Collinge raised her eyebrows as she spun the Astra round, the tyres crunching again. "Why?"

Striker brushed a hand through his hair, wondering whether his only sibling Lucy would still blame him for their dad's death. Taking a deep breath, he answered Collinge's question, "Because my nephew Deano knows a lot of these gang pricks... unfortunately."

Chapter Twelve

"Pull up round the corner, Lauren," said Striker, as they passed Lucy Striker's semi-detached council house. The streets in this part of town were narrow, almost claustrophobic. The houses were a mixture of housing association, council and privately owned – beige brick and box-like.

When the Astra eased to a halt, Striker got out and leaned through the window. "Give me ten minutes. I've not been here for a while, so I'm not sure what sort of reception I'll get. In the meantime, Eric, could you call the garage to see if you can get in touch with this supposedly sick manager, so we can take a look at the CCTV?"

Striker paced toward sixteen Stoker Avenue, surprised at how apprehensive he felt. The last time he'd called it hadn't gone at all well. He'd noticed the front door ajar, so let himself in, catching her with heroin paraphernalia scattered on the coffee table. He and Lucy had argued vehemently; she'd even blamed his teenage antics for contributing to their dad's death. This had cut Striker deep.

Old emotions flooded back as he reached the somewhat rickety gate. He pictured his beautiful sister of years ago – her tousles of strawberry blonde curls flowing past her shoulders, that stunning smile and perfect facial structure, their holidays with mum and dad: North Wales, Blackpool and the Lake District...

He thought of his dad, Harry Striker, a strict but fair man who loved the police and watched all the cop shows on TV. Harry had even tried to join the police force before Striker was born. From what Striker's mum Vera had told him, Harry had passed all the aptitude tests and the physical, only to fail on the medical because he was damn colour-blind, which seemed harsh. Predictably, when Jack Striker the teenager had become embroiled with the wrong crowd and had brought the police to Harry's door, it was the beginning of the end of their relationship.

Young PC Vinnie Stockley had attended the Striker family home to interview Jack about the shooting of one of his mates,

Lenny Powers in the multi-storey car park of Moss Range shopping precinct. Harry was understandably fuming. Once Stockley left, a row exploded and Jack stormed out. The last words Harry Striker had said to his son were: "Good bloody riddance. Now go and make something of your life!" Not long afterward, Harry Striker suffered a mild heart-attack and his health became fragile thereon.

Jack sought solace with childhood sweetheart Suzi Staunton, who'd provided an alibi for him regarding his suspected presence at the multi-storey incident. He owed a lot to Suzi – a hell of a lot. Not only had she lied to the police for him, and probably kept him out of prison, which would have obviously thwarted any chance of his current career, she'd also mothered their two beautiful children.

Once the dust had settled on the Lenny incident, their relationship had blossomed and they had bought a flat together in Eccles, where Suzi was a trainee solicitor. Despite Jack being as stubborn as his old man, in that neither would speak to each other – much to the dismay of perennial peacekeepers Vera Striker and Suzi – he was still determined to prove his worth to his dad. After numerous menial jobs – from window cleaner to shelf stacker to van driver to handyman – Jack finally applied for the police.

The day he passed the final interview, he knew that he *now* had something worthwhile to say to Harry. Though, as fate would have it, he found his dad collapsed on the kitchen floor of the family home. Jack's attempts at resuscitation were unsuccessful and, sobbing his heart out, he hugged his dead dad while clutching the tear-soaked acceptance letter from the police.

Young Jack used to call Lucy "Little Miss Perfect". She was certainly a daddy's girl. Unlike Jack, Lucy couldn't do any wrong. It was strange how things had changed. If Harry could see his "Little Princess" now, he'd turn in his grave. She was shacked up with his old mate DJ. And Striker knew *all* about him. Problem was, he knew all about Striker.

He knocked on the door, his mind flicking back again to the last time he'd seen Lucy. The shock at seeing her, the day her drug habit had graduated from suspicion on his part to confirmation, had hit him harder than a Mike Tyson punch. And now, he felt that punch again as he gazed in disbelief at the woman in the doorway before him.

Initially, he doubted it was her until the hair gave it away, despite having lost its vibrancy. To say Lucy looked gaunt would be kind. Her stunning features had been reduced to a look of near skeletal proportions. Dark bags under bloodshot eyes contrasted against a pallid complexion, scattered with pink blemishes. She must have weighed seven stone wet through. Those blue eyes they shared had lost much of their vividness.

"Jack, what do you want?"

"Charming. It's nice to see you too, Lucy."

"Nah… it's just, I wasn't expecting you." Striker also noticed her voice was slower, with a monotone aloofness.

He saw a couple of youths wearing dark hoodies stroll past, giving him the eye. "Can I come in for a chat?"

"Er… yeah, gimme a minute." With that, she closed the door on him and it didn't take a detective to ascertain what she was doing.

The 'minute' was more like five when Lucy eventually returned and 'welcomed' her brother inside. In the hallway, Striker immediately caught the unmistakable whiff of cannabis but ignored it. He was here for more pressing matters.

The décor was basically laminate flooring and beige walls, but what caught his eye was the enormous plasma telly in the far corner of the living room.

"Take a seat, Jack." He did, on a brown leather sofa that had seen better days. "Do you wanna brew?"

After a quick scan, he clocked the general mess, consisting of damp running down a wall, dirty clothes strewn across a chair, an ashtray full of cigarette butts and a floor that hadn't yet had the pleasure of meeting a brush. He declined his sister's offer, albeit with a touch of guilt. Her house reflected her priorities, and drug addiction beat cleanliness every time.

She went into the small kitchen to the rear, clinking crockery. She was still half in view through the open door.

"Nice telly."

"Oh yeah, DJ's made a few quid recently…" The sentence tailed off, as if she regretted telling her brother even that much.

He leaned back on the sofa to see her. "Is DJ not in?"

She was making herself a brew, not looking his way. "No, he's... just nipped out. Anyway, what brings you round here?"

"Wanted to see how my big sis was."

"That's not why you came, but I'm fine. Yeah... am fine. Why are you really here?"

"Well, there's no point in lying. I was hoping to speak with Deano."

"What about?" She rather noisily stirred her beverage and plonked the spoon into the sink and finally entered the living room, sitting to his right on a cream leather chair that didn't match the sofa.

"Just wanted an off the record chat, to see if he'd heard anything on the street about recent events." The lack of eye contact perturbed him, Lucy preferring to stare at what smelled like coffee in the mug she clutched with both hands.

"Events?"

"Is he in?"

"What events?" She finally looked up at him.

"You must've seen the news, Lucy." The local media had reported the two attacks, but were purely speculating, since GMP hadn't put out an official press release yet.

"Nah, I don't watch the telly much."

Striker glanced at the huge TV, but he actually believed her, as she obviously had other things on her mind. "There seems to be a dispute between the gangs that's getting out of hand and I—"

"Whoa, whoa, whoa!" She scowled and held up a spindly forefinger. "That's my bleedin' son, and even if he did know summat, I don't want my windows put through, or worse."

Striker sighed. "Where is Deano?"

"He's out." Her interest in the coffee resumed.

"Where?"

"Dunno."

"Come on, Lucy. There's two dead lads and, to be honest, we're struggling a bit. No one needs to know. It's off the record. Where is he?"

"Look, he's gone out with a few of the lads. I don't know where though, I swear."

"Who's he with?"

"Dodger and them lot."

Great. Roger Pennington, aka Roger the Dodger, had a reputation of dodging not only bullets, but also the cops. He was suspected of being part of the Moss Range Crew and had been linked to several shootings and serious assaults on their Bullsmead rivals. None of which had yet been proven.

"Okay, thanks. If I leave my number, will you ask him to give me a bell?" He passed her his card.

She didn't take it, eyeing him instead. "I really don't know if I can do that."

"If you can help, I'll be discreet I promise. You may be saving someone's life." He placed the card on a grubby-looking coffee table and bid Lucy farewell, glad the subject of their dad hadn't cropped up this time.

***

Having had no joy engaging any more gang members, nor with speaking to his nephew, Striker had reluctantly told Collinge to head back to the nick. He faced a midday meeting with Det Supt Brennan, DCI Cunningham and DI Stockley.

Brennan was the senior investigating officer, or SIO, to both inquiries. Normally, Detective Chief Superintendent Halt – the man who had asked Striker to apply for MIT – would be the SIO, but he was sunning himself on a Mediterranean cruise. Stockley would have the nugget of that Johnno character, from the second murder in Moss Range Park, as a positive lead, which would undoubtedly impress Brennan, whereas Striker had virtually nothing positive to contribute.

Bardsley had repeatedly called the petrol station, but getting hold of the manager was proving just as hard as newsagent Khalid Khan.

"You two may as well get some refs," said Striker resignedly, when they entered the hubbub of the canteen, where he grabbed a quick coffee from the vending machine. "Then chase up that CCTV. We really do need to view it, even if it means picking up the sick manager from his home and taking him to the petrol station."

After the meeting, he'd try again to track down Deano to see what he'd heard on the street, if anything.

He gave the details of the Bolands murder to the Operational Policing Unit so they could put it on the electronic briefing site, where it would be viewed by the afternoon shift onward. Then he nipped out to the back of the station for a quick fag, searching his mind frantically for something poignant to offer the brass. He stubbed out the cigarette, still having thought of nothing.

Chapter Thirteen

DI Vinnie Stockley was sitting outside Brennan's office, looking suave in his shiny grey Armani suit. Striker caught an unmistakable whiff of Brylcreem and saw that Stockley had flattened the usual quiff on his high fringe. Stockley was always messing about with the wispy quiff and Striker wondered why he just didn't accept his baldness and get rid. He smiled inwardly, recalling something Bardsley had said about fringes at the back of the head coming back into fashion. He sat beside his colleague on the basic tweed two-seater, while mirroring the half-hearted nod Stockley had offered.

"Vinnie."

"Jack." Stockley avoided eye contact, preferring to look at a portrait of the Queen on the wall opposite, while thoughtfully rubbing a finger on the side of his pointed nose.

"What's your gut feeling on the park case now? Any links with mine?" asked Striker.

"I'll tell you more when Brennan's ready, but suffice to say, there's definitely a link, of sorts."

Good. "You reckon?"

"Yes and it's probably the gangs."

Ah.

The door opened and Det Supt Brennan peered round – silvery hair, craggy features, expressionless, abrupt. "In you come then, chaps."

Striker felt uneasy. Granted, it was early days in the investigation, but as he entered Brennan's office, his gut told him this was going to be a tough case. As if to confirm this, Cunningham's face of stone greeted him – thick red lipstick, like graffiti on a wall. She was sat to the right side of Brennan's veneered desk. The room was stuffy and Striker wondered why a vertical fan in the corner wasn't on.

The super gestured at the two chairs across the desk from him and Striker took the one furthest from Cunningham. He briefly pulled at his collar, which suddenly felt tighter, loosening his tie a tad.

"Okay. The press are hovering like vultures, so who's first?"

asked Brennan.

Striker was about to speak, but Stockley blurted, "Well, sir, may I just inform you we've already established that our murder certainly appears to be a revenge attack as a result of the first murder."

Rather than being annoyed at Stockley's over-enthusiastic brown-nosing, Striker was glad of more thinking time and was intrigued as to why Stockley thought this.

Brennan leaned forward from his leather swivel chair, much comfier than the two DIs' hardback seats.

"Oh? Please elaborate, Vinnie."

"There was fresh graffiti at the scene that hadn't yet dried, and I've recovered a paint canister nearby that on first impressions seems to marry up."

"Seems?"

"Yes, it's the same yellow colour."

"Okay, that narrows it down a little, I suppose." Brennan glanced at Cunningham. "I take it the canister is now with the FSS being analysed?"

"Of course, sir."

"Along with samples from the graffiti?"

Striker clocked Stockley's hesitation and belated nod.

"What else have you got, Vinnie?"

Stockley told him about the freshly sprayed graffiti saying 'MRC' on the wooden climbing frame beside the body. He skimmed a hand smoothly through his thinning hair before continuing. "And we've also seized, and sent off, the rope used to hang the deceased. I've DCs checking on the knot used too, because I've seen it predominantly used in one area before."

"Oh?"

Now Cunningham leaned forward.

"The surgeon's loop."

The super and DCI frowned in unison.

"Fishing, sir. As a keen fishermen myself, I can confirm it's a strong knot used for the end of your line."

Oh please.

Brennan again exchanged glances with Cunningham.

"Are you saying that one of the Moss Range Crew is a keen fisherman, Vinnie?"

"It certainly looks that way."

Striker couldn't resist. "Either that, or he's a surgeon."

Cunningham scoffed, Stockley looked unimpressed and Brennan eyed Striker, who dipped his head, wishing he hadn't spoken. Years of working with Bardsley had rubbed off on him. Clearly there was no place for dark humour here. Lesson learned.

Stockley went on, "I'm just saying it's a possibility, and my DCs are currently checking this out as we speak."

Brennan looked pensive, then said, "Isn't it possible the killer, or killers, has internet access?"

Stockley shuffled in his seat. "Well of course, but it's a line" – he hesitated realising his unintended pun – "of enquiry, sir."

"Okay, but not one that'll win the case, Vinnie. Anything else?"

"Obviously the body is being given the once over too, and line" – again he hesitated – "searches are being conducted."

"Any witnesses?"

"Apart from Johnson, who was under the influence of drugs and was knocked unconscious from behind, there are no other witnesses yet, sir. There are no houses overlooking that part of the park either."

"Okay, thanks, Vinnie." He turned to Striker. "Jack, what have you got?"

Cunningham answered on his behalf and Striker threw her a look.

"Jack, tell us about the two youths who were sat on the wall on police arrival."

"I didn't arrest them because I didn't suspect them of murder. Plus, alienating them like that could have been counter-productive if we needed them as witnesses later."

"I do understand your sentiments, Jack, but I agree with Maria. I think you should have arrested them, especially with the media snooping for a story. That's why we've just sent Team Three to bring them in."

Striker was pretty stunned. *Was I so wrong on that call?* "If they were guilty of anything, surely they'd have done a runner, sir."

"Maybe, yet even so, we need to eliminate them and also ascertain exactly who they were with. You don't appear to have done either."

Striker hid a sigh.

Cunningham piped, "Have you established the IDs of *any* of the gang members who were present, Jack, like I asked?"

"We visited the Moss and I spoke to one, but didn't get much from him. I'll obviously keep trying." Striker purposely held back what Jerome Jackson had said about the two gangs meeting up to join forces, knowing this would go against the consensus of those present. That info wasn't reliable enough and he wanted something more solid to back up his vigilante theory. "I've also got a list here" – he reached into his jacket pocket – "of Bolands' associates."

"How many are there?" asked Cunningham.

"Forty-six."

"So that's forty-six possible youths who may have been with Bolands when he was murdered. That narrows it down, Jack." Her voice was almost patronising. "Now, do you see why we're arresting those two at the scene?"

"I have shortened it to twenty-five, but…" He noticed Brennan's stern expression. "But I do take your point."

Brennan blinked slowly, nodded. Striker continued, "I do have other leads to pursue though. Bolands' dad has agreed to drop off his son's mobile phone for the techies to analyse. The CCTV from the garage is usually of decent quality and still needs a good trawl. Bardsley and Collinge are onto that as we speak. Also, there's the shopkeeper witness, Mr Khan." He omitted the part about him having gone to Pakistan.

"The one you haven't spoken to yet?" It was Cunningham again.

Right. Time to speak my mind. "Bardsley briefly took a first account off him, which is why we have the description of that 'tall burly man'. Anyone could have sprayed 'MRC' on that climbing frame to make it look like the Crew were involved and throw us off the scent. How many gang members use a baton or a rope with a fancy knot, for God's sake? That's unheard of. It's always guns, knives and baseball bats. So I'm not convinced it's gang-on-gang. I still think the 'burly guy' could be our man and that both investigations should be linked."

"That's quite an assumption, Jack," said Brennan, "considering your lack of evidence."

"Both deceased males have ASBOs too. You are aware of that, aren't you, sir?"

"Coincidence… and to be fair, not much of one at that because it's odds on around here, don't you think? Look, Jack, we simply can't jump to conclusions and get carried off on a tangent." Cunningham and Stockley nodded. "So, we're *not* linking the murders. They'll remain as separate investigations. You find your 'burly man', and quick. I've got to face the press at sixteen hundred hours. Okay?"

Striker gave an imperceptible nod, then said, "Vinnie, that lad Johnson, who was with Chisel and then taken to hospital. Was he arrested?"

"No."

"Why not?"

"He's Chisel's best mate. A witness."

"Well, that's just like those two Bullsmead Boys, Mozerelli and Grinley at my scene. They were there and didn't flee the scene, like Johnson, even though they had the chance to. Witnesses. And could Johnson's head injury be conducive to a baton being used?"

"Come on, Striker, give it a rest," said Cunningham impatiently.

Stockley still answered, his voice raised. "He had a small laceration and a few inches of swelling, so it could have been any of number of weapons or objects that struck him. And anyway, I'll…"

"Enough!" Brennan said abruptly.

"With respect, sir, may I ask if Steven Bowker was already dead when he was hanged?"

"What are you on about now?" Cunningham shook her head.

"Sidney Mortham said that, as yet, it's inconclusive," said Stockley.

"I saw the marks on Bowker's face and he'd certainly been in a fight because they weren't like any injuries I've seen before in any hangings I've dealt with."

Brennan remained quiet, pondering, but Cunningham asked, "What are you saying, that the killer beat him to death and then risked being caught by hanging him?"

"It's possible… if he's making a statement."

"Right, I said, enough." For a moment, Brennan held up both palms. "Jack, concentrate on your own case. I won't tell you again. Those two youths will be arrested and interviewed when we get them, which will hopefully be today. You carry on following your leads and establish which gang members were at your scene. Hopefully, the two Bullsmead Boys can shed some light on this too. You'll obviously be informed by Team Three when those arrests are made, okay?"

Not much of welcome for the new boy here. Pity Mr Halt wasn't due back yet. "Okay, sir," said Striker, feeling his growing frustration turning into anger.

***

"You okay, Jack?"

Striker looked up from his mesmeric gaze at the blank wall and realised Bardsley had entered his office. His vacant stare continued, now aimed at his colleague.

Once the door was shut, Bardsley's voice softened a little. "You're not, are you, Jack?"

"That prick, Stockley, and Cunningham, trying to make me look inept in front of Brennan, and not a fuckin' lead to go on... Fancy a beer when we knock off, Eric?"

Bardsley grinned. "You're a mind reader. The Crown?"

"Now *you're* the mind reader. How did you get on with the CCTV? Please tell me something positive."

"Oh, it's positive alright. Positively positive! Should cheer you up." He waved a CD in the air and then inserted it into Striker's computer. He pulled up a seat beside Striker as it whirred into action.

There was a knock at the door.

"That'll be Lauren, she'd nipped to the ladies. I was gonna follow her in, but thought better of it."

"Behave, Eric." Shaking his head, Striker turned to the door. "Come in, Lauren."

Collinge opened the door and popped her head round before entering, as the CD played on the screen.

"Oh goody, just in time."

Striker beamed at Collinge, wondering what all the fuss was

about. She pulled up a chair and Striker got a pleasant waft of her perfume.

He watched intently, while Bardsley leaned across the desk to take control of the mouse. He fast-forwarded, studying the clock on the screen before pushing play at 22:27.

"This is it. Watch the top of the screen."

Striker could see a fairly clear picture of the petrol station's layout: four red-and-white pumps, two random cars, their drivers topping up. There was a slight haze as the artificial lights countered the night, but it was a lot better quality than some he'd seen. The backdrop, away from the forecourt's lights, was darkness. A group of lads appeared at the top of the screen. They walked across the forecourt toward the serving hatch, and became increasingly visible with each step. Eight of them, all in dark clothes and most wearing hoodies.

"This is where the manager switched cameras for us," said Bardsley. "They shut the main door at twenty-two hundred hours because of previous robbery attempts and the likes of this lot hanging about."

The picture flickered when the viewpoint changed to a window outside the counter area where the cashier served people, using a drawer facility for safety. Some of faces of the throng were clear to see, especially those with their hoods down.

"That's Grinley," said Striker. "And there's Mozo."

"Yeah, some of them bought crisps, fags and cans of coke and water, before moving on. There's nearly five minutes of footage here, Jack."

"Pause it." The screen quivered. "Is that Bolands?"

"That's what we reckon, Boss," said Collinge.

Striker glanced at the DCs, who were looking pleased with themselves.

"Good. So we know he was still alive at twenty-two twenty-nine. That's if that clock's right."

"Oh it is. I've checked and the manager said they'd fitted a state of the art system because his bosses were sick of the trouble, so the digital clock is always accurate." Bardsley pushed play.

"Strange that he's with the Bullsmead Boys though. They seem friendly enough with him too. Maybe Jerome was right about them meeting up to discuss a merger against the Salford lot."

"Yeah, we struggled understanding that one as well, Boss," said Collinge.

For the next three minutes Striker made notes and they discussed the possible identities of each of the youths. By the time this section of the footage ended, they had four definitely identified and another four possible names. The latter could be put on the electronic briefing for all officers to view, so confirmation would only be a matter of a few hours away, hopefully.

Striker was feeling much better about things as he watched the last of the youths disappear from view. Bardsley fast forwarded the screen again.

"Good stuff, guys."

"It gets better, Jack. Now watch the bottom of the screen."

Bardsley clicked play again and Striker edged forward in his seat. The digital clock was at 22:42 when a couple of figures ran across the forecourt.

"Not sure who they are, but we could work it out from the clothing or by closer analysis at Bradford Park, maybe later. Keep watching." Striker glanced at his colleagues in turn, curiosity strewn across his face.

A dark figure appeared, jogging. He was only just in view. Though this person wasn't a kid, it was a man – a tall burly man.

"That's our guy, Eric, it's got to be."

Bardsley nodded, grinned. "I told you it would cheer you up."

"You got stills?"

"Yeah, but not from this camera angle. Keep watching."

The mystery man jogged out of view.

"Where's he heading?"

"Looks like north, up Moss Range Road," said Collinge.

Striker made a mental note to check with council for any CCTV beyond the petrol station. The screen changed viewpoint again and revealed a much closer shot of the man running alongside the forecourt. Striker shuffled nearer, leaning in, as the man grew bigger. He was clearly wearing a balaclava and was dressed in a long black coat.

Bardsley paused the image at its optimal point. "Voilà," he said, producing three stills from his jacket pocket and handing them to Striker. He studied the photos. Two were close ups of the youths and one a copy of the shot now visible on the screen.

Striker stood up, turned to Bardsley. "You beauty!" He grabbed both sides of the DC's head and pulled him in for a smacker of a kiss on the lips.

Bardsley laughed out loud, saying, "Errgh."

Striker turned to Collinge, who was smiling. He leaned in a few inches, hesitating as their eyes met, before quickly looking back at the screen, fleetingly feeling warmth flush his cheeks.

Composing himself, he said, "Right. I know we can't easily ID him, but this changes everything. In some ways, it's okay that he's concealing his ID. I mean, why would a man wearing a face mask flee a murder scene?"

"Exactly," said Bardsley. "You were right, Jack, about it not being the gangs."

"And we've got continuity from Khan's account. We really need to speak with him now… Oh no, what time is it?" Striker looked up at the clock on his wall. It was five to four. "Brennan's speaking to the media in five minutes. Get a coffee, I'll be back in ten."

With that, Striker ran from his office, clutching the stills.

Chapter Fourteen

Taking the stairs two at a time, Striker was soon running down the corridor to the front-desk office. He burst into the room and Joanne, the frumpy-looking front-desk clerk, physically jumped, nearly dropping the plate of pasta she was eating.

"Sorry, Joanne, but has Mr Brennan started with the press yet?"

She swallowed what she was eating and tentatively shook her head. "No, but he's on his way down apparently."

Striker scanned the multiple cameras high on the office wall, showing all angles of the front counter waiting area and the outside of the nick. The media were there waiting in the car park, like a herd of scavenging hyenas.

He heard footsteps in the corridor, then a door opening. He saw Brennan appear on one of the screens, and on the adjacent one the media surged forward for the kill.

Striker sprinted out of the office and released a catch on the inner wall of the corridor beside the door. He entered the empty public waiting area – purposely vacated – and saw the back of Brennan heading toward a plethora of flashing cameras.

"Mr Brennan!"

The detective superintendent spun round, a look of incredulity across his face. "What?" he asked curtly, his arms open, gesturing at the multitude of reporters outside.

"Please, sir." Striker beckoned him over using his hand.

Brennan backtracked, saying, "This better be good, Striker."

Striker noticed an ITV film crew and a female reporter approaching the door, camera pointing directly at them, the reporter speaking excitedly into her microphone. He ensured the photos were out of the camera's view, hiding them behind his back.

He said in a hushed voice, "Sir, we've got some footage of the bloke that the newsagent Khan described. Plus, great shots of gang members, including" – Still mindful of the cameraman, Striker flicked through the photos for Brennan's benefit – "Bolands, Mozerelli and Grinley."

Deadpan, Brennan thought for a moment, glanced at the

111

media. "Good work, Striker."

"We have DCs Bardsley and Collinge to thank."

"Well good for them, but I've got a script in my head of what to say and we're sticking with the gang angle for now."

"With respect, sir, this man" – He held up the still – "is fleeing a murder scene while wearing a balaclava."

"Yes, but he could still be a gang member, Jack."

"What, dressed like that?" He pointed at the long trench coat.

"Look, leave the CD and the stills on my desk. I'll take a look afterwards. Now let me deal with this rabble, will you?"

"Don't you even want to show the photo to them and appeal for him to come forward, or see if anyone knows him?"

"No. Not yet. Now, do as I've requested, Inspector."

Exasperated, Striker's thoughts drifted to John Smith's bitter and the Crown.

***

Striker sent Bardsley a quick text, then went around the back of the nick for a cigarette. He purposely avoided the group of regulars gathered under the smoking shelter across the rear car park. Instead, he opted for a little alcove under the metal fire escape beneath his office.

He was soon joined by Bardsley and offered him a Silk Cut.

"Nah, can't get a drag out of them. It's like trying to suck treacle through a straw. I'll stick with my Bensons, thanks. Anyway, what happened with Brennan? Why have you still got the photos?"

"Don't ask." Striker took a drag of his cigarette. "He did say well done to you and Lauren, but he's sticking with the gang-on-gang theory."

"You're joking."

"I jest not."

"You know why he's in denial, don't you, Jack?"

"I can hazard an educated guess."

"He's shit scared of the media and, more importantly, the public thinking we have a serial killer on our hands." Bardsley blasted a double drag, the smoke caressing and intermingling with his beard before dispersing upward in the breeze.

"Sounds about right that. The tit-for-tit gang warfare would be no surprise, almost like old news. He won't admit it until it's absolutely necessary. Especially on his watch, while Mr Halt's still on his cruise." Striker drew on his cigarette, feeling the niggling guilt and disappointment at starting smoking again.

"Agreed. He's bottled it. He could've shown that photo there and then to speed things up. Anyway, I've just been to the OPU and they'll scan those stills onto the briefing site and hopefully that'll help confirm the IDs of the other four kids at the petrol station."

"Nice one. Thanks, Eric. We'd best hold back on the still of our man, until Brennan gives us the nod."

"Fair enough. When's he on telly?"

"I'm pretty certain it was a live feed, but I guess it'll be on the local bulletins later." Striker took one last drag. "Pub?"

Bardsley nodded enthusiastically. "Pub." They both stubbed out their cigarettes and headed back upstairs to finish off for the day.

After Bardsley had nipped back into the OPU with the stills for the briefing site, and Striker had placed the CD and photos of the suspect on Brennan's desk on the top floor, they were back in Striker's office.

Collinge had followed them in. "Boss, just thought you'd like to know, I've just checked the custody system to see if Mozerelli and Grinley have been arrested yet and it's a negative."

"Hey, cheers Lauren. I was just about to do that myself. Brennan's got the disc of the footage for the interviews, if they do get them in."

"Right then, I think that's us done for the day, guys. We're just going to the Crown for a quick pint, Lauren. Wanna join us?"

"Er... thanks, Boss, but I've got a date." She looked at them both staring at her, Bardsley raising his eyebrows. "It's only a meal after work, nothing special."

Striker surprised himself with a panicky twinge of jealousy and immediately suppressed it. "Who's the lucky fella?"

Collinge briefly looked away and ran a hand through her locks, saying, almost too nonchalantly, "Oh, er, nobody you know. But thanks for the offer. Okay if I get off?"

Bardsley was just about to say something, so Striker cut in.

"Of course, Lauren. You have a good night and I'll see you nice and refreshed at the morning meeting?"

"Refreshed? What, like you two will be? I've heard about your 'quick pints'," she said cheekily, throwing in the smile.

***

The Crown was on the southern edge of Manchester city centre and whenever they'd attended there in the past, the session had been a lengthy one. The alcoves were perfect, eavesdropper proof, and the music always light, usually swing, which suited them both. Black-and-white pictures of swing singers, old and new, covered the walls: Frank Sinatra, Dean Martin, Harry Connick Jr, to name a few.

The Crown was only ten minutes from the nick, up the A56. The predominantly wooden design, including beams, trim and flooring, along with the pastel orange wall lights, provided a relaxing look and warm feeling. Only being half full, it made serving fairly routine. They chose their alcove and sat across a mahogany table from each other, Bardsley making light work of the soothing fizz of Becks, while Striker felt the cool tang of John Smith's Extra Smooth running merrily down his throat.

"Stockley's always been up his own arse, Jack, so what would you expect from him anyway?"

"I know. And I know Cunningham will always bear a grudge, after what happened between us. But it was Brennan who surprised me today. I used to think he was okay, but even he was doing my head in. So I just needed a beer – with a friendly face."

"You call this friendly?" Bardsley pointed at his rugged, hairy mug, while contorting for effect and widening his eyes. "Enough to scare a bleedin' gorilla this. Just ask the missus." He chuckled at his own joke.

"That's another reason." Striker shook his head, smiling. "Your self-deprecating humour."

"And there's me thinking you were gonna put pen to paper 'cause you thought I wasn't politically correct."

"If I was gonna do that, Eric, I'd have done it years ago. Probably within the first few days of meeting you."

They both took a mouthful of their pints, then Bardsley asked,

"Can you remember that far back, old timer?"

"Cheeky git. I'm only thirty-five." They exchanged grins. "Anyway, how are you and Maggie getting on these days, now all the kids have fled the nest?"

Fleetingly, Bardsley's expression became forlorn and he took another gulp of his lager. Mischief soon refilled his eyes. "At least she actually touched me the other night. So things are looking up."

"Really?" Striker played along, with mock surprise.

"Yeah, well, I bumped into her on the stairs on my way to work. It's the closest I've been to sex for years. Can't speak for her though."

Striker nearly spurted his last swig of bitter across the table. "I'm the same, mate. No action for a good old while."

There was a slight awkward silence and Striker wondered whether Bardsley wanted to confide in him, which would be a rare occurrence. Instead, he opted for the safer bet. "Fancy another, Eric?"

"Does it rain in Manchester?"

As Striker strolled the ten metres to the bar, a student-aged brunette with eye-catching curves smiled at him. She was collecting glasses and brazenly looked him up and down, just as Robbie Williams' version of 'Mack the Knife' kicked in on the sound system. Striker found himself smiling back. Playing it cool, he quickly got the barman's attention.

"Same again, please, mate."

The clink of glasses beside him on the bar caught his attention and the girl was up so close he could smell her perfume. A new fragrance, not one he'd encountered before, but he liked it.

"Just finished?" she asked confidently.

"Huh? Oh, yeah, about half an hour ago. What about you?"

"Here all night. And you?"

"Will probably have a couple more."

"Good." She smirked, rolling her tongue in her cheek.

Striker was torn between doing the right thing and doing the wrong thing. So he did neither and turned back to the barman, who placed the pints before him. Once he'd paid, the girl was gone, cleaning a nearby table, and he half regretted not continuing the chat.

Bardsley's dirty smirk greeted him back in the alcove.

"Inspector Striker into paedophilia now? What will Mr Halt think when he gets back?"

"Sod off, Eric. I just said hello."

Bardsley took the head off his pint, wiped the froth from his top lip with the back of his left hand. "Oh really? You were drooling and I don't blame you. Those tits looked proper angry under that blouse. I clocked her as soon as we came in."

"Give over, Eric. You could be her granddad, you perv."

"And you could be her big brother. Worth a nibble though."

"You're a married man."

"And you're not, so why not?" Bardsley winked.

"Nah, it's not worth it. Anyway, I am technically still married. We never did divorce, you know. But since Suzi left, I just can't be arsed with women. Much better on my own, for now."

"All blokes need some relief."

"What are you calling me here, Eric?"

"I was referring to myself. I'm getting really adept at this DIY lark."

Striker shook his head again. "So things aren't right with you two then?"

"Very perceptive. You should be a detective."

He laughed, but Bardsley just stared into his pint.

A moment passed.

"I think she's been knobbing the window cleaner, Jack."

"Shit, Eric." His friend's face grimaced. "Fancy a smoke?"

"Good idea."

Taking their pints out to the rear beer garden, the chill of night soon hit them.

Striker pushed a button and the outside heater flared reddish orange, bringing near instant warmth. Bardsley lit two Bensons and passed one to Striker, knowing the DI's ten pack of Silk Cut had long gone.

Striker checked over both shoulders and saw that no one else was present. "How do you know, Eric – about Maggie and the window cleaner?"

"I caught him looking – no, staring – at her a few weeks ago, so I challenged him. He seems to have an answer for everything. You know, a cocky smart-arse type, so I gave him the benefit of the doubt."

"Is that it?"

"No. I came home from work and he was in the kitchen having a beer. One of *my* bleedin' beers, and they were giggling as I walked in."

"Right. Still not proof though."

"But Maggie looked different. Sort of glowing, like when we first met. And he supped up and left a bit too sharpish if you ask me."

"Have you confronted her?"

He shook his head. "You know me. It all just comes out as me being even more grumpy toward her. Instead of actually just having a heart-to-heart, you know?" He took a long drag and Striker thought he looked a little tearful when he exhaled, but it may have been the artificial lighting. "Anyhow, won't Brennan be on the repeat news bulletin soon?"

It was then that Striker's mobile chimed. He answered. "Jack Striker."

Bardsley looked up as Striker's face became stern, his head shaking slightly.

"Give me fifteen minutes, Becky, and thanks for letting me know," he said, before dropping the mobile into his jacket pocket.

"Jack?"

"Braeburn Road. Two more victims."

Bardsley instantly shook off his domestic problems and jolted into cop mode.

Within seconds, they plonked their pints on the bar and headed for the door. The pretty barmaid looked surprised when Striker breezed past her.

"Something I said?"

Striker briefly turned to her, but kept walking, backward. "Some other time, perhaps?"

"I'll look forward to it." Her smile faded and she appeared disappointed.

Though Striker knew that 'other time' wouldn't be any time soon.

***

"So one survived then?" asked Striker impatiently. The strobe flashes of blue police lights, from the vehicles preserving the scene, momentarily blinded him. The scene was already marked by a white SOCO tent about thirty metres away, half on the pavement and half on the road. Braeburn Road was a fairly wide B road that ran alongside Moss Range Park, with predominantly privately owned semis running its length, many with their lights on as the curious occupants watched the show through twitching curtains.

Tonight DC Brad Sterling was the night DO, while the rest of CID worked a mixture of day and afternoon shifts. Sterling would endeavour to keep abreast of any serious stuff and update a night crime log, until reinforcements returned in the morning to assist. And this was as serious as it gets. Sterling must have only just started his shift – talk about hitting the ground running.

"Yes, Boss, one survived. He's at the hospital under armed guard. Still unconscious though." Sterling brushed a hand through his lightly gelled blond comb-over, and Striker was mildly irritated on spotting a small Manchester United badge on the DC's tie.

Swiftly dismissing the triviality, he asked, "Which hospital, Bullsmead General?"

Sterling shook his head. "No, he's in Manchester Royal Infirmary."

Shit.

"You alright, Boss?"

The MRI brought back unwanted memories for Striker and he'd not been back there for many years. He shook the memories away before they began, knowing their ability to consume him. "Huh? Yeah, yeah, I'm fine. Do we have a name for the deceased yet?" Striker gazed at the SOCO tent, adjacent to the railings and bushes on the periphery of the park.

"No."

"So, what exactly happened, Brad?"

"It looks like an ambush. I've spoken to" – he checked his A4 daybook – "Betty Grange from number fifty-two Braeburn Road and she said she heard 'rowdy lads' passing and peeked from behind her bedroom blinds. Then she saw 'a large, dark figure jump from the bushes' and suddenly attack the two lads."

Striker was transfixed. "So we actually have a witness *and* a survivor?" He glanced at Bardsley, who nodded with a determined look. "Is someone taking a statement?"

"Yes, Boss. DS Grant came back on duty and took the old dear back to the station."

"So, from your initial account, how did she describe the attack?"

"The attacker punched the taller of the two lads, knocking him clean out. His head appeared to crack onto the pavement. He's the one in hospital. Then he swung 'a long black pole' repeatedly around the other male's head until he collapsed."

"Was it a baton?" asked Bardsley.

"Could've been. Nothing's been found and more officers from the late shift are on their way with dragon lamps for the search. Betty Grange was about forty feet away and it's obviously dimly lit. Unfortunately, her eyesight's not the best either and she's in shock. But that's not all."

"Go on."

"Once the second male had stopped writhing on the floor, the offender" – he checked his notes again – "coolly glanced over both shoulders, then straddled the lad, took out a large knife and eased it into his heart."

Striker swapped looks with Bardsley.

"Looks like we've definitely got a serial killer, Boss."

"A vigilante on a mission." Feeling vindicated, Striker turned back to Sterling.

"That's what we're all thinking too."

"Did he stab the other lad?"

"No, he straddled him, still holding the knife, and bent down. But he hesitated and looked around. Then, he quickly scaled the fence and ran into the park. Betty Grange said she'd heard a dog barking at that point, so…"

Striker thought for a moment, absorbing the info, processing the enormity of this escalating situation.

"Are Brennan and Cunningham aware?"

"The duty officer over at comms has been in touch with Mr Brennan, who asked me to call you. He couldn't get hold of DCI Cunningham, nor DI Stockley for that matter."

Hmm… "Okay. Cheers, Brad." Striker scanned the scene, his eyes resting on Response Sergeant Paul Roache. "Eric, do you mind co-ordinating house-to-house enquiries with Paul?"

"Not at all."

"After that, you get yourself off home, okay?" Striker was mindful they'd had a few pints and Bardsley nodded, obviously thinking the same. "I'll not enter the scene for now because I wanna check this lad out at the hospital. What's his name, Brad?"

Striker couldn't imagine how things could possibly get any worse, but was at least thankful they now had an eyewitness, despite her limitations. And, perhaps, the breakthrough they desperately needed would finally be forthcoming.

After another flick through his notes, Sterling said, "Don't forget he was unconscious, so he—"

"What's his name?"

"Dean Salt. He's in the ICU room three."

Striker was stunned, his heart plummeting on hearing his nephew's name.

This was now personal.

Chapter Fifteen

Striker thanked the nurse and tentatively entered the ICU at Manchester Royal Infirmary, the very same ward that his old pal Lenny was in all those years ago when Suzi's alibi saved Striker's arse. He fought hard to stem the flood of bad memories.

He'd been deliberating whether or not to phone his sister. Lucy had no way of knowing that Deano had been attacked, since he'd often staggered home in the small hours, sometimes not returning home for days. However, he prayed there had been some mistake, that the name was just a coincidence. Deep down, though, he knew. He decided on a positive ID from himself, before the harrowing task of informing Lucy.

He showed his warrant card to the two armed officers sitting outside ICU Room 3. They sat upright, nodded in acknowledgment. The bleeps of life-assisting machinery and medicinal smells greeted him as he opened the door; medical staff in green outfits, and a couple in dark blue, scurried around donning stern expressions. One, a female, saw his raised warrant card, nodded knowingly and pointed him in the right direction as there were four beds. He headed for the one on the extreme right and slowly pulled back the pale blue privacy curtain. He edged nearer, seeing that the patient wore an oxygen mask, his face bruised. The head appeared swollen under extensive bandages, and tubes and wires were connected to the body. He looked closer and his fears were confirmed.

"Deano," he whispered. His mouth dry, he swallowed and glanced heavenwards, momentarily. Seeing a cannula in his nephew's left hand, he walked around the bed and held his right hand, which dangled slightly from the bed. It felt cold, almost lifeless.

Fighting back emotion, he began to reminisce, recalling the day he became an uncle, cradling his newborn nephew in this very hospital. Suzi was drug free then, her happy beaming face mirroring Striker's, the latent stirrings of his own desire to be a parent back then simmering deep inside.

The many football matches he'd watched the young Deano play in began to whiz through his mind like an old movie: his first goal, his first winner's medal and his first injury. Striker had run on the pitch with the 'magic sponge' before carrying him to the side-line. The many Man City matches he'd taken him to came into focus. Not much success back then, but they'd had fun and the blues had even turned over their illustrious red rivals from across the city a couple of times, perking them up, reinforcing their faith.

A few recollections of family parties later and he returned to the now, releasing his grip on Deano's limp hand, sorry he hadn't been around for the last few years. The adolescent Deano had clearly gotten in with the wrong crowd, and Striker knew all about that. Only six months ago, Striker had received a courtesy call from Paul Roache to say that Deano had been arrested on suspicion of street robbery. Striker couldn't get involved in the case for legal reasons, but outside work he'd advised Lucy accordingly. Nonetheless, Deano was still convicted and was lucky to get away with just an official caution, which basically equated to a bollocking-cum-final warning.

The way Deano looked now reminded him again of Lenny Powers sixteen years ago. As Striker sat back in the chair, those haunting memories flooded back…

***

The door to Room 3 opened and Striker's mind zoomed back to the present as he saw a youngish nurse enter. His head was banging and he wished he'd not had those beers earlier with Bardsley. The nurse smiled somewhat forcedly and picked up a clipboard from the bottom of Deano's bed. She busied herself around Deano, doing her routine checks, occasionally glancing at Striker.

"I'm his uncle. Will he live?"

She hesitated, her voice soft. "He's taken quite a knock to the head."

"What do you reckon, though, off the record?"

"I shouldn't speculate, but there's a fair chance. People do come round from comas. We've stabilized him and got the swelling under control, so…" She became quiet, looking a little uneasy.

Striker nodded, realising he shouldn't really have put her on the spot like that. He'd speak with the doctor later. Within seconds the nurse was gone and Striker sank back into the chair, his mind briefly drifting again.

Striker's thoughts returned to Deano.

Despite the intensifying dread, he knew he had to make that phone call to Lucy. Either that, or go visit her in person.

The door opened and the doctor entered. Striker rose from his seat, not liking the doctor's grave expression.

***

Live on air, the press release from GMP was read out to the mass of reporters gathered outside Bullsmead Police Station by Det Supt Brennan, amid a flurry of flash photography.

"Tonight's unprovoked attacks on two innocent young men are currently being investigated by a thirty-strong team of very able officers. I can confirm, with deep regret, that one male aged eighteen has unfortunately died. A second male of the same age is currently in intensive care. We are not at this point linking it to any of the other recent murders, although this cannot be ruled out. The investigation is at an early stage and further information and evidence is being gleaned as I speak. I would urge anyone who knows anything about this to contact the incident room, where your call will be dealt with in the strictest of confidence, or alternatively call Crimestoppers anonymously.

"Family liaison officers are currently with the two families of the victims, and it would be inappropriate at present to elaborate further. Except to say I would like to take this opportunity to reassure the public that Greater Manchester Police are working flat out to catch the perpetrator, or perpetrators, of these despicable crimes, and that numerous extra patrols will be in force for the foreseeable future. To preserve the integrity of the investigations, I won't be taking any questions at the moment and a press conference will follow in due course."

A plethora of eager voices spurted out questions as countless camera clicks and flashes followed. Brennan raised a placating palm before turning to leave. The torrent of questions continued.

"Mr Brennan, when are you going to admit that Manchester has a serial killer at large?" ... "Are you close to an arrest?" ... "Do you have any advice for the local community?" ...

None were answered and Brennan retreated into the nick.

Striker switched off the large plasma TV. Having decided to tell Lucy in person at her home, he glanced across at his sister, her eyes bloodshot and baggy.

"We'll catch him, you know."

"Will you... really?" She sounded unconvinced.

"I promise."

"Well, you better fuckin' find him before I do, that's all I can say," DJ said through clenched teeth, as he tied the laces of his trainers.

Striker glanced at his old mate, but didn't speak. DJ was no stranger to drugs and looked just as gaunt as Lucy. As ever, he still shaved his head and still had the same criminal mentality. On the few occasions he'd seen him, since the Lenny shooting, DJ had been distant. Lenny aside, DJ knew Striker blamed him for Lucy's deterioration and Striker knew DJ was wary of him. He'd never been the same with him since Striker had joined the Job. Their old friendship was tucked safely away in the distant past, along with the dark secrets they shared. Words were rarely exchanged between them now, especially as they both knew they could easily bring one another down.

DJ's current anger was understandable. Deano was on life support with swelling on the brain; the doctors had given him a fifty-fifty chance of survival.

"You sure I can't give you a lift to the hospital, Lucy?"

"I said I'll take her." DJ eyed Striker.

Striker got the message. "Okay. I'd best get off, Lucy. I'm so sorry." He needed to return to work to establish who was dealing with these recent attacks throughout the night. He was weary and needed a vodka nightcap, then some shut-eye. He nodded at DJ, who was unresponsive.

At the door, Lucy looked at him, her face softening, eyes glazed.

Hugging his sister for the first time since their dad's funeral, he felt her frail bony body, the emotion deep within him bubbling.

Chapter Sixteen

After a meagre three and a half hours' broken sleep, Striker was back at the station mulling over the statements and copies of officers' pocket notebooks from the growing file currently strewn across his desk. He'd phoned the hospital and there was no change regarding Deano. He'd also checked the custody system and discovered that Mozo and Grinley hadn't been arrested yet. Had they gone to ground for some reason?

Amazingly, neither Cunningham nor Stockley had answered their phones last night, so he'd just picked up the new inquiry and run with it as the one larger connected case he'd suspected it was since the second murder.

Clearly now it was a chase to catch a determined vigilante killer, and evidence-wise they had next to nothing. However, as the scenes mounted, something was bound to arise that would lead them to the killer. DNA would be useful, particularly if the killer was on their database.

A tall burly man dressed in dark clothing, perhaps in his thirties. The attacks always featured a long dark weapon that was sounding increasingly like a baton, which is a strange weapon of choice if you want someone dead. Is he releasing pent up anger, enjoying the feel of the repeated strikes necessary to kill them? *Punish* them? Granted, in the latest murder possibly a kitchen knife was used too, obviously to make sure, like the rope with Chisel. Or had the rope been symbolism as he and Bardsley had discussed? He'd checked all recent hangings over the last year, but couldn't make a connection. Frustratingly, it all still seemed rather puzzling. Mixing MOs maybe? If this was to confuse the cops, then it was working... for now.

The possible baton aspect nagged him. They were easy enough for anyone to purchase these days, especially on the internet. And clearly cops used batons. Surely this wasn't the work of an officer who'd finally snapped? Exasperated, maybe, at the way the wheels of justice turned ever-so-slowly, and in some cases, seized up completely. Nah, this wasn't Hollywood, it was Bullsmead. He pushed this unwelcome, and highly unlikely, possibility to the back of his mind.

From the first murder, Striker was still waiting for forensics on a couple of cigarette stubs and a bottle of lager, and clothing from each victim had been seized for potential fibre comparisons, but the latter would take some time. The former items were likely to have been discarded by the gang of lads, not the killer. That could provide a few more potential witnesses, but they could easily say that's where they hang out most nights and that the bottle and cigarette ends had been there for days, rendering them useless.

He began to consider the possible characteristics of potential suspects. Who would suddenly start killing youths and why? Someone with a grudge, who'd been wronged somehow? This guy had been seen twice from a distance, though both times on foot. No vehicle had been seen. Why this area? Someone local? Had to be. Striker's knowledge of the B Division's scumbags was extensive, even so he was struggling to come up with anyone with the bottle to commit these types of crimes – someone unknown to the cops? Or someone who'd recently returned to the area perhaps?

The cogs turned slowly, in need of oil: evidence.

They'd already had a morning meeting, where he'd dished out numerous tasks to the officers present. He'd requested that Becky Grant chase up forensics from the first scene, and had delegated Lauren Collinge to liaise with the Operational Policing Unit on compiling a list of potential suspects. The criteria being offenders with a propensity to commit serious violence and who may have a grudge. It was a big ask and Striker expected an extremely long list, so had allocated another DC to assist.

Collinge had apologised for not being around last night and was coy about her mystery date, saying only that it had gone "quite well".

Bardsley knocked and entered, carrying more pocket notebook photocopies of the house-to-house enquiries conducted by uniform last night and from this morning's revisit.

"Anything relevant, Eric?"

"Just the odd one hearing noisy voices passing, but no eyewitnesses, apart from the old lady that Sterling and Grant spoke to," he said resignedly, sitting opposite his boss.

"This is the big one. The case that'll make or break me... us."

"I know, Jack. The press are all over it like a nasty rash. Have you read last night's Evening News?"

"No."

"There's a copy knocking about in the main office, but basically they are already linking the murders, and saying that we have a madman in our midst. The Sun started the speculation yesterday, but it wasn't front page news. It will be after last night though. They've already dubbed him 'The Hoodie Hunter'."

Striker raised his eyebrows, creasing his brow. He thought about possible repercussions with the gang fraternity, as there would almost certainly be an adverse reaction. "Tell me something I don't know. He's not just a serial killer, he's on a murder spree, mate."

They were both quiet for a moment, until Bardsley said, "Okay, good news. I popped into Khan's off-licence to pick up some fags on the way to work and he's back."

Striker's eyes widened. "So soon?"

"Apparently, he'd only gone to London to his brother's and didn't want anyone following him, so lied to his family about going to Pakistan."

Striker shook his head. "Have you spoken to him?"

"No, he was down at the wholesalers. But I did set up an appointment for a statement in half an hour."

Striker got up from his seat with renewed vigour.

A chat with Khan could establish, at the very least, if Grinley and Mozo were involved, or witnessed more than they'd been letting on.

He made a quick call to Brennan to inform him about Khan. His boss had sounded annoyed, not just at the mounting pressure of the case, but probably at both Cunningham and Stockley turning in late and missing the morning meeting. Shoddy, but *that* was their business. Striker had his suspicions, as they undoubtedly had about him, for very different reasons.

He grabbed his coat and left with Bardsley to find out exactly what the elusive Khalid Khan had seen.

**

"I'll take the lead, you take the notes," said Striker, alighting the

Astra. Bardsley promptly picked up his daybook and the two detectives entered the newsagents, hardly having noticed the rare Manchester sun. The door bleeped, alerting Khan, who strolled over from one of the aisles.

"Inspector Striker. So pleased to meet you, sir," said Khan in a strong Pakistani accent, proffering a hand, which Striker shook. Khan's wife was behind the counter, donning a polite, and somewhat nervous, smile.

Striker forced a half-smile in return, still wondering why this man had left his family when they were vulnerable to more racist attacks from the local youths.

Bardsley wore a look that implied, *And what about my handshake?*

Striker glanced at the newspapers on the counter, seeing the headlines on the front page of the Sun: 'Hoodie Hunter Strikes Again?' He wasn't surprised that the media had sensationalised events, inevitable really.

"Is your 'family business' sorted now, Mr Khan?"

"Yes, sir, and please call me Khalid." The shopkeeper had dark bags under his eyes, his face in a kind of permanent frown like that of a man with the weight of the world on his shoulders. "My wife told me you helped sort out our problem and that you wanted to speak with me about something very important, so I cut my break short."

Striker recalled Response Inspector Barney Briggs having mentioned he'd called in to chat and reassure Mrs Khan, then promptly deployed a couple of PCSOs to patrol the area for a few days. "Yes, it's about the attack outside your shop, the night before you left."

"Okay. I tell you what I know. Please." Khan beckoned the detectives to the back of the shop with a hand gesture and they followed him through a doorway with colourful dangling beads. The beads made multiple clicking sounds when pushed aside and a spicy aroma was initially pleasant, then so overpowering that Striker could almost taste the peppers.

Khan pulled out two seats for them at a dining table before sitting himself.

Striker headed straight for the crux of the issue. "So, Khalid, please tell us what you recall from the night of the attack."

"Yes. Gang of lads, you know, locals youths. I think may be

responsible for graffiti on my shop, but I'm not sure."

Striker glanced at Bardsley, whose pen was poised.

Khan continued, "But Inspector Briggs is onto that matter and I'm very thankful because—"

"Khalid. The attack. What did you see?"

Khan smiled, apparently realising his digression. "Two boys from gang were in shop when lots of shouting outside. I looked through blinds because I was close to shutting shop."

Bardsley had started making notes and glanced up to ask, "And what did you see, Khalid?"

"Well, I told you on night, but I was scared, very scared, and I didn't tell you everything because of this." He frowned even more, if that was possible, almost looking sulky now.

Striker felt this was going to be hard work, but it had some potential. He wondered how Collinge was doing with the list of potential suspects, though still nodded his head in polite encouragement.

"Gang had surrounded someone and were shouting, and I thought it was mugging or something. But then, man in middle started swinging black stick or something, like he was crazy guy." Khan did the repeated striking motion, even widening his eyes to emphasise his point.

"I see you just raised your left hand, so the killer was left-handed, Khalid?"

He studied both his hands briefly, then said, "Yes, yes, left."

"So who did he hit?" asked Striker, trying not to lead the witness.

"He hit them all and then they moved back few steps and I watched him hitting one boy particular, over and over, like he wanted to kill him." Fear shone in Khan's eyes as his account became frantic. "Other boys looked really, really shocked and they looked very, very scared indeed. The man must have hit boy twenty or thirty times and he shout as he hitting him."

Bardsley looked up curiously at Striker. "What did he shout?"

"Can I swear, please?" The detectives nodded in unison. "Shout 'Fucker' – over and over again." Striker raised his eyebrows. "Each time he hit him, he shout 'Fucker'. It was very scary shit, Inspector."

"It sounds it. And what did the other boys do then?"

129

"Well, one of them moved forward begging for him to stop, but he swung for this boy too and they all ran off in different directions."

"Then what?"

"The boy on floor was groaning and rolling in pain and man keep hitting him, until boy stop moving."

This was much better than Striker was expecting and he checked that Bardsley was getting it all, which he was, writing furiously. "When he eventually did stop, what did he do?"

"He looked round and I quickly closed blinds. Very quickly because I was—"

Bardsley finished the sentence for Khan. "Very scared? Understandable, Khalid."

Striker guessed Bardsley was rather peeved that Khan hadn't told him any of this when he'd done the initial knock-on, prior to Khan fleeing to his brother's. He glanced at his colleague, before turning back to the newsagent. "Then what, Khalid?"

"Few seconds later, I looked again and he running toward petrol station, very fast."

Continuity. Good. "And what did the two boys do, while you were watching?"

"They watch with me. They very scared, too. One was crying."

"Which one was crying?"

"The little one I think."

Mozo. "Is this them?" Striker pulled out two photos of their latest visits to custody that Bardsley had printed earlier.

"Yes, yes."

"Okay. Can you describe the attacker and tell me what accent he was shouting in?"

"That's easy. Mancunian. We've been here for twenty years and he shouted it like this...'Fuck-or, fuck-or.' Definitely Mancunian."

This was getting better and better. "And what about the man's physical appearance, Khalid?"

"Very big and stocky." He unnecessarily pulled his fists up to his chest and raised his shoulders to portray someone stocky. "Long black coat, with black trousers and black boots. The scariest thing was his mask, with holes in showing crazy eyes, like a balaclava, but that looked dark green, maybe, I think."

"Khaki?" asked Striker.

"Yes, yes, khaki, like the army colour."

"Could you tell us his height and his skin colour?"

"He about six-two, or three, or something, and white man."

"Hang on. But I thought he wore a face mask throughout?" asked Striker, as Bardsley looked up again, pausing, pen poised.

"He did, but eyes, you see."

"His eyes?"

"Skin round eyes was white. I saw this, when he looked at me."

Striker's own eyes lit up and he saw Bardsley glance his way, a glint in his too.

"He saw you looking then?" asked Striker.

Khan dipped his head, almost tearful, his frown intensifying. "Yes, sir. This made me very scared."

Bardsley motioned to speak, but Striker's subtly raised palm prevented any sarcasm. "That's only natural, Khalid. But we're here now. Would you be prepared to sign the notes made by my colleague, then later attend the station for a video interview, with a view to being a witness at court?"

"But what about my family?" He sounded panicky, his voice high-pitched now. "This guy is fucking loony-ball."

Striker caught Bardsley suppressing a smirk. "If it did come to that, Khalid, for cases such as this we have 'special measures'. We can protect you and your family, and even potentially relocate you, if necessary. You're our only key witness, Khalid. This is an extremely serious matter, as you know, and this man needs to be taken off the streets as soon as possible, for everyone's sake. Well, Khalid?"

"Er... I dunno..."

"DC Bardsley here will explain things in more detail."

"You say it's possible to move my family?"

"Relocation is an option, depending on how things work out."

He sighed. "Okay, sir. If you protect us, then I do it."

"Thank you, Khalid. You're doing the right thing." Striker patted him gently on the shoulder then turned to Bardsley. "Crack on, Eric, and give the video interview unit a bell." He lowered his voice and leaned in to the DC. "Now we know he's white, local and left-handed, I'm going to phone Lauren, so she can shorten that list she's compiling." He turned back to Khan and pointed at the back door. "May I?"

Khan nodded, still looking worried. "Of course. But sorry about mess out there, Inspector. We only use it for rubbish."

"That's okay." Striker took out his mobile as he exited the back door and entered Khan's dingy back yard. He saw a rat staring up at him and he shuddered. It was gnawing through a bin bag. Striker froze, instantly recalling the time he was bitten by one of the vermin while messing about in a disused building as a kid. The rat scurried through a gap under the yard door and into the alleyway behind.

Striker realised he'd not only held his breath, but had also broken out in a cold sweat, feeling the sheen on his brow with equally clammy hands. He even recalled torturing himself by reading James Herbert's rat trilogy as a spotty teen, in a bid to fight the phobia he'd had since the bite. Clearly it hadn't worked. He lit a cigarette, recomposed himself and his mind soon shifted back to the now.

He knew that the latest pieces of the jigsaw weren't exactly a breakthrough, although every little piece helped. At least it was clear-cut now, what they were actually dealing with. However, Striker sensed the killer had only just begun.

Chapter Seventeen

The next two days had been like pissing in a tornado, trying to ascertain which gang members had been present at the Bolands murder, among other things.

DS Grant had informed Striker that results on the cigarette stubs from the first scene had come back as either negative, or to "no one of interest". Basically, it was just a couple of kids off the estate, both of whom were twelve and had been arrested once for shoplifting.

DNA on the lager bottle was that of Luke Grinley, but they already knew he was there, sat on the wall with Mozerelli. Striker had liaised with Brennan to inform him what Khan had told him – then reiterated in the video interview yesterday – regarding the improved description of the killer, and that Mozerelli and Grinley were in fact just scared witnesses. Brennan hadn't apologised to Striker, but had called off the attempts to arrest the pair. The point that they'd evaded arrest, anyhow, had been rather embarrassing and was indicative of the area, in that even the low-level criminals around here had the know-how to dodge the cops. This begged the question: *What chance did they have of catching a professional killer if they couldn't find a couple of scrotes?*

Jerome Jackson, the gang member with the swelling to his right cheekbone who they picked up from the streets of Moss Range a few days back, had been interviewed again. He'd been identified by numerous officers who'd viewed the footage and stills from the petrol station. This time the interview with Jackson was official, at the station in the presence of his solicitor. He admitted being present at the Bolands murder and also to being assaulted himself, when trying to save his friend from the onslaught. Yet he was adamant at not wanting to press charges, or assisting the police any further. He did, however, corroborate reports, albeit off the record, that the weapon used was indeed a baton. A couple more names that had popped up were interviewed by Stockley's team, but they had apparently come up with solid alibis.

All this, added to the fact that Roger Pennington – or Roger the Dodger – had only loose affiliations to some of the Moss

Range Crew, confirmed that the gang theory had lost all mileage completely. Dodger had an ASBO – or in this case a CRASBO, for it was made on the back of a criminal conviction but amounted to pretty much the same thing – so that initial hunch, relating to the possible criteria of each victim's selection, still hadn't been quashed. The powers that be had come up with a new version of the ASBO called a CRIMBO, which Striker thought ridiculous.

Having hit a brick wall regarding the rest of the gang members at the first scene, the original list, compiled by DC Collinge and the field intelligence officers, had been modified accordingly. Consequently, they had established a top ten to interview about their movements at the time of each murder.

Along with Brennan's guidance, they had co-ordinated the interviews under caution. Nine of the ten had been spoken to and had provided decent enough alibis, all of which had checked out. Not that alibis around here were concrete, since invariably the family and friends of those under suspicion wouldn't think twice about lying to the police.

Brennan and Cunningham had also been keeping a close eye on Striker, to see if the Deano situation was affecting him, even saying that they had a 'duty of care' to offer Striker some compassionate leave. *Yeah, right.* He knew Cunningham just wanted him out of the way. With Deano still not having regained consciousness, leave was the last thing Striker wanted and he informed them of this as tactfully as he could without exploding. He had to admit though, his short fuse had shortened further with the added worry of Deano.

With Brennan having a rare rest day, annoyingly Cunningham was now calling the shots. She and Stockley had gone to track down the last of the top ten, who'd been spotted out and about in the city centre. Meanwhile, Striker had been delegated to attend a community meeting this afternoon, called by the notorious – but now supposedly reformed – former Moss Range Crew leader Jamo Kingston.

Kingston was a member of the Independent Advisory Group: 'Community members from the local area who provide advice and make recommendations to the Constabulary in order to assist them in creating non-discriminatory services', apparently.

The consensus of wisdom from the brass was that Kingston's involvement could bridge the gap between the predominantly white male police force and the multiracial community. Nonetheless, Striker had massive reservations regarding this decision, especially since he knew, as well as anyone, all about Kingston's shady past.

At least Bardsley would be by his side at the meeting, scheduled to start in three hours. He looked across his paper-strewn desk at the DC, who was chomping on a sizeable pork pie as if it was his last ever meal, and Striker wondered whether Bardsley's presence would actually be a good thing.

Bardsley looked at him, still chomping. "Why do we get the shitty little meeting, when there's proper police work to be done?"

"Don't ask," Striker said resignedly. "Cunningham can be very persuasive."

Hearing the kettle click off, Bardsley got up and headed over to the small fridge in the corner, which doubled as a brewing surface. They'd spent the morning assessing what they had so far, ensuring they'd not missed anything crucial or obvious.

"He's been quiet, Eric. Too quiet."

Bardsley stirred the coffee, splashing it round with the subtlety of a sumo wrestler doing a pirouette. He rolled his eyes, his Scouse tones as bullish as ever. "Now you've gone and said it, Jack. Jinxing us with the Q word."

"Well, nothing for two days. You don't suddenly stop what he's started. He's planning something."

"He may've just finished. Had enough. Completed his… er… mission."

"Nah, there's more to come. I know it. He could be taking time out because of Deano. Maybe he regrets it."

"Interesting philosophy. A serial killer with morals?"

"Perhaps. Either that, or he's up to something."

As Bardsley finished the brews, Striker drifted off again into a web of possibilities. It was almost certain the killer knew the area, and had a decent IQ, which narrowed down the possible perps drastically. Frustratingly though, no DNA profile had been forthcoming as yet and Striker wasn't holding his breath on the list they'd compiled coming up trumps. Or even the second list of ten that Brennan had the FIO's working on. Striker felt they'd catch this guy as a consequence of his mistakes. Problem was, he hadn't made one yet.

Bardsley handed him the coffee in Striker's precious Manchester City cup, passed to him by his long-time deceased granddad, the cup being a good thirty years old. The slapdash way it was passed to him caused a stray drop to splash onto Betty Grange's witness statement.

"Shit, Eric." Striker quickly dabbed the statement with the back of his light blue silk tie. "No wonder Margaret does the brews in your house."

"That's all she bleedin' does though."

"Things still not right?"

Bardsley sat down. "I know I'm not the best hubby in the world. A bit brash, always in work… I am polite though. I always tell her when I'm coming."

Striker half smiled, a little confused.

Bardsley continued, "Only problem is, I have to shout it because she's upstairs in bed and I'm on the settee."

Striker grinned, shook his head.

"And with trying to catch this psycho, I hardly ever see her, never mind make love. That's why I reckon she might be… you know…"

Striker felt for him, but didn't know how he could help, so opted for the only way he knew how: humour. "Nature of the Beast, Eric. You could always go back to uniform."

Bardsley stroked his beard. "Sod that, I'd rather be celibate."

Striker chuckled, pleased to see Bardsley smiling again, and purposely steered the conversation back to work. "There's definitely a pattern emerging. It's simple, but this guy must know someone close enough to access criminal records, as each one of his victims have been career criminals and menaces to society. Either that or, like us, he has a built-in radar for scumbags."

"People from the council have access to records of anyone with an ASBO."

"And so do all police officers and police staff in the UK. So that's about a couple of hundred thousand."

"That narrows it down then," said Bardsley, supping his brew.

Striker mirrored his colleague, the coffee tasting good, just the pep-up he needed to enliven him for that bloody meeting. "An audit trail would take ages."

"Time is one thing we don't have."

"Putting the ASBO theory to one side, he's certainly done his research and hit the bull's-eye with the victims. Except for Deano, obviously."

Both detectives became quiet, perusing the files of paper evidence before them.

The tabloids' 'Hoodie Hunter' nickname had stuck like superglue, and Striker had to concede, in the few days the killer had been active, the streets had become quieter. In some ways, the area had become safer for Joe Public. Decent folk were off the killer's radar completely and the vibes from media phone-ins, polls and news reports were, generally, favourable to this accomplished killer. Feedback from response sergeants on each shift had confirmed diminishing amounts of alcohol-fuelled youths had been hanging out on street corners, terrorising their respective neighbourhoods. Ironically, the Hoodie Hunter was achieving in a few days what GMP had struggled to do in years.

Striker castigated himself for almost fleetingly admiring the man's work. He swiftly reverted back to detective inspector mode.

"Keep sifting through, Eric, before we have to go to this damn community meeting." He'd tasked Bardsley with trying to make a connection between the victims. Striker opened a brown A4 envelope and was soon gazing down at the fanned photos of dead sons.

The office phone interrupted them and Striker picked up the handset.

Bardsley studied Striker's reactions, sensing something was going on.

A minute later, Striker hung up and stared pensively into space.

"Well, Jack?"

"The tenth one on our list…"

"Yes, Bobby Copeland."

"Stockley's just arrested him… for attacking a lad with a baton."

Chapter Eighteen

Civilian detention officer Vic Powers was deep in thought when he heard Sergeant Thompson shout his name. Bullsmead custody office was abuzz with detectives from the force's Major Incident Team, strutting around as if they owned the bloody place. Some of them hardly gave the likes of Powers a second glance, unless they wanted something, of course. Arrogant bastards.

"One minute, Sarge," said Powers, getting up from his custody office desk then placing the charge sheet he'd just prepared onto one of the many lined-up clipboards relevant to each detainee. "Just gotta update the hourly checks on the system."

After doing so, he strolled over to the sergeant, who was chatting up an attractive blonde solicitor. Thompson was sat on a high chair in front of his computer terminal, on the police side of the long counter, which curved at both ends to the walls of the staff office behind. On the other side of the counter was a spacious area with a couple of long benches fixed to the walls. This was where the calmer arrestees sat and waited, whether it was to see the police medic, to take a mandatory drugs test or to have their fingerprints, mugshots or DNA taken. The ceiling was high, creating an acoustic effect whenever the latest offender was bustled in, invariably intoxicated, shouting and cursing.

Thompson leaned on the counter, one arm bent to enhance his well-honed bicep; a posture Powers was familiar with, especially when a cute solicitor or interpreter was around. The sergeant turned to him.

"You look knackered, Vic."

"Yeah, didn't sleep too well, Sarge."

"Will you take that guy Copeland, who MIT locked up, from the holding cell to the exercise yard for a cigarette? Keep him sweet, eh? Stop him rattling the cells door again like a goddamn orang-utan." He glanced at the solicitor, who smiled knowingly.

"Sure, no probs. Think he's asleep as he's gone quiet, but I'll wake him." Powers walked through an archway back into the office, passing half a dozen colleagues, a mixture of cops and civilian staff, then out of the office door. The holding cell was a barred cell beside their office. It was ideal for keeping their eyes on troublesome or high-risk prisoners. There were plans to split the cell into three smaller ones, such was the demand, though the government cuts in these times of austerity had thwarted that.

He reached in his pocket, jangled the set of chunky keys attached by a long silver chain to a clip on his belt. When he found the correct one, he opened the heavy iron door.

Under a blue blanket on a thin plastic mattress, Copeland stirred, grunted. The blanket was flung off, revealing the detainee in standard blue sweatshirt, sleeves rolled up, and jogging bottoms, his own clothing having been seized for forensics.

"Come on, fella. Slip your trainers on and follow me if you want that ciggie." Powers got an unpleasant whiff from the pair of lace-less Adidas trainers parked outside the cell.

Copeland was a big man, well over six feet tall, early forties, portly, with balding ginger hair. The prisoner stretched from his slumber, got up, then followed sluggishly.

Powers opened another solid iron door leading to a lengthy corridor. Their footfalls echoed as they passed a long line of cells on either side, all with shoes and trainers outside them, and headed for the door to the exercise yard. The stale, sweaty stench was something Powers still hadn't become used to, and he held his breath as they passed. After another jingle of his keys, he clicked open a heavy door and let the detainee pass into the exercise yard.

The yard was square with brown brick walls, each approximately fifteen metres long, a large metal grill ten metres above. The prisoner took in his surroundings for a few seconds.

He turned to Powers. "I'm not gonna escape from *here*, am I?" he asked resignedly.

Powers shook his head. "No, fella. You've no chance, unless you're Spiderman."

His grin revealed two-thirds of a set of tobacco-stained teeth. "The name's Copeland, if you didn't know, Bobby Copeland."

"I know who you are," said Powers.

"So, where's me smokes, guv?"

He handed him the tobacco and Rizla papers he'd removed from the detainee's property bag earlier. "Roll away."

"You're alright, you, guv. Not like these Columbo types, trying to pin all sorts of shit on me."

As he stood by the doorway, virtually filling it, Powers watched this man before him, whose addiction to nicotine was evident in the way his hands were shaking as he rolled the cigarette. He didn't seem like one of the usual scumbags he'd become accustomed to dealing with as a detention officer. Powers was intrigued to know why this man had snapped and ended up here. Curiosity finally got the better of him.

"So what's your story, Bobby?" he asked, looking at the myriad of slashes on Copeland's arms. "And why do you self-harm?"

Copeland briefly looked his way, as if weighing him up. "Gimme a light, guv, an' I'll tell yer."

He flicked the lighter open and cupped his hands around the flame, while Copeland sucked frantically on the roll-up.

"Ah. Now that's a whole lot better," he said, exhaling smoke, before coughing. "I know it sounds stupid, but I find cutting meself is sort of comforting."

"I do understand *that*, working here, Bobby. It's more common than people think. Helps you forget. Kinda therapeutic, eh?"

Copeland looked surprised, nodded, as he took another drag.

"Come on then. How did you end up here?"

Copeland drew hard and gazed at the end of the shrinking roll-up. "Can I roll another?"

"Sure. It gets me away from the office, those phones and cell buzzers."

Copeland's nerves seemed to have settled and he rolled the second one much quicker. After Powers lit it, Copeland began his story.

"I'm basically here because of my brother. You may've seen it on the news a couple of years ago." He looked up, his voice monotone, forlorn, his posture hunched. "David Copeland, attacked for no reason, while walking home from the pub after watching a United match?" He glanced up again, looking for a reaction.

"Yeah, it does ring a bell, that. So he was your brother?"

"I just can't get over it, an' that's why am here. I just tried to beat up that bastard Sinclair." He hesitated, his features tightening as bad memories whirled. "Nine fuckin' days, I was at our Dave's bedside, while his brain swelled up in hospital. Nine fuckin' days. An' me mum went through hell, too. An' then those bastards walk free from court bragging about how 'untouchable' they are."

Powers shook his head. "Shit, Bobby. They got off with it? I didn't realise. I'm sorry. What exactly happened?"

He sucked on his cigarette, the drag audible, his voice rasping as smoke exuded as he spoke. "Our Dave wouldn't harm a fly. I know I've had a few scrapes with the law, but Dave was different. A top bloke. Two kids, decent job, everybody's friend. He was just walking home minding his own business when two lads came up an' asked him for a cig. He didn't smoke" – Copeland paused to take another inhalation – "an' he told 'em that, but they kept hassling him, then pushing him, an' it kicked off. In court they said he'd been the aggressor, an' he'd chased them. An' the youngest one, Sinclair, who was only sixteen at the time, said he was genuinely scared – of our Dave, for fuck's sake – and that's why he'd punched him."

Powers had heard so many examples of this before and he started to feel a bit wound up himself. "What happened then, Bobby?"

"Their lawyer said our Dave had a weapon, but nowt was found, an' they insisted *they* were fighting for their lives. What a loada shite. I know our kid, an' he would've just wanted to get home to Donna an' the toddlers – poor kids." He fell silent, just staring, at nothing.

"So how did—"

Copeland cut him short. "Once his head hit the pavement, they basically kicked the fuck out of him on the floor. I know this 'cos the older one, Bolands, the one that got rightly fuckin' murdered the other day, bragged about it after the case, an' it got back to me. But what swung it in their favour in court was that Bobby regained consciousness, then staggered in front of a taxi that hit him. Their bleedin' lawyer played on that, saying it was how he received the fatal blow to the head."

"Ah, reasonable doubt. Shit."

"You've got it. I've been suicidal ever since, 'cos those fuckers have taken away my brother, our Dave, me best friend, an' put our family through fuckin' hell. But I'll tell you one thing. Before I do kill myself, I'll kill that bastard Sinclair first. I will, you know. I used to box, you know. Manchester amateur champ, nineteen-fuckin-ninety, I was." Copeland held his fists up and did a bizarre bout of shadow boxing.

Powers forced a smile, watching diligently in case Copeland flipped. It wouldn't be the first time a prisoner had, and you never truly knew which ones were prone because most of them were screwed up mentally.

"I can empathise with your anger, Bobby, believe me. But karma will take care of them. You don't have to mess your life up for them. They're not worth it."

He suddenly stopped the shadow boxing, slumped against the wall, slid down onto his bottom. "My life's already messed up. They're gonna stitch me up with all those killings, you know, guv."

It started drizzling. Powers thought for a moment. "I know somewhere that might help you, Bobby." Mindful of the cameras, he took Copeland's hand and eased him up, then placed an arm around his shoulder. Turning their backs to the camera in the far corner of the yard, they moved into the recess of the doorway. Knowing it was a blind spot, Powers slipped his hand into his pocket and gave Copeland a business card, as he'd done on numerous similar occasions over the last two years.

Copeland seemed to understand Powers's discretion and glanced down at the card. "VOICES?"

"Yes, Bobby. Go there, mate, and I can guarantee that *your voice* will be heard. Now, come on, let's get you back inside."

Copeland shoved the card down the front of his jogging bottoms.

Walking up the corridor to the custody area, Copeland asked if he could use the toilet. With the holding cell not having a loo, Powers unlocked a vacant cell nearby and waited outside.

Powers heard voices emanating from the custody area. He looked up and saw a familiar face through the small reinforced window of the metal door that separated them. The detective was in deep conversation with three others from the murder squad. His face brought back bad memories for Powers.

The door opened and DI Stockley headed his way. "Where is he?"

"He's taking a dump." Powers pointed at the closest cell.

Stockley leaned in close and whispered, "Well, did he say anything to you?"

"Not a word," said Powers.

Chapter Nineteen

The meeting Striker and Bardsley had attended earlier at Moss Range Community Hall had gone about as smoothly as stroking a crocodile. With a mixture of Hoodie Hunter sympathisers and victims' families and friends present, it was like a time bomb waiting to go off. And go off it did. The heated debate had escalated into a slanging match for which, as usual, the cops were to blame.

Surprisingly, independent advisor Jamo Kingston, donning his trademark eyepatch, had actually been a peacemaker when the pushing and shoving had started. Dessie Bowker's presence, along with his cronies, had instigated this. Then, when a chap shouted out, "But he's only killing scumbags," Bowker tried to attack him and had to be restrained. Uniform backup was called as mayhem ensued with Striker and Bardsley in the thick of it. Two of Bowker's lot were arrested for public order offences. This included the one Striker had punched at the Chisel murder scene in the park. Unluckily for him, Striker had given him another crack to the same spot, under his chin.

So the meeting, set up to supposedly 'reassure the public', had actually had the reverse effect.

Striker looked down the corridor toward the cells of Bullsmead custody suite. He saw Stockley returning with Bobby Copeland and a civilian detention officer, who looked familiar. It was only when they were close up that Striker realised who it was.

Surprised, Striker turned away to lean on the lengthy custody counter, pretending to check his work phone for messages. Once they'd passed, he studied Copeland as he was led to the holding cell, its door clanging shut. He thought back to the photo of the killer from the petrol station. Somehow, he just couldn't put Copeland in that shot, wearing a trench coat and a ski mask. He was thankful that the detention officer returned to the back office, where the morning shift was handing over to the afternoon crew.

"What's up, Jack?" asked Bardsley.

"Oh, nothing important, mate."

Stockley rejoined them. "Here's a copy of the tapes from the assault interview," he said, giving Striker two cassette tapes, along with his arrest statement. "His solicitor handed us a prepared statement, admitting to the attack on Sinclair, stating it was a one-off due to frustration. He's not been locked up for any of the murders – yet. But with the links to the Bolands attack, we believe he's our man. We won't be disclosing this to his solicitor, though, until we have something more substantial to go on."

"We'll see."

"It's gotta be him. Both Bolands and Sinclair were found not guilty of killing his younger brother. It's too much of a coincidence. And, at one point in the interview, he said that the idea to use the baton came from him reading about the Hoodie Hunter. He brought the subject up, not us."

"We've still gotta prove it, though, Vinnie."

"Well, *obviously*." Stockley looked heavenwards, then at the smirking DC Steve Barron beside him.

Striker's glare instantly obliterated Barron's smirk.

Stockley scanned around, ensuring nobody was in earshot. "He also said that he could understand why the Hoodie Hunter is killing these scumbags, but his solicitor quickly advised him to shut up."

"Interesting," said Striker, though he wasn't convinced. "So what happens now, Vinnie? Where are we up to?"

"Steve's taking some uniforms to conduct a house search. The baton he used has been fast-tracked for forensics. You should have something back well before his twenty-four hours are up."

Striker waited for a constable to pass them and disappear around the corner into the custody suite. "So we're charging him for the assault and possessing the weapon in public, right?"

"Yeah, once the CPS give us the green light. DCI Cunningham wants you to drag it out a bit, to give us more time to obtain the evidence for the murders. In any case, she's anticipating Copeland won't make bail after charge, if we word it correctly."

"I take it you've spoken to Copeland and his solicitor about the voluntary interview, regarding his whereabouts at the time of the murders?"

"Yes, they've agreed, and seemed relieved we weren't arresting him, especially for the Bolands murder. But little does he know, eh, chaps?" said Stockley conceitedly.

"And that, plus the court file and liaising with CPS, is down to us because you've got your promotion interview, right?"

"Afraid so. If I pass 'the board' I could end up being your boss, Striker." Stockley wore a smug smile.

Like fuck. He looked at Bardsley and could tell he, too, was just as peeved. "Well, we wish you the best of luck with that, don't we, Eric?"

"Sure," said Bardsley, with a smile of his own as insincere as a crap door-to-door salesman's.

***

An hour later, having done the necessary spadework, Copeland was charged with actual bodily harm and possession of an offensive weapon. There had been a problem with Copeland's criminal record. It was surprisingly sparse of convictions, just a few minor drink-related offences and an assault over twenty years ago, so the CPS lawyer had been reluctant to remand him in custody. Striker had purposely not argued too vociferously to keep Copeland in, since he had a better plan. Subsequently, the decision was made to bail him to court next week with stringent conditions, including not contacting the victim, Sinclair or any other prosecution witnesses in any way.

Along with Bardsley, Copeland and his solicitor, Henry Guilfoyle, a suave-looking chap in his late twenties, they entered one of the interview rooms.

Once seated, opposite Copeland and Guilfoyle, Striker could smell the remnants of stale alcohol. He was fairly certain the odour was emanating from the dishevelled-looking Copeland, and not from Guilfoyle.

"Okay, Bobby, thanks for giving us the opportunity to speak with you. I must remind you that you are still under caution, as we will be asking you some questions relating to our ongoing investigation. This means your answers may be used as evidence in court. Do you understand?"

"I've already explained the situation to Bobby," said Guilfoyle.

"Just to let you know, this interview is not being tape recorded and you're free to leave at any time. Okay?"

Copeland nodded.

"Could you tell me your whereabouts last Friday night between nine p.m. and three a.m.?"

"That's easy. I was with Dorothy."

"Dorothy?"

"Yeah, Dorothy Lafferty, me lady friend."

"At her house?"

"It's a flat."

"Where?"

"Flat two, Bullsmead Court."

"Do you have Dorothy's phone number?"

"Yeah." He wrote it down, passed to Striker, who gave it to Bardsley.

"What about last Saturday night?"

"Dorothy's."

"All night?"

"All night."

"Okay. So if we speak with Dorothy, she'll vouch for you?"

"Of course."

Striker arranged them a coffee each, then led them to a secure consultation room down the corridor. Meanwhile, he and Bardsley found a quiet room of their own and got to work on the phone calls. Striker called the Forensic Science Lab to check on any results from the baton. Thankfully, the results were in. Two sets of DNA: one from Copeland, the other Sinclair. No surprise, just as Striker had anticipated. He made two more calls, while Bardsley had a very loud and deliberate conversation with Dorothy, constantly repeating himself as if he was talking to a five-year-old.

After a few minutes, Bardsley motioned to throw his mobile phone in exasperation, but didn't.

"That sounded like hard work, Eric."

"Just a bit. It would've been easier talking to a bleedin' stoned gorilla."

"Well, what did she say?"

"He was there with her on both nights. They 'got pissed up together', as she so romantically put it."

"Okay, so we let him go."

Bardsley stared incredulously. "What, based on his drunken

bird's say-so? He could've slipped out on the sly and she wouldn't have noticed."

"What, and committed three murders and an assault whilst drunk, without leaving us a shred of evidence? Come on, Eric. And, anyway, the baton he used only shows his DNA and Sinclair's, so we've actually got nothing on him."

"What about the house search?"

"I've just phoned Barron, and it's a negative."

Bardsley caressed his beard, deep in thought. "Even so, letting him go is a big call, Jack. Don't you think you should at least speak with Cunningham?"

"No, because she won't agree to what I have planned."

"And what's that?"

"I've just been onto Pete Murchy, the boss over at the Dedicated Surveillance Unit. We'll tail Copeland, just in case I'm wrong about him."

Chapter Twenty

"The subject is taking a left, left, onto Grosvenor Street...
temporary loss..." said veteran DC Philip Lowe, his pace
quickening.

On the opposite side of the road, also in plain clothes, the
diminutive PC Gill O'Brien crossed the busy junction. A horn
beeped angrily as O'Brien dodged the crawling cars in the traffic
jam. "Got eyeball again... He's heading toward Oxford Road...
and the damn carnival."

Lowe discreetly adjusted the skin-coloured earpiece in an
attempt to stop it crackling in his ear. "Did you say straight on,
Gill? The transmission was poor."

Twenty metres behind, lanky PC Daniel Freeman tapped the
covert microphone under his green sports jacket. "Think she
said he's heading for the carnival, Phil."

"Received, Danny. Just. The comms are crap." Lowe jogged
around the corner onto Grosvenor Street. He cursed on seeing
carnival-goers clogging the footpaths on both sides of the street.
He heard drums in the distance, saw flashes of the procession's
bright colours at the top of the street. Another crackle in his ear
was followed by the sound of O'Brien's broken voice.

"Didn't get that at all, Gill," said Lowe. "Repeat..." More
static. "Gerry, comms are down... Where are you?"

Sergeant Gerry Marland was co-ordinating matters from the
surveillance car, a black Ford Mondeo with an aerial on its roof,
supposedly providing their signal to each other. Marland was
with two other plain-clothes officers, there as replacements in
case the subject saw any of those following him. One had a
creased map of Manchester on his lap, plus an iPad, while the
other drove.

"We're stuck in traffic, Phil," said Marland, "and the trams and
these high buildings aren't helping comms."

The sound of the interference was becoming annoying, so
Lowe removed his earpiece and quickly zigzagged through the
growing crowd to the end of Grosvenor Street. The beat of the
conga drums intensified. He scanned the myriad of colourful
people in the carnival procession, heading along Oxford Street

toward Moss Range Park. He spotted O'Brien, whose eyes were darting left and right, clearly having lost Copeland.

"Shit," shouted Lowe, just as a child dressed in a plethora of red, yellow and Caribbean blue feathers passed, her mother frowning at Lowe and pulling the girl in close.

***

"Where the fuck's my money, you piece of shit?" growled Dane 'Woody' Woodthorpe through clenched teeth.

"Er, please, I can explain, Woody. What with the credit crunch and—"

A big right hook knocked sixty-year-old grocer Arnold Spinley off his feet. Spinley staggered backward into assorted vegetables. Carrots, tomatoes and potatoes fell on top of him as he hit the floor.

Woody strolled round the counter. "There is no credit crunch in my world, Arnold. And who the fuck you calling Woody?" he asked, kicking Spinley in the stomach. "It's Mr Woodthorpe to you." Woody popped the till open and plucked out all the available notes. Eyeing his snatched bundle, he said with a smirk, "That should do for now." His parting shot was a kick in Spinley's balls, adding almost casually, "Next week I want the money ready, okay?"

Spinley's reply was a barely inaudible "Ye-sss" as he was left to nurse his bruised vegetables.

Woody got into his black Subaru Impreza and revved it noisily, before wheel- spinning off to continue his rounds. His next stop was the Wagon and Horses pub.

A couple of minutes up the busy A56 leading north, a mile or so toward town, he glanced in his rear-view mirror and saw a car that he'd seen behind him earlier. He always checked his rear-view, usually for cops, since you never knew in his line of work. Was this cheeky bastard tailing him? Didn't look like a cop. Okay, let's test him.

Woody took a sharp left, checked his rear-view again. The car had gone straight on. Woody smiled, shook his head. Getting paranoid, too much coke and weed maybe. After a couple of swift left and rights through the outskirts of the Bullsmead estate, he was back on the A56. Two minutes later, he pulled into the Wagon and Horses rear car park and got out, knowing this one could be trickier than the old grocer.

This was a new customer and the seeds were planted only last week, when he'd dropped a few hints in the guise of smashing the pool room up with the boys. The landlord looked nothing special – although one of the boys had said he had a few brothers – and when Woody had told him he'd be back, the look on his face showed fear. Woody fed on fear, and feared no one.

He knew the boys were only a quick call away if things got tasty, but he'd not required backup in a long time. The going rate for a pub around here was a ton a week, so a little bit of resistance, or a couple of irate brothers, weren't going to stop him.

He lifted his athletic frame out of the Subaru, grabbed a smallish baseball bat from the compartment at the base of the driver's door. As he walked toward the entrance, he was surprised to see the car from earlier parked at the front of the pub. He studied the empty vehicle; it was definitely the one that he'd thought was tailing him. The very same black VW Golf GTI.

Chapter Twenty-One

The evening meeting had been called by DCS Halt, who'd been recalled from his Mediterranean cruise, after urgent talks with the chief constable. That's all Striker knew, save the possible announcement that the police's Mutual Aid policy may be utilised, whereby detectives from other forces would provide reinforced manpower.

Or should that be "person power"? Striker asked himself while climbing the stairs to the top floor. At the very least an announcement would be made by Halt regarding assistance from other detectives within GMP, as Striker had seen new faces dotted about the nick. Then again, their force was one of the biggest in the country, and taking the Mutual Aid option would be like GMP's proud hierarchy admitting an inability to handle such a big case.

And now, with another battered body being found dumped in the undergrowth near a disused rail track on the outskirts of Moss Range, Halt was back. Dane Woodthorpe, aka Woody, had been on the cops' radar for a while now, but someone had clearly beaten them to it. From what Striker could tell, having not been directly involved, the MO used on Woodthorpe pointed to their man. The consensus was that this man had to be Copeland, so Striker expected some extremely awkward questions being thrown his way.

Striker hadn't seen Cunningham as of yet. However, Stockley, back from his promotion interview that had apparently "gone great", had revelled in telling him that the DCI was seething at Copeland's release. Striker knew Cunningham would certainly make her views known to Mr Halt. Conversely, Striker wasn't overly worried Copeland was still out there because he was convinced he wasn't their man. Nonetheless, he wasn't looking forward to this meeting and was prepared to take some serious flak.

The conference room had a huge circular mahogany table that didn't really match the dark grey carpet. An overhead projector pointed an image simply saying, 'Operation Predator' onto a large screen at the far end of the room.

As he walked in clutching a notebook, Striker saw Stockley beside Cunningham and they both gave him the eye, therefore he purposely selected a chair directly in front of him at the opposite end of the table. The glare Striker received from Halt nearly knocked him off his feet. He felt his mouth starting to dry up and wished he'd brought a drink in. The humdrum of whispered conversations gave the room vibrancy. Striker had a quick scan and saw several new faces, confirming Mutual Aid had begun.

The only truly friendly face present was that of Becky Grant. Despite the earlier stern look, he was glad to see Mr Halt back, after Striker's disagreements with Cunningham and Stockley. Then he spotted his old response colleague Inspector Barney Briggs, sat at the far end of the room with his finger poised on a computer mouse. Briggs, obviously requested because of his know-how in using the projector and computer equipment, offered a sympathetic smile and nod that Striker returned. Halt was standing at the front near the large screen, reading an A4 sheet of paper.

Predominantly inspectors and above appeared to be present, plus a few DSs, including Grant, who lifted a subtle hand acknowledging Striker. He'd had to explain to Bardsley earlier that he hadn't been invited, much to his angst, and promised him a comprehensive scrum-down later.

With the remaining seats taken, probably twenty in all, Halt raised a hand and the room automatically hushed.

"Okay, everyone. Thanks for coming. Firstly, let me introduce you to Edward Nosworthy, a criminal profiler from the National Crime Faculty." Halt gestured near the front to a fat balding man pushing sixty. Nosworthy half raised his hand, probably knowing some officers would frown upon his presence.

Striker stopped himself from rolling his eyes, instead he sighed discreetly. Good old detective work would catch the killer, not geographic profiling, forensic psychology, cognitive mapping and statistical analysis. There was no time for all that.

Halt checked the room for dissent. "In truth, Edward should have been with us earlier." He tossed a look at Cunningham. "But since he's only just arrived, he won't be providing us his insights just yet. However, he'll be part of the team until matters are resolved, so let's make him feel welcome." Again, Halt scanned the room.

"Now, I won't harp on about the importance of what faces us because you've only got to switch on the TV or pick up a paper to see the storm this vigilante has caused. The Hoodie Hunter they've dubbed him. Quite fitting, I suppose." The tone of his voice briefly became sarcastic. "This guy thinks he can fix Broken Britain. Hmm...

"One of the problems we face is that some of the public secretly support him, going off his 'fans' on social networking sites. Evidence is in short supply and I'll be asking each of you what you've got later. Communication is the key on this. Tomorrow the Sun" – Halt's facial expression was one of disgust – "are publishing a letter, supposedly sent from the killer."

The low whispers started up again and Striker sat forward in his seat, spotting a few shaking heads.

"At least they kindly gave us the original, which is being examined at Bradford Park as I speak. Unfortunately, we were unsuccessful in our attempts to block publication of the letter. Anyway, have a read for yourselves – Barney." He nodded at Briggs, who clicked on the mouse and the letter appeared on the screen. The room fell silent as they all read it intently.

Dear Sirs,

The government is weak. Weak leaders are half the problem. Respect and discipline have evaporated from society. Harsh tactics are the only answer. I make no apologies for mine.

The destructive characters you're dealing with here simply don't care. They want to inflict serious harm on people and understand only one language. I know because I am fluent in that language too. However, I have discipline, respect and morals – they don't. There's been talk of forcing them into two years of national service, but we can't just use the forces as a dumping ground for these idiots. That would be an insult to the professionals already serving their country.

Harsh behaviour requires harsh treatment, but we don't have corporal punishment and our prisons are an absolute joke. You've tried and failed, so now it's my turn. I know for my plan to work I'll have to be relentless, or "prolific", as some serial killers are described. But they are invariably insane and I detest the thought of

*being mentioned in the same breath as them. I have principles and
I'm only doing what many wish they had the balls to do.*

*I call upon all those wronged by our ineffective justice system to
bear arms and seek retribution.*

*I see the papers have given me a name – whatever. I suppose I
need one.*

Soon.

HH

"Any first impressions?" asked Halt.

Striker began. "He's connected to the military in some way."
Twenty pairs of eyes looked his way.

Halt seemed to sigh, his expression still stern. "Interesting,
Jack. Why's that?"

"His terminology. The start, 'Dear Sirs', plus he doesn't want
the offenders being dumped into the forces. And he seems hot
on discipline and professionalism."

Halt slowly nodded, considering Striker's observations.

Stockley jumped in. "Of course, that could all be just a
smokescreen to throw us. After all, he's already shown that he's a
cunning bugger, hasn't he?"

"I don't doubt that." Halt smoothed a hand through greying
hair.

"He's military." Striker said doggedly.

Cunningham joined in. "Well, if it is a smokescreen, then
Jack's certainly been suckered, like he was by Copeland."

One or two officers shuffled awkwardly in their seats. Striker
bit his lip, hard, and then swallowed discreetly.

"Maria! Later."

Later? Great.

Halt looked around the room, sensing unrest. "Just to update
you, we already have teams searching for Bobby Copeland, but
he's not been seen since his release. You've all got the photos of
him, right?" Everyone nodded. "Okay, now back to the letter."

Becky Grant spoke out. "I'm with Inspector Striker. Speaking
as ex-military myself, the experience is etched into my soul, and
it's difficult to shake the doctrine and principles gleaned. Even if
you try, it still creeps through into your language, like it seems to
have done in this letter."

Cunningham rolled her eyes upward, twisting her neck slightly for emphasis. "Well, what with Jack's hunch and your soul, Rebecca, we should have the killer in custody before bedtime."

"Now, now, everyone. Settle down."

Striker noticed some of the new faces looking somewhat uncomfortable. "Just remind me, Maria. Aren't we all supposed to be on the same side?"

Her expression tightened. "Sure we are, Jack. But if he is military, then why is he using a baton and a rope?"

It was a good question.

"Right. We're all entitled to our opinions. And there's a lot more to get through. Barney, hand out the copies of the letter." Briggs gave a bundle of A4 sheets to Cunningham, who took one and passed them on.

Halt continued, "Keep a copy each and re-read it as many times as you wish, and show your teams. If anything at all springs to mind, then let me know."

"I don't like that 'Soon' sign-off, at the end," said a new face, a chap in his mid-thirties, his accent broad Yorkshire. Possibly Leeds.

"That worried me too," replied Halt.

"Could just mean that he'll be in touch again soon," said another new voice, this time a craggy-featured Lancastrian, beside the Yorkshireman.

"Hopefully, but I think this guy communicates by his actions," said Stockley with a hint of derision. "The most worrying part is him calling for 'all those wronged to bear arms and seek retribution'."

Striker actually agreed, but stayed silent.

The remainder of the briefing was taken up with a laborious step-by-step breakdown of each scene, evidence gleaned, outstanding enquiries and plans of action. Then there was the reallocating of resources, including the newer colleagues from outer forces. Plus, the delegation of teams to deal with each murder, and organising debriefs for the end of each day. The designated incident room was thankfully here at Bullsmead, which pleased Striker. What didn't please him was the fact he'd not yet been mentioned.

"Okay, everyone. Overtime's not an issue, so I'll be expecting a concerted effort. Now, let's go catch him."

Daybooks snapped shut and pens were slid into pockets as people went about their business with renewed zest. Striker glanced over at Halt, who was already looking his way.

"Jack, can you stay? I want a word."

Chapter Twenty-Two

The conference room was clear except for Halt, Cunningham and Striker. He stood up to face them as they approached and stopped side by side about two metres from him.

"How many complaints have you had in your career, Jack?" asked Halt.

A little confused, Striker answered, "Er, say about one or two a year since I joined, so perhaps less than twenty. Why, sir?"

"Because today we've had three more."

"With respect, sir, there's a school of thought that if you're not getting complaints, then you're not doing your job properly."

Halt's face transformed from serious to sympathetic. "Look, Maria's updated me on... events... and with the fiasco of that community meeting, then the release of Copeland, plus your nephew having been attacked, we've decided that you're off the case."

Striker glared at Cunningham, who mirrored the look back tenfold.

"Cut the hard face, Maria. Copeland's not our man."

"Oh, come on, Jack. His alibis are based on the word of a drunken woman and as soon as he's released there's another body. He's our prime suspect."

"It's not him. Just look at the letter." He held it up. "There's no military connection, for one, and he's not that articulate. For God's sake, he's a piss-pot alcoholic, totally incapable of these murders."

Halt held up a large hand. "Look, Jack, you are wrong. Not only is Copeland clearly connected to Bolands and Sinclair, but we've just discovered that his partner, Dorothy Langton, was also having casual sex with our second victim, Steven Bowker."

Striker was stunned, but stood his ground. "It's still only circumstantial evidence, though, sir."

"Look, Jack, I'm sorry, but we feel it's become a little too personal for you and think you should take a week's leave."

"No! With respect, sir, I can catch this maniac. I have the local knowledge. You're making a big mistake."

"We just want you operating on full steam. Go to your family.

They need you."

"What, and _you_ don't?"

Halt's voice became hushed. "Jack, young lads are dying here, and we're not getting any closer to the killer. To be honest, from what I can see, we've got sod all to go on as yet, except for this Copeland character."

He could feel his fuse shortening, his mouth parched, voice hoarse, "But I've barely got going on this!"

Halt dipped his head briefly, sighed. "Exactly, Jack. The case is too big for you at the moment, especially in your frame of mind."

He was struggling to remain calm. _This is surreal. There's bugger all up with me!_ He turned away briefly, took in a deep breath and tried to stem the rising anger; he had deep respect for Halt. "Right. Thanks for your honesty, sir. At least I know where I stand now. If I agree to this break—"

"The decision's already been made, Jack."

Was Cunningham smirking? Striker's fuse was burning out rapidly. He thought of Deano still lying comatose in hospital and the promise he'd made to Lucy about catching the perpetrator. "So who's taking charge of my team in the interim, one of those newbies?"

Cunningham chipped in, this time definitely smirking. "Vinnie will fill in for you, while you're away."

The fuse incinerated. "Oh, that's fuckin' marvellous! You really know how to kick a man in the balls, Maria. That prick Stockley dealing with my family? Thanks a bunch."

"Striker!" shouted Halt.

He thundered out, the door bouncing on its hinges.

"STRIKER!"

He ignored Halt's cries as he thundered down the corridor. That's all he needed. Stockley with a one-way ticket into his family, to snoop around at will until he found something.

***

The Grosvenor Casino in town had a new décor in various shades of blue, but the layout was exactly the same as when Striker was last there six months ago. The bubbly twenty-something receptionist Linda recognised him and offered a welcoming smile before taking his jacket and buzzing him through the secure door.

Exhilaration rushed back like an old friend, albeit a troublesome one that had gotten you into a whole lot of trouble. A mass of colourful lights and computerised chimes and bleeps greeted him, making him blink a couple of times to focus, the half bottle of vodka he'd supped in his apartment now kicking in. The repetitive clinking of pound coins hitting the winning tray caught his attention and he turned to see a Chinese bloke putting an excited arm around a female half his age. She gave the man a peck on the cheek as four yellow and black 'BAR' symbols shined brightly in a line before them.

Striker climbed the three steps to the bar area that had a dozen or so people, mainly men, dotted about. This was a good vantage point, overlooking the numerous roulette tables. He heard the low drone of gamblers deliberating with friends regarding their next move, while light swing music played in the background. Sinatra.

"Hey, Jack! Longa time no see. What brings you back?" The barman was collecting glasses from a nearby table, his dulcet Italian tones chirping Striker up somewhat.

"Hiya, Franco. Long story, mate."

"Let's see… voddy Red with two cubes of ice, isn't it?"

"Well remembered." Striker always opted for vodka Red Bull in here to keep him awake for a long session. In any case, they didn't have John Smith's on draft.

He scanned the bar area. On the far side, behind a mahogany cordon, a large group of females filled a lengthy table full of scrumptious-looking food. The tempting aromas drifted his way, reminding him he'd not eaten since lunch ten hours ago. He looked at the ladies scoffing and thought that he may have a nibble later.

Franco placed the drink on the table he'd just cleared. Striker took a sip, cold and tangy as it eased down his throat, invigorating him. He put his hand in his back trouser pocket, prompting Franco to raise a placating hand.

"Nah, Jack. It's onna the house. Good to see you, my friend."

Striker lifted his glass and smiled, albeit forcedly. "Cheers." A young couple brushed past him on the stairs to the bar, so he turned and headed a few metres to another of his old vantage points. He leaned on a rail overlooking the gambling arena and placed his drink on a ledge beside a spider plant. A strange and slightly uneasy feeling of being 'back home' swamped him. His anger was subsiding, the murder enquiry and his supervision's lack of confidence in him ever so slowly fading from his mind.

He watched the tables, studying the croupiers, memorising the winning numbers and waiting, until the tingle of excitement within him grew irresistibly.

Having knocked back another drink, he headed down the steps to the gambling area to change some cash to fiver chips. He'd brought £300, though decided to change a ton and see how he went. When he headed for the chosen table, he spotted an old pal, resurrecting memories, some never forgotten.

"Bloody 'ell, Jack. What a blast from the past."

Ged the Giant towered over him. It was good to see him after all these years; the memories flooded back – some good, some bad. He noticed a few grey hairs had invaded Ged's dark brown mop.

Ged proffered a sturdy hand, grinning. "How's tricks, mate?"

They shook hands. "Well, you know…" A twinge of guilt jabbed Striker for not keeping in touch. "How long's it been… twelve years… more?"

"About that."

"Married? Kids?"

"You can tell you're a cop, with all these questions."

"I'd have asked them if I *weren't* a cop, mate."

Ged nodded. "Yeah, you were always the inquisitive one. To answer your questions, I'm not married and I've no kids. I heard about you and Suzi splitting. Sorry."

"That's life."

After an awkward moment, Ged digressed. "Do you still go watching City?"

"When I can. Chance would be a fine thing at the moment. The Hammers aren't doing so well, are they?"

"I try not to think about it. West Ham always seem to let me down. Bad time to be missing City games though, mate, what with all that money coming in for new players. You busy at work then? You're an inspector now, aren't you?"

"Now who's asking the questions? Yeah, we're very busy."

"What, with that Hoodie Hunter fella?"

Striker inwardly sighed. Social conversations always turned to work for a cop. If he was an electrician, he doubted Ged would be asking him about light fittings. Would a window cleaner really be quizzed about his window round on a night out? Or a bricklayer asked about walls? "Yep," he said, purposely keeping it brief.

"Bad shit, all that, innit? But you've gotta admit, Jack, the streets are a bit quieter, aren't they?"

"Don't say you agree with what he's doing."

"All I'm saying is that it was only a matter of time someone fought back, what with the way it's all been going."

It was time to change the subject. He certainly didn't want to fall out with Ged so soon after seeing him again. And he obviously hadn't heard about Deano yet. "Do you still see any of the others?"

"Er, yeah. Wozza, and DJ. He's the one who's kept me up to date about you."

"I sometimes see DJ, but I've only seen Wozza once since..." His voice tailed off.

"Since our Lenny was shot?"

"Yeah, sorry for bringing it up," he said solemnly.

"It's okay. I think that night changed something in all of us didn't it, mate?"

"Definitely."

Another slight lull ensued. Striker glanced at the roulette table as a female croupier leaned over to clear the table of all the losing chips. They soon rattled and clinked down a hole out of view, much to the disappointment of the half a dozen punters.

"Do you reckon you'll catch this Hoodie Hunter guy then?"

Why the fixation? "We always catch 'em in the end."

"Are you close though?"

Striker ignored the question, looked at the tables again. He clicked the handful of chips together. "Fancy a flutter?"

"Yeah, why not?"

Chapter Twenty-Three

Striker's head was still somewhat hazy from last night's session, the feeling of regret over the £300 loss not helping his mood. He pulled his ageing Cherokee onto Barnfield Grove, a distant flutter in his heart like an ailing butterfly, not quite dead yet. On his approach, he caught the first glimpse in three months of his marital home. A myriad of memories, both joyous and painful, engulfed him.

He eased the Cherokee to a halt outside the front garden, shocked at what he saw, having to do a double take. He struggled to suppress his bubbling anger.

Beth was the first to see him as he opened the car door. He watched her angelic little face light up, followed by her excited shouts of "Daaddeeeee!" She ran from the front porch down the garden path. This prompted Harry to pause his game of basketball with Greg Bannatine, the two of them in vivid red Man United shirts: literally red rags to the bull that was Striker. *Where the fuck was Harry's City shirt?* Striker had bought it after weeks of pleading from his son, about six months ago from City's souvenir shop beside the Etihad Stadium, dubbed 'the Blue Camp' by some. Striker had even got Harry's name on the back of the shirt and his son had been thrilled to bits – 'had' apparently being the operative word.

Wearing a concerned look, Suzi appeared at the front window. Striker opened the front gate, which unsurprisingly still squeaked, reminding him of his numerous attempts to thwart the nagging sound with WD40. Within a heartbeat, Beth had jumped into his arms, a surge of warmth and emotion gripping him, momentarily dissipating his disdain.

"Daddy, I've missed you *so* much." Her voice was high-pitched and emanated tenderness.

"I've missed you too, princess." His words were hushed, disguising crackles of emotion.

"I've missed you more."

"I doubt it, love."

"I've missed more than... than the whole ocean."

"I've missed you more than the whole earth."

"Well, I've missed you more than the... the whole universe."

"Okay, so you win." Striker tickled her armpit, inciting a fit of giggles.

"Beth, come here, darling." It was Suzi at the front door, cutting short his rare loving moment. She still looked radiant, despite the stern face. Beth slowly released her grasp and headed to her mum. Striker glanced toward the lawn, where Harry avoided eye contact, opting to continue tossing the basketball back and forth with Bannatine.

"Jack," said Bannatine, with a nod and a smug expression.

Striker nodded back, hoping Harry might just look his way.

"So, for what do we owe the pleasure?" asked Suzi, with a dash of derision.

"I just wanted to say hello to my kids, if that's okay?"

"I thought we agreed to specific times, Jack. Not that you remember them."

"I know, and I am sorry, but..."

"Please!" Suzi held up a halting palm. "Spare us the excuses. We've heard them all before."

Striker bit his lip, turning his attention to Harry. He strolled onto the lawn, noticing a few bald patches appearing. He recalled laying it with Eric Bardsley one rain-sodden April afternoon. "Hey son, so how's school? You on blue books yet?"

Harry ignored him, slam dunking the ball into the portable basket, another thing Striker had bought.

"Harry, you're dad's asking you a question," said Bannatine.

"I think he heard me, thanks, Greg," said Striker sharply, not looking at him.

Harry offered him a fleeting glance. "School's school, innit? And yeah, I am on blue books now, actually. Mum and Greg have been helping me."

"That's great, son. So, what's with the United top?"

Harry slammed the ball down hard and it bounced high off the grass, over the wood-panelled fence and into next door's garden. In a huff, he headed toward his mum.

Bannatine turned to Striker. "He's doing okay at school, Jack. He just needs a bit of time to—"

"Yeah, thanks for the update, Greg." Striker turned, headed for Suzi.

"In you go, kids," she said. Harry went sulkily, while Beth appeared reluctant, glancing back at her dad, sorrow and confusion in her sparkly blue eyes.

"Jack, did you get the letter?" asked Suzi abruptly.

"Yeah, I got it this morning."

"Did you read it?"

"I got the gist." He lied.

"Well, you should know by now about legalities, especially in *your* job. It clearly states: 'Once a week by prior arranged appointment'."

"Suzi, they're my kids too."

"You've had your chances, Jack, but you just keep on letting us – them – down."

"But I'm trying to catch a bloody serial killer! Don't you understand? And I came to tell you he's put our Deano in intensive care."

"Right, cool it." Bannatine placed a hand on Striker's shoulder, which he shrugged off with a glare.

"Oh... Jack... I'm..."

Striker was gutted at the way he'd told her the news. "He's at the MRI, if you wanna visit him."

Her tone softened, was almost sympathetic. "Please tell Lucy that I'm thinking about them, okay?"

"I will."

A brief silence followed and Striker considered asking to see his kids, but didn't. That was the first hint of sympathy Suzi had shown him in well over a year.

"I do still think it's time you spoke with your own solicitor. Now, could you please leave?"

Back into 'cow mode'. Didn't take long. Striker stepped forward a pace when she turned to go inside. "It doesn't have to be like this, Suzi."

"Come on now, Jack," said Bannatine, blocking Striker's path. "You're not in the casino now." Bannatine gestured at the Cherokee.

Admittedly, Striker used to escape from the troubles the Job presented by frequenting the casino. However, he'd curbed this behaviour, realising the error of his ways. Well, apart from last night's lapse.

As he eyed Bannatine, he felt his fuse burn out and shaped to punch him, but he could hear Beth sobbing from behind the front door. He chided himself for swearing and nearly losing it. Instead, he shook his head and walked away.

Bannatine followed. The gate squeaked shut and Striker pivoted, catching a glimpse of Harry's solemn face gazing out the front bedroom window.

He leaned toward Bannatine and whispered through clenched teeth. "Greg, I can just about handle you screwing my wife, but if I ever see my son wearing a United shirt again, I'll fuck you up good 'n' proper."

***

Striker gazed into his tropical fish tank as he sat on his brown leather two-seater supping a glass of John Smith's Extra Smooth. Three empty cans lay on the glass-top coffee table before him. Dean Martin's 'Memories Are Made of This' stirred memories of his own. He pictured the legendary crooner, not too dissimilar to his dad, save the tux and riches.

Harry Striker had loved the old Rat Pack. Probably why Striker himself had a huge collection of their CDs stacked to his right beside his music system. The speakers were rigged high on the wall, either side of a pencil portrait of Beth and Harry junior, who regrettably his dad had never met. Striker had been brought up listening to Harry's music, secretly enjoying the relaxingly sentimental tones, but not telling his mates for fear of ridicule. They were all into Oasis and their 'Cigarettes and Alcohol'.

Somehow, Striker felt closer to his dad now, as Martin concluded his take on memories, no doubt a whisky swaying in his hand – or was it apple juice? Sinatra's 'New York, New York' kicked in, Harry's favourite, bringing him in, even closer.

If only his dad could see him now. Gone were those days when Harry would sit steeped in worry, chain-smoking in the kitchen, waiting for his son to return home from his latest escapade. Oddly, Striker felt more of a connection with him once he'd died. Maybe this was because those macho shackles that had hindered their relationship were long gone. He wondered whether Harry would be proud of him. He wished they could chat now, as adults, about Striker's latest exploits. Yet, if he did know, perhaps his dad wouldn't be so proud after all.

Sliver the loach was aptly named by Beth when he had shown his kids 'Daddy's new home', and to his left Sliver played among the backdrop of shooting bubbles. He studied Sliver's movements, the loach sliding unnoticed among the diverse community of guppies, mollies, neons, white clouds and gouramis. All were oblivious to the mopping up job Sliver was doing around them. The multi-coloured stones and scattered marbles below gleamed from Sliver's work. The algae and scum, blighting the inner glass of the tank, had been well and truly cleaned up by the industrious loach. Sliver was relentless in his daily mission to cleanse the tank, along with Mr Plec, who Harry had named. Striker considered whether the other fish within the community appreciated Sliver's efforts.

Then, he thought of the Hoodie Hunter and the letter.

Soon, his mesmeric state was interrupted by his mobile.

"Jack Striker." He plugged his left forefinger into his free ear to block out the music.

"Boss, it's Lauren," Collinge was whispering. "Just thought you'd like to know our man's been at it again. Last night. Can't speak now, but will try and meet you for lunch."

Jeez, this guy was relentless. Striker could hear people busying themselves in the background. "Right. Twelve o'clock, at Mario's café in Eccles, okay?"

"Yeah, should be."

"Thanks for calling."

"No probs. Gotta go, Boss."

"Gimme a name, Lauren… of the latest victim."

"Barry Gartside. See you later."

The phone beeped to an end in his ear. This Hoodie Hunter was certainly fearless, he'd give him that much. Gartside was an infamous amateur boxer turned bad boy. The man was seldom crossed by anyone. A notorious bouncer turned prolific burglar-cum-robber to feed his drug habit, Gartside had a long list of victims in his wake. He'd been inside a few times, but had become more elusive and adept, despite everyone at the nick knowing he was still bang at it.

Striker leaned across the settee, switched the music off and his dad drifted from his thoughts, until the next time. Standing up, he strolled over to the open-plan kitchen behind him to get another can of bitter. He opened the fridge door, paintings stuck on it from his kids, but nothing recent. Returning to the settee, he thought hard, and after pouring the can he jotted down the names of the murdered lads, looking for links.

Gareth Bolands aka 'Gasbo'... Steven Bowker aka 'Chisel'... Roger 'the Dodger' Pennington... Dane 'Woody' Woodthorpe, and now Barry Gartside. Not forgetting the injured Deano. He thought about that old drunk Copeland. Never mind the rest, but surely Gartside alone would've eaten Copeland alive.

Why the change from young Hoodies? Woodthorpe was twenty-six and Gartside twenty-eight. Was the killer just ridding the streets of scumbags? The dead were certainly not chosen randomly. The victims must have been specifically targeted because the killer had hit the jackpot in each instance. He'd certainly done his homework.

Striker took his drink back to the settee, picked up a copy of the letter from the coffee table. Turning on his flat-screen TV, he switched it to BBC News, waiting for any mention of the case.

He didn't wait long. Halt and Cunningham filled the screen, the murder incident number running along the bottom, a mugshot of Copeland in the upper right corner.

"Bloody fools!" He finished the beer in one, slammed the glass on the coffee table. Trying to channel his frustration, he turned the volume down, making more notes in a bid to sort his thoughts before the meeting with Collinge.

His scouring of the internet, since he'd been unceremoniously dumped off the case, had produced some very interesting results. He just hoped Collinge would accept his proposition, despite its obvious perils.

Chapter Twenty-Four

Eccles was the town where Striker was born thirty-five years ago, before the family uprooted and headed for Bullsmead in the mid-eighties. The council had finally offered the relocation they desired, for no other reason than that of cheaper rent.

Looking around Eccles lately, he'd noticed its deterioration, as with many small urban towns; the boarded-up shops and derelict buildings were testament to that. Local government funding seemed to be saved for Manchester city centre, Salford Quays and the opulent areas surrounding the Trafford Centre, a huge shopping complex across the Manchester Ship Canal. "We're off to the posh side of the wart-or," Jack used to tell his infant school mates when they asked where he was moving. But in truth, Bullsmead was undoubtedly rougher than a tramp's chin and made Eccles look like swanky Hale.

Across Barton Road Swing Bridge, on the Trafford Park side of the canal, the emergence of the huge retail estate that was the Trafford Centre – a miniature town centre in its own right, attracting shoppers from all over the country – had hit the less glamorous precincts hard – very hard. Compared to the pre-Trafford Centre and pre-credit crunch days, Eccles was a ghost town. Nonetheless, one thing it did still have was true northern character in abundance, something money couldn't buy.

Only established outlets had survived and, thankfully, Mario's Café was one of those. In Eccles town centre, Striker watched the world pass by through the café's expansive rectangular windows. A plethora of smells teased his taste buds, from fish, chips and curry to sausage, egg and beans, but Striker wasn't here to eat. It was discreet and out of the way, which was key.

A group of hoodies swaggered past the window, one spitting on the pavement while another grabbed one of his mates playfully around the neck as they moved out of view. Striker wondered when all these killings would stop and whether the Hoodie Hunter would branch out of South Manchester into the likes of Eccles. Then he saw Collinge scurrying past the window to the door, her face serious, yet still easy on the eye.

He waved at a waitress, asked for another pot of coffee as

Collinge walked in and headed his way. She wore no make-up, didn't need it, her wavy brown locks up in a bun, fresh-faced from the winter chill. Looking good.

"Hi, Lauren. Thanks for coming. Take a seat."

She scanned the nearly empty café, removed her coat and easily slid her trim figure along the tight double seat. "This your new office, Boss?"

Striker grinned, purposely avoided looking at her slender legs. "You could say that. My mum used to bring us here when we were kids."

"You've got a good memory." The smile again.

"Cheeky sod." He glanced around, checking that nobody was within earshot. "I've just ordered some coffee. Tell me about Gartside."

"A local chap, returning from a night out, found him hanging from a substation on the border of Moss Range and Bullsmead at about four o'clock this morning, with his guts hanging out. Wasn't a pretty sight."

He was glad he'd not ordered a late breakfast. "Doesn't sound it."

"Uniform attended and preserved the scene, and the night DO got there about half an hour later."

"Hanged again? What's he trying to tell us by hanging some, but not others?"

"Not sure yet, but he's certainly a risk taker."

"Yeah, but you'd think he'd wanna get in and out quickly. That substation's quite remote, just like the park where he hanged Chisel."

"Where he had more time, maybe?"

"Maybe." Striker brushed a hand through his hair. "Must've been a strong rope, Gartside was a big fella. There's no way Copeland did it."

Collinge dipped her head.

"Lauren?"

"They're all convinced it's him, Boss," she said resignedly.

"Please, it's Jack." He took a deep breath, calming himself. "I know *they* do, but do you?"

She hesitated; he didn't like it. "Could be. You've gotta admit, though, everything does point his way."

"Not you too, Lauren? It's all circumstantial."

"Best to keep an open mind though, eh?"

"Definitely." He changed tack, wanting her onside. "Who was CID cover last night?"

She hesitated again; he wondered why. "Brad Sterling."

"Did Cunningham turn out?"

"Yeah, her and Stockley arrived about six apparently, an hour after SOCO." Her tone became lighter. "I'm sorry about what happened. Me, Eric, Becky and some of the others think it's bang out of order."

"Only *some* of the others?" He left the question floating, not expecting an answer. "Well, it won't stop me. But I will need your help, Lauren. If you're willing, that is."

"Whatever you need, Boss, just ask," she said, almost seductively, or was that just Striker's imagination?

Still calling him "Boss"? A group of chattering mums entered with their children and formed an untidy queue at the counter.

Striker lowered his voice. "Lauren, what I'm about to tell you has to remain between us until the time's right, if at all. Okay?"

"What about Eric?"

"I'll speak to him soon enough. But it'll just be the three of us because the less people who know, the better."

"Okay, not a peep to anyone. Go on."

"Hold on. First things first. Any new leads?"

"From what I can gather, SOCO have some fibres from the substation brickwork at the Gartside scene, and a few swabs of blood found a few metres from his body are being fast-tracked."

"So there may've been more than one person present?"

"Possibly, but it could still Gartside's blood, before he was strung up."

"And what about—" A young, flustered-looking waitress arrived with the coffee. Striker gave her a polite smile and thanked her. He poured the coffees, watching the waitress go out of earshot to deal with the noisy group. "What about the others, anything?"

"Well, Mozo and Grinley were released without charge. All we got was same description that Khan gave us. A tall stocky man in a black trench-style coat, but they said his face mask was dark green, not black, and that he had Magnum boots on.

Grinley also said he used a baton, 'like the police use'. They definitely didn't know him and they reckoned it was a 'fully grown man, not a lad'. I think that quote was from Mozo."

"Who interviewed?"

"Who do you think?"

"Stockley?"

"In one. But thankfully, Becky Grant was second jockey. That's where I got the specifics."

"Fair enough. You could argue they got more than I – we – got from them, so the arrest was justified after all. Maybe I was wrong on that, but I didn't want to alienate them as witnesses."

"You weren't wrong, though, were you? You said they weren't involved and your judgement was correct. They *were* witnesses, like you said."

Collinge had a knack of lifting his spirits, something very few people could emulate. They both sipped their coffees. The noisy throng of mums and kids at the counter were still ordering, a takeaway Striker guessed as they'd not yet sat down. The odd clang of pans and plates emanated from the kitchen area beyond the counter.

"What about the Woodthorpe murder? Not heard much about that one."

"Me neither really. Team Three took that one. Believe he was found beaten to death near the railway, probably with a baton again. He was then stabbed through the heart, like Dodger. The spot was secluded, but no hanging, so…" She shrugged.

"Hmm, okay. Heard they'd interviewed a few gang members too. What was the upshot of all that?"

"Basically, it's pretty much like Jerome Jackson said to us when I drove you around the Moss. The two gangs were meeting up to discuss joining forces over the doors in Manchester city centre. Both gangs have their own bouncers on certain patches, but remember that Bobby Campbell shooting a while back?"

Campbell, aka Meat Balls. Striker nodded. Although he didn't have any direct dealings with the case, he knew he was from the Moss and that nobody had yet been convicted of his murder.

"Well, it seems like both South Manchester gangs from our patch were gonna take on the Salford gangs who, intel suggests, were responsible."

Striker was surprised Jackson's story was true, especially since the Bullsmead Boys and the Moss Range Crew had been at war since he could remember. "And what about the rope used to hang Chisel? Anything back on that? Was the same type of rope used on Gartside?"

"I just know it's a popular rope and, no, he used a different one on Gartside. And before you ask, the knot was the same, but again, common enough. Anyway, come on then, what were you about to ask me? The suspense is killing me." She gave him the smile, only it had a nervous edge to it.

"Just between us, promise?"

"Cross my heart and hope to die."

"Please don't say that, Lauren. You've not heard what I'm gonna ask you to do yet."

Chapter Twenty-Five

"I've been trawling the internet, looking for anyone or anything that may help, and I think I've stumbled across something." Striker sipped his coffee, leaned forward a little, checking over both shoulders. He was a tad disappointed that the lively group of women and children had decided to eat in, though thankful they'd settled on the far side near the entrance.

"What, exactly?" asked Collinge, also leaning closer.

"Well, I was trying to think what would motivate someone to start murdering the local scumbags and I re-read the letter over and over. Then, on a whim, or a hunch if you like, I searched the net for local support groups for victims."

"So you believe our man's been wronged in some way. Makes perfect sense."

"Yeah, and I found a few action groups scattered around the north, a couple in the northwest, but only one based near here, on the outskirts of Greater Manchester."

"Where?"

"Wilmslow."

"That's where I live." Collinge looked anxious, her eyes tightening, brows scrunching. "What's the group called?"

"VOICES."

"What does that stand for?"

"Victims of Injustice Can Ease Suffering."

"Seems reasonable. And?"

"That's what I thought, initially. They meet up monthly at an old Masonic temple off the A34."

"Think I know it."

"Okay. But they've also got a chat forum and this is where it gets interesting. They were talking about the Hoodie Hunter on it, defending him."

"Oh." She seemed nonplussed. "But *everyone's* talking about him. And isn't that understandable, with it being for victims of crime, who are probably bitter about what's happened to them or their loved ones? He does seem to have the public, and some parts of the media, split doesn't he?"

"True, but one guy was a little *too* pro-Hoodie Hunter for my liking, virtually singing his praises."

She took a sip of her coffee. "Did you join in the chat, Boss?"

"Please, Lauren, call me Jack. We're in a café and I'm on gardening leave, or so it seems."

She blinked, nodded. "They'll have you back soon enough."

"Perhaps not 'soon enough', eh? And, no, I just lurked a while. But I will join in the chat tonight and if I get the same vibes, I may need you to go into one of their meetings as a victim."

She sat upright, eyes widening. "What, you mean off the record?"

He opened his arms. "Can't get authorisation from here can I?"

Collinge stroked a hand across her creasing brow. "With respect, Jack, why can't you go into the meeting yourself?"

Striker shook his head, his turn to look thoughtful. "I can't because I think my old mate Wozza was on the forum. If so, he'd obviously recognise me. He was chatting on there about a friend of ours who was shot in the head years ago."

***

Striker plopped some bloodworms into the tropical fish tank, watching the crimson mass disperse and wiggle in unison down toward certain death. The vigilant neons, as always, were first to go in for the kill, the less alert mollies last to join the feeding frenzy. A few of the bloodworms nestled in shells, skulking in the shadows, but it was only a matter of time until the inevitable onslaught reached them too. No stone, or in this case shell, would be left unturned.

Mr Plec and Sliver the loach showed no interest in the wriggling bloodworms, instead they continued focussing on their mopping-up process, aimed at the scum in the lower echelons of the tank.

He poured himself a vodka and Diet Coke, and sat at his computer. Turning it on, the whirring noise as it powered up was followed by the universal chimes of Windows opening. Waiting for the screen to upload, he gazed out of the second-floor apartment at the huge Beetham Tower, seeing little movements in the myriad of windows from miniature people going about their business, the rare winter sun shimmering off the impressive. Tetra-style building.

He considered Collinge's reaction to his suggestion of her possibly infiltrating the action group. Initially, she'd looked a little uneasy, but he reassured her that both he and Bardsley would be nearby as backup, if at any point she wanted out. Sometime soon, he'd have to give Lucy a call and check in on Deano again. Though, as bad as he felt about that, it would have to wait for the moment.

A couple of clicks later, he was on the VOICES website. He joined the site choosing the random name 'Davey', for no other reason than it was the first name that popped into his head. He'd made up a Hotmail address incorporating Davey, but wasn't too bothered about leaving any technical footprints that could be traced back to him via his IP address. If anything positive arose from this, then the computer analysis would just be used as evidence in court, and the judge and jury could decide on its legitimacy.

He knew he was akin to a hippo crossing an iced lake, but what did the brass expect him to do: forget the whole thing and sleep like a baby? Nothing would probably come of this anyway, yet something told Striker it was worth a shot.

On the forum, Wozza had used his real nickname in the early hours when Striker had last logged on, but trawling through the various threads now, he didn't appear to be on there. Nonetheless, Striker read through the thread titles, his eyes resting on one in particular: 'My son was killed and the bastards got off'.

'Edith' had started this thread and was understandably irate. Striker saw a green tick beside her name, signalling her online status. Time to make contact. He began typing.

Having read about her son being jumped by a gang as he returned from football practice in the tough Manchester suburb of Wythenshawe, and how the police arrested eight youths but charged no one, Striker typed a short message: *So sorry to hear of your loss, Edith. I do hope your son's attackers are brought to justice.*

Within seconds Edith responded: *Thank you, Davey. So do I. Not seen you on here before – welcome. Have you lost someone close as well?*

Time for calculated bullshit. It felt slightly immoral duping an innocent victim, but the moral high ground was with Striker, in that his motive was for the greater good.

Davey: *Well, this is the first time I've 'spoken' about it. My nephew was attacked and pretty much left for dead too. He's never really recovered. I'm still coming to terms with it. I know it can't be compared to your loss, but it's still devastating seeing him struggle through life.*

Edith: *Oh, Davey. We all feel the same pain and it's crucial that you don't carry that pain with you – you must share it to lighten the load on yourself and it's good you've taken that first step. If you're in the area, why don't you come to one of our meetings? You'd get so much out of it. I don't know how I'd have coped without them.*

Davey: *Thanks for those kind words, Edith. It's nice of you to offer, but I'm a fair few miles away.*

Edith: *Oh, these meetings are open to all and are very therapeutic.*

Davey: *How many attend them?*

Edith: *Usually a dozen or so, and sometimes it can be as many as twenty.*

Davey: *I dunno about talking about this in public though.*

Danny Boy: *Hey, mate. We're a friendly bunch n you don't have to say anything.*

Davey: *Hi, Danny Boy. That's reassuring. Thanks, but still not 100% sure.*

Edith: *It's entirely up to you, Davey. Just an option that's open to you. Think about it – we don't bite!*

Davey: *LOL.*

Wozza: *Davey, welcome. You can just use this forum to get things off your chest, fella. Many people do that, especially those scattered around the country.*

Davey: *Thanks – all of you. You really are decent and I'm feeling better already.*

Edith: *I told you!!!*

Davey: *So who runs the meetings – if I was gonna turn up?*

Wozza: *Usually Vic, but if he's got other commitments, then Danny fills in.*

Davey: *Right. Vic? Is that a woman?*

Danny Boy: *It doesn't really matter who runs it cos all the meetings have the same format n serve their purpose.*

Davey: *Okay, thanks again. Gotta go now, but nice chatting to you all and hopefully speak again soon.*

Striker didn't want to push his luck, but why did this 'Danny Boy' character seemingly jump in about the names of the organizers? And why weren't they on the website in the 'About' section? It simply stated that 'VOICES is a place where like-minded people meet up for a cathartic fortnightly session.' No names given: maybe this was simply to protect the victims' identities, or could there be another reason?

Suddenly a comment from Danny Boy flashed up – *He's still online* – and disappeared within a blink.

Striker scrutinised the screen, noticing a 'whisper' icon at the top right of each comment made, plus 'delete', and a 'report post' facility. He tested the whisper option out with a message to Edith. He clicked on her last comment: *I told you!!!* The new comment box opened with 'Whisper to Edith' at the top. He wrote, *Sorry for doubting you. I appreciate your welcome.*

Twenty seconds later.

Edith to Davey: *No worries. We love new members. Hope to see you at a meeting soon. X*

Davey to Edith: *I'm sure you will.*

So it appears that Danny Boy may have been whispering to someone, maybe Wozza, about Davey. Could have been innocently chatting about the 'newbie', but Striker wasn't so sure.

After checking the list of dates for their next meeting, Striker logged off VOICES, deciding to check out another forum he'd found, one he had a vested interest in. He typed in the Google search bar: 'BDSM forums.'

Chapter Twenty-Six

Striker fired up the hired Vauxhall Vectra and flicked the wipers to intermittent to clear the light drizzle. He hadn't wanted to use his own car for this particular excursion.

Leaning a hand out of the driver's window, he key fobbed the private car park barrier up and headed off. On Liverpool Street he passed a group of schoolchildren, obviously heading for the Museum of Science and Industry, thirty or so excited voices drifting into the Vectra. The teachers, or helpful volunteer parents, dressed in luminous green jackets, were guiding the kids away from the city centre traffic.

The Beetham Tower soared above him as he turned into the inevitable queue on Deansgate, an immaculate burgundy-bodied Harley Davidson fleetingly catching his attention outside Manchester Motors. After a few impatient minutes, he left most of the congestion in his wake and sped beneath the bridge beside Deansgate railway station, a noisy tram thundering the bridge's girders above. Not wanting to think of his dad at this moment, he ignored the swing CDs in his glove compartment, opting for an eighties music collection instead. Duran Duran's 'Hungry Like the Wolf' began to belt out.

He headed south along the A56, on his right the futuristic and predominantly glass design of the Salford Quays towers proudly piercing the skyline. Because of its close proximity to the city centre, 'The Quays', as the locals called it, was a haven for city centre high-fliers, actors and the like. This list included a few from popular local soap opera Coronation Street. Both the BBC and ITV had their studios there, giving the place a distinctly prosperous feel. The Quays was set at the end of the Manchester Ship Canal, overlooking a picturesque and expansive basin where huge cargo ships used to dock and turn in years gone by. But typical of Manchester, looming behind was the tough Ordsall Estate in the neighbouring city of Salford.

Chester House, Greater Manchester Police's old HQ, flashed by to his left, making Striker picture the much swankier new HQ at Central Park in Newton Heath, where no doubt numerous media vehicles would be camped outside with reporters hoping for a word with the chief constable.

A cloak of bitter memories engulfed him as Old Trafford, Man United's ground, came into view to his right. Indelible recollections of too many Man City defeats there flicked through his mind; the tangible excitement of derby day within the city never seemed to live up to its billing for the blue side of Manchester, until recently thankfully.

Striker cursed under his breath and put his foot down to escape the shadow of the huge stadium. Known by football purists as the 'Theatre of Dreams', it faded into the distance. To him and his fellow blues, it was cynically nicknamed the 'Swamp', due to its old muddy pitch, and City fans also teased their red counterparts regarding its location in Trafford, not Manchester. However, City's state-of-the-art stadium was built for the Commonwealth Games held in Manchester in 2002 and was much easier on the eye than the sprawl of ugly scaffolding-like supports on the roof of their rivals' stadium. There was always a flipside to intense rivalry, and with City still renting their home from Manchester City Council, the reds cheekily retaliated by referring to it as the 'Council House'.

Old Trafford slipped into the distance as Spandau Ballet's 'True' kept Striker company, and he recalled smooching to it with Wendy Wilkinson at the school disco. As he drove, he fleetingly wondered what life would have been like if he'd stayed with his first love, but after a flashback of him fumbling for his clothes on hearing her dad's footsteps nearing her bedroom, he smiled and began to concentrate on the now.

The now that had seen five boys murdered and his nephew hospitalised. The now that had seen him unceremoniously dumped off the case. The now that saw him embarking on a private investigation, with the real possibility of Striker himself winding up in prison, and not the killer. Thoughts of football and his first love faded as Striker firmly focussed on the now.

Before long, he was on the M60 – a vast motorway which ringed Manchester – where the drizzle transformed to heavy droplets, pounding his windscreen and roof, his wipers now on full pelt accompanied by an annoying squeak. Such was the downpour's distortion of his vision, he had to lean forward and squint to view the motorway turn-off sign for the A34 to

Wilmslow. Just as Queen's 'I Want to Break Free' began to boom, he noticed the Vectra's digital clock was on the hour. He flicked the CD out and the radio automatically reverted to the BBC GMR news headlines. His resolve intensified when the bulletin was all about the Hoodie Hunter.

The Sun had apparently run with the letter headline that Halt had warned them about two days ago, despite, as Bardsley had informed him, GMP's desperate attempts at gaining an injunction to block the revelation. According to the radio, no one from GMP was available for comment, though a press conference was due this afternoon. Striker was honest enough to admit he was glad that he wasn't the one facing the cameras, and he felt sorry for whoever got landed with the job. The unfortunate person with the responsibility would probably be the chief constable, such was the enormity of the escalating circumstances.

Striker pulled the Vectra onto the A34, still a couple of miles to his rendezvous point with Bardsley. He listened to the female broadcaster sensationalising the story with "Hoodie Hunter" this and "Hoodie Hunter" that, scaremongering the general public in true media fashion. He knew that now the story was out in the public domain, the proverbial brown stuff would hit the fan big time, and cause quite a mess to say the least. This, along with the knowledge his colleagues were chasing the wrong man, made Striker put his foot down, despite the incessant rain. The sooner he could find out more about this VOICES group, the better.

***

Striker saw Bardsley's green Job Astra parked beside some trees, a second before its headlights flashed him on his approach. Bardsley indicated and slowly turned down a pot-holed country lane.

Striker followed, instantly feeling the random bumps testing the Vectra's suspension. They drove slowly through a canopy of sycamores, poplars and oaks, and soon passed the impressive-looking Masonic temple that loomed somewhat eerily to his left. Striker recognised it from the photo on VOICES website. The Astra slowed to a crawl, Bardsley's protruding right arm waving

Striker forward.

They drove further down the lane, which split dense woods to the left from vast farmer's fields to the right, and they came to a halt at a closed wooden gate. Striker pulled alongside Bardsley and they both opened their windows. A strong smell of manure wafted in from the fields, where cows were dotted here and there.

"Remote isn't it, Eric?" A cow mooed in the distance as if to reinforce his point.

"And smelly too."

"Wonder what they are trying to hide."

Bardsley raised his eyebrows. "That's what I was thinking."

"Hmm… maybe nothing." Striker quickly scanned the area. "But, then again, this may just be a bit *too* dodgy for Lauren."

"You having second thoughts, Jack?" No one else around and the 'Boss' tag was dropped like clockwork.

"There's a lot on the line for all three of us if we mess this up, Eric. I don't wanna bring you two down with me."

Bardsley looked concerned. "We're a team. And, anyhow, we can have a quick nosey and if nothing comes of it then no one need know."

"True. I still believe we need to do this, and we don't have enough suspicion to do it lawfully so…"

"Ways and Means Act 1984." Bardsley winked then grinned devilishly.

"Exactly. 'The book' is out of the window for me now."

Bardsley put two cigarettes into his mouth, lit them, and leaned across, passing one to Striker. "What do you mean, 'now'? Always bleedin' was."

Striker took his cigarette, drew on it, smiling. "It's worth the gamble. How long have you been waiting?"

"Long enough to guess that no one's knocking about if you wanna take a closer look. No cars in the car park and no CCTV cameras, as far as I can see. Looks like they have motion-sensor lights around the front car park. Probably need 'em too, could see it being quite dark here at night."

Striker gazed through the woods to their left, seeing the backdrop of the temple, peering through the trees. Its varying shades of beige nineteenth-century brickwork looked rather mossy and weather beaten. "Yeah, it's a bit creepy looking, even in the daylight."

"Shall we have a closer look?"

Striker considered Bardsley's initial observations for a moment. There were no obvious signs of anyone else being present. Of course it was possible that someone could still be there, but Striker doubted it and nodded. They both got out of their cars and headed on foot toward the temple, the gravel underfoot crunching as they approached.

The building itself had a gothic look, probably a few hundred years old, the masonry a mix of browns, greens and greys, uneven, yet still picturesque.

Striker carefully checked the black metal handles on the huge, oak double doors. They were cold to touch and a quick twist of them told him the doors were locked. They headed around the back, passing numerous stained-glass windows, until they reached one with a transparent piece which enabled them to see through. Striker looked first and saw a large hall with a high ceiling. There were about twenty upholstered burgundy chairs in a spacious circle, including three chairs behind an old wooden desk, obviously where the people running the meeting sat.

"Anything interesting?" asked Bardsley, his tones hushed but still coarse.

Striker's left index finger shot up to pursed lips. "At least *try* to whisper, Eric. There's a hall, some seats and a few doors. One that obviously leads to the main entrance, plus one that could be a fire exit and another marked 'Toilets'. There's what looks like a" – Striker craned to look – "small stage at the far end, with the curtains closed. There's a small drinks bar too. Nothing untoward. Here, have a nosey and see if I've missed anything." He moved aside.

Bardsley peeked inside, then looked to his right and walked gingerly a few paces before pointing at another door. Striker nodded, turned and gestured for Bardsley to follow him back to the cars.

Once they were thirty metres or so clear of the temple, they talked as they walked. Bardsley regarded the vast fields to their right, cows mooing intermittently. "I know there's only the country road leading here, but the actual access to and from the temple is pretty good, isn't it?"

"Agreed, Eric. At least three doors in and out of the hall, plus two more exits from the building itself. Lauren should be fine."

"Remind me why it has to be Lauren. Wouldn't it be better if I did it?"

Striker thought for a moment, then said, "Nah, Eric, I've something else planned for you. Anyway, one of my old mates might be there."

"Eh?" Bardsley looked surprised.

"I'm sure it was him, chatting on the VOICES forum I told you about."

"Who?"

"Wozza."

"Oh… right. Chris Worsall. Gotcha." Bardsley's voice was loaded with inquisition. "Wasn't he there when your mate got shot way back? When Stockley was a spotty probationer and gave you a hard time?"

Striker had only told one officer about this and that was Bardsley, until recently hinting at it to Lauren out of necessity. "Yes, Eric, way back. Wozza never really got over it." Striker stared blankly for a moment before continuing. "That's why I think he's involved in the VOICES group. They never did catch the bastards who shot Lenny, you see, and it's been pretty hard to bear… for us all…" Again, Striker gazed into space.

"Okay, Jack." Bardsley patted him on the shoulder as they reached the cars. "When we gonna do this thing then?" asked Bardsley as they opened their car doors.

"The meeting's tonight at eight."

"Bleedin'ell, Jack, that's in five hours."

"Exactly. No time like the present." Striker winked at him. "Keep your phone charged. I'll be in touch."

The Vectra and the Astra crawled past the Masonic temple with the continuous scrunch of gravel under tyres, until they disappeared up the bumpy country lane.

***

A solitary magpie was perched on the sill of the lone window within the body of the temple's spire. Once the two suspicious cars were out of sight, the dark figure peering through the window faded back into the room, returning to his work with renewed vigour.

Chapter Twenty-Seven

Since his doctor gave him the news about the prostate cancer, he knew he'd have to rapidly speed things up regarding his 'project'.

The symptoms had already begun: urinating more often, especially at night, and sometimes it stung like hell too. The chemotherapy would start in two weeks and he'd eventually lose all his bodily hair. No big deal as he'd always preferred a shaven head, ever since his time in the army.

He'd saved up a few of his days off work, specifically for this week, to start his project with a bang. And no one could doubt the fact that he'd certainly done so. However, with the vibes he was getting, he knew the cops were closing. So the least he could do was visit his mum, especially after their telephone chat earlier, when he'd sensed something was wrong. He'd not told her about the cancer though, as she'd had enough to contend with in her life.

He rang the bell twice before knocking on the bungalow's front door three times in quick succession – an agreed code for his mum to know it was him. He heard her quaky voice, muffled behind the door.

"Okay, son. I'm coming."

The bungalow was in a line of twelve council properties in a supposedly secure complex. He was pleased when she'd been finally accepted for this place, since she'd had problems with youths in their old family semi in Bullsmead. His mum had met his dad, Donald, by chance, or fate as some people would call it, but not surprisingly at a snooker hall in Moss Range. Donald was never out of 'Potters' throughout his life and had always taken the boys there at least once a week. It was his younger brother Josh who'd proved to be the gifted one, the one with raw talent.

Josh was just sixteen at the time and had never really gotten over dad's sudden death. A heart attack while with his trusty friends at the snooker club, was quite a fitting way to go. Dad's fellow players soon arranged an annual competition in his honour. The brothers had made a pact to always put on a brave face for mum.

He heard his mum chinking the numerous bolts and chains that he'd fitted to the door himself. The door finally opened, revealing her welcoming smile, her wavy grey hair dotted with curlers.

"I'm so glad you came, son."

"Doing your hair again, Mum? Going somewhere nice?" He produced a bunch of red and white carnations from behind his back.

"Ooh, carnations, my favourite." She took the flowers, immediately giving them an exaggerated sniff. "Aah, wonderful. Oh, you're such a good boy. You always could brighten up my day. And, yes, I'm off to bingo this afternoon, then to the meeting tonight, of course. You going?"

"Not sure, got a lot on at the moment."

She gazed at the carnations. "These are truly lovely." He stooped and kissed her on the cheek before hugging her and receiving a peck on his own cheek.

"You need a shave, lovey – not like you. Come on in, and I'll flick the kettle on."

As she shuffled through the modest hallway toward the kitchen, he checked the bolts of the front door were all working correctly by yanking on the two chains, pulling them taut. When he was satisfied, he joined her in the kitchen. She was delicately putting the carnations in a sculptured glass vase. The smell of cooked fish teased his nostrils, reminding him he should pick up a takeaway on the way home, if he had time.

"Got this from Barnardo's for a pound. Beautiful vase like that, for a pound. Would you believe it?"

"A bargain, Mum," he said. He was impatient to know if something was wrong, noticing an unusual lack of eye contact so far. It was probably nothing. Perhaps Doris had been ignoring her at bingo again, causing mum to be paranoid that she'd done or said something to offend her. Invariably, from his experience of her dotty bingo partner, it was Doris who was the problem, her mind deteriorating faster than a druggie's.

She placed the flowers on the window ledge above the sink. "Tea, lovey? Earl Grey okay?"

"That'll be fine, Mum, thanks."

The kettle boiled and she took a couple of cups from the hooks below the wall unit. She began pouring the hot water into a flowery-patterned teapot, and half turned to him.

"You sounded a bit down on the phone this morning. You okay?"

She looked away and stirred the tea. "Nothing you need to trouble yourself with."

"Well, since you've said that, you know I won't leave till you tell me."

"Oh, where's your big mug?" She pretended to look for it, even though it was directly in front of her on one of the hooks, which he'd also fitted, beneath the wall unit.

"Mum, come on, it's right in front of you."

"So it is, silly me. The Alzheimer's is kicking in."

He smiled, stood up. "I'll pour them. You sit down and tell me what's up."

They were soon sat opposite each other across the short drop-leaf kitchen table, supping their brews.

"You seem a little preoccupied yourself, lovey. How's the job going?"

He sipped his brew. "Fine, both me and the job. I've taken a fortnight off to sort a few things out."

"Well good for you. It's nice to have you back home and settled somewhere with a bit more normality in your life. I used to worry about you over there in, erm… Pakistan, you know."

He shook his head. "It was Afghanistan, Mum. But I'm home now, aren't I?"

"Yes, and I can sleep a lot easier, knowing you're not at war anymore."

It was his turn to drop eye contact as he pretended to look at his watch. *If only you knew, Mum.*

"You're not thinking of going so soon are you?"

"Not yet. I want to know what's up though. Now, please."

She took an extra-long audible slurp of her tea.

"I saw one of them today, you know."

His adrenaline rushed. "Who? Where? What did he say?" The chair scraped on the floor as he jolted to his feet.

"Steady, son. Sit down, please."

He reluctantly sat down, eager to know more.

"I was walking home from Spinley's grocers with Doris—"

"I've told you to get the bus. Or phone me to pick you up."

She raised a hand. "Let me finish. I saw a group of youths approaching. Didn't give them a second glance, till I heard one of them say, 'I don't fancy yours much.' They were just being cheeky, but another said, 'I've already...'." She looked tearful.

"Already what?"

"'I've already... fucked the little one." She shook her head. "It was then I glanced up and our eyes met."

Through grinding teeth, he asked, "Which one was it?"

"That big one, or 'Big-un', whatever they call him."

He stood up again. "That cheeky piece of—"

"Calm down, son. He was obviously referring to messing my... our... lives up."

"Yeah, Mum, I know what he meant. Was that it?"

Her voice was quivering now. "Well, he definitely recognised me. They all strolled past laughing and I..."

She broke down, head in her hands, her frail body shaking. He hugged her and as she sobbed his fury boiled inside.

At the front door ten minutes later, his mum had composed herself. "Ooh, that was another big hug, lovey."

Agreed, it was, for he knew there was always the chance things could go horribly wrong, and he wanted to saviour every moment with his mum, in case it was his last. His plans may have to change. A whole new debate began in his mind...

Kingston or Big-un?

Chapter Twenty-Eight

Thankfully, after a quick call to DS Becky Grant, Striker was relieved to discover that there had been no further attacks attributed to the Hoodie Hunter reported throughout the day. There was yet another bogus 999 call, the tapes of which were being analysed, and it was being taken a little more seriously than previous ones, apparently, due to the specifics and nature of the call. However, it was probably a hoax, just like the rest.

Striker had considered involving the trustworthy DS in his undercover op – he'd not given it the customary operational name due to it being unofficial. In any case, the computer responsible for spitting out these names down in Hendon, London, probably wouldn't have 'Operation Dodgy' in its repertoire.

Ultimately, he'd decided against involving Grant. The less people who knew about this, the better, and he trusted Bardsley like a brother. He trusted Collinge too, but she was only here by necessity, and he felt more than a tinge of guilt at 'using' her in this way. Especially, if his hunch about the characters off the VOICES forum was to reveal any semblance of substance.

At the same spot they were at earlier, Striker, Bardsley and now Collinge sat in the hired Vectra, the woods to the left hiding them from the temple. It felt much more remote in the dark, only the odd 'moo' emanating from across the fields to the right breaking the silence, adding to the eeriness.

Somewhat awkwardly, Striker shuffled side-on in the driver's seat to study Collinge in the back. "Okay, Lauren. Are you ready?"

"Now or never, Boss."

He frowned at her. "We're off duty, right?"

"Looks like it."

"You know what I mean."

"You're aware that I've not done much UC work before, aren't you... *Jack*?"

Bardsley lit a Benson and Collinge tossed him a dirty look, opening the rear window.

"I'm fully aware of that, Lauren, but you're more than capable and you did do the surveillance course a couple of years ago, didn't you?" She nodded. "I should know because I got you on it, so now's your chance to put it into practice. I've got every confidence in you." He smiled at her. "Now, got your cover story straight?"

Lauren took a deep breath and said, "I'm Laura Jackson from Urmston and I lost my beloved younger brother, Brian, aged seventeen, in a gang fight when, in the summer of 2009, he got jumped in Moss Range and was stabbed then left for dead." She took an audible breath, exaggerated in a subtle attempt at sarcasm, perhaps. "He died in hospital two days later and they never caught the *baaa-stards* who murdered him."

"Impressive, Lauren. I actually believe you, love. I'm filling up here," said Bardsley, sucking on the Benson.

Lips pursed, Collinge held a hand up in a mock threat to slap Bardsley, who dodged to the side, grinning mischievously.

Striker nodded approvingly. "Perfect, Lauren. You can do this. Just get a feel for what they're about and report back. Put your phone on vibrate, but like I said, have the number ready on speed dial to ring on this pay-as-you-go, if you need us." He held up a basic-looking black Nokia. "We'll be nearby. If there's a break in the meeting, use these." Striker handed her a pack of cigarettes and a lighter.

"I'm not smoking, Jack."

"You don't have to. Just light one up and go for a leisurely stroll, then give us a quick bell, if you can, to update us. If not, no worries, we'll just wait till the end."

"Okay," she said, but there was something amiss in her tone.

"You'll be fine. I have every faith in you. It's just for intel really. Nothing will happen to you, I promise. Just wanna rule these guys out of the equation, and if we get something more to go on, then great. We'll be very close by, honest. You ready, Lauren?"

She didn't look very ready, a nervy expression hardening her soft features. "Let's do it," she said with forced conviction.

***

The call box door squeaked shut and he undid the top couple of buttons of his black trench coat, his funeral coat that held the memories which spurred him on. After composing himself with an intake of the chilly night air, he dialled the number. Three rings later, an official-sounding female answered.

"Emergency services, which service please?"

He put on a pseudo-Scottish accent he'd been practicing on and off for days. "The po-lice."

A few beeps later, another female, same officious tone. "Greater Manchester Police, which town please?"

"Moss Range, Manchester."

"What's the nature of your call?"

"It's about that killer on the news – the Hoodie Hunter, I think they call him."

"Oh, really?" She sounded surprisingly unconvinced. *Silly bitch.*

"Aye, really."

"What about him?"

"He's attacking a wee lad on Moss Range Park."

"Okay, and your name is?"

"That's nae important, but ye'd best send someone down here sharpish."

"How do I know this isn't another crank call? We get loads, you know."

"Ye'll know when ye get here, 'cos there'll be another deid lad."

"Okay, okay. How do you know it's him?"

"He uses a baton right?" Silence on the other end. "Well, he's using it right now. I saw him. It's him. Listen…" He pushed play on his Dictaphone and distant, intermittent screaming ensued.

"Okay, can you still see him?" There was urgency in her voice now.

"Naw."

"Can you stay on the line, until we get patrols there?"

"Naw." With that, he hung up.

He was beginning to enjoy this; it had given a perverse sense of fun to proceedings. Thinking up new ways to outwit the police and the fuckwits had brought a new feeling of accomplishment to his work.

Ten minutes later, he was driving in the opposite direction toward the city centre, having passed half a dozen speeding police vehicles, blue lights and sirens in full flow, plus a couple of plain cars carrying whom he suspected were detectives. He could've sworn he'd seen the unfortunate DI Jack Striker's replacement Vinnie Stockley among them.

If so, job done.

He pulled the black VW Golf GTI into a side street, checked his mirrors and got out. He descended the steps of the dim, dank subway and what others would construe as fear intensified, as he heard the gang's bullshit-spewing voices. Unlike many, he knew fear was his friend and was just adrenaline heightening his senses, preparing him for battle.

No time for symbolism and games now.

In preparation of what was to come, he rolled down his hat, which doubled as a balaclava.

Chapter Twenty-Nine

"The Hoodie Hunter? He sounds like a real pussy to me, man."

"I'm telling you, Castro, he's one mean muvver. Doesn't fuck about. Takes out three at a time. According to papers, he—"

"The papers? Rah, yeah right, man, it must be true then." Castro drew hard on his spliff as he leaned back on the soft leather sofa and put his feet up on the Jamaican-patterned beanbag on the floor. He liked to call his flat an "apartment", but deep down he knew it was just a flat, despite the address being Grosvenor Apartments – a sales ploy, nothing more. Still, it was kitted out lavishly from ill-gotten gains, and the Moss Range location was hardly salubrious, ensuring the suspicions of the authorities were kept in check. "C'mon, shock me. He did what?"

"Well, they said he took out three hoodies in one go on the other side of town, but the cops denied they were all down to him. Said it was gang shit."

"The Hoodie Hunter?" he said disdainfully, clicking his tongue on his teeth. "Okay, so he took out three hooded sweatshirts, in one go? Sounds like an aggressive shoplifter to me, innit." Castro grinned at his own joke, revealing gold front teeth amid a dark goatee. "Hoodie Hunter, my arse." He sneered under his own dark hoodie.

"What about our runner boy, Gasbo?"

"That could've been anyone who killed him, man. Little twat, sneaking around behind my back, trying to sort shit out by teaming up with the enemy. Fuck him."

Big-un was worried. All the papers had said this "one-man crime wave" was responsible for up to a half a dozen hits this week alone and he knew the net was closing in on the likes of the Moss Range Crew. They'd done some bad stuff and this appeared to qualify them for whatever this crazy guy was doing. He stroked a hand over the tattooed letters just below each of his knuckles on his right fist – 'YMRC' – signifying membership. The 'Y' stood for 'Young' as he'd been in it since he was thirteen and now helped run the show, second only to Castro.

"But, bro, he single-handedly fucked up the Bad Bastards on the east side," said Big-un.

"Rah, rah. Yeah, yeah, yeah. Those pussies? Blam, blam, fuckin' blam. Heard it all before, man," said Castro, sucking the dregs of the spliff. He had to admit, though, their rival gang had been a bit quiet recently, since two of their main men had been smoked by someone. Granted, it saved him a job, but he knew it wasn't any of his crew. He'd heard the Bad Bastards had been branching out their business into the city centre. They'd dissed a few bouncers from Salford, so that was the most likely reason they'd been smoked, not this vigilante prick. He killed the weed stub in the ashtray on his lap.

"Aw, bro, I had twos-up on that."

"Fuck you and your bullshit, Big-un. You sound scared, man."

"Am not scared… just a bit… wary, innit."

"Rah, a bit? Well, if that pussy ever fancies his chances, then I'm ready." He stood up, withdrew the Browning revolver from his waistband and pointed it at an imaginary target. "I was fuckin' born ready, man. Just ask Leroy Bright… or Mad Dog McPherson… or Benny Jacobs…"

Big-un knew he couldn't ask them. He watched nervously until Castro tucked the Browning back into his waistband. Castro had been rather paranoid lately as whispers about a hit on him had gained ground.

"Anyway, I'm off to drill me baby-muvver," said Castro with a smirk.

"Which one?" asked Big-un.

"Laticia, of course." He leered. "Need a fix of her Babylons."

"Don't blame you, bro." Big-un pictured them: impressive to say the least and well worth a juggle. He should know, since unbeknown to Castro, he'd juggled them himself.

"Meet me back 'ere in a couple of hours, okay? And bring some funds for tomorrow."

"Do I ever let yer down, bro?"

"Never. So let's keep it that way, man."

Their fists met in a show of macho respect.

Big-un left Castro's flat, smirking to himself about Laticia's Babylons, as he headed to meet up with the boys. They'd jack a few pissed-up students, inflict some pain, sniff some coke, then back to Castro's flat to discuss business, like they did most nights.

***

Striker and Bardsley skulked in the undergrowth of the woods, having moved twenty or so metres toward the temple, before finding sanctuary behind a large sycamore. The early evening sun had long since disappeared, the darkness their ally.

"No," whispered Striker abruptly, as Bardsley threatened to light a cigarette.

"Come on, Jack. I'll cup the flame."

"I said no, Eric. We're too close and they may see it. Can't you wait? How addicted are you? Jeez."

"Look who's talking."

Striker gave him the eye, annoyed with himself for going back on the cigs.

Bardsley huffily replaced the cigarette into the packet. The two detectives peered through the trees as the crunch of gravel underfoot signified the arrival of attendees about fifteen metres to their left.

As planned, Lauren had headed along the short lane, then along the main road to her own car parked around the corner in the car park of a country pub. If anyone spotted her, she was under instructions to say that she was just checking the location for the meeting before having a bite to eat at the pub. However, the text message Striker had just received saying, *All clear, no worries, I'll be fine. Really, I'm okay now, thanks,* had lifted Striker's spirits somewhat. He'd remained waiting in the dank woods with the flatulent, chain-smoking Bardsley. Striker had been in more romantic situations in his life, but not for a while.

"And no more bloody farting either!"

"Okay, Jack. But you know I love a good Indian... tindaloo... loo by name and loo—"

"Shh. And get your bloody head on, Eric."

Bardsley was always like this before any type of job that had the potential of going pear-shaped, and there'd been a few over the years, though none of them were of this potential magnitude. Striker knew it was his colleague's way of beating the demons, the nerves that every cop felt at times like these, especially with so much riding on it. He also knew, despite Bardsley's tomfoolery, that he was a damn good cop and Striker couldn't think of anyone else he'd rather be beside, flatulence aside.

A couple of cars approached, so Striker took out two small pairs of binoculars, handing one to Bardsley. The temple itself looked somewhat eerie, its rugged appearance now shadowed with shifting shapes as more cars pulled up.

A couple of doors slammed and Striker manoeuvred the binoculars into position until he saw two women in winter coats and scarves, possibly mother and daughter. He then looked at three men in long black trench coats, standing at the large wooden doors of the entrance, reminding him of doormen. Or bouncers, or door security personnel, or whatever they were called now. Voices travelled in the night, but the exact words were incomprehensible.

He scanned again, this time seeing Collinge locking her car, then lifting the collar of her coat to fend off the chilly night air. She headed for the temple's entrance.

Striker flicked the binoculars back to the three men, one of whom prodded another as if to alert him, and all three looked sternly at the approaching Lauren Collinge.

Chapter Thirty

On his approach down the subway steps, he could hear their voices growing louder. There was laughter too, but not for long. He knew they'd be here because reconnaissance was one of his fortes.

He saw the first one, then the second and soon clocked that there were five in total.

Careful.

They were listening intently to a big lad in the middle who was gesticulating as if describing beating somebody up. The words "Rah, rah" and "Innit" were prevalent. His instant recognition of the large youth known as 'Big-un' from the Moss Range Park estate sparked a surge of excitement within him.

Control and focus.

The others were dressed in the usual dark sports gear, with their hoods predictably up. He stopped at the subway's entrance, craning to identify his prey from twenty-five metres away. He withdrew a small pair of lightweight NVG7s and soon sussed the one he had no interest in had a bright stripe across his hood.

He then saw that two were going through the pockets of a young curly haired lad he hadn't initially spotted. The lad was clearly petrified, probably a student.

Right.

"Oy, dickheads!"

They pivoted in unison, looking surprised.

"Want some?"

"You fuckin' with us, man?" shouted Big-un.

"What do you think, you bunch of low-lives?"

The student was discarded like litter. They all surged forward as one, a mass of arms, legs and aggression, their profanities resounding off the subway's graffiti-stained walls.

He turned and ran like a fox being hounded, albeit a very cunning one. He took the steps three at a time, soon passing a cul-de-sac on the right...

One...

He ignored the second right turn...

Two...

He heard them closing in…

Three…

He headed into the third cul-de-sac, passing the rows of terraced houses and parked cars, and stopping at the dead end. Breathlessly, he withdrew a baton from his left sleeve – his preferred weapon, not only due to its silence, easy concealment and his dexterity with it, but also because with each hit, he felt the satisfying shockwave of their pain.

He waited.

The noisy throng emerged at the top of the dark street.

"There he is, the cheeky fucker." Down they ran, their footsteps echoing in the narrow street.

He stood his ground, baton at the ready. They slowed up, still cursing, a wariness creeping into their psyches perhaps.

Big-un drew a blade, glistening under a streetlamp. "You're fucked now, gobshite."

He backed off from the gang, sucking them in, slowly edging around them, baton outstretched, slicing the night air with threatening swings. Eyeballing Big-un, he saw a flicker of fear. With deliberate, confident paces, he subtly manoeuvred them into the opening of an adjacent alleyway, a few metres to his right. They spread across the alley's entrance. One tried to sneak behind him, but the baton cut audibly through the air.

'Wanker! Am gonna shank you," said Levi, clicking a flick knife open. He knew all his targets' names, and more, much more than they would ever know.

He jockeyed them back a few paces, with a few nifty forward steps and vicious swings of the baton, further into the alley, capitalising on their hesitancy.

He took a step back himself when spotting a third knife appear in the hand of Renshaw.

"He's bottling it now. Ha. His arse has fell out. Fuckin' slice him, bro," said Big-un.

Two metres away, if that, their anxious faces just visible in the darkness.

Big-un lunged forward and the others followed, yelling, grimacing. Side-stepping Big-un, he grabbed his arm and jerked it behind his back, wrenching it up to his neck until it cracked.

He threw in a kidney punch for good measure with his baton hand.

"Aaargh." Big-un's blade clanged onto the asphalt and he dropped like a bag of shit, clutching his broken arm. At the back, Levi shaped to throw something, so he ducked and a bottle smashed beside him on a wall. They surged forward and a 360-turn impacted the baton onto a couple of stray skulls. Spotting Big-un trying to get up, he stamped on the broken arm, producing a girlie squeal.

The gang were getting too close.

Next phase.

He expertly swung his baton, connecting on the nearest cheekbone with a thud, his arm juddering on impact. Shanks cursed, holding his head, the others hesitating again, giving him a second to remove a brick in the wall.

"That won't fuckin' stop us, you muppet," yelled Levi.

Behind the brick was his trusty Glock 17, the silencer already fitted. "This fuckin' will though!" In one swift movement, he retracted his baton and slipped it up his left sleeve into its adapted sheath. Gripping the handgun in both hands, he took aim. All swagger was gone now, their fear-etched faces frozen. Levi and Shanks turned to run.

"It's a dead-end, boys – just like your lives."

"No, man, please—"

Three sharp, muffled shots, one for each forehead, the recoil expertly controlled. They dropped like dominoes.

Whimpering, Big-un tried to clamber up the wall, but fell to his knees. He cowered as he slowly looked up.

Someone was sobbing deep in the alley. It was the last lad standing, the one with the white stripe on his hood, his face pallid and still as the moon.

"Go now. Speak to no one or you won't be so lucky next time. Go sort your life out." The lad shot off like shit off the proverbial shovel.

He scanned his work, the useless young bodies strewn randomly, reminding him fleetingly of Kabul. A satisfying thought grew in his mind, that of the numerous crimes prevented and the many victims spared by his actions. Then he gazed at the end-terraced house beside him. Stemming the flow of a thousand memories, he spun round and pointed the Glock at the scampering Big-un. He was trying to sneak away, still clutching his shattered arm, still whimpering like a puppy.

"Pleeease… don't…"

Control and focus.

Now, let's move this thing forward.

He fired a couple of slugs that whizzed past Big-un's head, pinging into the wall behind. Big-un halted, crouched and raised his good arm to cover his face.

"Fuck me, man!"

"No thanks, you're not my type."

"You're Him, aren't you? The Hoodie Hunter."

He glanced up the street, noticing a few lights had come on. "Yes, I'm Him."

"Aw, nooo… Can… I go now… Pleeease?" asked Big-un, pathetically.

"What do you think?"

He strolled over to Big-un, who recoiled and resumed his snivelling, ironically, akin to many of his own victims.

Chapter Thirty-One

Striker switched the binoculars from Collinge to the three men at the temple's entrance. Thankfully, their expressions had softened somewhat, one even smiling as Collinge took the first of the three steps to the entrance. Another proffered a hand and she appeared to glance Striker's way before tentatively shaking it.

Striker tensed up a little, briefly looked to his left to see Bardsley watching events through the binoculars he'd given the DC earlier. Striker again observed the playing scene, compunction prodding him as one of the men in dark trench coats opened the huge wooden doors, ushering Collinge inside, out of sight.

He zoomed in on the face of one of the other two men who remained outside. He twisted the focus dial and froze for a second, recognising the face. It was his old pal Wozza. Moving his view slightly to the left, he had vague recollections of the other man, but couldn't quite place him. He briefly considered whether he knew the one who'd taken Collinge inside and regretted not having zoomed in on his face to check.

The scrunch and drone of two more cars on the gravel alerted him and he watched more people arrive. They received similar greetings to Collinge, although perhaps not as warm and friendly. Or was he being paranoid?

He heard a low vibrating sound, turned and saw Bardsley placing his binoculars on a sycamore branch. Bardsley reached into his pocket, his face lighting up from the glow of the phone.

"It's Becky. I'd best answer it, Jack," whispered the DC, huskily.

Striker nodded, himself wanting to know why she'd called.

"Go on, Becky… right… okay… bleedin'ell… I'm on my way."

"What's so important?"

"Can I take the hire car, Jack? They need all available resources. Looks like our man's been on a killing spree. Three more dead."

"Shit." He dipped his head, leaned on a branch of tree. Knowing he had no choice, Striker threw a look at the temple and then reluctantly tossed Bardsley the keys.

***

Having discreetly parked the hire car in a side street near the nick, Bardsley had picked up his Astra and now surveyed the scene before him, barely believing his eyes. Vivid blue lights flashed intermittently around the cordoned-off street as lighting was being erected in the blackness of the alleyway, the resting place of three young men. Five spent cartridges had already been located by Armed Response, swiftly being identified as from a Glock 17 pistol.

Late-shift CID officers were conducting house-to-house enquiries while clutching their turquoise daybooks. From what he'd gathered, Maria Cunningham was already trying to prepare a press release with GMP's Press Office, after being inundated with calls. Syndicate Three had joined Vinnie Stockley's team, having been pulled off a knife murder in Salford, as the enormity of this escalating situation reverberated to the chief constable at HQ. SIO Halt had no doubt been called at home and been in touch with the chief, who'd ordered the callout of every available detective, bar those who'd been drinking, the latter invariably amounting to quite a few. Bardsley knew more Mutual Aid assistance from surrounding forces would also be required, now the media machine was on full throttle.

Then, to Bardsley's amazement, the police radio in his inside pocket announced another scene in the Grosvenor Apartments and two more bodies, both shot.

Jesus. This was unprecedented, even for round here.

And Jack Striker had missed it all. Was the temple really connected to all this? Bardsley doubted it. As much as it must have been frustrating for Striker to not be involved in the case anymore, Bardsley had only gone along with the Striker's – somewhat rushed – op out of misguided loyalty and to give his pal a sense of involvement. How could they be involved anyway, if these killings had occurred when Bardsley and Striker had been watching those bouncers at the temple? Clearly the killer was nothing to do with this VOICES group.

Bardsley saw Vinnie Stockley heading his way, the DI speaking brusquely into his mobile. He held a finger up, suggesting he wanted Bardsley to remain there while he finished his call.

"... So you'll sort the second scene out and let Mr Brennan know? ... Okay, Maria, yes, yes, I'll see you later..." He glanced at Bardsley. "You too." He dropped the phone into the inside pocket of his slate grey suit. "Bardsley, I need you to assist with the CCTV checks at the shops along the main road."

Bardsley looked up at the DI. *What again? Twenty years in the Job and all I seem to do is trawl bleedin' CCTV.* He couldn't be arsed arguing. After all, he had enough on his plate wondering whether his missus was shagging the window cleaner. Here was yet another night he'd be late home, and it was supposed to be a rest day.

"Sure, Boss. I'm onto it," said Bardsley with fake enthusiasm.

"Get onto the council too. There are street cameras along Moss Range Road."

"I know. I've worked around here for nineteen years."

"Less of the backchat. We're trying to catch a serial killer here. You got a problem with that, Bardsley?"

"Nah, sorry, Boss. Just a few domestic issues on my mind, that's all."

"Haven't we all? At least you've got a future in the Job. Unlike your mate, Striker, who's probably in the casino drinking vodka, drowning his sorrows." Stockley leered.

If only you knew. "What do you mean by that?"

"Been chatting to his drug addict sister and dodgy brother-in-law about the attack on their son Deano and Striker's shady past," he replied smugly.

"Oh, that's very nice of you. Stitching up a colleague by abusing his family's trust, while prying into Jack's background. What a nice bloke you are, Vincent." Bardsley's anger bubbled, and watching Stockley's face stiffening up any thoughts of rank evaporated. "So how do you feel about all these murders on your watch then?"

"Be very careful, Detective. I can do some digging on you too. Just go and get those damn CCTV checks done."

Bleedin' tosser, thought Bardsley, heading to his Astra and reaching for his mobile.

Alone in the dark woods, Striker watched the third bouncer exit the temple to resume his greeting pose with the other two. After missing the chance of getting a closer look earlier, Striker instantly zoomed in the binocs and was taken aback at whom he saw.

What the hell was Ged the Giant doing here?

He instantly recalled their exchange in the casino and remembered thinking at the time that Ged was a little *too* pro-Hoodie Hunter. He thought back to having caught Wozza whispering on the forum to that Danny Boy character. Could that have been Ged? Or even the killer himself? After all, Striker was also on the forum in a different guise, but for obvious reasons. Nah, surely not. His old mates wouldn't be into something this heavy, would they?

Yet another car arrived accompanied again by the crunch of the tiny stones within the car park, which was becoming surprisingly full. He ducked momentarily when headlights shined his way through the trees. Two big blokes in long dark coats got out of a BMW. One went to the front passenger door to help an elderly lady out by extending a strong arm, which she held onto before leveraging herself out. What was it with all these black trench coats? Was it a bouncers' convention?

He watched the lady being linked by the two men. She was clearly important to them. Then it struck him. She was probably Edith off the forum, had to be. Once she was led inside, the bouncers on the door followed and the huge wooden doors slammed shut.

Striker was just about to edge through the woods into the thicket in front, in order to head for the rear and hopefully get a closer look, when he remembered where he'd seen the third, unidentified man on the door. It was one of Lenny's older brothers.

Haunting memories flashed back, merging with the new thoughts of this investigation, in a mishmash of speculations he could barely keep up with. Nonetheless, one thing seemed perfectly clear: his mates were here because deep down they, like him, still felt that gnawing guilt at being powerless to stop that bullet impacting Lenny's skull all those years ago.

The craving for a cigarette was strong, but he soon quashed it.

The trees rustled above him as a chilly breeze wafted through the woods, the sycamore's branches creaking slightly. A shiver shot up his back. He upturned his jacket's collar in a feeble attempt to ease the cooling night. Gazing toward the temple, dark gathering clouds seemed to be moving faster than normal above it, threatening yet more Manchester rain. The multicoloured glow of the large hall's inner lights lit up the thin, rectangular stained-glass windows down the side of the temple.

With his friends clearly involved in this VOICES group, the nagging question was: *Were they genuinely seeking comfort and catharsis in the company of like-minded people, or was something more sinister going on?*

He understood that perhaps, with vulnerable victims present, there was a need to reassure them by providing security on the venue's door. So maybe his imagination was leading him to the wrong conclusions.

Just as he felt his mobile vibrating in his pocket, he heard shuffling behind him. He pivoted enough to see a baseball bat for a micro-second, inches from his forehead. It was followed by a painful thud so sharp that it was accompanied by a bright shockwave in his mind's eye…

… then darkness.

Chapter Thirty-Two

Castro's iPhone finally rattled on the dark oak coffee table in front of him and he saw Big-un's name on the screen as the mobile slowly spun with the vibration. He paused Black Ops 2 and a dead soldier flickered on the fifty-inch LED television, then he tossed the Xbox control onto the settee beside him and answered the phone.

"About fuckin' time, bro. Thought you'd got nicked or summat. Where've you been?"

"Hi, Castro," said the deep voice.

He stood up, confused. "Who the fuck's this? Where's Big-un?"

"You'll know me soon enough. As for Big-un… for a 'big-un', he's a right cry baby, isn't he?"

"Yo, dickhead. If you touch him, you're dead meat. Do you know who you're fuckin' with, man?"

"It's too late for Big-un. And, yes, I do know you, *man*, that's why I'm coming up right now."

The phone went dead. Castro couldn't think straight and felt a rare surge of panic. Who the fuck would have the balls to take out his number two and diss him like that?

He withdrew his Browning and paced the flat. A quick glance out of the window revealed nothing. Shit, who was this muv—?

Suddenly, it struck him like a bullet to the head. "It's that Hoodie Hunter guy!"

An unfamiliar fear engulfed him; even so, his rage obliterated it. "Okay, Mr Hoodeee-fuckin-Hunter. Let's see who the man is. I'm not just some punk-arsed-muvver you can trample all over – *I'm* the man!" As he spoke, he could see the pistol shaking in his grip.

There was a bang on the door. Castro's heart flipped. He wished he'd gone easier on the weed today. He pointed the Browning and edged toward the door.

Another bang.

He shuffled sideways to the wall, away from any line of fire. He needed to check the spyhole. He took a sharp intake, moving swiftly to take a quick look. What he saw made him jump to the wall beside the door. He registered a snapshot of a man in a balaclava, holding a handgun.

His options were limited and he instantly knew what he had to do. He'd have to get the boys to clear the flat of money and merchandise pronto before the cops got here. But this was self-defence right?

Bizarrely, he pictured Laticia's Babylons, wishing he could nestle into them now. But he knew he had no choice.

"Fuck it!"

Castro cracked out six shots, splintering the door, each bullet piercing through. There was a faint smell of burning wood, the gun hot in his shaking hand. Adrenaline pumped and he felt sickly. Silence, except his own heartbeat. Cautiously, still pointing the pistol, he peeped, but saw nothing. He slowly unlocked the latch and jolted the door open.

Relief.

"Woo-yeah, man." Castro eyed the prostrate body. No movement, definitely smoked. A black trench coat with blood seeping out. He jumped onto the body and began to dance. "Who's the man now, Mr Hoodeee Hunter?"

As he danced, he noticed the floor was wet and got a whiff of something. He crouched and touched the carpet, then smelled his finger. He laughed manically, his gold front teeth glowing, and he resumed his celebrations with even more vigour.

"I was right about you, man... the Hoodeee Hunter's pissed himself... what a fuckin' pussy!"

***

He watched the halfwit dancing over the corpse and rolled down the dual-hat balaclava, then readied the Glock 17. He stepped out from the doorway into the corridor.

"Look at you. You're all the same," he hissed in disgust, causing Castro to pivot like an owl on speed. Silencer still fixed, he popped a slug into the gang leader's gun hand, the Browning bouncing a few feet away. Castro shrieked, clutched his hand, his eyes wide with shock. A woman's petrified face appeared in a doorway down the hall.

"Get back in and you'll be safe," he yelled, and her door slammed forthwith.

A man's muffled voice: "It's okay, Beryl, I've called the police."

The handgun was still trained on the squealing Castro. "Pull back the face mask," he said, gesturing with the Glock's barrel.

Like a good boy, Castro peeled the balaclava back, revealing a duct-taped mouth. He lifted it further and Big-un's vacant eyes looked up at him.

"Now pass me my other Glock."

Castro had tears in his eyes. "Look... Fuck you, man. Who the hell do you—?"

"Okay, I'll get it myself." He blasted Castro in the midriff and strolled forward. "That's from our Josh..."

Castro buckled, gasped for air, his expression a grimace with a dash of disbelief, both hands clutching his blood-spewing gut. He staggered back against the corridor wall.

"... And this one's from me." The second shot hit the top of Castro's brow and he collapsed in slow motion.

He stepped over the bodies, resisting the strong urge to spit on them, and retrieved the empty Glock he'd forced Big-un to hold. Still no DNA for Jack Striker's lot. As he heard faint sirens, he gazed down the corridor at the wall.

It's always surprising how far brain and skull fragments fly from the back of your head when shot at close range. An odd mix, like cheap ketchup and mushy peas, spattering a white-washed wall, is never a pretty sight, but it can be perversely satisfying to see in this relentless process of mopping up.

He headed along the corridor to the fire exit, the face of his next targets already clearly formed in his mind.

Chapter Thirty-Three

Bardsley dropped the mobile phone back into the pocket of his black leather jacket as he was buzzed into the council's CCTV offices in Manchester city centre. A security officer dressed in a similar uniform to a constable, including black body armour and epaulettes, nodded and escorted him up two flights of stairs.

That was the second time he'd tried to call both Striker and Collinge. Strange – neither of them were answering their mobiles. Surely the meeting would be over by now. Maybe they were still in earshot of the temple. He would try them again later. He'd also phoned Margaret, but there was no answer from her either. This had really started the old paranoia cogs turning; especially since earlier she'd told him she was "just going to catch-up on the soaps I've recorded", so she should have been beside the landline.

After the security officer had punched in a few digits on a door's keypad, they entered a vast room with numerous fifty-inch screens on two walls. There was a long line of CCTV operators chatting while spasmodically watching the screens. All of them turned to eye Bardsley, who strolled in holding his daybook. Momentarily, he wondered what they were thinking. He guessed that suppressed envy could be in the minds of any wannabe cops present.

The security guard introduced him to a tall, hard-faced chap wearing a slightly creased blue shirt and dark blue tie, who reminded Bardsley of a poor man's Vinnie Jones, facial scars and all.

"Hiya, fella. Barry Stone." He held out a chunky hand, which Bardsley shook, feeling the man's strength as he squeezed a little too hard.

Was Stone a wannabe cop? "DC Bardsley, MIT. What have you got, Barry?"

"I followed this incident from the start 'cause I saw a bloke wearing a face mask, hanging about near the subway." His voice was as common as the types Bardsley nicked. Rightly or wrongly, he speculated that Stone had a record in years gone by – probably assault – but had sufficiently cleaned up his act to snag this job.

"Did you phone it through?"

"Nah, not initially."

That's why you're a security guard.

"But I think we might have summat for yer."

"Good. What?"

Stone pressed a series buttons, rewinding the picture. A few of the operators to Bardsley's left began talking excitedly, huddling around a screen as it kicked off yet again between drunks in the city centre. Bardsley glanced up; it looked like a tasty fight, but his gaze soon returned to the screen directly in front of him.

Stone pressed play and a large-framed man wearing a long black coat strolled from a side street, with some sort of man bag across his shoulders. Or was it wrapped around his waist? It was hard to tell because of the distance.

"That's him, I reckon."

"Who?"

"That Hoodie Hunter fella."

"And you still didn't call it in?"

"Well, I didn't know at this stage."

"And how did you know it was the Hoodie Hunter we were after tonight?"

"It's all over the news, man."

Jeez, already? Bardsley watched as the man on the screen walked down the subway steps and stopped in an alcove before peering into the tunnel. "So you didn't zoom in?"

"Not yet, but in a minute I do when he takes out a pair of binocs and puts on his face mask. I actually think they're probably NVGs 'cause I do a bit in the TA, like."

Inwardly cursing at potentially missing a chance to get a close-up of the guy, Bardsley's blank expression told Stone that he wasn't interested in his pastimes. To be fair though, Stone wasn't to know and at least they had some footage to analyse.

"There you go." The camera zoomed in as the man stood, legs apart at the subway's entrance, appearing to shout something. He suddenly turned and quickly took the steps before heading back the way he came and turning into a side street out of view.

Bardsley leaned in as the group of lads stormed out of the subway, gesticulating and shouting something. The system didn't have sound, of course, and he couldn't see clearly enough to recognise any of them. The camera followed them until they turned into the same side street a few seconds later.

Never to return. "Hang on. Rewind it to those lads."

Stone did.

"There's five."

"Yeah, and…?"

But he only killed three, so we have two witnesses. "Can you enhance footage here?" Bardsley suspected they couldn't, but thought he'd ask, such was the speed of technology these days.

"Nah, fella, but we wish we could, like."

"Did you get any footage of anyone exiting the side street later?"

"Nah, I only kept the camera pointing that way till the coppers arrived."

His work done here, Bardsley got a CD of the footage from Stone and filled out a yellow exhibit label, getting the security man to sign it. He took his contact details, thanked him and was escorted out.

Outside, he felt the night's chill and lit a cigarette. *So now, who gets this info first, Stockley or Striker?*

It was a no-brainer. He dialled the number, hoping this time he'd get through.

***

Striker drifted in and out of consciousness in the musty gloom. His fuzzy mind flashed back and forth, deep into the past then back to the present. A hodgepodge of random thoughts, snippets of conversations, interspersed and fused together.

"… Good bloody riddance!" yelled his dad from the front door, as young Jack fled the Striker family home, his mum sobbing in the background…

"… Let's go, Jack… for God's sake!" pleaded Lenny from the rear of the Escort that Jack was struggling to control…

… The life support bleeped intermittently. Lenny lay prostrate in the hospital bed, his brothers' blurred faces glaring at Jack, fingers pointing accusingly…

… Or was it his nephew Deano in the bed? Lucy was there

now. DJ suddenly appeared grabbing at her arm, forcing a syringe of heroin into it. Mouth agape, Lucy fell onto the bed, clutching her pregnant belly...

... Jack sat against the park wall with the rest of Sunnyside Boys. It was after the Lenny shooting. Ged's face was up close, pale in the moonlight, contorting as he spoke. "And when my cousins find out, the shit will hit the fan big time..."

... In slow motion, the leather football soared through the rain toward Striker... he jumped majestically, ignoring the kidney punch as he rose. Adeptly craning his neck, the ball slapped his forehead then diverted to the top corner of the goal, rippling the net. Falling back into the quagmire with a splat, the mad eyes of the huge defender atop of him seemed vaguely familiar, burning into his psyche. The weight of the man's impact winded him and he tried to squirm free, like wrestling with a crocodile...

... Back in the hospital now... He peered closer at the body in the bed... Was it Lenny again or Deano? The life support machine sounded one long continuous bleep... He felt panicky, unable to see who it was... Frantically pulling the oxygen mask and bandages from the face... It was him... Jack Striker...

"... Daaddeeeee," screamed Beth and Harry..."

Striker stirred from his stupor, momentarily, just as something furry brushed past his nose and began clawing at his cheek.

Then darkness fell again.

Chapter Thirty-Four

Striker felt something pressing on his chest and his wrists. He was frozen, powerless to move. The internal throbbing of his forehead was the only noise. He'd had migraines before, but this was something else. He could murder a drink, his mouth virtually saliva free. His senses began to kick in. Awareness, signs of clarity and then ensuing panic swept him. He was face down, a cold concrete floor beneath him.

He could smell stale food, its mustiness irritating his nose. His face felt sticky, the skin tight, sore; he guessed it was dried blood. His throat was parched and his hair matted with more blood from the blow to his head. His forehead was throbbing and he tried to raise his right hand to gently check the lump he knew was there. However, his hands and feet were bound and aching. He remembered the dreamlike flashbacks, but shoved them to one side as realisation of what had happened to him kicked in.

The pressure on his chest was his own body weight because he was face down. Smelling mustiness, he sneezed, coughed. Recalling being hit in the woods outside the temple, he frantically struggled to pull himself free, but it was no use. All he could do was force himself up to a sitting position, that alone feeling like a mammoth effort.

"Lauren… Shit." He heard his own croaky words, hardly recognising them, and was momentarily surprised he hadn't been gagged. If he'd been taken, then surely Collinge had too… or worse. Please, no…

Despite his grogginess, he forced himself to think and tried to look around. A thin vertical beam of light emanated from what looked like a door several metres in front. It was difficult to tell exactly how far, but at a guess maybe six or seven metres. He bent his right hand and managed to touch his left wrist, feeling the taut rope that had disabled him. After a deep breath, he used all the strength he could muster to pull at the rope.

A minute of trying elapsed and he cursed in exasperation. It was no use. His eyes slowly began to adjust to the darkness and he saw something move. A small shape accompanied by a hollow scurrying. He saw another shape and heard rustling.

Mice? A shudder ran up his back. Please no… Rats, heading his way!

Since being bitten by one as a kid, then reading the trilogy from his favourite author growing up, James Herbert, in an attempt to dispel the fear, he'd developed a distinct dislike of the rodents bordering on phobia. He felt a cold sheen of sweat forming on his brow and could hear his heartbeat quickening.

Their clawed feet tapped away, growing louder. Somehow, he exerted himself enough to rock into a sitting position and quickly kicked out with both legs, which seemed to divert the creatures away. Where the hell was he, in some kind of old food store? Or the temple's basement, maybe? He could be anywhere.

Thankfully, the scurrying eased as if the rats were wary of him, too. His eyes continued to adjust to the gloom, improving visibility slightly. What looked like boxes were piled up to his left and shelves to his right. And, yes, that was definitely a door facing him. An inner rage fizzed. Who'd have the balls to kidnap a cop? How long had he been in here? And what the hell had happened to Lauren? Emotion gripped him.

He'd messed up big time. He'd let Lauren down. He'd failed her and the force with his half-cocked plan. He wondered if the serial killer he'd failed to catch was the one who'd attacked him and dumped him here. If so, what would happen next? Had he been put here simply because he was close to catching the killer? Or was Striker next? If so, why was he still alive?

He heard the rats again, edging closer, gaining confidence. Panic swamped him, an unfamiliar sense of helplessness. It was then that he thought of little Beth and Harry, and two things happened that hadn't since Lenny was shot sixteen years ago.

A solitary tear rolled down Striker's cheek…

… and he began to pray.

***

FOCUS!

Striker inwardly castigated himself for being a wimp. Even though nobody had witnessed it, *he* knew it had happened. He'd cried, not much, but it still counted and qualified him as a soft-arse. He'd cried for his children, for Lauren and for being such a damn failure. He'd blown his marriage and now his career, and in all likelihood his life. Unless, that is, Bardsley had become suspicious and was on the case.

But what if he hadn't? He was the only other one who knew what they'd been up to. Striker dipped his head for a minute or so. As well as his throbbing head, his shoulders and biceps ached at being stuck in this position.

He shook the pitiful thoughts away then began pulling and jerking with every fibre of energy he had at the ligatures disabling his wrists and feet.

Nothing, except for pain in his joints. But one thing he'd never been was a quitter – probably why the gambling got out of hand years ago. Striker hated losing, and if this was to be *it* then he wasn't going down without a fight.

He shuffled over on his backside toward the door, each movement producing a shudder that his headache didn't appreciate one iota. He heard the rats scurrying away. The little bastards would grow more confident and inquisitive soon. As he lumbered along, he felt around for anything that he could use to prise or cut the ropes incapacitating him, but found nothing.

After a few minutes of forward movement, he leaned onto the door and caught his breath. The crack where the door met the frame was just wide enough for him to partially see into the next room, which appeared empty. A few chairs around a rickety-looking table with three empty bottles of Stella on top. He strained his eyes to see to the sides of the outer room and spotted an old tweed-style sofa and what looked like the tips of a pair of black Magnum boots on the floor.

One of the boots moved. He winced, realising someone was wearing them. And whoever it was, started to head his way.

Chapter Thirty-Five

Bardsley was beginning to feel somewhat concerned. Not only were both Striker and Collinge not answering their mobiles, they were now switched off. He'd put the Margaret issue to one side for now and reluctantly reported back to Stockley regarding the CCTV footage. Stockley seemed to be fretting and appeared out of his depth. Bardsley had heard the rumours about his nickname on the division – 'Feathers' because he was always flapping – but this was the first time he'd really witnessed confirmation.

All available officers had been kept on duty until further notice, to assist with the two new scenes. The media were hovering like vultures and more officers from surrounding divisions had been drafted in to assist with the manhunt for Bobby Copeland.

He'd been assigned to ensure that uniform had thoroughly checked the shops for CCTV and to co-ordinate house-to-house, which he'd done, albeit in haste. He knew he was supposed to report back to Stockley again, but he was now driving at double the speed limit deep into South Manchester, back toward the temple in Cheshire.

Fifteen minutes later, he pulled the Astra into the gloomy lane leading to the temple and soon crunched into the empty car park. The lights activated at his presence, bringing welcome brightness. By the look of the place no one was present, all inside lights being off. He quickly jumped out and checked the large wooden doors, but they were firmly locked.

Back in the Astra, he drove around the much darker rear and, again, no signs of anyone present.

"Where the hell are they?" he muttered.

Taking a torch from the Astra's glovebox, he meandered through the wooded area to where he'd last been with Striker, the damp foliage slushy underfoot. Shining the beam around, he saw nothing untoward and returned to the Astra.

A notion struck him. He'd seen them flirting for a while and if nothing had come from Striker's little mission then maybe, just maybe, they'd hooked up for a few drinks. He remembered that country pub around the corner, where Collinge had been prior to her entering the meeting, and checked his watch. Gone midnight – it'll be shut now.

However, if an impromptu date *had* been the case, then why hadn't they answered their mobiles?

Doh! Of course. Bardsley shook his head knowingly. They'd be having dessert. You lucky bugger, Striker!

He prayed he was right, but something still nagged and he didn't like the feel of it. Why hadn't Striker called to update him or to even ask him about the latest on the case? Sure, if he was having a 'special moment' with Collinge then he wouldn't want Bardsley to know, but…

He studied the eerie Masonic temple, the trees swaying and rustling above him, and he wondered if this place did have something to do with the case after all. But what could he possibly do now? He certainly couldn't tell the brass about Striker's op.

His mobile rang and he saw that it was Stockley's work number. "Shit." He ignored the call and jogged back to the car, reassuring himself that Striker was a top notch detective, who could handle himself.

Heading back to the B Division, his mind slowly returned to how he could persuade Stockley to stand him down from duty, so he could get back to Margaret and try and sort out his godforsaken marriage.

***

Striker shuffled awkwardly in his sitting position, away from the door, his urgency enhanced as a key rattled in the keyhole behind him. He felt naturally apprehensive, but all the earlier wimpy thoughts had been vanquished, replaced by a gritty determination to survive. He was still perplexed as to why he'd been taken, by whom and what involvement his so-called friends Wozza and Ged had in this surreal situation.

He managed to reach his original location. Still sitting, he leaned against something with a cool, hard surface, possibly a metal barrel or drum of some kind. He tried to stifle his breathlessness.

The dark musty room became awash with light as the door opened. Striker dipped his head to shield his temporarily blinded eyes.

The deep voice was local, cool as you like and almost apologetic. "I had no choice."

Striker raised his head slightly to view the large silhouette of the man whose head was turned away. Striker's eyes still struggled to adjust to the sudden light, though he was certain of one thing. He knew that this man wasn't Bobby Copeland.

He cleared his throat. "No choice?" he managed, somewhat croakily, mouth as dry as a lizard's arse in a sandstorm.

The voice raised an octave, though still guttural. "You know what I mean, DI Striker."

Ah, so he knows I'm a cop. "No choice but to assault and kidnap a police officer?" *What did this headcase want?* Striker raised his head, squinted and achieved better focus. The man was about three metres from him and it was no surprise to Striker that he was wearing a balaclava. The guy had to have gigantic balls to be doing what he was doing.

"Met our little friends yet?"

"Huh?"

"The rats. They're wild buggers. Feed 'em on meat, you know. Surprised you've still got a face, Inspector."

Jesus! He tried to remain cool.

"So how did you know, Striker?"

"Know what, er... sorry, we haven't been introduced."

The kidnapper sniggered. "I admire your sense of humour in the circumstances."

"Comes with dealing with shit, day in, day out. Mopping up the streets."

He hesitated, dark eyes opening further into a brief glare. "Tell me about it. I know the feeling very well."

"Yeah?"

"Yeah."

"How's that then?"

"Doesn't matter... and *I'll* ask the questions. So, how did you know?"

"Any chance of a cool beer?"

"No. Answer the question. You sound like a Tory MP."

Striker smiled, falsely. "Know what exactly?"

"Come on, Striker. Let's not play games." His voice was raised now.

The first signs of a temper, best go easy. Striker played for time, to subtly take in his surroundings while the room was partially lit. "I'm not in a position to play games, fella. You're clearly the boss here, but please, I'm not sure what it is I'm supposed have known."

"Okay, I'll rephrase it. Why were you watching the temple tonight?"

Was he one of the trench-coat doormen? I don't recognise his voice, so it's not Wozza or Ged. Could it be one of Lenny's brothers? Or someone else from VOICES? Maybe the owner of the temple? Am I in the temple's cellar now? Should I ask about Lauren?

"Well?"

"Just a bit suspicious of what was going on in there, that's all."

"Why?"

"Why do you think?"

"I said I'd ask the questions, Striker!"

Temper, temper. It could be him — our man. Sod it. "I thought you could have some connections to the recent spate of murders."

"Murders?"

"All these innocent young lads — you know."

"Innocent? They were far from innocent."

"How do you know that?"

"Right! No more questions, smart arse!"

"And where's Lauren Collinge? If you touch her, I'll—"

"You'll do what exactly? Look at you. You're a fuckin' mess."

Striker's heart jumped as he saw the dark shape of a handgun appear in the man's right hand. He tilted his head down slightly in a submissive gesture, but still eyeballed him approaching.

Striker felt a sturdy boot into his sternum, well and truly winding him, and he jolted back against the metal barrel, his head clunking painfully against it. Pulling at the ropes around his wrists, Striker couldn't even rub his head, now throbbing on *both* sides.

Shit, I wish I wasn't tied up. I'd nail this bastard. "You seriously need… to book some… anger management classes, fella."

Towering over Striker, he waved the pistol. "Where's that fat

Scouser you were with?"

"I'm telling you fuck all. Who do you think you are anyway?"

"Like I said, you gave me no choice. And, stop with these questions."

"There's always a choice."

The Magnum boot flew at his head with a *whoosh*, impacting on his chin, jolting him back against the barrel again. He half-registered his attacker's parting shot – "And don't try anything stupid because I'm the one with the fuckin' gun remember" – as, for the second time that night, Striker left consciousness behind.

Chapter Thirty-Six

His extensive research had not only led him to his targets, but he also had an acute awareness as to who was working on the case. Striker had left him no choice, interfering before his work was done. He had to give him credit as, even though he knew that he'd been careful enough to leave very few clues, the DI was a shrewd operator to get so close so soon. But he was off the case, so there's no way it was an authorised obs post. He was running his own private investigation. *Never off duty, eh?* Just like himself. Striker certainly had tenacity, but he already knew that from marking him at football.

However, these were only complications and although, admittedly, time was running out, it was nothing he couldn't handle. He'd been trained to adapt. There would be enough time to conclude matters satisfactorily; he'd make sure of that. That Stockley would be shell-shocked at what he'd just done, and up to his eyeballs in it. But they'd seen nothing yet and soon enough they wouldn't know what hit them.

He pulled the black GTI into the cul-de-sac of semis, struggling to see the house numbers. He spotted the house he wanted in the corner. The street was quiet. *Good.* A light was on upstairs, the rest of the house was in darkness.

He slipped on his balaclava and checked his Glock 17 and silencer, purposely close to him, now the cops were closing. He took the retractable baton from the glove compartment, sliding it up his left sleeve into its adapted sheath.

Fully armed and ready, he got out of the Golf and walked purposefully up the drive. After a swift scan behind him, he scaled the five-foot fence with ease and dropped into the back garden, the trickle of a water feature the only sound.

He checked the back door, finding it was predictably locked. Leaning closer, he could see a key inside the door through one of half a dozen square-panelled windows. He shook his head at people's naivety and took out the Glock. He shot the nearest glass panel to the lock, creating minimal noise due to the silencer and modest size of the chosen window, and then he reached inside.

Within seconds, he'd opened the door and put the pistol in his deep coat pocket. He retracted the baton knowing the occupants wouldn't be armed. He withdrew a pencil torch and flicked it on, then made his way through the kitchen, living room and into a hallway, where he could hear low groans emanating from upstairs. He crept up the stairs, mindful of any sudden creaks in the timber beneath the carpet.

At the top of the stairs, he realised the groans were those of pleasure, repeated every second, predominantly female. The light in the front bedroom was on, so he peered through a crack in the partially open door. A big white buck arse pounded away, grinding deeper with each jolt.

So maybe Bardsley wasn't too concerned about Striker after all.

***

Still recovering from the hefty boots, Striker was gagging for a drink and the bodily aches were really kicking in now. His migraine throbbed.

He again recalled his dreamlike reminisces, but this time he didn't dismiss them. The one he thought he'd long forgotten was from Ged after Lenny had been shot: *When my cousins find out, the shit will hit the fan big time.*

He pondered it a while. The third bouncer outside the temple was Danny Powers, who was Ged's cousin and Lenny's brother. Striker recalled Lenny had two brothers, both older than Striker, so he didn't know them that well. He'd heard one ran the Wagon and Horses in Moss Range, and knew the oldest was in the army. *The army?* Striker thought back to the letter sent by the killer.

One thing he did know was that the very youngest of the four brothers got jumped by the Moss Range Crew, after going onto their patch for a money match at snooker. The kid – Josh Powers, if memory served – comprehensively beat at least three of the gang and won a few grand. Not surprising really, since he was on the verge of turning professional, having both a sponsor and a coach. The Crew didn't like this one bit. After the beating – with his own snooker cue and several brands of training shoes – the kid was left with fractured orbits in his left eye. Once it had dawned on him that the dream of turning pro was over he'd hung himself... *hung himself...* and the older Powers brothers were obviously devastated, as was Ged.

Striker remembered this so clearly because he was the one who'd dealt with the case as a DS in CID. More importantly, he'd never brought the offenders to justice due to insufficient evidence.

The sturdy ropes were still tied tightly around his wrists and ankles, and were really getting on his nerves, to the point where he could have screamed like a madman. He'd shuffled around searching for anything to cut the ropes with, to no avail. Rubbing them on the metal barrel hadn't worked, nor the wall and wooden beam to his rear.

His chest ached from the Magnum boot's impact. There was no need for that, but Striker's goading was to test and get a feel for whom he was actually dealing with. In a way, it had partly worked.

He was still undecided as to the identity of his kidnapper. It was more than feasible that he could be the killer, but Striker wasn't sure. It seemed increasingly likely that there was a connection to Striker's past too, although what bugged him most presently was Collinge's fate.

At least Bardsley would eventually realise they were missing, but how long would that be? A sudden thought of his mobile struck him and he awkwardly felt inside his jacket pocket with his inner right arm, unsurprisingly finding nothing. He also knew his wallet containing his warrant card – and more importantly a snapshot of Beth and Harry – was gone from the back pocket of his jeans, as he couldn't feel any bulge. If the truth be known, what with the concrete floor, he couldn't even *feel* his own rear end anymore.

No! Now he knows what my kids look like.

He was becoming more weary and desperate than he'd felt at any point in his life. At least he'd managed to see the layout of the room a little when the door had been opened. The room was about ten metres square and there were many scattered barrels about, not just the one he was propped up against. There appeared to be an opening to his far left at the end of a decrepit-looking wall, as though there might be a further room beyond.

The cardboard boxes to his right were brown with a black emblem on them, which was hard to distinguish, possibly crisps.

He was convinced he must be in the temple's cellar. He heard the shuffling of a rat again and shivered, yet it brought with it a eureka moment. It was absolute madness, but worth a shot given the desperate circumstances.

He manoeuvred himself up close to what were hopefully crisp boxes, and began biting the boxes. He spat out cardboard and bit again, repeating the process over and over.

Five minutes later, he was covered in bits of cardboard and had a bag of crisps rustling between his teeth. He carefully leaned back and let the packet fall slightly onto his upper chest. He leaned back further, feeling the muscles in his stomach tighten as he held a half-sit-up position until the crisps slid a little and balanced directly below his chin. He slowly increased the pressure between his chin and his upper chest, hearing a low popping sound, followed by a waft of beef and onion.

He lay on his back, feeling more pain in his momentarily squashed hands, and carefully let the crisps slip from chest to the floor. He shuffled round so he could grip the packet with his fingers, and when he was sure he had a decent grip, he bent forward as much as he possibly could, until the crisps covered the rope around his wrists. He could feel the slight scrape of crisps between his wrists and hands.

Recalling what the kidnapper had said, he then began rubbing his forearms against the wooden beam behind him. Knowing the beam had made scant headway into fraying the robust rope around his wrists, he knew it would be more successful cutting his skin. He grimaced and cursed, while scraping the skin of his forearms. But he continued, nonetheless, feeling the wood scuffing and tearing into his flesh. Wincing through grinding teeth, he stopped only when he felt the blood trickling down each arm toward the wrist ligatures.

He took a deep breath in anticipation of facing his fears head on. The odds were firmly against success, but it was the best option he could muster in the circumstances. True, they may not be partial to beef and onion crisps, but from what his taker had said earlier about meat, just maybe, they'd come for his blood.

He feared he was finally cracking up as a question arose that he never thought he'd ask himself.

How do you beckon rats?

Chapter Thirty-Seven

Bardsley's pleas to Stockley had resulted in a vacant stare from the DI, the knockback about finishing for the night not quite "fuck off", but may as well have been. He'd been designated to take a statement from the occupants of the terraced house beside the alley of the first scene, as apparently they'd "heard a kerfuffle". Just as he was about to knock on the door, his mobile rang to the tune of 'You'll Never Walk Alone', the anthem of Liverpool FC. One of the uniforms protecting the scene threw him a dirty look, obviously a United fan.

Bardsley answered it.

"Hi, is that Eric Bardsley?"

"Yeah, who's this?"

"It's PC Ben Davison, the one from the scene in the park where—"

"Yeah, I know who you are, Ben. What's up?"

"You need to come home. There's been an incident at your house."

"What? Is Maggie okay?"

"She's fine, just a bit shaken."

"What's happened?"

"You've been burgled. Just get down here and I'll wait for you."

"I'm on my way."

"You're not going anywhere. What about that statement?" asked Stockley, breaking off a conversation with one of the SOCOs.

"Gotta go, Boss. I've been burgled."

"I need that statement."

"I *need* to see my wife!" he shouted, heading up the road to his Astra.

"Bardsley... Bardsley! BAAARSDLEY!"

***

Frustratingly, and unsurprisingly, the rat idea was proving to be the long shot Striker had suspected it to be. He'd heard them shuffling about, but none had been bold enough to come his way as yet. He'd even tried to play dead, having recalled one being up close the last time he'd come round, but still no joy. The sneaky buggers were obviously cleverer than he'd given them credit for.

In his desperate state, he obviously wasn't thinking straight, his thoughts a jumbled mess. His head was still throbbing from all the knocks he'd taken, though somehow he was becoming accustomed to the pain.

He heard faint footsteps. The line of light around the door's seam shadowed slightly. A key turned in the door. He turned his head away to soften the flooding light.

"Just checking you've not had any silly ideas, Striker."

It was him again, the same voice. Striker looked up and saw the handgun in silhouette. The man still wore a face mask, and this time Striker got a glimpse of his skin below the eye. *Caucasian. Narrows it down further. Every little helps.*

He shined a torch around the room that Striker was increasingly convinced was a cellar. *The ripped crisp box!* The torch soon found it.

"You should've said you were hungry. I'd have cooked you one of the rats. Met 'em yet?"

Striker nodded. *Surely he wouldn't guess Striker's desperate plan. It was too ridiculous.* "Thirsty and bored shitless."

"And that's how you'll stay until I'm done." He moved a few paces forward, still checking with the torch.

"Done what?"

"More questions. You can tell you're a detective."

Striker wasn't lying about being bored. He was sick of tip-tapping around this nutter's stupid game. "Until you've finished killing more young men?"

"You think I'm that killer off the news, don't you?"

"Yeah, why else would you kidnap me?"

"Maybe *you've* wronged me in some way."

Striker didn't like his matter-of-fact tone. He was seriously beginning to doubt whether he'd actually get out this alive. He needed this bastard up close.

"I've never intentionally 'wronged' anybody."

"Maybe not intentionally."

More games. Come closer so I can trip you up and rip your bloody throat out with my teeth. "Don't suppose you could slacken these ropes off a bit could you? They're a just a touch uncomfortable."

"Suppose not. Not arsed about your comfort."

"So remind me then, about me wronging you."

"Let's just say that not much has changed, has it?"

"Meaning?"

"Well, just look at the case you're on now. You've not caught the offender for that either. A common theme running throughout your career."

"You're talking crap. I've got an excellent conviction record."

"Talking crap, eh?"

More anger. Come on, closer. If this guy was the killer, then Striker felt certain he wouldn't kill a cop because from the letter he seemed to have some sort of warped moral values. Come closer...

The alternative was to be all submissive and compliant. But Striker didn't do submissive and compliant. "Yeah, complete crap."

"You cocky fucker," he spat.

Something clicked in Striker, a giant penny dropping. "So which of Lenny's brothers are you then?"

The gunman exploded. "Now you've really left me no choice!" he yelled, pointing the pistol at Striker.

Then he fired two shots.

Chapter Thirty-Eight

Bardsley had quickly returned to the nick and parked up the Astra, before getting into his Fabia and speeding to the outskirts of the division in record time. He was warned by supervision against living so close to the division in which he worked, but with less travel time it compensated somewhat for the usual long hours. Anyhow, the local dicks were separated just enough from his newish estate on the border of Stockport, it being set back on a hill. With one road in and out, the only people that entered were residents or legitimate visitors, so anyone from the estate would stand out like a tramp at a black tie event.

He passed Ben Davison's panda and pulled onto his driveway, swinging open the driver's door before he stopped. Within a few seconds, he'd clocked one of the small panelled windows smashed on the back door and went inside. Davison was sitting at the pine kitchen table, taking a statement from Maggie, who was opposite in her dressing gown, her head dipped.

"You okay, love?"

They both looked up, Davison nodded.

Eyes bloodshot from crying, Maggie said, "Yeah, yeah am fine, Eric," unconvincingly.

"Did you see anyone? What've they taken?"

Davison answered. "Margaret didn't see anyone, just heard them. She's a bit shaken. We're just going through what might be missing, but up to now that amounts to nothing."

"Nothing? Did you disturb them, Maggie?"

"I must have done, if they've not nicked anything," she said half-heartedly.

Something didn't feel right. Maggie looked sheepish. "I'll take a look around."

Five minutes later, Bardsley was back in the kitchen. He purposely watched Maggie as he spoke. "Nothing missing that I can see. Strange burglars these. Going to the trouble of breaking in, then stealing nothing."

"They must've heard me get up and call the police. That's all I can think of."

"That's a result then, of sorts, eh Eric?" said Davison, taking a sip of the brew Maggie had obviously made him, in Bardsley's favourite Liverpool FC mug. He'd let Davison off, knowing the lad wasn't into football.

It just didn't feel right. Twenty-five years of marriage and he still couldn't tell if his own missus was lying or not. *Some bloody detective I am!*

"Suppose so. As long as you're okay, Mags," was all he could muster.

"Can I finish the statement, Eric?"

"Yes, of course, Ben. I'll do a fresh brew. Coffee okay?"

"Please."

Davison turned to Maggie. "So you were in bed asleep when you heard this noise…"

In bed asleep? The paranoia started again. *Why didn't she answer her mobile earlier? Was she in bed with him?*

Bardsley flicked the kettle on and then went upstairs. Entering their room, he could see the bed covers were a little ruffled. He checked underneath the bed and pulled back the duvet – nothing untoward. He studied the carpet and saw that the beige had turned slightly pink as if something had been spilt and rubbed dry. He bent down and sniffed the stain. Initially, all he could smell was a slight mustiness, but he kept sniffing. There was a hint of the familiar metallic scent that all cops knew.

Back in the kitchen, he finished making three coffees and plonked two on the pine table, Davison still writing away, not noticing Bardsley had switched his cup to a plain old brown one. Despite nothing being taken, there was always paperwork to do.

"Did he come into the bedroom, Maggie?"

She looked startled. "Who?"

"Who? The burglar, of course. Who else?"

Avoiding eye contact, she said, "No, no. I stayed there till PC Davison arrived."

"Well, what's that reddish stain upstairs beside the bed?"

"Oh, that?"

"Yes, that."

"That's just some red wine I spilt."

"Since when have you been drinking red wine alone in bed?"

"Not often. Just now and then."

Was she blushing? "And, why didn't you answer the phone

earlier?"

She sipped her coffee, then said, "It was on charge."

"Was the landline on charge too?" No response. Bardsley turned to Davison. "Take it you're calling SOCO out?"

"Erm, there's nothing specific for them, except the glass samples I suppose, but I could take them."

"Call them out, Ben. They can take a sample from the carpet while they're here."

"Why? No one came into the bedroom," insisted Maggie.

Bardsley's eyes fixed on his wife. "Why? Because I don't believe it's red wine. I think it's blood."

***

Bardsley watched through the living room window as Davison pulled away in his panda. Feeling deflated, he turned to Maggie, who was sat on the sofa, looking like a naughty schoolgirl outside the head teacher's office.

Bardsley glanced above the mantelpiece at the photo of them both on their wedding day. He turned to his wife, cursing his heart for still loving her, despite his growing suspicions.

"You worried about the results of that carpet stain once it's been analysed?"

She looked up, her face harder than usual. "Not at all. It's just wine, Eric." Maybe he was being irrational, his suspicious mind, honed at work, now bleeding into his marriage more than ever. It had always been there, although perhaps now he was going over the top with this wonderful woman with whom he'd shared a quarter of a century. Together they'd reared three children, who'd blossomed into responsible adults any parent would be proud of.

"I'm going to bed, Eric. I feel drained with all this. You coming up?"

He looked at her, unable to think straight. "No. Think I'll stop on the settee for now, love."

***

Bardsley stirred as his mobile's tune persisted. He felt as though he'd only had an hour's sleep and, realising he was on the settee, his first thoughts were of Maggie.

He reluctantly reached out to the coffee table and answered the phone, grumbling a croaky, "Hello."

"Bardsley, it's DI Stockley. We need you back at the nick. We have a serious problem. How soon can you make it?"

"Huh? Why, what's up?"

"Lauren Collinge has been reported missing."

"What?"

"When did you last see her?"

Wake up! He couldn't tell him because it would compromise Jack and his unofficial investigation. "Er... Let me just get a brew and I'll be down."

"Scrub the brew. Get down here, and quick."

"Who's reported her missing?"

"Brad Sterling. Now, hurry up." The DI terminated the call.

Brad Sterling? What's going on?

After a quick rinse of his face and a gargle in the kitchen sink, Bardsley fired up his Fabia and was on his way.

He lit a Benson and opened the driver's window, the cool night air waking him fully. As he drove through the virtually deserted streets, except for the odd taxi dropping off revellers from town, he tried to make sense of Stockley's revelation. How could Lauren be missing? He'd left her and Jack at the temple. Had something gone wrong there? Had he completely misjudged the importance of Jack's secret op? Maybe there was more to that place and that VOICES group than he'd initially thought. Or had Lauren and Jack finished up there and gone home, and then something had happened to her? How did Brad Sterling know she was missing? He was CID cover for the night, so would have been at work.

He tapped in the code into the keypad that lifted the barrier. Pulling into the nick, he felt rather foolish that he'd assumed Lauren and Jack had finally 'got it on'. So where the hell was she?

He parked up, jogged to the rear door nearest to their part of the building before typing in another code. Once inside, he went through another security door and took the stairs two at a time. Out of breath, he entered the MIT office. Surprisingly, for such a late hour, there were numerous officers bustling about – some on phones, others in deep conversation. He saw Stockley talking to Cunningham and Brennan at the far end of the room and made his way over.

Slightly out of breath, Bardsley asked, "Sir, what's happened?"

Brennan turned to him. "Thanks for turning out, Eric. DC Collinge hasn't been seen since nineteen hundred hours last night."

She has. Just get a feel for things first. "Isn't she at home asleep?"

"Clearly not, Bardsley. That's why we've all turned out." Cunningham, true to form, making him feel like a dick.

"When did you last see or hear from her?" asked Brennan.

Bardsley hesitated, smoothed a hand across his beard. "Can I just ask why Brad Sterling reported her missing? How would he know?"

"Why are you stalling? Tell us!" Brennan sounded impatient.

"I need to know, then I'll tell you."

"I don't like your attitude here, Bardsley. We haven't got time for games." Brennan eyed him. They all did.

"Please, it's important."

Brennan sighed. "Look, in brief, Sterling had arranged to call at Collinge's home before his night shift this evening, so went for a quick coffee and she's not been seen since."

Bardsley saw that Cunningham's face looked stonier than usual, if that was possible, and noticed Stockley watching her too.

"Okay, sir, but how do you know she's definitely missing?" asked the DC.

"Dennis, you don't have to explain yourself to him," said Cunningham sharply.

The detective superintendent exhaled audibly, looking vexed. "Being honest with us, Sterling told us he'd arranged for them to meet up if things got quiet at work, and Collinge said that she'd definitely call him in any case. But she didn't, so when Sterling went round, she wasn't there. And her family have no clue either. So, tell us what you know, Eric. NOW!"

She simply has to be with Striker. Perhaps they did hook up after all. "It's awkward, sir."

All three glared at him, eyes widening. "Bardsley, what are you hiding?" asked Cunningham.

Maybe something had *happened at the temple.* "With respect, sir, I just don't wanna drop anyone in it… but I think she's with Jack Striker."

***

Bardsley drove Stockley, the sulky-looking Sterling and a uniformed officer from the night shift, toward Striker's city centre apartment. He was cursing himself for having to actually do this, despite being left with no option.

He pulled into the street of the Striker's home and, on seeing the sign post, he felt fleeting warmth at the sight of his birthplace's name: *Liverpool* Street.

Knowing it was a private car park with a key fob system, Bardsley parked on the street at the front of the trendy apartment block. The Beetham Tower loomed large at the top of the street, much bigger than Bardsley had remembered, most of its lights now off due to the early hour.

"Right, bring the wham-ram," said Stockley to the constable in the rear as they all got out of the Astra.

"What do you need that for?" asked Bardsley, pointing at the heavy steel implement used for forcing entry.

"I'd have thought that would be obvious."

"You can't go smashing Jack's door in."

"If he doesn't answer, then I'll do it with—"

"Pleasure?" Bardsley finished the DI's sentence for him, but Stockley didn't respond. Bardsley shook his head. "He'll be in… with Lauren," Bardsley said, hopefully. He glanced at Sterling, who looked away, clearly worried about what they might discover.

Having had time to think and come to his senses more, he'd recalled that neither Lauren, nor Jack, had answered their calls. This, along with the dubious op at the temple, then Lauren being reported missing, made him doubt whether they'd now be in bed together. Perhaps he'd been naive, missed something crucial, like he had done with Maggie. Maybe he was losing his sharpness or, God forbid, just getting old.

Either way, he'd dropped his mate in it. Striker could be caught sleeping with someone from his team, which wasn't exactly the crime of the century, yet even so it may be construed as unprofessional and at the very least would be fuel for the gossipers. Or, Jack's secret op could become common knowledge, which would be a whole lot worse for all three of them. It was a lose-lose situation. Bardsley prayed Jack would just answer his door.

After they'd climbed the six outer steps to the apartment's communal entrance, Stockley asked, "What number?"

"He lives at flat twelve on the second floor."

Stockley pressed number twelve repeatedly on the keypad, creating a low buzzing sound. A minute of pressing passed and he started trying the other buzzers. After a few minutes, the voice of a woman, clearly half asleep, answered.

"It's the police. Can you let us in please?"

"Oh, erm… hang on a minute…"

Bardsley saw a room light up on the first floor above them and the curtain was pulled aside discreetly, a woman's face peering briefly. A moment passed, then the communal door released with a buzz. Stockley opened it and they followed him in; the officer carrying the wham-ram, rather awkwardly because of its weight, entered last.

Inside it was plush, a spotless cream carpet and matching walls. They passed sixteen pigeon holes to the left and a notice board to the right, sparse but for a couple of posters about city centre events. They were soon up the carpeted stairs and standing outside number twelve. Stockley banged on the door three times.

Nothing.

He knocked another three times, throwing looks at the others. Normally they'd opt for the letter box next, but there wasn't one. Bardsley had seen that each resident was designated a pigeon hole down in the communal hall for post.

"Right, Constable. Wham-ram it."

"Steady on. Give him time to answer."

"We need to find DC Collinge," Stockley snapped, before moving aside as the officer holding the wham-ram edged into position and began checking the door for the appropriate point of impact. Sterling donned a look of concern a few paces back.

Bardsley banged on the door a further six times. There was

still no answer. "Can't we try the neighbours first?"

"No. Now move," ordered Stockley, with a poorly disguised glint in his eye.

Bardsley stepped aside as the uniform moved in, carrying 'the Enforcer'. There were several types of wham-ram, including the dual device, but this was the easiest to carry and was most officers' preferred option. The constable pointed at his chosen spot, two thirds up the door beside the keyhole. His face a picture of concentration, he gritted his teeth as he lined it up and did a mock run, slowly swinging the Enforcer back and forth to the desired point.

Bardsley rubbed his beard, watching the officer, who glanced at him saying, "They don't call me 'One Arrow Aaron' for nothing, you know." Aaron impacted the door with everything he could muster and, after the loud crash of splintering wood, Aaron nearly followed the Enforcer into Striker's apartment, a satisfied look on his face. The door had almost split in two and hung at an angle on one hinge.

"If they weren't awake, then they will be now," said Stockley as the officers poured in.

Bardsley headed down a corridor full of framed police commendations and certificates, as well as a collage of Striker's kids, Beth and Harry, while the others took a room each. He knew, from previous visits, where Striker's bedroom was. He heard Stockley shouting, 'clear' intermittently, on checking rooms. Bardsley tentatively opened the bedroom door, aware of Sterling peering from behind him.

He viewed Striker's bedroom, turned to see Sterling's face showing a glimmer of relief that soon transformed to panic. The empty double bed was far too neat to have been slept in. Bardsley instantly thought back to the temple.

Now he would have to tell them everything.

Chapter Thirty-Nine

PC Ben Davison was peeved that he hadn't been allowed to go to the Lakes today to propose to Louise. It was symptomatic of the Job that all rest days had been cancelled because of this serial killer on the loose, which was understandable considering the latest unprecedented development. Two officers were officially missing, sending shockwaves through GMP. Most of the night shift were being utilised for an op run by Mr Halt. That was as far as Davison's knowledge of it reached, for it had been classified as restricted info.

Everyone at the nick was growing increasingly concerned about the officers, the attractive DC Lauren Collinge and her decent boss, Jack Striker. Davison liked the DI, who obviously hadn't forgotten his roots like some, having been true to his word about telling Sergeant Roach about Davison's good work at the scene of the park murder. Subsequently, Roach had promised to submit a report to Mr Halt to consider Davison for a divisional commander's award. Hopefully *that* would impress Louise!

However, on the downside, Davison had been asked – or told – to do a night shift and he expected a late finish. Okay, so the overtime would come in handy, especially if Louise said yes, but he was running short of leave and wondered when would he actually get a chance to have a social life. Because of the shifts, his erratic sleeping patterns and the drain of being a cop, he'd hardly seen Louise at all recently. He was starting to understand why so many cops separated from their partners.

He envisaged himself proposing, down on one knee, top deck of a boat on a Lake Windermere that was glistening in the Cumbrian sun amid the backdrop of stunning mountains. Nervous at messing it up, *and* the outcome, he'd played it in his mind a hundred times.

"Louise, we've been together for two years now… We've had some wonderful times together… I'm not one for sharing my feelings, but when it comes to you… well, I… want to share the rest of my life with you… Will you marry me?"

One of the boat's crew looked on from the cabin, his finger

poised on a CD player waiting to unleash 'Congratulations', while another furtively lit the sparklers on a cake. The many tourists on the upper deck looked his way, cameras at the ready, secretly clutching party poppers, some smiling, staring agog…

Louise flicked a hand through her sunlit blonde hair, a stunned look on her face that flickered with a hint of confusion. "I'm very flattered, but just remind me who you are again…"

A lone vehicle shook him from his musings, suddenly appearing with a squeak of tyres from a side street, the driver clearly in a rush. He accelerated the panda and saw that despite him doing 40 mph, the black hatchback was still pulling away, probably twenty above the speed limit.

Davison cranked up the revs to sixty, flicking on his blues 'n' twos, a rush running through his body. He closed in on the car, trying to identify its make and model, squinting in a fruitless attempt to see the registration mark.

Mindful of the force's policy on pursuits, he assessed his surroundings and then pushed the hands-free button on the panda's gearstick to alert comms via his vehicle's radio set.

He shouted over the klaxons, "One treble-eight six, control."

"Go on, Ben," said civilian Maureen Banks, his favourite comms operator.

"Vehicle making off at speed… Moss Range Road… heading north… toward the city… it's a black hatchback… no further description… standby…" He gripped the steering wheel and eased the accelerator pedal down.

"What's your speed, Ben?"

"Oh, er, sorry, Mo. It's sixty-five. The limit's fifty here. Dual carriageway."

"Repeat, Ben, all I got was your two-tones."

"Sixty-five… six, five… received?"

"Gotcha. Road conditions?"

"Slightly wet, but it's stopped raining. Traffic's very light, no pedestrians."

"What's it done, Ben?" It was Bob the Dog, interrupting.

"It's just made off on seeing me."

"Mo, I'm en route from Bullsmead Road."

"Received, Bob. Any VRM yet, Ben?"

"Standby!" Davison hit seventy and began to close in on the

hatchback.

Thirty metres away. "One occupant, looks like a male."

"Keep it coming."

Twenty-five metres. "Part VRM: mike, kilo, zero, eight…"

"Got it. Did you say male driver?"

"Affirmative." Davison eased his foot to the floor, seeing hazy streetlamps and houses whizz past in his peripheral vision. Twenty metres. "Seventy-three miles per hour."

"DI Stockley, control. Back off, Davison, I'm calling this pursuit off."

"Ben, did you get that?"

"Juliet, victor, yankee."

"Received, but DI Stockley said you've to end the pursuit, Ben."

"End it, Davison. You've breached force policy. That's an order!"

"Sir, he's slowing down… fifty-seven… vehicle taking a left, left onto Richmond Road… temporary loss…"

"Four double-zero seven, about five minutes away."

"Received, Bob. Sir, can they continue?"

"What speed?"

"Ben?"

"Only thirty-five… right, right onto Boldman Street…"

"DI Stockley?"

"Okay, continue."

"Mike five, making the area."

"Nice one, we may need a van. Ben, that VRM comes back to a Skoda Octavia in white."

"Vehicle stopping, Boldman Street."

"Four double-zero seven, four minutes away."

"It must be on false plates, Mo. It's a VW Golf GTI in black."

***

The last thing he wanted to do was kill a cop.

But his work for tonight was not yet complete. With the cops closing, it had been imperative that he'd made the jump to the last batch on his list, the ones that the police could actually find a link to. It wasn't a problem, as he knew a conflict situation was always in a state of flux. He was adaptable and nothing would stop him from completing his mission. The midlist scumbags would be the fortunate ones, for now. They were just mere irritants, stains on society. He simply couldn't risk being caught before the ones who really mattered had been dealt with, particularly after last night's turn of events and the little predicament he now found himself in.

He sighed and stared up at the wispy clouds snaking past the moon, as the lone officer got out of his patrol car. Blue lights flashed around, bouncing off the two large industrial buildings, between which he'd purposely stopped on the deserted street. Checking his mirrors, he watched the officer edging toward him.

He slipped the knuckleduster onto his right hand and checked the baton was in position up the left sleeve of his coat. He calmly placed his man bag into the footwell of the passenger seat. The Glock 17 would remain in the glovebox, for now.

The officer was bound to react on seeing that he was wearing a balaclava. Checking his wing mirror, he saw that the cop was up close, just a few paces away.

He swung open the door, into the cop, knocking him sideways. He leapt out of the car, throwing a straight right, the knuckleduster impacting the cop's left cheekbone. He instantly flicked the baton from his left sleeve and clicked it open. Still on his feet, the stunned cop reached for his CS gas, but the baton was already crunching into his collarbone. The metal fist followed up with a nose-bursting blow and the cop fell to the ground.

He stood over the young constable, whose eyes rolled back. No resistance remained. He stooped down, unclipped the noisy radio from the body armour and threw it twenty metres down the road. The desperate concern in the woman's voice faded and the radio clattered in the distance as it landed then skidded to a stop.

Another police car exploded into the street, wheel-spinning to a stop with a handbrake turn. The occupant, a much older officer, was already rushing out, clutching his baton and yelling in a Scottish accent, "Urgent, back up! Officer down, Boldman Street. Get an ambulance."

The cop was just five metres from him, so he turned and

headed for the Golf. The door still open, he dived inside and reached for the glove compartment. As he felt his legs being grabbed, he fumbled for the Glock.

"Ben, it's alright, pal," roared the cop. "I've got the bastard."

He kicked out, buying crucial seconds. Forcing himself round, he faced the oncoming officer, pointing the handgun at his forehead, stopping him dead.

"You've 'got' no one. Now back the fuck up."

The dogman's face hardened, but he didn't move, just froze, glaring.

"You deaf, Constable? Don't make me do it."

The old cop stared into his eyes. "I guess you're Him, aren't you? They're gonna catch you. Don't make it worse for yourself. Just give me the gun." His voice was surprisingly unwavering.

"Not a chance. I've not finished yet. Now, move away, old timer, or you'll never get to see your pension."

The veteran slowly retreated, holding the stare. "So now you've gone from attacking scumbags to assaulting police instead? You're gonna lose that public sympathy if you're not careful."

"Stop trying to stall me. You lot are just in my way. It's nothing personal. Now go help your mate." Hearing more sirens approaching, he slammed the door, fired up the Golf and screeched off.

Chapter Forty

The metal barrel beside Striker had two gunshot holes spouting liquid, bizarrely reminding him of an old western he'd once seen starring Clint Eastwood. The sudden hiss of liquid had drenched Striker completely. His ears were still ringing from the bullets that had very nearly taken off his face. His heart was palpitating faster than he thought possible. Experiencing the gun's discharge close up reminded him of Lenny being shot all those years ago, and the piercing bangs still resounded in his ears, doing his headache no favours.

Thankfully, either the gunman was a lousy shot or Striker's theory of the man not wanting to kill a cop was correct. Either way, he'd certainly made his point, and some. The latter was the most probable, as the way he'd held the pistol was textbook, with the opposite wrist supporting the firing hand. Striker didn't doubt this man's dexterity of aim and he was almost certain this man was the killer. With that in mind, Striker simply had to escape, and quick or he'd probably end up as rat food. He struggled to shake those unforgettable scenes from Herbert's rats trilogy from his weary mind.

His guess at his kidnapper's possible identity had clearly hit a nerve. If Striker was correct, then who knows what a desperate man would do next for self-preservation, even if cop killing was against his moral code.

Once the rounds were discharged, the gunman's silhouette had disappeared through the door, the ensuing darkness and solitude engulfing Striker again as the door slammed shut, offering him a strange solace. The only sound was the flow of the liquid from the barrel that was slowly diminishing in intensity.

Striker was drenched, but wasn't too bothered since he recognised the smell of the liquid and licked his lips. He smiled, then leaned over and let the tiny waterfall pour into his gaping mouth, savouring its refreshing taste as his thirst was welcomingly quenched. He'd lost all sense of time. His eyes had adjusted better than he'd thought to his new place of residence – albeit temporary, he hoped.

Again, he pondered Lauren and her possible whereabouts.

Was she also tied up in some cellar somewhere? Or worse? He dismissed the thought, unable to handle it. And what about Copeland? Were Striker's colleagues still wasting time hunting him, while Striker was stuck in this godforsaken shit hole?

His predicament, combined with his scrape with possible death, had made him feel a little emotional, philosophical even.

His children had been at the forefront of his mind throughout the conscious hours of his incarceration. A tinge of guilt jabbed him, a reminder from within that they should have been paramount in his thoughts always, not just now. Nonetheless, he'd been pushed out by Suzi – admittedly after his own regrettable dalliance – and had since thrown himself deeply into his work. And now, with her lover Bannatine on the scene, Striker felt even more distance between them than ever before.

He cursed. The liquid behind him became a trickle and his mind drifted toward his mum. He wished he'd met up with her more often for a brew and a chat. Good old Mum. The only one who'd forgiven his shortcomings throughout the family feud that had erupted after Lenny was shot. Striker's late father had been seriously peeved at having the cops sniffing around his family home. So much so that he'd chucked teenage Jack out into the big wide world, with those reverberating words: "Good bloody riddance!"

Those damn words had cut Striker deeply at the time. Three years later, just after he'd got himself a flat and become a police officer – basically to show Dad he wasn't worthless – the oak tree that was Harry Striker went and died on them. The melancholy surrounding his dad's sudden heart attack was deep-rooted.

The noisy liquid abated, the barrel now empty. His befuddled thoughts shifted and he began to ponder his precarious relationship with Lucy, wondering where it had all gone wrong. Perhaps he'd been too stubborn, like he'd been in the three years away from his dad, despite his mum's efforts to reunite them. He should have swallowed his pride much earlier, which may have prevented his big sis deteriorating into a life revolving around drugs with DJ.

He hoped he was wrong on that one, but he'd already met hundreds of so-called 'druggies' in his job and the signs were disturbingly evident: loss of weight, dishevelled appearance, spotty complexion and unpredictable disposition. Unfortunately, Lucy ticked all the boxes. If he could somehow wangle his way out of this mess, he would make a concerted effort to help her.

He'd heard before of people staring death in the face and somehow coming through with renewed purpose, then righting all the wrongs in their life. What he would give for that opportunity himself. He'd tragically missed that chance with his old man, and the profound sense of making Dad proud that he'd carried all his life had intensified rather than diminished since their bust up. Maybe it was time to concentrate on the living. Striker desperately wanted to be included in this philosophy too.

The concerned, craggy features of his dad looked serious in Striker's mind's eye: "Dig deep, son." He used to shout this to him from the sideline, whenever his junior football team was losing.

Striker took not only a deep breath, but also his late father's advice.

As far as he'd seen, when his abductor had visited him the room had no windows, and he felt sure of what type of cellar it actually was. When his host had shown his unique brand of hospitality a second time he'd learned more about the room's layout, it having been partially illuminated.

In the far corner was definitely an opening of some sort that almost certainly led to another room. The walls had no decoration and were just plain old brown brick in bad need of pointing. What struck Striker was the supporting wall that ran halfway down the middle. He was unable to see behind it; even so, it offered possibilities. The hefty supporting pillar, in line with the wall toward the far end, revealed a gap between the pillar and the wall. Hopefully it allowed access to the other side. The obvious hindrance was his ligatured wrist and ankles, which had been chafing with a vengeance, despite the cold liquid providing some relief.

Even considering his numerous aches, his senses seemed heightened, invigorated by the refreshing liquid he'd gulped, and simple logic told him at least the type of location, if not his exact whereabouts.

What had clinched it for Striker was the smell and taste of the liquid that perhaps he knew rather too well: his beloved John Smith's.

Maybe there was a God after all.

The irony being, to escape he would need all the Dutch courage he could muster. The bonus being, the spewed bitter had soaked the rope, enabling him to ease his wrists from side to side.

Chapter Forty-One

It must have taken Striker more than half an hour of frantic manoeuvring to finally slip his hands free from the ligature, then another ten minutes to free his legs. The relief was momentarily tangible, and now at least he would have a fighting chance.

He ached all over, so much so that his troubled mind didn't know which ache was worse: his pounding head, bloodied nose, sore chest or his abraded wrists and ankles. So he just concentrated, ignoring as best he could the stiffness in his legs and the dizziness. Arms outstretched in front of him, he lumbered toward the pile of boxes beside the room's supporting wall. More crisps. The many silver beer barrels, and the one he'd sampled earlier, had clarified beyond any doubt that he was in a cellar of an establishment that sold alcohol. He felt that in all likelihood it was the temple, as he'd seen a bar area through its windows – what must have been yesterday – when checking the place out with Bardsley.

The lighting was virtually non-existent and he'd felt around for light switches to no avail. He strained his eyes to see more, but was confronted by shifting shapes and shades of blackness. With his hands still outstretched, he edged tentatively forward, feeling the rugged brickwork for the gap between the wall and pillar. The only sounds, as much as he tried to stifle them, were his own footsteps and haphazard breathing, the latter dangerously loud, enhanced somehow by the gloom.

He felt cobwebs brush his face and hastily wiped them away. He heard scurrying in the far corner behind him. A prickle ran down the back of his neck, despite the rats not mattering quite so much now he was mobile. As he edged forward, he was mindful he could do with a makeshift weapon of some kind. Hopefully, something more effective than the cans of coke he'd used the last time he'd been confronted by a handgun in the Bullsmead newsagents years ago. He tried desperately to search for implements to assist an escape bid, anything, but the darkness was his enemy.

Something made contact with his left foot and rattled across the stone floor. He froze, winced. Groping blindly, he searched for the culprit as the noisy object clattered to halt.

A bloody tin lid! Fingers crossed he'd gotten away with it. Gingerly turning right, he finally entered the second section of the cellar behind the supporting wall.

A glimmer of excitement flickered inside him. High in the far left corner, he saw a rectangular beam of light, not too dissimilar to the door where his opponent had entered. The leakage of light, from what he hoped was a door of some kind, illuminated the cellar enough for him to see there was a direct route with no obstacles on this side of the wall.

He picked up the pace until he was standing below the hatch, where he realised the beer barrels came in and out. There was an old wooden sloping fixture in front of him, the hatch ten feet or so above. He saw a ledge beneath the hatch door, where the light was at its brightest and on which appeared to be three plastic crates of bottles. Alas, there didn't seem to be a handle or knob to open the hatch. A closer inspection was required.

It was then that Striker heard the footsteps.

***

There was no direct evidence, but the warrant application had been flowered up somewhat and the magistrate they'd awakened – with an initial phone call, then in person – had given them the green light. With it being an emergency, Mrs Grafton-Jones authorised it expeditiously, especially when being told about the two missing cops.

Halt had told Brennan, Cunningham and Stockley to continue with the murder enquiries, insisting on attending the strike on the temple himself. He was in the front passenger seat of a plain Mondeo being driven by Bardsley. They'd rustled together a team and conducted an impromptu briefing. In the back of the Mondeo was DS Becky Grant. They were directly behind three armed response vehicles, with another three double-crewed, liveried vans following, in case transportation of prisoners was required. Ambulance control were made aware and put on standby, if necessary.

Bardsley had informed all concerned about the temple's three potential exits: the obvious double doors to the front and the two separate rear doors.

The risk assessment was obviously high and all officers wore their body armour. No one was expected to be living at the temple, although they couldn't be sure of this, so had to be on alert for any eventuality. The current owner of the building, a local businessman who was unknown to the police, didn't hold a firearm's licence. He was apparently "away on business" and would be spoken to later if need be. Radio silence was to be maintained unless absolutely essential, until the strike commenced.

The right turn to the country lane was approaching so, as planned, Bardsley flashed his headlights. The ARVs turned into the lane and Bardsley followed, stopping amid the canopy of trees just short of the car park. The rest of the convoy remained behind him until given the all-clear by the armed officers.

The dozen firearms officers were to conduct an armed strike in – Halt checked his watch – two minutes.

"Just hang on here. And silence, remember."

The only noise for the next few moments was the distant whirring above from the force helicopter. They nearly all still referred to it as "India 99", but in 2012, like everything it seems, air support was centralised and became NPAS: National Police Air Service. Regardless, Bardsley knew any aerial recordings of the temple strike would assist immensely in a future court case and also that any escapees would struggle to outwit the chopper with its multi-million-pound dexterity, including the priceless heat-source camera facility.

"Go, go, go!" suddenly blasted out of their radios from the armed officers. Repeated bangs and smashing could be heard, along with shouts of "armed police!"

Bardsley exchanged glances with Halt as they waited, hoping.

The atmosphere in the Mondeo was morose. The half-hour wait had been longer than anticipated, but was understandable considering the temple's size and the amount of rooms to check. Plus, they'd not had time to obtain any plans of the building.

Their radios came to life: "Sergeant Rhodes to Mr Halt."

"Go ahead, Dave."

"Sir, the main building has now been checked. We've just an outside hatch to force, so we can check the cellar. There are officers on the inside too, but it seems the basement has several rooms. Then we'll check the spire and the area will be sterile."

"All received, thanks for the update," said Halt, his brow creasing. He turned to Bardsley. "Let's just pray Striker and Collinge are in that cellar."

Chapter Forty-Two

Striker headed toward the source of the footsteps, hastily clambering up the wooden beer barrel delivery fixture. However, halfway up he slid back down, his trainers still wet from the bitter. Redoubling his efforts, despite the aches from the beatings, he tried again, this time moving to the edge where he could partially grip the lip at the far right side of the fixture.

He heard muffled voices. The wood splintered in his hand and he stifled the sharp pain. He gripped tighter, pulling harder in order to reach the ledge at the top. There *was* a handle. He looked heavenward briefly before pushing upward on the hatch. It rattled, but didn't open.

Bastard! It was locked from the outside. He heard the voices, less stifled now as if passing the outside of the hatch, the odd word becoming intelligible. Quickly considering his options, he realised what he must to do.

It was risky, but he began rattling the hatch.

He just hoped his kidnapper didn't hear.

***

Twenty minutes later, their radios boomed into life. "All clear. All clear. Area safe."

Bardsley fired up the Mondeo's engine and sped forward, took a quick left and parked outside the front of the temple, amid the familiar crunch of stones under tyres. They all got out, seeing Sergeant Rhodes from Armed Response exiting the temple, holding his arms out and shrugging.

"Nothing, Dave?" asked Halt.

"No, sir. The cellar's empty. But there's still the spire to check."

"So the all clear was called early, then?"

"Well, the spire's window is out of view from here, so I thought it would be safe for you to come closer, sir."

"Okay, I'll have that."

Bardsley heard a firearms officer shout up on the radio for Halt. He passed the chief his radio.

"Halt speaking, go ahead."

"I think you'd best come up here, sir…"

***

After desperately clattering the hatch up and down, Striker soon realised the source of the voices and footsteps were intoxicated people returning home, possibly leaving the establishment itself. Their drunken ramblings faded into the distance.

He heard the key turn in the cellar door and punched the hatch three times in panic, banging it up and down about an inch each time. Then he lay flat, hoping he was out of view, but knowing he'd surely be found by his captor, regardless.

He heard the low repetitive thud of his heart. With his face flush to the narrow ledge beneath the hatch, every intake of breath drew in particles of dust, increasing the dryness of his mouth, dirt sticking to his blood-curdled face.

"What the fuck?" erupted from the shadows of the cellar.

Striker flinched. *Think, think, think…*

"There's no way out, Striker!" The voice was muffled, the tone clearly very pissed off. And its owner had a very good point.

He heard the sound of boxes being thrown around. He knew he had seconds to come up with something resembling a plan of action in order to survive. Carefully reaching for two bottles from the crate beside him, he clutched them in either hand, before lying face down again.

Impulsively, he placed one of the bottles of lager in his mouth and started to bite the aluminium top. The metallic grinding caused a shooting pain through his gums. He stopped for a second of respite before persevering, this time angling the bottle to gain more leverage. His head jerked back and lager spewed from the neck with a minimal hiss. He placed a thumb over the top and gave the bottle a rigorous shake until he felt the pressure build up against his thumb.

He sat up, carefully lifting the hatch the inch it would permit. The oozing light, possibly from a streetlamp, teased him. Another quick shake, then he jammed the neck into the inch gap, allowing the lager to spurt outside. He hoped this wasn't the temple as he prayed for more passers-by.

A circular beam of light flashed erratically on his side of the supporting wall, near the opening he'd used. Shuffling feet, clanging objects and crunching boxes echoed throughout the cellar.

Striker reached for more bottles and managed to get three out of the crate. The fourth one clinked and the torch beam shot across his eyes.

Footsteps approached, the growing voice louder. "There's a pig in 'ere. I can smell it."

Striker braced himself, clutched a bottle in either hand. The torch beam flashed around, randomly illuminating the room like a helicopter over a war zone; no doubt the artillery was to follow.

He saw the brief shape of the man as the torch darted round. A dozen feet way, edging closer. Was he carrying a weapon? It was hard to say, though Striker had to assume as much.

He sounded no more than few feet away now, close to the bottom of the wooden fixture. Striker could hear him panting like a wild dog. The torch beam pointed toward Striker, who instantly lowered himself flatter, hands over his head.

Striker cowered, feeling the air whoosh close to his ear. *He's swinging some kind of weapon.* Glimpsing the man's position beside the glare of the torch, Striker sat up and launched a bottle.

Surprisingly, it seemed to strike its target on the head.

A low groan was followed by a crash on the wooden fixture below Striker. Something clattered onto the floor.

Striker fleetingly considered rushing him and taking his chances. *Not yet.* He threw a second bottle and it smashed against the supporting wall. He threw a third that hit the shadowy figure as he got up, causing the torch to dance in the air, the bottle fizzing on the floor. The torch was directed for the floor. He was looking for the weapon, meaning he didn't have the gun.

Now!

A desperate madness gripped Striker as he grabbed bottle after bottle from the crate, blindly lobbing them into the darkness, the odd yelp on impact. He heard footsteps scrambling up the wooden fixture, bringing him to his senses. He jumped up, smashing a bottle onto the man's head. The judder of impact shot up Striker's arm and the neck of the bottle remained in his hand. The man crashed backward like a human skittle.

The torch shined directly into Striker's face and another whoosh zoomed toward him. He felt a vicious pain shoot across his left temple, accompanied by a flash of light in his eyes and suddenly felt nauseous and dizzy.

His attacker clambered back up the fixture. Striker desperately jabbed him in the face with the remains of the bottle, hearing a squelch and shriek. Then he lunged with his right foot and kicked the bastard back down.

Hearing banging from above, Striker was astonished to see the hatch suddenly jerk open, light flooding in, making him squint.

"Jesus Christ, Jack! Come on, mate."

A welcome hand reached out and Striker clasped onto it, clambering up through the opening and onto the pavement. Totally disorientated, he was pulled to his feet and guided to the open rear door of a car.

He didn't look behind him as he was bundled into the rear seats lengthways. A thrown object pinged off the car's bodywork. The car did a wheel spin and sped off.

Striker realised his top was dripping in blood from his head wound and just about managed to summon the energy to say, "Thanks, lads," before passing out.

Chapter Forty-Three

Bardsley followed Halt and Grant up the spiralling metal staircase to the highest point of the temple. They entered the room at the top, which had old decaying stone walls. The heavy wooden door had evidently been forced by the searching officers.

And there she was.

Lauren Collinge was sat on a shabby burgundy Victorian-style chair. Not quite Queen Victoria – her hair dishevelled, face grubby and solemn. The firearms officers were frantically undoing ropes attached to her ankles.

"Thank God," said Halt. "Lauren, you okay?"

Collinge looked up, half smiled nervously, tears in her eyes, her pride preventing their descent. Voice croaky, she said, "I am... now, sir."

"We found DC Collinge in there, sir," said one of the armed officers pointing at a cubbyhole, the small door hanging in pieces having been forced open.

Becky Grant was on her knees, placing an arm around Collinge's shoulder while whispering tender encouragement.

Bardsley made eye contact with Collinge, winked and then patted her gently on the back as he passed. He stooped to peer inside the cubbyhole, seeing it was cramped and dingy. There was an empty chocolate bar wrapper beside a cushion that matched the chair Collinge was currently sat on.

He turned back to her. "So that's where you were hiding, Lauren. The things people will do to avoid a bit of overtime."

Halt glared at him. "Bardsley, please!"

Collinge laughed and one or two of the armed officers joined in with chuckles, forcing Halt to mellow and just shake his head.

The firearms sergeant rushed in, carrying a bottle of water. "The ambulance is on its way and so are SOCO," he said, handing the bottle to Collinge, who began gulping it like she'd spent a day in the Sahara.

Bardsley studied a map on the wall, noticing red plastic markers pinned at various intervals. He looked closer, soon recognising a few street names in South Manchester. He rubbed his beard, studied it a little longer.

Halt cleared his throat. "Thanks gentlemen, could you please leave us for a few minutes?" The armed officers looked up, hesitated then filed out. Bardsley and Grant stayed.

Halt asked one of the exiting officers for sterile gloves and he reached into a pouch on his belt. Halt took the gloves and put them on. He began checking the drawers of an antiquated oak desk to the left as he asked, "Lauren, are you up to answering a couple of questions?"

She looked anxiously at Bardsley, wondering how much he'd told them. Bardsley nodded discreetly.

Halt clocked the look between them. "It's okay, Lauren, I know all about Striker's unofficial operation. It looks like the stubborn bugger was right with his hunch. However, I can't condone the way he went about it. Just hope we find him soon. Now tell me about this meeting."

Taking a sip of water, Collinge almost spurted it out. "What? Is Jack missing too?"

"Oh, sorry, Lauren. I didn't want to unduly worry you so soon. But unfortunately, yes he is."

She dipped her head, looking stunned. "Oh my God, I hope he's okay."

"He'll be fine. He's made of sturdy stuff is Jack," said Bardsley, hoping he was right.

Halt shoved a drawer shut and slid open another. "Now, about this meeting."

"Well, there were about twenty people there and they just went around the room introducing themselves by first name only, then saying why they were there. It was held in the temple's hall."

"Who was in charge?"

Bardsley studied the map while Halt continued checking the drawers as Collinge spoke, Grant wearing a sympathetic expression beside her.

"A guy called 'Danny' seemed to co-ordinate things, but there were a couple more bouncer types, whose names I don't know, who seemed to be involved. It was mainly men, some new and some who seemed to know the organisers. During the midway break, some of the men had a sort of sub-meeting while the bulk of those in attendance went to the bar or for a cigarette."

"Sub-meeting?"

"Yes, they appeared to be huddled together in a room at the back, sort of whispering. It may've been something and nothing, who knows?"

"How did you end up being kidnapped?"

She took another swig from the bottle. "As everyone was leaving, Danny asked me to come into that room at the back to sign the visitors' book and pick up some 'welcome literature'. I had no reason to think anything untoward was happening and I was going to tell DI Striker just that, when I was grabbed from the rear on entering the room. I felt a wet cloth across my mouth and nose then I awoke feeling very groggy in the darkness." She indicated the cubbyhole.

"Okay. Can you describe this 'Danny' character?"

"Sure. IC one, over six foot, stocky, dark wavy hair, pale complexion and he was definitely Mancunian. Had a bit of a beer gut, too."

"Don't suppose you recognised him?"

"Unfortunately not."

Bardsley's radio emanated from his jacket pocket: "Ambulance in attendance."

"Thanks, Lauren," said Halt. "You best get checked over. Can you walk or do you want them to come up?"

"I'll walk, sir," she said, getting up and looking instantly unsteady on her feet.

"Let me help you, Lauren," said Grant, placing her arm around Collinge's back.

Bardsley also assisted, hooking an arm under Collinge's armpit. "Sit down, Lauren. I'll get them sent up." Reading Halt's mind he said, "I know there's already been too many people on this crime scene, but it's best we get Lauren sorted, agreed?"

Halt nodded. "Sure."

They eased Collinge back onto the chair. Bardsley strolled over to the spire's window and looked out, seeing the ambulance and a firearms officer he recognised. He 'point-to-pointed' the officer via the radio facility to speak one-to-one, and requested that the paramedics come up. The car park lights had lit up the area and Bardsley tracked the bushes to the point where he was standing with Striker yesterday evening.

The crafty twat had been watching them.

Halt pulled out a black book from one of the six drawers and started carefully thumbing through it.

Bardsley turned to study the map on the wall again. "Sir, these red markers, they're the murder scenes."

Halt's gaze was fixed on the book. "I know. Look at this." He showed Bardsley two pages listing the names of known criminals. Bardsley scrutinised the list: some had 'ASBO' next to their names, others the name 'Josh', the rest 'Lenny'.

"Bloody 'ell, there's twenty-five on that list, sir."

"I know, and he's certainly done his homework. The first few are dead and then he seems to have made a leap to five of the six at the end of the list."

"He knew we were onto him," suggested Bardsley.

Then, it suddenly hit Bardsley like a smack across the face. He'd been the only one of the three detectives involved in Striker's little op who hadn't been 'shut up'. The killer must have been the one who'd broken into his home. Obviously looking for him, the cheeky bugger. But how did he know where he lived? Had he followed him home? Was he connected in some way? He thought about Striker's friends at the temple, his past and his friend who'd been shot years ago... *Lenny!*

"Kingston's the last one on the list," said Halt.

Bardsley pointed at a green marker on Kingston's address on the map. He swapped looks with Halt, saying in unison, "He's next!"

Halt took out his mobile. "I'll phone Cunningham and tell her to get a team together."

Bardsley took out his own mobile. "I'm checking on the missus."

Chapter Forty-Four

Striker heard muted voices, familiar yet distant.

The haze in his mind began to gradually clear and he became aware of the discomfort. His left shoulder and chest ached, his wrists, arms and ankles were sore. He had a biting headache and his nose throbbed. He'd felt better. He could smell antiseptic, or something similar, and had an odd medicinal taste in his mouth. A strong hunger pang rumbled in his belly. He struggled to open his eyes, though managed after a few moments.

"Jack, thank the Lord." Vera Striker looked heavenward and leaned in to hug her son.

"Mum," he croaked. "It's really good to see you." He felt a rare moment of warmth engulf him.

Vera pulled away, removing her glasses to wipe away tears with a handful of her lilac sweater, probably knitted by her own hands.

A nurse in a light green uniform who was easy on the eye smiled at him. "Mr Striker, do you mind if I do a few checks?"

"No, check away. And, please, call me Jack."

The nurse began, popping a thermometer in his mouth and rolling up the sleeve of his blue hospital gown. He wondered briefly if the nurse had changed him. His eyes were still somewhat hazy, his mind foggy. A myriad of thoughts began to cascade.

Still tearful, Vera said, "Suzi's been, Jack. She didn't bring the kids, but she sends her best wishes. She left those flowers."

Pleasantly surprised, Striker looked on the window sill and saw a bunch of red, yellow and white carnations in a vase. "Very nice of her." He turned back to his mum, realising he had a cannula in his left hand. "I'm sorry for not seeing you as much as I should have done. I promise I'll—"

The nurse looked at him and smiled as she checked his blood pressure.

"Oh, give over, Jack. You're a busy man. I know that. Your dad would have been proud of you, you know."

Striker felt emotion rising, but controlled it. "How long have I been in here?"

"Oh, a few hours, that's all."

"Am I at the MRI?"

"Yes, dear."

He saw Bardsley waving a bunch of grapes at the window outside the room, a daft grin on his face. The DC then raised a banana and his eyes widened, clearly eyeing the nurse's pert bottom.

Vera looked round and Bardsley instantly changed to sensible. "Do you want me to leave you to it?" she asked.

He felt awkward, though he did need to speak with Bardsley as soon as possible. "If you don't mind, Mum. I really appreciate you coming. It means a helluva lot to me. How will you get home?"

"Oh, erm, Albert brought me," she said sheepishly.

"Albert?"

"From the church… he's just a friend," she said, a little too hastily.

The nurse pretended not to listen, but Striker saw her hesitate while she filled in a chart that had been clipped to the bottom of the bed.

"Mum, it's okay with me, honestly. Dad's long gone."

"It's not like that, he's just a friend. Really."

He smiled.

"Oh, and Lucy sends her love."

"Really?"

"Really."

"How's Deano?"

"Oh, of course, you don't know. He's come round now."

He felt a surge of relief. "That's great news."

"The doctor said he should make a full recovery. Your friend's been talking to him I think."

Striker looked at Bardsley, who was now exaggeratedly eating the grapes.

Vera got up and gave Striker a peck on the cheek. "It's great to have you back, Jack. Now, you just look after yourself and get well, okay?"

"I will, Mum. Thanks for coming. I'll take to you Mario's café for a meal soon. Promise."

"Now that would be nice." Vera Striker nodded, turned and

waved once she reached the door. She left, being replaced by Bardsley, who was blatantly ogling the nurse.

"I'll leave you to it, Mr Striker. Could you please take these?" She passed him two white tablets and pointed at the bedside table where there was a jug of water and a glass.

"Sure." He felt the bandages on his head. "So I take it I'm good to go soon?"

"Not yet, Mr Striker. I'll tell the doctor you're awake." She smiled sympathetically as she left with Bardsley's eyes burning into her bottom.

"Okay, cheers."

"You look like shit, Jack."

"Thanks, Eric. I love you too."

Bardsley tossed the grapes and banana onto the bed. "Fame at last, eh, DI Jack Striker?"

"Huh?"

"You've been all over the news, mate."

"Have I? Great. Now every bloody scrote in the country knows I'm a cop." His mind was slowly clearing and just seeing his sidekick had started the investigative cogs turning again. Still, his time incarcerated was, so far, only coming back to him in brief flashes. He recalled the overwhelming, panicky feeling of being trapped... snippets of conversation with the kidnapper... his deep, matter-of-fact voice... being shot at... the rats... the dreams and reminisces...

"Before you ask, we've found Lauren and she's fine."

"Thank God for that." More relief flooded him. "Where?"

"In a cubbyhole, up in the temple's spire."

He thought for a moment. "Was I in the temple's basement then?"

"No, Jack. You were in the cellar of the Wagon and Horses in Bullsmead. Let me fill you in..."

Striker just stared and listened intently, still trying to gather his thoughts, piece things together.

"... I'll be honest, Jack. Initially I just assumed you were getting your end away with Lauren."

Striker raised his eyebrows, shook his head. "What do you take me for, Eric?"

"A red-blooded male? Anyway, I was wrong. Here, I've got

you a suit for when you're good to go." He tossed a bin liner onto the bed.

Striker opened it and saw a familiar charcoal grey Armani suit, light blue shirt, matching tie and black slip-ons. "You've been in my apartment, Eric?"

"Yeah, sorry, we had to force your door, mate. Stockley got a buzz out of that by the way."

"Bet he did."

"Watch your back with him, Jack. Especially now, he'll be jealous of you being proven right and stealing his thunder."

"I know. Don't worry, I can handle him… and Cunningham."

"Anyway, we still haven't a clue as to who the hell brought you here. Care to enlighten me?"

"Huh? Wasn't it you lot?"

"No, Jack."

"You were dumped next to an ambulance at the side of the hospital. The ambulance crew heard a continuous beep of a horn and got out. They found you on the pavement."

Striker was flabbergasted. He suddenly got a flashback of being bundled into a car, but the image evaporated before he could grab hold of it.

"Any ideas?"

"No."

"By the way, Syndicate Four caught up with Copeland. He was drinking with the tramps under Bullsmead arches. He protested his innocence, of course, and with the latest developments Halt authorised his release. He's threatening to sue us for harassment."

"I'm not surprised. What 'developments'?"

"I was at the temple with Halt and Becky Grant when the firearms search teams found Lauren in the spire. There was a map in the little office up there, detailing all the crime scenes and a black book listing the hits. So it looks like you were right about our man, Jack."

Striker sat up, pulling the tubes leading to the medicinal trolley with him. "I bloody knew it." He felt vindicated, although still wondered about repercussions from the brass. "But I guess Halt's gonna be pissed at me?"

"Not at all, Jack. Well, that's not the impression I got. I think he's looking at the bigger picture, and rightly so."

Striker nodded slowly, relieved. He'd have to fall asleep in hospital again soon, if all this good news was what he'd wake up to.

"Get this... there were twenty-five names on the list, so already you've saved a fair few lives. But do you know that one-eyed Kingston guy who's an independent advisor to the police?"

"Of course I do."

"Well, he's the last name on the list and Halt's got a team sat on his home address as we speak, just in case."

"Just in case?"

"Yeah, it's just precautionary to cover all bases. Can't see the point really."

"Oh, and why's that?"

He grinned. "Because we've got the bastard who kidnapped you both."

"You have?" *This is getting better and better.*

"Oh, yes. Danny Powers, the landlord of the Wagon and Horses. Lauren's identified him as the leader of the VOICES group from the temple."

"Brilliant. Makes perfect sense." He didn't mention that the man was Lenny's brother, but he guessed Bardsley knew of the connection. "And he has a military background right?"

"Well, actually, no, from what we can tell. Info has been scant on him so far and he's not talking at all."

Striker became momentarily quiet before saying, "So he's not in custody then, he's in hospital right? I recall shoving a bottle into his face."

"He's still in hospital under armed guard. What's made it more awkward is that the doctors are being a bit arsy because his face is such a mess. It's full of glass shards, apparently. You really did a job on him, Jack."

"He didn't do too badly with me either. Please tell me he's in *this* hospital, Eric."

"Yeah, but it's a fair walk from here. Right on the other side of the hospital. Why you asking?"

"I need to see him. Like you say, 'just in case'," said Striker, pulling the cannula from his wrist, clambering out of bed and starting to get dressed.

Within two minutes, after ignoring Bardsley's pleas, Striker was heading for the door. A Pakistani doctor donning a surprised expression said, "Detective Inspector, I need to check—"

"Sorry, doctor, I'm self-discharging. Thanks a lot for your assistance."

Bardsley shrugged at the doctor and followed Striker out of the ward.

"Which way, Eric?"

"Follow the signs for A 'n' E, if you must."

"I must."

Despite the plethora of aches, Striker started jogging. Three minutes later, they were approaching the Accident and Emergency Department.

"Now where?"

"Take a left then a right and you'll see them," said Bardsley, struggling to keep up.

Striker saw two firearms officers standing outside the entrance to a ward, clutching their Heckler and Koch MP5 submachine guns.

"Morning lads, DI Jack Striker, MIT." Realising he didn't have his warrant card, he waited for Bardsley. "He'll vouch for me."

"It's okay, sir. I recognize you," said one of the officers, opening the ward door. "Third door on the right."

"Thanks." Striker was halfway down the corridor.

"Jack! Wait, will you?"

He let Bardsley catch up and they both entered the room, where two more firearms officers were sitting, one reading a newspaper, no MP5s, just Glock 17s strapped to their legs.

A man in bandages sat in the bed, looking like a mummy.

"Hi, Danny. Sorry about the face. Did your brother put you up to this?"

He didn't reply.

"Lads?" Striker gestured with his head for the officers to leave.

"We're under strict instructions from Mr Halt not to take our eyes of him."

"Well, you were just reading the paper. Two minutes. It's important to the investigation."

They looked at each other and both nodded. "We'll be outside the door. Two minutes, right, sir?"

"Cheers, lads. But I may only need one."

Once they'd shut the door, Striker went in close. "Danny, I know you're no killer, but you're up to your neck in it, fella. Was it your older brother who kidnapped me?"

Still nothing.

"Jack, it's him. He was caught red-handed."

"Eric, Shut it!" He leaned right up to the arrestee's face. "Talk to me, Danny. Look, you'll get a fifteen stretch for kidnap and attempted murder and you'll only serve half that – unless, of course, you take the rap. In which case, you'll never see the light of day again. Was it your brother?"

He turned his head away.

Striker yanked at the bandages and pushed his fingers into Danny Powers's wounded face. "Talk to me, Danny."

"Aaargh! You fuckin' lunatic!"

The two firearms officers rushed in. "Sir, this is out of order!"

Striker probed again into Powers's face.

"Aaaaargh! I caaan't. He'll fuckin' kill me. He's outta control." Blood oozed through the bandages.

"Do you want me to do it again?"

One of the armed officers pulled out his Glock and pointed it at Striker. "Sir, I strongly recommend you stop this, now!"

"Aaaaargh! Yeah, it was our Vic, now fuck off, you headcase."

Striker released his blood-soaked hand. "Thank you."

Chapter Forty-Five

Vic Powers flipped the mobile phone in anger and tossed it onto the dashboard.

Still no answer. What the fuck was Danny playing at? He'd told him, in no uncertain terms, to keep his mobile charged and by his side at all times. Probably fell asleep. Or had he bottled it? It wasn't every day your brother asked you to look after a kidnapped cop without offering a decent explanation. "Trust me, Dan" probably wasn't sufficient under the circumstances. But his bro owed him big time, from all those favours over the years, especially when it came to clearing dickheads from his pub each time Vic had been on leave from Two Para. That 'Woody' character being the latest, as he'd unwittingly self-referred onto the original hit list of twenty-four.

By now, he suspected Danny probably knew what he'd been up to, particularly considering the abduction of two cops. Anyhow, if things went pear-shaped, he'd ensure he himself took the full blame and he'd tell the cops how he'd coerced Danny into assisting him.

Prison didn't scare him one bit, despite the cancer. He wasn't naive. He'd prepared himself for this eventuality, psyched himself up. It would be fun: he'd be like a kid in a sweetshop.

His eyes flicked from the Golf's rear-view mirror to the wing mirrors every few seconds as he powered through the Manchester streets, his overactive mind drifting…

… He recalled leading his weary mother, Edith into her seat beside Josh's fiancée, after the announcement that the magistrates had reached a decision. He hadn't been confident because the evidence had been largely circumstantial and witnesses scarce, obviously intimidated. What had wound him up from the start was that the case should've been manslaughter in his eyes, seeing as Josh's suicide was a direct consequence of him being jumped and beaten to a pulp by these fuckers.

The humdrum of the court room had waned and everyone stood up in respect as the magistrates took their seats. The head guy peered over his spectacles at him, Mum and the family as they sat praying for justice.

The five faces of the accused mirrored each other with glib looks. One even managed a smirk. Another eyeballed him and he held the gaze, electricity between them, until a court security chap clocked it and blocked his view.

Something about the way the head magistrate chose his words, plus the reluctant tone he'd used, suggested things were not good. When the head juryman delivered the verdict of not guilty – due to insufficient evidence – Edith physically slumped, along with his heart. The "whoop-whoops" of people in the gallery and the raised arms, sneers and leers from the five defendants high-fiving one another were as close to 'too much' as a man could take. All his powers of discipline and constraint were required.

Deep down, everyone associated to the case knew they were guilty, although proving it was obviously another matter. Detective Sergeant Jack Striker offered apologies to Edith, but she was too distraught and angry to acknowledge him as he slinked off to screw up yet another case, no doubt.

Powers had concentrated on the public gallery, at the standing people who were still cheering. And there he was, wearing his trademark eyepatch and grinning with an upraised fist of victory as his latest 'works in progress' escaped from justice: Kingston, the so-called reformed character, who served the community so well.

Yeah, right. He knew all about Kingston, the old Moss Range Crew leader who had become the darling of the media, a local figure offering hope within the community in the fight against gang warfare. He'd been on chat shows, in the papers and had been portrayed as a shining example of hope, proving a leopard could actually change his spots. Bollocks.

Just because a man had had a few kids and found God didn't mean he could fool everyone by suddenly becoming a good person. There were always consequences from actions, and Kingston would soon learn this reality.

From his extensive research, he'd discovered Kingston had been the one who'd pulled the trigger of the only Smith and Wesson pistol present at the scene of Lenny's shooting in Moss Range multi-storey all those years ago. The bullet in Lenny's skull had been from that same make of pistol, but the cops couldn't prove it. The intel had come from the streets, yet no one had the balls to testify in court.

He'd also been either linked to, or been a suspect in, two other shootings, one fatal. And now he was feeding his overinflated ego by parading himself to the public as some sort of messiah. Well, not for long.

He'd wanted Kingston to squirm; he always had to be the last. Doing him early would've brought obvious links and the others would've been spared poetic justice.

He was frustrated that some of the other ASBO pricks hadn't had their comeuppance, but he could live with that. The list of twenty-five was maybe pushing it, even for him.

He thought of those five smug faces in the dock: Castro, Big-un, Levi, Shanks and Chisel. Well, they weren't so fuckin' smug now, were they?

The ASBO boys, like Bolands, Dodger and Gartside, had been hit-listed to help the local community, in a much more effective way than Kingston professed to be doing. Plus, he needed to throw the cops off his true scent, letting them think someone was just randomly mopping up the streets of the scumbags blighting the community.

Apart from Chisel, he'd left all those that could've been linked back to him till last. Chisel just had to go early, though. He was a particularly nasty piece of work and a one-man crime wave. The bonus was that Gartside, Dodger, Shanks and Castro had been prime suspects in four separate murders recounted by members of VOICES. After the initial shock, he could see the hidden satisfaction in their eyes.

As he approached Kingston's home, he cursed at the sight of an unmarked police vehicle opposite, twenty metres down the road. They stood out like a black man at a BNP rally. He dropped into second gear and turned off along a side street, then accelerated away.

Why were they there? Were they onto him? Or was Kingston up to his old tricks again? And why wasn't Danny answering? The clock was ticking. What to do.

He'd play things cool, have a damn good think. He'd not arouse any undue suspicion by throwing a sickie. He'd go to work as normal and finish things off later, at Kingston's bullshit little community project.

***

Powers was pondering his next move regarding Kingston when Sergeant Thompson shouted him over.

Thompson, as ever, was sitting on a high chair in front of his computer terminal, police side of the long custody counter.

"Can you do the hourly visits, please, Vic?"

"No problem, Sarge."

Powers exited the staff office and opened the heavy metal door before heading down the corridor. He began checking each cell by peering through the spy holes.

He'd been working here for nearly two years since quitting the Paras after Josh had hung himself. He'd beaten himself up for not being there for the younger brother who he'd idolized back in the day. Pre-Kabul, he'd gone to as many snooker matches as he possibly could to support Josh, often taking his mum with them, until that fateful day when the Crew jumped him, ending his career and basically his life.

While out in Kabul, he'd had time to think it all through and discuss it with his no-nonsense buddies. The injustice of life, the way British society had deteriorated, the way the scumbags ruled the streets and how the authorities pussy-footed around. The public's fear was tangible and he knew someone would have to do something about it, using the only way he knew that worked. Fight violence with even more ferocious violence.

To glean the intel required, he knew the ideal job would be as a civilian custody clerk and he'd waited patiently for the opportunity for well over a year, while he planned his mission.

Admittedly, things had gone a little off track, but once he'd done Kingston, he'd go seriously low profile and reassess the situation. He'd have to release that tenacious bugger Striker and the young DC first, of course. Cop killing had never been part of the plan.

He'd been a little apprehensive about coming into work, but he could tell all was well here. However, there was growing concern that he'd not yet heard from Danny.

Striker hadn't made a big deal about his findings as he was sure Halt and the rest of the brass would've stopped him even entering the nick. After all, he was technically on gardening leave and should have still been in hospital. Nonetheless, he wanted to do this himself, his way, smoothly and with minimum fuss. Consequently, he'd deal with whatever the brass chose to throw at him.

Being in charge of the custody area, Sergeant Thompson had been told out of necessity, and the look of utter astonishment on his face still lingered. Striker had to dissuade him from his initial preference of involving the brass, saying they had no time to rustle up and brief a team before Powers got an inkling they were onto him.

Striker had made calls to Ben Davison and Bob the Dog after Bardsley had filled Striker in on the details of their altercations with Powers. Both officers had sufficiently recovered from their trauma and, despite being given the day off, had jumped at the chance of being involved in the arrest. Davison and Striker looked like 'the walking wounded'. Bardsley had been with Striker throughout, plus he'd had Powers sneaking around his house frightening Maggie. Meanwhile, Bob the Dog had nearly seen his dreams of retirement go up in smoke from Powers's handgun.

Yes, it was unorthodox, but so was Striker. And why the hell should the likes of Stockley and Cunningham get any credit when they'd done sweet FA on this case?

The main thing was the team he'd hastily assembled were trustworthy. The four of them, along with Sergeant Thompson, watched Powers on the CCTV monitors. He was walking around the cell block, somewhat ironically checking on the criminals' welfare. Thompson had sent Brenda the civilian custody clerk back into the staff office, saying that he needed to study some CCTV for a few minutes.

"Ready, lads?"

Davison, sporting a shiner any boxer would be proud of, clicked open his baton and flicked at the press studs of the leather cuffs holder on his utility belt.

Bardsley nodded, rubbing his beard thoughtfully.

Bob the Dog revealed his Billy Connolly grin. "I'll go to the van dock and get Rhys ready, in case he decides to run that way."

Thompson looked as apprehensive as a student officer about to deliver his first briefing to the shift. The disbelief in his voice graduated to anger. "If this guy *is* a serial killer, then shouldn't we get Firearms down and let the hierarchy know? It's in *my* custody office and it's on my arse."

"Thommo, it's *my* arse that's on the line, not yours, mate. It's my call, so stop fretting. Right, come on, let's do it."

***

After finishing from the hourly checks, Powers had not returned to the staff office, opting to go through a side door toward the kitchen area near the CCTV room to make a brew. As was customary, he thought he'd ask whoever happened to be doing their two-hour stint on the cameras if they wanted a brew.

However, on entering the somewhat compact room, he was surprised to see Sergeant Thompson sitting at the long, dark blue Formica desk facing the cameras.

"Sarge, why are you on here?"

Thompson couldn't hide his shocked expression. He hastily scanned the plethora of screens before him as he stood up, the chair wheeling backward and clattering a radiator behind. "Ah, Vic, I'm just, er, filling in 'cause Brenda needed the loo," he said, while pushing the buzzer to the charge desk.

Thompson sounds nervous. Something's not right here. Powers looked at the screens and saw a couple of figures in the custody area. One of them was a uniformed officer and the other was... *Jack fuckin' Striker!*

Thompson lunged forward in a bid to grab Powers. The sidestep and swift right uppercut thwarted his attempts, sending the custody sergeant sprawling across the desk and into unconsciousness.

Powers had anticipated this eventuality at some point. He studied the screens while pushing a button marked 'UP' on the control panel. An expansive metal shutter began to rise at the far end of the thirty-metres-long secure van dock area. He headed

271

for the door leading to the van dock, hearing Brenda's robotic-sounding voice on the control panel intercom saying, "Go ahead, Sarge," as he exited the CCTV room.

The sudden barking of a police dog heightened his senses. It was straining at its leash, held by Bob the Dog, whose face contorted. The noisy shutter continued its mechanical rising behind the dogman, beyond the car park... *freedom... and Kingston.*

"The game's up, Powers," shouted the dogman, withdrawing his baton.

"Like fuck it is," he said, running toward the growling dog.

The German shepherd jumped up onto his hind legs and Bob unhooked the leash. Powers volleyed the police dog into the air, Rhys howling as he backflipped and landed upside down with a yelp.

Bob swung his baton, hitting Powers in the chest, seemingly winding him. But Powers lashed out a backhand to the cop's cheek. He ran under the now fully opened shutter and sprinted through the car park to his Golf.

An office worker arriving for the day said, "Morning, Vic."

When he ignored her, she gave him an odd look which transformed to shock on seeing Rhys speeding toward them. She cowered and stooped in fear, holding her hands out as Rhys shot past her. Breathless, Powers virtually jumped inside the Golf and slammed the door, a split second before the dog thudded into it.

Five seconds later, the Golf was zooming toward the exit gate. He slammed on the brakes, opened the driver's window, punched in a code and waited impatiently for the metal gate to open. He heard raised voices behind him and Rhys barking. Checking his rear-view, he saw Striker and a few others frantically running toward their vehicles. But the wide gate was now half open and he sped off to finish his mission.

Chapter Forty-Six

Jamo Kingston eagerly opened the shop he'd converted, via a government grant and lottery money, into his offices. He was expecting a busy day ahead, having half a dozen appointments booked with local youths regarding his – and hopefully his clients' – journey of atonement. Then, this afternoon, he was expecting a journo from the Manchester Evening News to do another interview, further publicising his award-winning project.

Today is gonna be another good day, the Lord willing. Kingston adjusted his eyepatch and looked up, his gold incisor gleaming in the rare Manchester sun.

He opened the shutters at the front of the building and, as he did with glowing pride every day, held a prolonged gaze at the colourful wording on the sign above: 'The Moss Range Community Project'. The flag pole above the sign proudly displayed the green and black, split by the yellowy gold saltire, of the Jamaican flag, flapping in the breeze. He also had a Union Jack below it, so as not to alienate potential clients.

The police had been outside Kingston's house for most of the night. They'd informed him this Hoodie Hunter madman had his name on some hit list. They said they were duty bound to inform him, but when he'd asked them if the killer had been caught, they surprised him by saying that he had. They asked him to keep it to himself and he called DCS Ronald Halt to insist they use their resources elsewhere.

He knew the police presence outside his family home last night was not only to reassure him, but also to sweeten him and keep him onside. The position of being an independent advisor to the cops brought the perk of being buddies with their main men and privy to many of their secrets. That's how desperate the law was to get the local community onside. And with his past, he knew they needed him more than he needed them.

Back inside the project's main office, he sat proudly at his desk, a photo of himself and his four smiling children staring back at him. The mothers weren't present in the photo as they were all different and it would've been impossible to co-ordinate *that* snapshot! Anyhow, they'd have been at each other's throats, another reminder of his wayward past; a past he'd protected his children from as best he could. He wanted them to grow up with their father as the right kind of role model, the backdrop of the Christian church in the photo and what they called "Daddy's Project" both testaments to that philosophy.

He flicked open the diary on his desk and saw the name Lee McPherson, hoping that he wouldn't be a no-show. At fifteen, McPherson had certainly showed signs of hanging out with the wrong crowd, already having a rap sheet containing three street robberies to his name. McPherson's mum had booked the appointment, which always increased the probability of a no-show because the client hadn't booked it themselves. Even so, Kingston was making headway with these young pretenders and he wouldn't stop in his relentless search for redemption.

The sound of screeching tyres outside the office made him look up from his desk.

***

Striker saw Bardsley's disdainful expression mirroring his own, after Powers had screeched out of the police car park. He cursed himself as he and the DC jumped into the Astra. Striker wondered if the recent bangs on his head had clouded his judgement. He knew he'd been the one to finally identify the killer, but letting him escape was unforgiveable. He was already in enough trouble as it was, what with his unofficial continuance of the investigation while off duty, and then bringing in officers who'd been told to take a day off.

"Bleedin'ell, he's out of sight already," said Bardsley, heading for the exit gate that had automatically closed. Bardsley reached out of the driver's window and punched in the code, seeing Davison and the Bob the Dog in the liveried dog van behind, blue lights flashing impatiently.

"Come on, come on!" The DC banged the steering wheel as the gate sluggishly opened. He turned to Striker. "Kingston's, Jack?"

"Yeah, but not his home address. He'll be at his office by now."

"Okay," he said, squeezing the Astra through the tight gap of the half-opened gate.

Realising his plan had gone to rat shit, Striker withdrew his police radio. "DI Striker, control."

"Er… go ahead, sir." The male comms operator sounded surprised to hear from him.

"The suspect in the recent spate of murders is heading to the Moss Range Community Project on Moss Range Road. I urgently need ARVs to make that address, and let Mr Halt know, would you? I also want response officers to attend Kingston's home address as a precaution. Any non-armed officers attending the Community Project should RV at a safe distance. We'll say Moss Range Park gates, okay?"

"Okay, sir. I'm onto it."

"DI Stockley, urgent."

"Go ahead, sir."

"Talk-through with DI Striker."

"I'm listening."

"You sure about this, Striker? We have the offender under guard at the hospital, haven't we?"

"He may be involved, Vinnie, but he's not our man."

"Comms, update the log to show myself and DCI Cunningham en route."

"Done, sir. DI Striker, does the suspect have a name?"

"Yes, it's Vic Powers. And, yes, it's our very own custody clerk."

Radio silence.

***

The window of the office door smashed through, such was the force of the sturdy boot. Kingston vaguely recognised the twisted face of the huge man who'd stormed in. From his gang days, he also recognised the handgun that was pointing directly at his forehead, forcing him to cower in his chair. It was a Glock 17. Himself, he'd always preferred the Browning 9mm.

"The door has a bell, you know," said Kingston. It wasn't the first time he'd stared down the barrel of a gun.

"Up the fuckin' stairs now, you prick."

"Okay, okay, go easy, man." He glimpsed the photo of his

smiling children as he was yanked up by the throat.

Stumbling up the stairs, they reached the landing that had three doors leading off. He was pushed to the door at the front above the offices.

"Keys?" asked the madman.

"This isn't ma flat. The master keys are on ma desk downstairs."

A gunshot fired, the door splintered ajar and Kingston was shoved through it. He saw the man reach inside a bag hooked over his shoulder. He whipped out a thick rope. Kingston was pushed onto a bed and felt the rope land on him.

"Put it around your neck."

"What? No way, man. What's all dis about, anyway?"

He pointed the gun and blasted Kingston in the leg, his kneecap exploding beyond pain. Kingston screamed and writhed on the bed, blood pissing out of his knee. He saw the man looking out of the front window before lifting it open. Kingston tried to crawl off the blood-soaked bed, but felt his legs being grabbed, pulling him back. The man gripped the rope and stooped to tie it round the bed posts.

"Pleeease... Who are you, man? Why are you doing this?" asked Kingston as the noose was hooked over his head to his neck then yanked tight.

"Remember Lenny Powers? Remember Josh Powers, and you supporting your gangster wannabes at his court case?"

Kingston recalled both boys with deep regret. "I've changed," he said, desperately pulling at the rope. "I've stopped all dat." He felt himself being lifted off the bed. "I've got... kids now... pleeease!" He was above the psycho's head now.

"They'll be better off without you."

"No..." he spluttered. "Please... I'll pay you..."

"Fuck you and your dirty cash."

"Oh, ma fuckin'... Gorrrrrrrd!" yelled Kingston as he was flung out of the window, just as his ten o'clock appointment arrived below.

Chapter Forty-Seven

"Holy shit!" said Striker, as Bardsley pulled the Astra up thirty metres short of the Community Project. Kingston was swinging between a Union Jack and a Jamaican flag, his legs bizarrely riding an invisible bike, hands pawing helplessly at the rope around his neck.

"Get closer, Eric."

"He might be armed, Jack. Shouldn't we wait for Firearms?"

"Just get bloody closer!"

Bardsley accelerated and pulled up outside the Project and Striker jumped out. The dog van screeched to a halt behind and Davison got out with Bob the Dog. Rhys was soon leashed up, panting excitedly following Striker and Davison into the shop.

Kingston was clearly too high for them to reach, so Bardsley radioed for more patrols, an ambulance and the fire service. He also asked for an ETA for Armed Response and was told five minutes. He got out of the Astra and jogged to the door.

Before entering, he glanced up at Kingston whose wriggling had lessened, eyes bulging, tongue protruding. Onlookers began gathering, drivers rubbernecking, some stopping and getting out, an occasional scream here and there. A teenage boy stared silently in horror by the door.

Helplessly watching Kingston, Bardsley nearly said, 'Hang on in there, fella,' but stopped himself. He told the lad to "leave, pronto" as it wasn't safe. Unfortunately, there was no way they could save Kingston in time, so he rushed inside.

Striker took the stairs three at a time. Behind, Davison withdrew his CS gas canister and baton. Barking enthusiastically, Rhys almost pulled Bob upstairs.

On the landing, a metal step ladder led to an open loft door above.

Striker climbed halfway up then looked down. "Ben, quick, pass me your torch... and that baton... in fact, just give me your utility belt."

Without hesitation, Davison whipped his belt off and passed it up to Striker. "Now, go and see if you can help Kingston." He pointed along the hallway leading to the front of the building.

Bob the Dog said, "The ladder might be a decoy, I'll check the rest of the rooms with Rhys."

Striker stood on his toes at the top of the ladder and peered into the loft. He flicked the torch around at shapes that shifted and threatened. There was a skylight, wide open. A figure appeared and pointed a handgun. Striker winced, no time to jump out of view.

Bardsley rushed up the stairs, seeing Striker's legs dangling from the loft. Hearing a gunshot, he froze. The bullet powered through the ceiling and hit the wall, creating two small clouds of plaster dust.

"Bleedin'ell, Jack. Get down, leave it to Firearms!" He saw the DI's legs disappear up into the loft. "Jeee-sus, Striker."

Bardsley mentally derided his borderline obesity, knowing he wasn't agile enough to pull himself up into the loft to help his mate. Frustrated, his thoughts reverted back to Kingston. A metaphorical light-bulb lit above his head. He grabbed the step ladder and ran, albeit awkwardly, back downstairs.

Seeing more people gathering, he yelled at them to leave. Some did, others didn't. He had no time to argue.

He leaned the step ladder below Kingston who was virtually motionless. Davison donned a panicky expression above, leaning out of the window, trying to pull the rope up. The young lad, who Bardsley had told to leave, was halfway up a drainpipe, tears in his eyes, struggling to reach across to Kingston.

"Hey, get down now. I need your help," the DC shouted to the youth.

Bardsley ran to the Astra, started the engine and pulled it onto the pavement directly below Kingston. Hearing multiple sirens approaching, he got back out and scrambled onto the bonnet, which audibly sagged. He clambered onto Astra's roof and it buckled noisily under his weight. The teenage boy was now waiting on the pavement and had twigged Bardsley's idea, passing the step ladder up.

Police vehicles skidded in unison to a halt, including ARV Range Rovers. Bardsley focussed on his balance as he climbed the wobbling ladder on the car roof. He reached up and grabbed Kingston's dangling legs, pushing them upwards in a bid to ease the tension on his neck.

But the reformed gangster felt dead.

**

Striker jumped up in the loft and gripped both hands on the rim of the gaping skylight. He pulled himself up and quickly scanned. The grey slate tiled roof was steep, a chimney stack located up the slope from him. The buildings were adjoined, creating a long block. He frantically shot looks both ways. To his left, he saw nothing. To his right, he saw Powers, stooped, edging away, clutching the handgun.

Striker reached into his jacket pocket and withdrew the radio. "DI Striker, comms. I'm on the roof of Kingston's offices and Powers is approximately forty feet away, moving north and armed with a handgun. Received?"

"All received."

"Detective Chief Superintendent Halt, interrupting."

"Go ahead, sir," said the communicator.

"Jack, considering the suspect is armed, I want you down from there."

Striker thought for a moment. "I'll just track him from a safe distance, sir."

"Safe? You're unarmed on a bloody roof chasing a man with a gun!"

"Sir, but he's getting away."

"Air support should be there by now and ARV supervision can take it from here."

He heard the force helicopter overhead. Picturing Armed Response, discussing tactics and risk assessing on the street below, he said, "Sorry, sir, you're breaking up…"

"Striker, come down now, and that's an order!"

Striker sidled crab-like, leaning into the roof to maintain his balance. He felt gusts of wind testing him, and was thankful the tiles were dry, providing essential grip. Powers was about fifty feet away and had worked his way to the ridge, where he seemed to move quicker. Striker copied this technique himself. From his vantage point he could see numerous police vehicles below and officers dotted about. Some were creating a cordon, while others moved pedestrians away and redirected the growing queues of traffic.

He heard the cackle of a gun and dropped onto the roof. The bullet cut viciously through the air beside him, ricocheting off the chimney stack behind. He looked up and saw Powers disappear downwards. Had he gone into another skylight or just onto a lower roof?

Striker stood up, continued forward. Glancing upward at the force helicopter, he hoped it had the bastard in its sights.

Chapter Forty-Eight

Davison saw Bardsley rather awkwardly taking Kingston's weight below and felt the rope's tautness ease in his hands. Standing on the bed that was wedged tight to the wall, he quickly turned and jumped off. He'd struggled to untie the rope previously, due to his unwieldy position under the bed, but now he found he could lift the bed and access the knot more easily.

Bob the Dog entered the first-floor bedroom, tying Rhys's lead to a radiator pipe.

"Here, Ben. Gimme that." Bob took the elevated bed's weight and Davison went to work unhooking the rope from the upturned bed post. A few seconds later, Davison had the rope in his hand and Bob eased the bed down to the floor, pulling it from the window to create better access.

Davison leaned out of the window and saw a group of his colleagues holding on to both Bardsley and Kingston, the latter looking as floppy as a rag doll among a mass of black uniforms. There was an ambulance parked up nearby with two green-uniformed paramedics at its rear holding the doors open.

"Think we were too late, Bob," said Davison resignedly.

"We did all we could."

"Now then, what about helping DI Striker?" Davison headed for the hall.

Following, Bob said, "You heard Mr Halt. Armed Response will deal with it from here, lad."

"Where are they then? He's on his own, Bob. Come on. This is what I joined the Job for."

They both looked up at the loft opening ten feet above them. They bounced stern looks and Davison said, "You've got your pension waiting and I'm the tallest."

"Think of Louise."

"I am, Bob."

"Ach, Ben. You're as mad as Jack Striker." The dogman shook his head and crouched, cupping his hands together.

Davison placed his foot onto Bob's hands and was thrust upward with a Scottish "Uu-saaah". He grabbed onto the rim of the loft and did an English version of the same exerting noise that they'd coined together in the work's gym.

The rookie constable clambered into the loft.

***

Striker soon sussed the quickest way to run across the lengthy ridge and got into a rhythm, one foot either side. Closing on the point where he'd lost sight of Powers, his right foot gave way on a loose tile. He cursed, slipped and rolled down the roof like a kid on an inflatable slide. The sky somersaulted in his vision. His radio clattered down the tiled slope and disappeared over the edge. He scrambled his feet frantically, using his leather shoes as brakes. He heard gasps and screams coming from below as he continued, albeit more slowly, skidding toward the edge. The buckle and cuffs of the utility belt scraped the tiles, slowing him further.

About five feet short, he came to halt, looked down and exhaled. He took a deep breath before turning and climbing back up to the apex.

Within a minute, he saw another skylight ajar and guessed that was where Powers must have gone. He lay on his stomach and crawled closer so he could peek inside. When he did, a sturdy hand grabbed his hair and wrenched him downward.

Chapter Forty-Nine

Powers pointed the Glock at Striker, who lay in a heap, groaning on the wooden floor.

"I've got to hand it to you, Striker, you're a tenacious bastard. But I already knew that from when I marked you at football, didn't I, eh?"

Striker sat up, staring at the muzzle of the handgun. "If you recall, it was me who 'marked' you."

Powers laughed exaggeratedly. "Yeah, I know. I've still got the stud marks," he gestured with the pistol toward his right leg.

"Come on, Vic. It's over, fella." Striker shaped to stand up.

"Now, that's where you're wrong, Jack. It's far from over," Powers said, forcing the DI back down with a foot to the chest.

The whirring of the police helicopter overhead emanated through the open skylight.

"You're surrounded. You got Kingston, and probably got me the bloody sack."

Powers grinned. "Yeah, your methods are somewhat unorthodox, to say the least."

"Look who's talking."

"Especially, since you've been dumped off the case."

Striker fixed a stare. "Tell me something…"

"Shoot."

"Poor choice of word, Vic, but tell me… why the baton?"

"Am I under caution here?"

"Not yet."

Now Powers eyed Striker. "Don't suppose it matters now. My weapons of choice are obviously guns, so when I saw a baton in the locker room a year ago, I thought, why not? You wouldn't be linking me to it, being ex-forces. I practised using it on my punchbag for a year and, as you know, got pretty damn good with it."

"You used a cop's baton?"

"Sure. I bet some of you guys wished you could use it the way I did."

Striker didn't answer.

Powers dipped his head for a second. "Sorry about your

nephew, by the way. He just happened to be there."

Striker bit his lip. He then thought about Danny Powers, thankful Vic didn't know what had happened in the cellar, or the hospital for that matter. If he had heard, things would have certainly been much different here. Striker guessed that he probably wouldn't broach the subject, so as not to incriminate his brother.

"Apology reluctantly accepted, since he's okay now. Good job he is, though."

"Don't you ever learn? You're in no position to make threats, Jack."

"You always have a weapon. Why not put the gun down and let the best man win?"

Powers shook his head. "Good try. It's tempting, but I can't risk that. My list is still incomplete."

"So you carry on, until you're shot dead. Because that's what will happen."

"Yeah, but now I have a hostage. A window of opportunity to escape."

Striker considered rushing him now. He wondered whether the covert body armour he was wearing could stop a bullet from such close range. But from what Bardsley had told him, Powers preferred the shot to the forehead.

"There's no way you'll get out of this now. There have been too many killings. Ten is it now, with Kingston? You can't carry on doing this."

"They were all scum, Striker and fuckin' deserved it, and the world is a better place without them. I didn't hear too many objections from the city's decent folk either. Reckon they secretly admired my work. Bet some of you cops did too."

"Come on, we can't condone cold-blooded murder. If we did, there'd be anarchy on the streets. Who do you think you are anyway, Charles-fuckin-Bronson?"

Powers edged the gun closer, face expressionless, eyes fixed on Striker.

"Anyway, why mess about hanging Kingston when you knew we were chasing you?"

Powers sighed, lowered the gun slightly. He took a pace back and shrugged, his taut features relaxing a touch. "It's no big deal... *if* I'm caught. I had to make that statement with Kingston, just in case. It was always the plan, but maybe not so rushed. It'll be all over the internet already. I saw some of the gathering crowd below recording it on their phones. People need to know there's a consequence for scumbags like Kingston. My kind of justice is much more effective than yours, don't you think? I mean, just look at that farcical court case when Castro and his pricks jumped Josh. You're a decent detective and even you couldn't get them convicted."

Striker stared at the loft's dusty floor then looked up and said, "You can never justify murder."

"So, you're telling me I've not done the public a service, mopping up the scum from the streets? Come on, Jack, there's barely a hoodie in sight around here now. I bet you're secretly pleased with my work, especially with Kingston."

"What do you want me to say? That the bastard had it coming?"

"Well, yeah. They all did."

He was talking freely. Good. "You've certainly been busy. I don't know how you managed it. Who've you had helping you?"

"I acted alone."

Just as Striker was about to probe further, a metallic voice interrupted them, echoing from outside: "VICTOR POWERS, THIS IS DETECTIVE CHIEF SUPERINTENDENT HALT. YOU ARE SURROUNDED BY ARMED OFFICERS, WHO HAVE BEEN BRIEFED TO SHOOT TO STOP IF YOU DO NOT CO-OPERATE. RELINQUISH YOUR WEAPON AND COME OUT WITH YOUR HANDS ON YOUR HEAD."

Striker lowered his voice, "Come on, Vic. At least end it by saving your own life. Do you think Lenny and Josh would want you to carry on the killings?"

Powers became momentarily quiet. Clearly deep in thought, his temples and jawline appeared to almost pulse. Then he said, "I won't tell them about your shady past, you know, Jack." For the first time, there was an air of resignation in his voice.

"Don't think that matters now. In our own ways we're both, as they say, 'fucked'... I may even see you in the slammer."

They chuckled in unison, albeit nervously, Striker clocking that the Glock was now dipped.

"Watch each other's backs, eh?"

"Yeah, something like that. So why didn't you kill me when you had the chance?"

"I still have the chance now." He jiggled the gun in the air.

"You're an ex-Para, aren't you? And you shot at me twice."

"True. I aimed to miss. Killing cops isn't on my agenda. You know that."

"I could just take that gun off you now then?"

"Try it if you want."

Striker stood up and Powers pointed the Glock. "Striker, no, stay the fuck there!"

Striker edged forward. "Come on, Vic. It's over. Now, give me the gun and we'll walk out together."

***

Davison looked heavenward past the chopper and stood up above the skylight. Forcing thoughts of Louise away, he took a deep breath.

Then, feeling a rush, he plummeted onto Powers's head, both of them collapsing to the floor. Striker grabbed Powers's gun hand and twisted it. Davison gripped the killer in a headlock, but struggled to hold him as he raged and grappled. The gun went off and splintered a nearby joist. Striker withdrew the baton from the utility belt Davison had lent him earlier. Powers broke free, cursing, and rolled Davison so he was on top of the constable. Striker clicked the baton open and whacked the raising gun hand. Powers let out a grunt, though still held the weapon, directing it at Davison's head. Striker swung the baton again, connecting with Powers's head, knocking him backward into a diagonal wooden beam. The DI dived onto him, feeling the boarded floor giving slightly underneath. He gripped the Glock's barrel, the vibration of the next discharge rattling his palm violently free as the bullet hit the wall behind them.

Davison wriggled out of the melee with an exerting groan. He punched Powers repeatedly in the head and face. Striker stooped and bit Powers's gun hand, feeling the bitter tang of blood in his mouth. Powers cried out, the Glock dropping onto the boarded floor with a thud. Striker took a hefty right to the nose, making him stagger back. Davison extracted the cuffs from Striker's belt, expertly clicking one onto Powers's left wrist. He yanked on the cuffs and Powers fell sideways. Striker straddled Powers's back and both officers pressed him into the floor. The DI grabbed Powers's left arm and forced it awkwardly behind his back. Davison yanked on the cuffs, wrenching the right wrist closer. He struggled briefly until the welcoming click of the second cuff finally incapacitated Powers.

Both officers were sprawled across the boarded floor, their elbows leaning on Powers's back. Struggling to catch his breath, Striker turned to Davison.

"Do you want to... do the honours... Ben?"

His heart rate still racing, Davison tried to compose himself, pleasantly surprised at the offer. "With pleasure, sir." He leaned closer to Powers's left ear. "Victor Powers, I'm arresting you on suspicion of ten counts of murder... You do not have to say anything... but it may harm your defence... if you do not mention... when questioned, something which you later rely on in court... anything you do say may be given in evidence... do you understand?"

Silence.

Striker prodded Powers in the gut with the baton. "Any reply, Vic?"

"Yeah. The world is better off without them."

Chapter Fifty

Bardsley was standing amid the growing mass of police officers on the opposite side of the road to the long block of shops. Media cameras had already arrived to join with the gathering public on both sides of the one-hundred-metre cordon. News travelled fast around these parts, the proverbial bushfire slow in comparison.

Bardsley was virtually in the centre of the scene, in among the half a dozen armed response vehicles, a couple of divisional vans and a few plain cars. A fire engine was parked up to his left, its crew still inside, now redundant, since Bardsley and co. had managed to, somehow, get Kingston down. Kingston had been hastily rushed off to hospital, amazingly still showing signs of life.

Bardsley's main concern was Striker and the equally over-exuberant Davison. Mr Halt had just spoken into the hand-held loud speaker, informing Powers that firearms officers had surrounded the building.

He'd earlier caught both Stockley and Cunningham deriding Striker, basically saying he was finished. He'd defended his friend vehemently, probably to the detriment of his own career, saying that even added together, they didn't have half Striker's gumption. However, deep down he feared they were right, though to gloat about it was just bang out of order. He'd also got the impression that Stockley's dealings with Striker's sister Lucy and her family had provided further ammo to fire at Striker.

The force helicopter did yet another circuit of the skies directly above, no doubt filming the scene in its entirety. Bardsley noticed a Sky News chopper doing the same in the distance, but with undoubtedly more critical eyes. He was glad it wasn't there earlier, when he was struggling to save Kingston. However, he did see some young locals recording him on their phones. No doubt he'd be on YouTube before long.

Firearms officers had covered the front and rear of the block, as well as evacuating all the occupants who were now huddled together in a couple of large police people carriers parked to the extreme right of the cordon.

Unexpectedly, a door opened at the front of a hardware store about ten shops down from Kingston's Community Project. Armed officers instantly pointed their weapons in unison. Bardsley craned to see between cops' heads until relief swept him. A beaming smile spread across his face, accompanied by a knowing shake of the head.

Slowly exiting the store, Striker raised his left arm, his right clutching Powers, who was cuffed to the rear. Davison held his right hand aloft while his left held onto the killer. All three had blood tricking down their faces. A few "whoop-whoops" were heard as the trio crossed the road. Sergeant Roache opened the rear doors of a divisional van just as someone starting clapping.

The applause spread among the crowds on both sides of the cordon and then Bardsley joined in, grinning. Within a few seconds, the mass of officers were clapping, including Halt, who looked on, almost disbelievingly, at the unusual phenomenon. Bardsley mentally noted that neither Cunningham nor Stockley were clapping.

Powers just stared straight ahead, impassive.

Firearms officers shadowed the trio all the way as the other cops parted creating a path up to the van. Striker placed a hand on Powers's head to dip it slightly as he helped the vigilante into the rear of the van. Davison wore a proud grin as broad as the sentence awaiting Powers.

Striker wiped his brow, half-heartedly held up an acknowledging palm. Next, he began to trudge over to Halt, probably to see if he still had a job.

An explosion of gunfire made everyone pivot and cower. Bullets clanged and ricocheted off the back of the van.

Striker flinched at the repeated blasts and then span round to see the manic Dessie Bowker charging at the police van, pistol in hand, emptying the gun's magazine in the direction of Powers.

"You killed my son, you bast-aaard!" yelled Bowker, his face twisted, eyes bulging.

All cops took cover, some just hitting the deck. Screams emanated from the crowd of onlookers, many spinning to flee the scene. The van doors weren't shut yet so Powers was the proverbial sitting duck. Still cuffed, he jumped out, blood dripping from his right shoulder where he'd taken a hit. Striker sprinted to Powers and dived across him as more shots fired and Bowker closed in. Striker felt a shockwave to his chest, a reverberation in his ribcage, just before he landed, dragging Powers with him. Firearms officers unleashed a volley of sharp, accurate shots to Bowker, his upper body an eruption of blood as he fell, almost in slow motion, onto the crimson tarmac.

If Bowker the gangster hadn't retired before, he definitely had now.

Bardsley rushed over to Striker and Powers, as relentless, haunting screams filled the air, intensifying the horror. The detective crouched down and leaned over the two sprawled bodies on the road. "Shit, Jack... Jack? Are you okay, mate?"

Chapter Fifty-One

Once Powers had been released from hospital, having had the gunshot wound to his right shoulder tended to, the series of interviews had begun, with Halt taking the reins and choosing Bardsley as his second jockey. To be fair to the vigilante, his full and frank confessions to the murders had gone a considerable way to patching up what the press had cruelly called "a shambolic inquiry".

It turned out that Powers had been devastated by Lenny's shooting all those years ago. To say he was disappointed at the police's failure to catch the shooter was an understatement. He'd bubbled with frustration and anger while out serving in Helmand Province with Two Para, where he'd endeavoured to channel his rage into his work as a soldier. However, when he'd heard that his little brother – the talented snooker player Josh – had been attacked by the Bullsmead Boys, he'd been given compassionate leave. Then, the bombshell from the specialist came when Josh was told he'd never play snooker again, due to the fracture of the orbits in his right eye.

Desperate to rekindle his younger sibling's snooker career, Powers tried everything to assist. He paid for special glasses to ease the double vision, but as Josh's frustration grew at being half the player he was, Powers's wrath grew tenfold. Second and third opinions from eye specialists came and went, all saying the same thing. The eye would gradually sink into its damaged socket and finally settle, but the double vision would always be there, intermittently at best.

Josh was inconsolable and the depression finally broke him, culminating in him taking his own life. It was their mum, Edith, who'd returned home from bingo one afternoon to find her youngest son hanging from the banisters of the family home. It had been the very house that overlooked the alleyway where Powers had executed Shanks, Levi and Renshaw, before kidnapping Big-un to use as bait for Castro.

Powers received the call about Josh's suicide while on an operation in Helmond Province and had completely flipped at the news. After disobeying orders from Command, he'd jeopardised not only the operation but also the lives of his colleagues by charging into a Taliban stronghold. That day he shot dead five of the enemy and two of his colleagues were injured in the battle. After lengthy discussions, his army career was terminated and he returned home.

From then on, he began to plan his mission in earnest. He knew that in order to glean the required intelligence regarding the crimes committed against his brothers, he would have to find a way in. Because the recruiting of the "twice as expensive" police officers had been suspended due to economic cuts, he applied to become a civilian detention officer at Bullsmead nick. In hindsight, it had proved a better option, being on the periphery, lower profile, with less chance of snooping colleagues.

During one of the interviews, he'd even told Eric Bardsley that he'd broken into the detective's house in a bid to "temporarily silence" Bardsley, who he'd seen with Striker in the bushes outside the temple. But Powers was surprised to see a naked young man jump out of Bardsley's bed to confront him. Powers had promptly struck the 'lover boy' with his baton before fleeing the house.

Bardsley had camouflaged his anger by joking in his own inimitable way. "Thanks for the heads up, Vic, but I was already onto it. And, anyway, when are you gonna pay me for the carpet cleaning and the broken back-door window?" Unbelievably, Powers actually offered to pay!

Powers had insisted that he'd had no desire to harm any police officer, doing only what he had to do in order to complete his mission. He apologised profusely for all the injuries received by officers who'd "unfortunately got in my way". Plus, he felt particularly remorseful for the attack on Striker's nephew, Deano. Nonetheless, when it came to the non-completion of his 'mid-list', he was disappointed in himself.

Striker, still sporting a nasty bruise on his chest where one of the late Dessie Bowker's bullets had taken a chunk out of his body armour, had his own series of interviews to contend with. He was quizzed at length by Professional Standards. And, although he'd squirmed more than once at their jobsworth-style interrogations, he felt he'd held his own. They were particularly interested in exactly who had rescued Striker from the cellar and dropped him off at hospital. But "concussion and shock are a formidable combination", Striker had told them. He knew they'd spoken to his colleagues, particularly Vinnie Stockley. His counterpart had delved deeply into Striker's past when interviewing his sister Lucy about the Deano attack.

Still, Striker had already played his ace card. When he'd been digging on the internet and had found the VOICES website – now closed by the authorities – he'd also found something else intriguing on a very different forum.

He'd known Cunningham was into kinky sex after he'd awoken from their drunken one night stand all those years ago with his hands tied to the bedposts. The crazy bitch was dressed in bondage gear, holding a whip and dripping hot wax on his bare chest. He'd left that fast, he'd nearly taken the bedposts with him.

So, after joining the BDSM forum under a false name, Striker discovered that both Cunningham *and* Stockley were members under the guises of "Madam Justice" and "Mister Obedient". He'd loved to have shared this revelation with Bardsley over a pint, though that would have been the equivalent of putting it on News at Ten.

This info was all he needed to keep Stockley quiet, his pointy face flushing red when Striker had addressed him by his kinky alias in his office.

This had boosted Striker, along with the fact that he'd hung onto his job "by a piece of burning cotton", as Halt had succinctly put it in the Crown earlier. They'd all surprised Striker with a celebratory shindig, greeting him with cheers and raised glasses on his entrance. Feeling somewhat embarrassed, and not being one for a fuss, Striker had gone with the flow for half an hour or so and, of course, sank a couple of John Smith's.

Bardsley told him he was going to give Maggie a second chance, since the Casanova window cleaner was now off the scene. "But, on one condition," Bardsley had said with a cheeky grin. "She cleans the bleedin' windows!"

Becky Grant, who'd been co-ordinating the security at the hospital, informed Striker that Kingston had actually survived. Even so, he'd spend the rest of his days in a wheelchair.

Poetic justice, thought Striker.

It was as nice to see Ben Davison with his new fiancée, Louise, as it was to see Cunningham and Stockley looking sheepish in the corner. It was also good see Lauren Collinge having fully recovered from her kidnap ordeal. What wasn't so good was the sight of her huddling so close to Brad Sterling.

Ah, well.

Despite the tempting eyes of that curvaceous barmaid gazing through the crowd, Striker made his excuses, knowing something much more important awaited him.

When he'd been discharged from hospital, he'd been surprised to receive a phone call from Suzi.

"You okay, Jack? You've been all over the news," she'd asked, her voice filled with a concerned tenderness he'd not heard for years.

Apparently, Sky News had run a live feed of the Powers's capture. It included Striker not only chasing the vigilante across the rooftops, but also later leading him out with Davison, then Striker diving across the killer and taking a bullet from Bowker. The latter part was edited considerably and just reported verbally, due to the graphically violent content. The whole thing had been more poignant to the viewers with the added ingredient of that "kidnapped cop" seeking retribution on the vigilante. Beth and Harry had apparently watched the whole thing open-mouthed during the post-school news bulletins. Suzi had lifted Striker's spirits by saying that both kids – not just Beth, but now Harry too – had wanted to see him. Harry had even ditched his red United shirt and put on his sky blue City one instead.

Back in his apartment, 'Mack the Knife' was playing on the CD player as he waited for his kids to arrive for their first ever sleepover at Daddy's apartment. He plopped some frozen bloodworm into the fish tank and watched it disperse. Mr Plec and Sliver the loach took cover while the rest feasted frantically on the smell of blood.

He wondered whether it would be Suzi who'd bring the kids over. It would be nice to see her. The paradox of his kidnap ordeal was that it had given him time to think, time to reflect on his life and the relationships therein, the people that mattered. And he knew Suzi, the mother of his children, his first love, would always be right up there.

The apartment buzzer sounded, surprising Striker. Were the kids here early?

Peering through the blinds, he was blown away at whom he saw, distant memories whizzing back. He ran a hand through his dark locks, considered not answering. The buzzer rang again, sounding louder somehow.

He walked tentatively into the hallway, where he took a deep breath before picking up the phone from the wall. "Wozza, me old mate. Come on in," he said, with fake enthusiasm, pressing a button to release the communal door. "There's a lift on the left."

A minute or so later, Striker opened the front door, feeling awkward and trying not to look shocked. The ageing process hadn't been kind to Wozza, his ginger hair cropped close to hide his receding hairline. A few wrinkles had appeared and he'd developed a paunch, not that it mattered. What did matter was who he'd brought with him – in the wheelchair.

Wozza glanced down. "Look, Lenny, it's Lord-bloody-Lucan." He returned his gaze to Striker. "Have yer got Shergar hiding in there with yer, too?"

Striker forced a smile.

Lenny appeared to smile back. He donned a red, Santa-style bobble hat. It jiggled from side to side as if he was excited. Wozza pushed the wheelchair along the short hallway.

Striker glanced down at Lenny, who was dribbling. "How's he doing?"

"He's full of the joys of the upcoming festive season, aren't you, Len?" he said, jerking the wheelchair a little.

Lenny rolled his head from side to side, akin to Stevie Wonder but without the harmonious tones, the white bobble on the hat swinging.

"Come on, Wozza, how *is* he doing?"

"Ask him."

Striker felt uneasy. He walked over, crouched a little and asked softly, "How are you, Lenny?"

Lenny rolled his eyes and spluttered some saliva onto his top lip then sidled his head again.

"Does that answer your question?" said Wozza, expertly wiping the spit away with a readied tissue.

Striker turned toward the sink and dipped his head to wash a cup over-rigorously. Guilt engulfed him at not keeping in touch with his old mates.

He poured milk into two cups, hesitated, gesturing at Lenny. "Does he...?"

"No. He can't. Gets his nutrients via tubes. He's sorted. I did it before. I'm his full-time carer now."

"Ah, right. Good on yer, Wozza." He poured hot water into the cups, the steam rising into his face momentarily.

"How did you know where I was?"

"Your Lucy gave me the address."

"I didn't mean that. You know what I meant."

"It's safe to be honest with you, then... *Inspector*?"

"Come on, we're mates, right?"

"Alright. Ged and I had our suspicions because of some of the things Vic was saying and doing at the action group's meetings."

"What *was* he saying and doing, then?"

"Look, Jack. Don't turn this into an interrogation or I'm outta here. You've caught him now so let's leave it at that. I came to see how you are, bud. Plus, I'd thought it would be nice to reacquaint you with Lenny."

"Okay, okay. You're right, and I'm glad you came."

"And I wanted to return this, discreetly." He handed a wallet to Striker.

Surprised, Striker took it, checked its contents, seeing his warrant card was still there. "Thanks, but where was it?"

"Look, at the last VOICES meeting, I overheard Danny Powers on the phone, saying that someone was skulking in the bushes outside the temple. I didn't think much of it, until later when I found your wallet on the floor of Vic and Danny's office. So I told Ged and we got in touch with DJ. Remember the pledge we made on the park about always sticking together, no matter what?"

Striker nodded, remembering it well, for it was the night Lenny was shot.

"Anyway, the three of us went to Danny's pub. He was really edgy and scared, drinking whisky. When we confronted him, he said he'd no clue what we were talking about. So we left, arguing about what to do. We were even gonna call the cops, but... Anyway, we heard banging and smashing coming from the cellar.

The hatch rattled, so we yanked it up and there you were."

Striker stared into space, in deep contemplation.

"We knew nothing of Vic's crazy business until that night, I promise you." A moment passed. "Our secret – right, Jack?" he asked, looking unsure.

"One thing I can keep, Woz, is a secret." Striker reached across the table and they shook hands.

Wozza smiled, withdrew a present, crudely wrapped in Christmas paper and gave it to Striker, who noticed Lenny lolling his head from side to side again.

Striker tore the wrapping off, beamed and shook his head. A framed snapshot of Striker, Wozza, Lenny, Ged and DJ on Bullsmead Park. They were all posing, trying to look like tough guys, but looked more like a naff boy band.

"The Sunnyside Boys."

Epilogue

On A Wing the food was so-so. Vic Powers was treated with the respect he deserved, both by the screws and the inmates. He'd caught some of his fellow prisoners giving him the odd stare, sizing him up. They didn't hold his gaze for long as they knew what he was capable of. They were weak and they knew he knew it. They also knew that he wanted to kill them more than they wanted to kill him. This was a unique situation for these pretenders – someone even more aggressive than them, but with brains to boot. No wonder they were shit-scared of him. Nonetheless, he wasn't complacent – far from it. He expected someone soon to attempt to make a name for himself. Especially since he'd already started the chemo and may have appeared more vulnerable.

But he was ready. He was always ready.

Sitting in the prison library, he picked up a copy of the Manchester Evening News. He smirked knowingly at the headline.

And they thought *he* was a handful. God help them...